A Fabulous Fling

Geraldine Bedell has been a feature writer and columnist for the *Independent on Sunday*, is now a journalist at the *Express*, and has written for many other newspapers and magazines. She is married, lives in London and has four children.

GU00372865

A Fabulous Fling

GERALDINE BEDELL

HarperCollins*Publishers*

HarperCollins*Publishers*
77–85 Fulham Palace Road,
Hammersmith, London W6 8JB

www.fireandwater.com

A Paperback Original 2000
1 3 5 7 9 8 6 4 2

This novel is entirely a work of fiction. The names,
characters and incidents portrayed in it are the work
of the author's imagination. Any resemblance to actual
persons, living or dead, events or localities
is entirely coincidental.

A catalogue record for this book
is available from the British Library

ISBN 0 00 651408 1

Typeset in Sabon by
Palimpsest Book Production Limited,
Polmont, Stirlingshire

Printed in Great Britain by
Omnia Books Ltd, Glasgow

For Elaine

It was just one of those things,
Just one of those crazy flings
One of those bells that now and then rings,
Just one of those things.

It was just one of those nights,
Just one of those fabulous flights
A trip to the moon on gossamer wings,
Just one of those things.

Cole Porter

Julie

This lunchtime I had the best sex I've had for months. OK, fair enough, the only sex I've had for months. But it was flashing holograms in space-best, hypersonic looping-the-loop, formation-flying in the stratosphere-best. Or so it seemed, at the time.

At the time, it seemed like the best sex I've *ever* had – except that the rest was all so long ago, it's hard to tell. And I don't really want to admit that it might have been the best ever. Because where would that leave the sixteen years with Richard?

So now I'm thinking it's just fresh in my mind.

The sex episode really started yesterday, at the meeting about the new road. I was late, because Arthur fell over in the back garden and got grit in his graze and then he wouldn't let anyone clean it up except me, but my friend Mel had saved me a place in the hall.

'What kept you?' she demanded in a fierce whisper, as I slumped on to the chair beside her. 'You almost missed him!'

'He's here?' I craned round the room.

'Of course he's here! He's the whole point of the meeting! And he's about to speak!'

I realised then that Mel wasn't talking about Richard. I was the only person for whom Richard was the whole point of the meeting. Mel was here to see Ed McGregor. And sure enough, the environmentalist-superstar was up on the platform, waiting patiently for Suzy Sharp to finish a speech she was making in a weirdly sonorous Winston Churchill voice.

'House prices will fall and the green will be covered in concrete,' Suzy intoned. 'But we in Britain . . .'

'She's been practising this for days,' muttered her husband Dennis, behind me.

'. . . have a long and honourable tradition of peaceful protest . . .' And here Suzy went off at a bit of a tangent about the Magna Carta and the suffragettes, before introducing 'the presenter of *Local and Global,* and radical green' – which I thought made him sound like a shade of emulsion – 'Ed McGregor!'

Mel nudged me excitedly. She watches *Local and Global* every Wednesday and always seems to know where the famous environmentalist is on the planet. Though she's the most happily married woman I know, has a baby daughter, and hasn't so much as glanced at another man since she met Ian, she gives the impression that Ed would only have to call her from the Antarctic needing help with some penguins or an ice shelf and, within the hour, she'd have bought the plane tickets and chartered a sledge.

I, though, was not at the meeting at St Christopher's Church Hall to see Ed McGregor, other than out of a vague voyeurism. I was at the meeting because I thought Richard might be there. It's true that Richard hasn't lived in Langley for seven months, but he surely has to come back some time, and a three-lane mini-motorway slicing through the wood was once something he would have cared about.

But I'd now scrutinised the back of every head in the room, and it was clear he hadn't chosen this particular evening to return to us from fashionable Clerkenwell.

I did my best to distract myself from thoughts of my husband by staring at Ed McGregor. He was in his mid-to-late thirties, tall and loose-limbed, with black tangly hair and heavy-lidded eyes behind glasses, which he took off and dangled in his fingers as he draped himself over the microphone. He was saying something about how much the road would cost and how many hundreds of houses would have to be demolished, then something else about carbon dioxide emissions from fifteen-mile traffic queues, and then another thing about bulldozers and earth-movers.

Mel whispered: 'He's one of those.'

'What?'

'An earth-mover.'

'He's OK.' He wasn't that special. He was an adventurer, an outdoors, restless type, quite sexy to watch from a distance, but who made you secretly glad you were with someone restful like Mel's Ian, or Richard. Or in my case, at the moment, not with.

Ed finished by saying that, to be really effective, the resistance had to come from local people. He could do nothing without us. Mel raised her eyebrows at me swoonily.

Then Suzy got up and started again: 'The people of Langley have been fighting this road for years . . .'

'And where were those bloody dole-scroungers then?' Dennis muttered in my left ear.

He meant the people with matted hair and plaited dreadlocks who were perching on the windowsills and squatting in front of the stage because they were too radical to sit on the orange plastic chairs, whose heads were shaved up the sides and zigzagged across the top; the ones you could tell didn't come from Langley from their multiple facial piercings.

Even as Suzy was finishing off about the stupidity of building a huge great motorway just to shave ten minutes off the journey into central London, her audience was already getting to its feet, gathering up its bags, and discussing whether Ed McGregor was sexier in the flesh or on television.

'In the flesh,' Mel said. 'And in my view, the more of it the better.'

'Richard not back then?' Dennis asked me conversationally.

I shook my head. It was encouraging, at least, that people still thought it was a possibility. But Emma's almost young enough to be Richard's daughter. Sooner or later, surely, she'll be old enough to leave the love nest.

Suzy clinked and jangled over to join us – she's part of a pyramid jewellery-selling operation – still flushed from her shared platform with Ed McGregor.

'Children not here? Richard got – what d'you call it? – access?'

'My mother's at home.'

'Oh well.' She looked at me pityingly. 'It'll be all right. Eventually. Emma's hardly . . . suitable, is she? In the meantime, have you thought about Ginny? You can't keep dragging your mother over here every time you need to get out . . . Oh, Ed!' she squealed, catching playfully at the sleeve of the famous environmentalist and centripetal force, who happened to be passing. 'Can I introduce Julie Ellison?' She beamed. 'She's got *lots* of time to help with the protest.' She lowered her voice. 'She's having a trial separation from her husband.'

'And it certainly is a trial,' I said, smiling through gritted teeth.

Ed's eyes, which were velvet-dark, held mine for a fraction longer than was necessary.

'Why are you doing this?' I asked him stupidly. 'Protesting?' It was all the talk about Richard, I think, and separation, and the disappointment of his not being here.

'People don't want a motorway slicing through Langley Wood and covering the green in concrete,' Ed said reasonably.

'No, they don't. But you can't stop it.'

Ed McGregor raised his eyebrows. Close-up, he was so handsome, it made me want to laugh.

'We've written hundreds of letters,' I pointed out, 'and we've been to public inquiries and stood outside the library with banners. We've even handed in a petition to Downing Street. It's all over. What difference d'you think squatting in a bunch of condemned houses on Cherry Drive is really going to make?'

Why was I doing this? I'd only just met the man and

I was behaving like he'd come up and punched me and then run over my dog.

'You don't think it's worth standing up for what you believe in?' Ed asked. 'Even if it doesn't look as though you're going to get it?'

I shrugged. I don't even have a dog. I was suddenly exhausted. He probably thought I was trying to flirt with him. Richard wasn't here, Arthur had got me up at six-thirty this morning and I wanted to go home.

I was saved from having to defend myself by the arrival of a beautiful, unfeasibly thin girl. She had a long neck, creamy skin and nearly non-existent hips. She was wearing jeans pushed down low to expose her really quite offensively flat midriff, and a tiny tie-dyed T-shirt (were they back in?) without a bra. It was clear that her breasts had never known the seductive pull of gravity – although to judge by the proprietorial way she put her hand on Ed McGregor's arm, the same might possibly not have been true of the seductive pull of Ed McGregor's hands.

'Could we talk about where we're going to put the office?' she asked, looking through us with the serene confidence of someone who knew she was more important than us. Then she flashed us a brilliant and utterly empty smile, and drew him away.

'You were very confrontational,' Suzy said disapprovingly. 'They're here to help us, you know.'

'Actually,' I said, 'I think I gave in too easily.'

Mel bounced up, wide-eyed. 'Julie, did he *speak* to you?'

'Have you signed up to provide soup?' Suzy asked

6

Mel severely. 'And have you seen this season's pendants?'

'They're lovely! I adore zirconia!' Mel lied warmly, deftly steering me away from Suzy. 'What did Ed McGregor say?'

'Nothing,' I said sourly. 'He gave me a sort of lecture about transport.'

'As in transport of delight?'

'No. We should go. Honestly, Mel, it's a cliché being a suburban mother who fancies Ed McGregor. Next thing you'll be wearing tracksuits to go shopping.'

'Joining a David Lloyd Centre to have an affair with the tennis coach!' she said. 'Got your car?' she added furtively.

'Yeah. You?'

'Yeah. See you tomorrow then, maybe.'

In fact, the person I saw tomorrow was Ed McGregor. I was putting the milk bottles out on the front step at eleven-thirty, and he was walking up my garden path.

'Leaflets.' He waved a sheaf of yellow papers. 'I'm delivering them. I didn't know you lived here.'

'No, well, you wouldn't.' I took one; it was advertising another meeting. 'Don't you have minions to do this?'

He smiled. 'We're very democratic. I take it you won't be coming?'

'No, I . . . Hey, bloody hell, look what you're doing!'

Ed McGregor – had he been leaving? Waltzing sideways? – had managed to kick two milk bottles off the step on to the path and smash them.

'Oh, I'm so sorry!' He bent down and picked up

some of the larger pieces of glass. 'Let me help you clear them up.'

I shook my head violently. 'No, it's fine, really.'

I still hadn't washed my hair, and I was wearing my most ancient pair of ripped jeans and an old shirt of Richard's. To be absolutely truthful, I wasn't entirely sure I'd quite got round to cleaning my teeth. I looked like a human compost heap.

But he insisted. 'I'm not leaving you with this mess. Have you got a dustpan and brush?'

'It's fine. Honestly.' Go away. Please. Come back when I'm wearing mascara.

I went inside to get something to sweep up the mess; infuriatingly, when I came back, he was still there, and he'd cut his thumb. He took the dustpan and brush out of my hands, swept up the broken glass and tipped it into the dustbin.

'Very masterful,' I said ironically.

He lounged against the wall and looked at me sideways. 'Please ma'am,' he said in a Deep South accent, 'could I have a glass of water?'

'Oh, for God's sake!' I wanted to reply, but didn't. 'Come in,' I muttered instead, and even managed to ask, more or less graciously: 'Do you need a plaster? Is it water you want, or something else? Coffee?'

Somehow, I already knew the answer.

'I'd love a coffee, thanks. And some water.'

And Ed McGregor pulled a chair out from the kitchen table and sat down.

'I hope you're less clumsy than that when you're swinging around in the branches saving trees.'

'I was distracted.'

8

'By what?'

'You.'

I blushed, but then decided he must mean because I was an eyesore.

He said: 'I was thinking you gave in too easily last night.'

'I couldn't see the point of arguing.'

'Like you can't see the point of fighting the developers?'

He watched me as I splashed hot water into the coffee pot. He had eyes like a cobra. Did I mean cobra? Or some other snake? 'What *can* you see the point of? What doesn't overwhelm you with a sense of futility?'

I got out cups noisily.

'Pursuing passions seems to you to be a waste of effort?'

'No, that's not true. I'm perfectly passionate.'

'About what?'

'My family.'

'Your children?'

'And my husband.'

'Ah. How long have you been separated?'

'That's none of your business.'

'But he's coming back?'

'That's none of your business either. Yes.'

What was I doing with this man in my kitchen, insulting me and generally being seismic? I felt muddled, and hot, and furious.

'If I went round pursuing my passions, as you call it, everything would fall apart,' I said, banging the cupboards shut. 'People depend on me and most of the time

I manage not to let them down. Milk, sugar? If I went *haring about* after things, it would all disintegrate.'

I put a mug of coffee down in front of him. I was going to get my own and sit down across the table, but before I had a chance, he grabbed my wrist. I stared at him, startled and confused, and made to pull away.

'Don't you ever feel – I don't know – *desperate*?'

'Well, I suppose sometimes,' I said doubtfully. What did he mean?

'Do you never think it doesn't matter what happens tomorrow?'

'No,' I said truthfully. 'I don't.' He was standing up now, and looking down into my eyes, making me think, weirdly, of famine and darkness, fire and deserts. 'I suppose, though,' I said carefully, 'I do sometimes think, "sod it".'

And then he kissed me. For a moment, I was too startled to respond. Then I kissed him back.

So then he kissed me on the throat, and then his hands were grazing and bruising my skin under my clothes, and that seemed to unlock his voice, and he was talking and talking, about how much he wanted me, and had ever since he first saw me last night, and how he didn't understand it, because this sort of thing didn't normally happen to him, this urgency, this longing, and then about what exactly it *was* he wanted to do and in what order and from which direction first.

And then, quite a lot of it, we did.

A little over an hour later, I shifted on the kitchen table. If Ed McGregor lay sprawled on top of me for much longer my left shoulder blade would get stuck in the wood and fossilise.

But I was happy. I am a suburban housewife – no, a *deserted* suburban housewife. I am in my late thirties, which is almost forty, and I can practically tuck my breasts into my trousers. But I had driven Ed McGregor – *the* Ed McGregor – to the edge of distraction. If only half the things he'd told me were true, I was Olympic standard at sex.

I looked down our tangled, naked bodies and was slightly surprised to see that they weren't covered in scorch marks.

Ed opened his eyes and frowned, then sat up.

'You're fantastically clumsy,' I said dreamily. 'You knocked that full cup of coffee on the floor. Another breakage.'

He kissed the end of my nose. 'I think that was you. And fantastically clumsy isn't what you were calling me twenty minutes ago.'

'No, that's true. Apart from the fantastic bit.'

He eased himself off the table. 'What came over us?'

'You did. More than once, actually.'

'You too, I seem to remember.'

He started picking up his clothes from the floor and pulling them on. His penis dangled long and damply between his legs. It made me smile.

I eased myself off the other side of the table, wishing the light wasn't quite so strong through the back garden window, wondering if he could see the caesarean scar. I looked around the kitchen and realised we still had a mug-tree. Richard had given it to me when we were at university.

But he wasn't looking at that. He'd picked up a book from the work surface.

'You reading this?'

It was a newish work by a famous biologist.

'No. Richard is.'

'Oh.' He put it down quickly.

'Is it good?' I asked.

'What? Oh, sort of. Interesting. Wrong.'

'Another cup of coffee? To make up for the one you didn't drink?'

He smiled at me, slow and deeply sexy. 'I'm not sure I ever really wanted one in the first place. But no. I ought to go.'

'All those leaflets to deliver.'

'Huh? Oh, yes. And to go home to Chelsea to change, and over to White City; I'm in studio later on.'

I nodded.

'Sometimes,' I said carefully, 'I suppose I do think it doesn't matter about tomorrow because this is only a one-night stand.'

'Actually, it's morning. Lunchtime, to be precise.'

'Bloody hell, so it is! We don't normally behave like this in Langley.'

He frowned. 'But I suppose the one-night principle could still apply . . .'

I got dressed quickly, so as not to show my disappointment. After all, I'd mentioned the one-night thing first. And I was a married woman. I had three children. I didn't want an affair. I didn't have time, what with the school run and everything.

But the sex *had* been fabulous. It would have been

12

interesting, at least, to see whether we could do it to that sort of standard again.

I stood up, biting my lip in confusion.

He smiled, and kissed me briefly on the mouth. He'd had a good time too – there wasn't much doubt about that – but I had the feeling that now that we'd agreed that it was only a one-lunchtime stand (sit, lie, kneel) he couldn't wait to get out of there.

Yet again, I felt I'd given in too easily.

Kate

Mum's sitting on the bathroom floor surrounded by piles of washing and staring morosely at the side of the bath. I asked her what she was thinking about and she said, 'Chelsea.' I hope she's not planning to get interested in football in a desperate attempt to meet men.

She's been in a funny mood for a week. I think it could be something to do with the road protest: she's been very furtive about the meeting. Perhaps she's finally realised how important the environment is. She used to think the ozone layer was something you got on your mahogany from using furniture polish.

I hope she isn't going to fall apart after all this time. You'd think she'd have got used to Dad being gone after a year. But her friend Mel obviously thinks she's having a crisis, because she brought round a vile liquid called St John's Wort a few days ago, which she said was like Prozac, only herbal, and Mum has been looking spacey ever since. I am fourteen, which is an age when girls need their mothers to be conscious.

When I found her sitting among the dirty T-shirts, I suggested maybe she should see a therapist. I only meant it would be someone to talk to, so she didn't have to tell it, whatever it is, to the side of the bath, but she snapped that she didn't think *she* was the one who needed therapy. So much for her and Dad staying friends.

If parents are going to split up, they should have better manners and not complain about each other in front of their children, so making us feel guilty for loving the other one. Mum tries to keep her feelings under control, but she is useless at it.

Julie

I was shocked at myself. How had I been so *loose*? Five minutes in his company, and allowing myself to be seduced . . . what must he think of me?

I had a pretty good idea, actually, because he hadn't called. Nearly a week now, and no word. Which, even though we'd agreed it was just the once, was still faintly insulting.

But there was no point in dwelling on it, going round and round in circles, when there were so many other things to be worrying about . . .

Richard, for instance. He was standing on the front path, with Emma beside him, grinning and clutching his arm and showing off a cleavage you could lose earrings down. He smiled down at her indulgently. Richard is tall and blond, with blue eyes that always seem to be swimming with feeling – perhaps because he isn't very good at articulating it and it swills around a lot.

'Children ready?' he said briskly to me.

I ushered them towards the door: Arthur purposeful

and sturdy on fat little legs, Kate vivid and hormonal, and Ben tripping over his shoelace. I reached out to catch him as he fell, but Emma got there first.

'C'mon, Benjy,' she said thickly though a mouthful of chewing gum, leading him down the path to her new convertible BMW. Her skirt was so tiny and stretchy, it could have doubled as an elastic band.

'You weren't at the protest meeting,' I said, too desperately, to Richard's retreating back.

'What's that?'

'About the road.'

'Huh?'

'The motorway extension.'

'Oh . . . Did he turn up, that environmentalist?'

'Ed McGregor.'

'Any good?'

How good, you will never know.

I might be ashamed of myself now. I might disbelieve everything that Ed McGregor had said, most particularly that he didn't do this sort of thing often, but at the time it had seemed natural, almost inevitable. And fabulous.

But perhaps, thinking about it, one day Richard *would* know. Perhaps that was why I'd done it. After all, a married woman needs a reason to have hot sex on the kitchen table with someone who simply happens to have turned up on her doorstep with a leaflet. And, actually, I'd had a *good* reason: now, if I wanted, I could grab Richard's hand and tell him that I understood, I'd done it too, I knew how these things happened. And now we were quits, couldn't we just forget it and go back to before? I forgave him.

This wasn't the moment though, because at this particular time Richard didn't want forgiveness from me, or anything else – apart, possibly, from spontaneous combustion.

The children waved from the car, but Richard studiously kept his eyes on the road. He wasn't interested in the years, the effort invested in our relationship. He was the emotional equivalent of one of those rogue traders who bring down banks. He'd disregarded all the time-honoured rules: there was to be no more careful husbanding for him. He'd cashed in. He was a speculator in emotional futures now, and derivatives too, probably, whatever they were. There was certainly nothing very original about Emma.

I went indoors and made a cup of coffee, thinking despondently that, for me, not much had changed since Richard and I had been cast opposite one another as Antony and Cleopatra for the university drama club. I was still Cleopatra, age not withering and custom not staling my infinite variety etc. Inside I was, anyway. For Richard, unfortunately, custom had not merely staled me, but covered me with speckly bright green mould.

When we met, he'd been going out with someone else. But then she'd dumped him, and I'd thought Richard was Antony (bloody Shakespeare) and he'd thought I was – what? available, probably. And he *had* seemed quite exciting back then: he used to sell the *Socialist Worker* outside Tesco's, and I used to fantasise about us ending up in Paris, a sort of latterday Sartre and de Beauvoir, debating ethics and influencing world governments through a haze of Gitanes. After Tesco's, it seemed the logical career progression.

But then Richard gave up the Socialist Workers for the Anarchists, and after that the Liberals, and he tried to become a local councillor, but he never got the votes. So he proposed to me in the china department of John Lewis instead and became head of history at Langley Boys' Grammar School.

Deep down, I was still Simone de Beauvoir, wanting only to sit in Les Deux Magots over an absinthe to come up with, say, a ground-breaking book on feminism. But Richard felt defined by his job and his Edwardian semi in Langley, and belittled by them. As Mel says, it's stupid to be defined by your job when you've got three children and a home to run, but that's men for you. Anyway, he became increasingly reluctant to see any of our old friends who'd become politicians or television executives or fat-cat lawyers or investment bankers, especially if they lived in Islington or Fulham.

And we moved to Langley, because Richard was offered a good job here.

'Anyway,' he said, on the day we moved in, 'I don't see why living in an almost outer suburb of London has to diminish us.'

But I suspect, deep down, that he wasn't convinced he belonged anywhere more glamorous.

And then one Saturday morning, he was stowing cornflakes in a kitchen cupboard – we were just back from Sainsbury's – when he suddenly sat back on his heels and said: 'I'm sorry, Julie, I can't do this any more.'

'I know,' I sympathised, 'it's bloody annoying. It's Arthur: one minute it's all Choco-Krispies, the next he won't eat anything except Frosties.'

19

'No. All of it. You and the children. Lying.'

Lying? Me-and-the-children-all-of-it?

'I'm in love with Emma Neil.'

When he looked up, the muscles were strained across his face and a pulse was thudding in his neck. He must have thought about how to manage this beforehand (though I can't believe he meant to say it with his head in a cupboard), but even he was horrified by the irreversibility of what he was doing.

'Since when?'

'June. When she came to talk to Year Nine PSE about drama college.'

I put out a hand to steady myself. The oven, hob and fridge had fragmented into lines and planes, a baffling geometry, all distorted and off-beam. The cups on the draining board were busy breaking up into a cubist jumble. The plates, the saucepans – all the apparently solid things that used to support our marriage and prop us up – were suddenly insubstantial and fragmentary, all jagged surfaces and acute angles.

I'd thought beforehand that I was prepared for bad things. I'm always imagining disasters involving mad cow disease, flesh-eating bugs, and bits of space detritus tumbling through the stratosphere straight on to our house. But somehow I just wasn't prepared for Emma Neil.

I once shared a stall with her mother at Langley Grammar School Parents' Association Summer Fayre. Good as New, I think it was called, which we decided summed us up as well. Wrongly.

Emma and Richard first met when he taught her history in an experimental teaching exchange with

20

the boys' school. I can't imagine she was a very apt pupil. Her favourite kings came filter-tipped and the only dates she had time for involved boys in cars.

Yet she was probably Langley Grammar's most glittering success. Two weeks before Richard announced that he was leaving us to set up home with Emma in what the *News of the World* was subsequently to call a romantic hideaway, her picture was on the front page of the *Langley Advertiser*. She'd landed a part as someone's long-lost step-sister in *EastEnders*.

I like to think that what Richard mainly sees in her are film premieres and pictures of his kitchen in *Hello!*. But actually, he was having an affair with her *before* she was famous. He found me boring by comparison even when she was a school-leaver with chipped nail polish. I am a housewife in Langley, with its Sunday morning car-washing ceremony, its turf-laying sacrament, and its convenient proximity to the retail parks of the North Circular, and I disappointed him.

As a parent, you want to be good enough. That's the buzzword-thing: good enough is actually very good. Richard and I, it always seemed to me, had a good enough marriage. It may not have been thrilling or spectacular, a wild rampaging other-world of sex and violence, but it worked.

What right did Richard have to be dissatisfied with good enough?

Two hours later, I appeared to be still at the kitchen table with a cup of coffee thinking about Richard. Specifically, now, I was thinking that this thing with Emma has gone on long enough. It's downright insulting to lose your husband to a peroxide bimbo with nothing more to recommend her than a toned musculature. Secondly, he's mine. And thirdly, I love him. *Obviously*, I love him. He's the father of my children and we've spent sixteen years together and that's surely not meaningless? I've heard of taking a wrong turning, but this was *marriage*, a bloody Himalayan trek. We weren't in a position to divert.

I considered the pros and cons of accidentally-on-purpose poisoning or gassing myself, the tearful hospital scenes as he begged me to return to consciousness and absolve him. But he might not make it to intensive care on time. He might be waylaid by an urgent squash game with George Michael or lunch with Posh Spice. I also ran through the possibilities of hair dye, facelifts and liposuction, but I could have total body reengineering and still not be able to compete with Emma. Especially if I had total body reengineering I wouldn't be able to compete with Emma, who looks as though she's been on a sunbed even when she hasn't, and whose breasts look silicone, even though they're real, and whose nose is so perfectly, naturally retroussé that you'd swear it could only have come off the operating table of a world expert in rhinoplasty.

And then I considered sex with Ed McGregor in the new light of its having been a masterplan to lure Richard back, but I got a bit distracted by needing to go over it in very, very explicit detail . . .

Oh God, this was so self-destructive. It was a fling. It could never have been anything else. He knew I was married and I knew he could have pretty much anyone.

Anyone like me, anyway. Whatever he'd said (and he'd said so much; that I was lovely and breathtaking and this didn't normally happen to him, this connection with another person – *connection*, he'd actually used that word) I knew, or should have known, that it was just a line.

'I suppose it's one of those life-experiences everyone should have,' I said gloomily to Mel, because even though I obviously didn't want to have an affair with him – couldn't afford to, in the light of my continued plans for Richard – I was mildly insulted that he didn't want to have one with me.

'Perhaps he's worried that you'd be too much of a distraction. He wouldn't be able to concentrate on lying down in front of the bulldozers, or whatever it is he does.'

'Perhaps it was my mug tree. So hopelessly seventies. Perhaps he realised I'm older than I look.'

'In which case, you're better off without him.'

'*Obviously*, I'm better off without him.'

Once a week had gone by, I abandoned any pretence that he was just playing it cool. Sex for him was *always* that electrifying; no, usually it was *more* electrifying. That had been run-of-the-mill, production line, factory-second stuff.

When I first met Richard (as he explained when he left me), I'd been interested in all sorts of things – politics, movies, Samuel Beckett, the possibility of being discovered by Steven Spielberg. Now I'm chiefly interested in keeping the coloureds out of the hot wash and getting the children to bed by nine o'clock. I ceased to be the aspiring actress he married, and became the woman who cleans the kitchen floor. Never mind that I only became so boring because boring was what he seemed to want; boring, apparently, is what I am.

As Richard would no doubt have known, and told me, Ed McGregor was never going to call.

Ben

Mum's friend Mel is here again. They're in the kitchen, talking about Ed McGregor being sexy. Or Mel is. Mum doesn't think anyone's sexy except Dad, which is lucky, as she's married to him. Well, not at the moment, but usually.

If I wanted to wear an earring and live up a tree I bet they wouldn't think it was sexy. They'd send me to my room.

Ed McGregor and the protesters are trying to save the chestnut tree on the green. After that, they're going to squat in the houses in Cherry Drive until they're dragged out. I didn't know the tree was so old, or a chestnut. But it's a beautiful tree (if I'm thinking of the right one) and obviously it shouldn't be chopped down. Cars give children asthma and shrink our brains, even though they are quite useful and we couldn't get to Dad's flat on public transport, at least not without changing twice.

(And come to think of it, some cars, such as Ferraris, Jaguars, etc are really more beautiful than the tree. I have never collected model trees.)

When the protesters move into the houses they will live on floors in sleeping bags and make concrete bunkers and padlock themselves to furniture bolted on to the floor. Some people will attach themselves to dangerous walkways. It sounds brilliant. I have volunteered my bike lock, because Sam Everitt says Ed McGregor explained that bike locks are important to allow people to chain their necks to the branches etc. I wanted to volunteer my neck as well, but Mum said that twelve is too young to have a broken neck.

Perhaps I can be a road protester when I grow up. You don't need many qualifications.

Julie

Fran is one of the people Richard's spent the last ten years trying to avoid. She's too damn successful. She's never married, has a bank account instead, and lives in a four-storey white stuccoed house in Notting Hill. She sends all her laundry out for someone else to deal with, and her idea of home cooking is to get a celebrity chef to send round a lobster.

Fran buys clothes from designer collections when they're in season, not in the sales, and looks brilliant in them because she's whippet-thin, with shoulders like coat hangers and legs that belong on a pylon. The sort of money I budget for food for five people, Fran spends on reflexology, cranial osteopathy, acupuncture, colonic irrigation and skincare. As a result, she's always buffed and polished and gleaming.

It's a sign of Fran's loyalty – we've known each other for ever – and her general niceness that she still sees me at least once a fortnight and refused ever to be put off by Richard's ridiculous inverted snobbery about people who aren't teachers. But, without meaning to, she sometimes makes me feel like a fat old suburban reject. I wasn't sure I was up to telling her I'd been dumped by another man, and this time, without getting much relationship in first.

'You sounded depressed on the phone,' she remarked this evening, unpacking, from a Harvey Nichols bag, one bottle of vintage champagne, one tub of olives and one packet of posh crisps.

This was my cue to tell her about Ed McGregor. Except that I wasn't convinced she'd appreciate the *seriousness* of my motives. She'd think he was the housewives' heart-throb and I was the housewife.

I tried to work my way round to it. 'How did this happen to me, ending up in Langley with three children and a husband?'

'You know what?' She popped an olive into her immaculately painted mouth. 'You should get a job.'

'You sound like my mother.'

'Your mother talks a lot of sense. A lot of rubbish too; but she *is* right that you were mad to give up work – especially for Richard, who only ever wanted to turn you into a drudge.'

'Hang on . . .'

'He did, and you know it. He wanted you to be one of those women who serves fondant fancies and beams at piles of whiter washing.'

'Then why did he leave?'

'Because he didn't succeed and you're still beautiful and talented. You're funny and smart and a wonderful mother.' She picked Arthur up from the floor, where he was nibbling a leaf that someone had walked in from the garden.

28

It *is* true that Richard was always the one who wanted to get married and have children and move to Langley and for me to give up work and develop a relationship with the ironing board. He'd hated me having a proper career, even though when I gave up acting I was earning more than him. But I'd wanted our life to be comfortable and contented, so I gave in and left work. I was as guilty as he was; I honestly thought I was doing the right thing.

'You've really got something, Jools . . .' Fran insisted. Could she be drunk already, or did people in advertising sometimes lapse into this overdone, mwah-mwah manner?

This was my cue to tell her that Ed McGregor had obviously thought I had something too. (What, though? Open legs?)

'. . . The trouble is, you're insecure. You don't believe in yourself. Any chance you get for a bit of emotional analgesic, you take it.'

'What do you mean?' I said indignantly.

'S'amazing really,' she added, 'considering your background.'

She meant because my mother was the first feminist in Letchworth, always quoting Betty Friedan over the washing-up and Germaine Greer as she whizzed round Sainsbury's. But, somehow, my mum reconciled reading Andrea Dworkin with having dinner on the table for my dad when he got in from work. Unfortunately, I lack her sleight of hand, and exist in a puddle of contradictory ideals.

'Your marriage became a way of avoiding life, which is the opposite of what it should be.'

How the hell did she know? It wasn't as if anyone had ever *wanted* to marry her.

'Honestly, Jools, why don't you get a job?'

'What job could I get?' I asked irritably. 'I'm at the age when people get downsized. And they're the ones who are qualified to do something in the first place.'

'Didn't that bloke next door ask you if you were interested in working on the local paper?'

'I wouldn't know what to do.'

'Don't be daft. You can find things out, and you can type, and people are always telling you things they shouldn't. It's because you've got a nice face.'

'I don't think that's enough.'

'And you've been successful before. The RSC is successful. They'll be impressed by that, funny little local paper. This is exactly what I mean about emotional analgesic: you take the easy way out. You should jump at it.'

Experience-wise, I've been bloody bungee-jumping lately, but I didn't get to tell her about that because the doorbell was ringing, and when I went to answer it, Ben was on the step, his cheeks streaked grubby with tears, sniffing the snot back into his nostrils and gulping it down his throat.

'I g-g-got mugged!'

I led him down the hall and sat him down in the kitchen.

'These boys . . . two of them . . .' He was crying and he wiped the back of his hand across his cheek, smearing grime from his eye to his ear.

'Did they hurt you?'

'They asked if they could go on my skateboard and

I let them and they *took* it!'

'We must call the police!' Fran said.

'Why did they *do* that? I never did anything to them,' Ben complained.

'I'm afraid that's not necessarily how it works.'

How it works is that if you look too sweet, too trusting, too good-humouredly available to life, and you happen to be a twelve-year-old boy, you get picked on.

Ten minutes later, a couple of police officers called by and listened gravely to what we had to say. But they couldn't offer much hope of catching the culprits, still less of retrieving Ben's skateboard.

'This is why I need a man around!' I said to Fran, when they'd gone and Ben had disappeared upstairs to wash his face. 'He needs his father. He's getting too much of me and it's turning him into a wuss.'

'It's not as if he doesn't see his father,' Fran said – but then she wants to persuade me I don't need Richard back. 'He never used to get picked for football teams before.'

'In trying to make him into a good man – empathetic, unafraid of his emotions, tough but tender – all I'm doing is turning him into a lousy boy, unable to shout "tits out for the lads" at passing women, and incapable, when people ask for a go on his skateboard, of smacking them in the mouth. And every time something goes wrong for him, which is more or less once a day, I assume it's my fault. Children whose parents aren't together do worse at everything.'

Fran swigged her champagne. 'What you need,' she repeated smugly – there are times when she really quite gets on my nerves – 'is a job.'

*　*　*

'Mum,' Ben said later, when Fran had gone, 'can I still go to the Ed McGregor meeting tomorrow?'

'What?' I jumped, which was ridiculous (I really should have put it behind me by now). 'I don't think so.'

'Why not?'

'I went to one of those meetings and they're a waste of time. It's just Suzy Sharp making speeches.'

'But you said! When Kate and I couldn't go before!'

'I've changed my mind.'

Ed McGregor would think I was pursuing him. I'd feel like a stalker.

'But everyone at school talks about it! I'll be left out again!'

'I'm sorry, Ben, but I'm not going.'

'Is this because of my skateboard?'

'What? No, of course not.'

'Why, then?'

'Oh, Ben, please . . .'

He brightened. 'Could I go with Sam and his mum?'

'Oh God,' I said wearily (how could he think I'd punish him for being mugged?), 'if you must.'

Frankly, I don't know why he's so interested. It's boring as hell. Carbon dioxide bloody emissions. He's probably got it mixed up with something else. He probably thinks the green belt is something to do with judo.

'But they have to drive you home,' I said severely. 'I'm not going anywhere near that hall.'

Two days later, when Ben had described to me for the twenty-fifth time how Ed McGregor planned to save the chestnut tree on Langley Green by building a house in the branches of old planks and sheets of corrugated tin, I snapped: 'Don't you think Ed McGregor should grow up?'

So then I had to go out into the garden to stop myself from bursting into tears, and to dig off some of my bad temper, and I happened to see Tony over the fence, mowing his mother's lawn.

I edged sideways, fiddled negligently with my clematis, then said: 'Were you serious when you said the *Advertiser* needed some help?'

Tony switched off his mower. 'Would you be interested?'

'I might.'

I've spent the last thirteen years picking up toys. A much more important question was whether they'd be interested in me. I didn't share Fran's faith that all I needed for success was a nice face.

Tony joined me at the fence. 'It's not glamorous,' he warned. 'And Pete, the editor, still gets a bit confused about whether women are in offices to make the tea.'

'I'm world-class at tea-making.'

'And the pay's terrible.'

'You're making it sound irresistible.'

'And there are silverfish in the lavatories.'

'You're desperate, aren't you?'

Tony grinned. '*I* am. There's no one for me to talk to. I'll tell Pete.'

I went indoors and called Suzy Sharp about Ginny, her neighbour, whom she is always trying to foist upon me for childcare. Suzy says Ginny makes Mary Poppins look like a slut.

Kate

Mum's been offered a job on the local paper. God knows how. She has no skills. Grandma will be really pleased, because she is a feminist and believes women have to be freed from financial dependency to have true equality. She makes Mum feel inadequate. It is a relief that my mother is never likely to make me feel inadequate.

I'm hoping Mum will have more money when she starts her new job. Trainers are getting more and more expensive. The only other thing she needs now is a man, but that will be hard at her age. She is quite pretty, for a mother, but skin begins to biodegrade after the age of thirty-five, which means she is already carrying around several years of decay on her face. My friend Rachel says she wears cool clothes, like granddad shirts and vests and combat trousers. She certainly has her own style, which is not everyone's, but quite often she looks like a plumber.

I am hoping that the new job, though only part-time, will leave her with less time to think about me, because now Dad's living in a warehouse space she thinks she has to be Captain Sensible. She says I can't get my ears pierced because when she was at school girls who did that always got pregnant. I have tried to tell her that this is not how pregnancy happens, but it appears she knows even less about sex than I thought.

This evening Suzy Sharp brought her next-door neighbour round for an interview to look after Arthur when Mum's at work. Suzy barged in, pointed at a spot on the sofa for Ginny, the neighbour, then sat down between her and Mum like a human shield.

'Do you have any brothers or sisters, Ginny?' Mum asked.

Suzy said: 'She has two older sisters.'

'And have you looked after children before?'

'She's been involved with my two, helping out.'

'But you haven't actually had any training?'

'I don't think that's important,' Suzy said. 'It matters *much* more to have the right kind of personality. Don't you think? They teach a lot of nonsense on those courses – no smacking . . .'

'Perhaps Ginny could answer herself . . .' Mum suggested. 'What about discipline, Ginny? What would you do if Ben or Arthur simply refused to do something?'

Ginny looked terrified.

'Oh, well, obviously she doesn't *approve* of smacking! She doesn't go round looking for *opportunities* to hit them! She's not one of those child-battering nannies. You shouldn't be so literal-minded. All I meant was, a lot of that theory isn't necessarily important when you get on the job.'

It was hopeless. I don't think Ginny got the chance to answer a single question. Suzy told Mum Ginny's entire family history, and all about her media studies course and how she planned to fit this job round it, and she even promised that Ginny could help out in the evenings whenever Mum needed babysitting. (I hope she'd checked with Ginny beforehand.) The only time I heard Ginny utter a sound was when Mum asked if she had a boyfriend and the corners of her mouth turned down, her eyes filled with tears, and she made a kind of strangulated noise in her throat.

'Bit of trouble lately,' Suzy admitted. 'But we're getting over that now. Aren't we?'

Ginny nodded dismally.

The one good thing about her was that she hadn't been in the room five minutes when Arthur went over and climbed on her lap. He sat there nuzzling his face into her chest and rubbing noses with her until Mum finished shooting questions at her and Suzy finished answering them. Then he took her hand and led her upstairs to meet his dinosaur collection.

So Mum agreed to give her a trial, and Suzy said why not have her babysit next Saturday, because she, Suzy, was having a barbecue and there was someone she was dying for Mum to meet. Mum looked absolutely horrified and told some lie about being busy on Saturday, but Suzy carried on, her voice getting louder to cover Mum's protestations, about this bloke Mum will 'love', apparently. She is the most bossy woman I have ever met.

After Suzy had lassoed Ginny in again and led her away, I asked Mum how she'd got so domineering, and Mum said she'd decided she was a force in the community. I said, 'What, like ethnic cleansing?' and Mum said it was partly to avoid turning into someone like Suzy that she was going out to work.

Julie

I was waiting for Mel at Polly's, the tea shop in the High Street. Polly's has only been open fifteen months, but it's got up to look like a Cotswolds farmhouse kitchen circa 1935: gingham tablecloths, high-backed settles with cushions, lace curtains and young girls in pinafores bustling about serving fat sponges, jam scones and tea in Denbigh Ware. The last time I was at Polly's it was with Richard, discussing our Situation. We had lots of those meetings in the first few months. We called them discussions, but, actually, they were more like lectures, with Richard listing his aims and requirements while I stared at him stupidly, wondering what had gone wrong. Anyway, he'd got bored with the meetings eventually, and they now seemed as much a part of the past as Polly's heritage butter pots.

I hadn't, as a result, had a graceful opportunity to tell Richard about Ed McGregor, even if there'd been anything to tell.

I *had*, though, managed to get a job. And now Mel wanted to hear all about my interview – not, actually, that there was all that much to tell about that either. It had lasted approximately seven minutes.

I'd worn jeans, on Tony's advice, but I was still overdressed. Pete's shirt seemed to be covered in baked beans.

He shook my hand, avoiding my eyes, sat down heavily behind his desk and blurted out: 'Tony says you can help him and you don't need IT training.'

I began my little speech about what I could contribute to the *Advertiser*, but he interrupted: 'We don't pay much.' He picked up a paperclip and unbent it nervously. 'I don't know why we can't get *young* people. We should be able to attract someone other than bored housewives.'

'Excuse me . . .'

'All right, I don't mean you, obviously. We'll give you a trial. Two weeks. That'll be long enough to tell if you're crap.'

And that was it.

I went home and employed Ginny, who is fair, loose-limbed and hefty, like someone in a 1930s poster for youth hostelling. By the time I've paid for a sandwich at lunchtime, the odd beer for Pete and the vast remuneration negotiated for Ginny by Suzy Sharp, I'll be about six pounds a week better off.

'Are you taking commission?' I asked Suzy suspiciously when she refused to budge from her unreasonably high pay demands for Ginny to come in for a few hours after school and the two mornings when Arthur's not at nursery.

Suzy gave one of her little tinkling laughs. 'You know what, though? I think I'm rather good at this. When

I've finished with the road protest, perhaps I should get a job as an agent.'

When I told Mel, she suggested: 'She could call herself Agent Orange.'

Ginny is so far from being the Mary Poppins of Metroland that I am half-expecting her to turn up for work accompanied by Suzy. I have still not heard her speak.

'The boys need a mum,' Kate objected acidly last night, when she was annoyed with me about my illiberal attitude to ear-piercing. 'Someone who stays mum isn't quite the same thing.'

Still, after she'd gone home from the so-called interview, Arthur said:

'She's nice, that lady. Is she coming again?'

I can only think she must communicate with him at some extra-sensory level, by hitherto-undetected toddler rays. And if she makes him feel settled and happy, I really don't care if she never says a word to me.

'I wonder, sometimes, what we're here for,' someone was saying behind me, over the back of the settle. For a moment I thought she was having an existential crisis in Polly's Tea Shoppe, which would be understandable, if unusual. But then she continued: 'I can't stand the place.'

The person who was speaking had an over-enunciated, upper-class voice, not the usual slipshod London-fringes you expect to hear on a Tuesday afternoon in Langley.

'The commuter-belt smugness, the Rotary Club husbands and the women with their conversations about paint effects and garden size.'

'It's so bloody anonymous,' someone agreed. 'Scotch pines and tidy streets. Miniaturised Voysey villas.'

I froze. I knew that gravelly, back-of-the-throat voice. The last time I'd heard that voice, it had been whispering fabulous obscenities in my hair.

'Yah. You could be in any one of half a dozen other places and you'd never know the difference.'

It was the person with the self-supporting breasts and sticking-out cheekbones. Had to be. She was bound to have that kind of bored, supercilious drawl. And she was talking about us.

I considered poking my head over the top of the settle and re-introducing myself to Ed McGregor. I could hardly be accused of stalking him here. I'd arrived first.

'The women are the worst,' the girl continued. 'That Sharp woman. Thinks because she once ran a cake stall she can run a road protest.'

'Sssh!' Ed said, laughing. But he wasn't disagreeing. He wasn't saying, 'Oh, no, you're wrong about that: you should see them naked on their kitchen tables.'

'Either that or passive-aggressive,' the girl went on. Behind her, concealed by the high settle, I flushed brilliantly. What did she mean, passive-aggressive? Was I this? Was this what Fran had been trying to say with all that stuff about emotional anaesthesia, or whatever she called it? It'd been a very rude way of referring to my husband, anyway.

'Sometimes I wonder what we're doing here,' the girl went on loudly, 'preserving their little enclave of respectability and comfort: the High Street with ye olde tea shoppe and the florist's and the hairdresser's . . . it's so fucking anodyne.'

'And no better when you get inside the houses,' Ed agreed. 'Stripped pine and mug-trees. And ornaments. All those bloody ornaments.'

My cheeks flamed. How *dare* he? How could he do that, come into my house and pretend to be having a good time, then make fun of me with his snobby friends?

'Oh well,' Ed McGregor sighed, 'come on, let's go and save it.'

There was a scuffling as they got up from their seats, and a ping of the door as they left the shop.

I sat low in my seat, hating him. If there had been any idea left in my mind that I might, somehow, one day, repeat the Ed McGregor sex experience, it was gone. I never even wanted to see him again, let alone have him touch me. My flesh crawled at the idea that I'd let such a horrible person anywhere near it.

Mel slipped into the seat opposite me, her eyes shining.

'You'll never guess who I've just seen!'

'Ed McGregor.'

'Oh!' Her face fell. 'You might have pretended! Was he in here? Did you speak to him?'

'I'm never going to speak to him again. He made fun of my mug-tree.'

'Your what?'

'Mug-tree. You *know*,' I said exasperatedly, 'thing you hang mugs on . . . Oh my God!'

'What?'

'I've just remembered. Richard's mother's figurine-thing. Lladrò, I think it's called.'

'What are you talking about?'

'In the kitchen. On a high shelf. It's absolutely vile but they cost a fortune and Richard's mother gave it to us. I couldn't throw it away, and Richard insisted on leaving it out in case they ever dropped round, and of course he didn't take it to Clerkenwell, it's not white . . . I'd stopped noticing it, you know how it is. That must have been what he was talking about. That's why he never called. He can't stand the idea of having sex with someone with ornaments.'

'You're mad.'

'Was he with that skinny girl?'

'She's called Nettle.'

'Ha! vicious by name . . .'

'I thought you didn't care about him?'

'I don't. I just wanted to have someone to show off to Richard about. And Ed's as famous as Emma, but old enough to have sex without getting the other person arrested. But now I wouldn't have sex with him if we were the last two people in the world.'

I told her, briefly, how he had made fun of our trees and villas.

'He villa-fied us?' Mel gurgled; sometimes she has no respect for my emotions at all. 'Do you think he and Nettle are – you know, together?'

'I hope so,' I said bitterly. 'They deserve each other.'

Ben

Why does Mum have to get a job? We've already been abandoned by one parent. And she's hired someone called Ginny to look after us, who isn't even qualified to do it. Mum asked if I had any objections and I couldn't think of any right there and then, and she assumed that was the same thing as not having any.

She's been behaving very strangely since the road protesters arrived. She doesn't like Ed McGregor for some reason. It's probably because he's sexy: he reminds her she hasn't got a husband.

If the road comes through Langley it will affect house prices in the whole area. Ed McGregor doesn't talk about that much; he is more interested in air quality. But everyone else does, and it's the sort of thing Dad cares about. He still jointly owns our house; he's always going on about it. So perhaps he and Mum will be united by the struggle to keep the property market healthy.

Then if they got back together I might not lose so many things, e.g. my skateboard. I used to lose things before, but not so often, and there's always stuff on the news about the children of divorced people failing at everything, so I suspect my parents are actually to blame.

I'd only gone out on the skateboard in the first place because Mum had shouted at me for dropping a bottle of milk on the floor. It was in the part of the kitchen that slopes, so the milk went under the fridge. And then I thought those boys in the park wanted to be friends, and I was pleased because I don't have that many friends – only Sam Everitt, and he's not that keen to hang round with me because then Adrian Farr picks on him as well. And now it's even harder to make new friends than before because I have two homes and if people want to ring up they don't know which number to dial. Even I can't remember them both.

Today, Adrian laughed at me because I fell over my desk in the classroom and it gave me a nosebleed. Everyone else laughed too, so I went to the toilets and locked myself in and imagined Mum and Dad going to court to fight over who should look after us, and neither of them wanting to.

What you want from your parents is a Nintendo 64 and trips to Disneyland Paris, not going off with other people. And now Mum has invited this Ginny person over tomorrow night so she can go to a barbecue at Suzy Sharp's house. Why does she want to go out? She is a mother of three. I only hope she is not going to meet another man before she's had a chance to get back together with Dad because of the house prices.

Julie

'You must go. If you've said you would . . .' Kate scrutinised her split ends. 'Is it OK for Rachel to come over?'

'Anyone else?'

'No. We need to revise for our French test.'

I bet it was a French kissing test. A boy had telephoned several times recently.

Kate's possible plans to become a teenage pregnancy statistic aside, I *really* didn't want to go to the Sharps'. Even Richard, in his previous man-at-suburbia incarnation, used to say their life was switched off at the mains. We only knew them because Dennis and Richard used to play squash, and now we didn't even have that. Richard always used to claim he spent entire evenings waiting for Suzy to invite everyone to throw their car keys into a bowl, because, he said, it was inconceivable this was all there was to it.

Unfortunately, since Richard left, Suzy has been behaving as though she has adoption rights to me. I feel a bit guilty about resenting this so much, because she means well and she has admirable energy. I just wish she'd find another outlet for it. Powering the national grid or something.

'She's going to try and pair me off!' I told Mel in a panicky phone call when I was really supposed to be getting ready.

'I thought you *wanted* to sleep with someone else, to find out whether it was as good as it was with Ed?'

'I'm *sure* it is.' I was reluctant to think that Ed was special after the appalling way he'd behaved. (Some explanation, apology, acknowledgement would have been *polite*, at least.) 'Anyway, can you imagine Suzy coming up with anyone that I'd remotely want to seduce?' I envisaged this man portly and avuncular, with broken veins.

'But if you don't go, you'll never know,' Mel said reasonably. 'And if you keep running away from possibilities, you'll *never* find someone to torment Richard with.'

That was true, and it was what Fran would have said too, so I changed into a pair of combat trousers and a sludgy green silk shirt. It didn't look right. It's difficult to know what to wear to the Sharps', because Suzy favours blazers with brass buttons from Planet, but I don't have any of those and, in any case, I think the Sharps invite me for some sort of imagined funkiness. I changed the shirt for a T-shirt and the trousers for a black stretchy pair but they didn't look right either, so I put the first lot back on again, by which time I was late.

Suzy and Dennis live in a detached house with a circular driveway in the front and a large Edwardian-style conservatory at the back. I went through the side gate to the garden, feeling nervous, knowing that I am still an object of grim fascination in Langley, the woman whose husband left her for a soap star. I have all the horrific allure of a motorway pile-up.

The men were outside on the patio, where Dennis was flame-grilling flamboyantly, watched by Brian, an estate agent who lives next door to the Sharps, and Patrick, who's something in banking. It's a primal thing, men and barbecues. Mel says someone should make a gas cooker that taps into this male memory of roasting mammoth on the neolithic savannah.

Nicki and Jo were sitting on cane chairs in the conservatory, watching their men complacently, like women who think separating is something you do to eggs.

'Just waiting for a few more people,' Suzy said, winking at me. 'Guacamole, anyone?'

Nicki crunched on a celery stick. 'Did you invite Ed McGregor?'

'Yes, he couldn't come, but he was very nice about it. "Another time," he said. Did you see he was in the *Harpers & Queen* top ten bachelors in Britain?'

I grimaced. Ed McGregor was about as eligible, as far as we were concerned, as the Pope. Never in a million years would he be able to make it to one of Suzy's neighbourhood barbecues.

'I don't like him much,' I said, reluctant to be co-opted by the Ed McGregor groupies.

Nicki scooped up some more dip on her cheesy biscuit. 'Why's that?'

'He's conceited and supercilious and he's just *using* us,' I said, more vigorously than I meant to.

Suzy said: 'We can't stop the road on our own.'

'We can't stop the road anyway. He's exploiting us to get his name in the papers yet again and to seem like an action hero. We're just his pawns.' Or in my case, porn.

'He *cares* about improving the environment,' Jo said. 'He makes all those television programmes about it.'

'He cares about improving his image.'

Suzy shot me an irritable glance, but then something caught her eye across the garden. 'Oh goody,' she chirruped, and skipped forward to meet a man who was coming across the grass.

This, I thought glumly, was my future: to be confronted with a series of preposterous romantic prospects by Suzy and other women whose own lives were so dull that they had to get their kicks from my efforts to avoid sex with hideous men. My role from now on was to be the Houdini of the unwanted sexual escapade, providing sly satisfaction for Suzy and her friends, whose husbands may have been dreary old couch potatoes but at least stuck to their own couches.

And then I saw him properly. He was tall and slim, with Scandinavian-brown skin, dishevelled dirty-blond hair and blue eyes. He was gorgeous.

Suzy dragged him across the lawn with the air of a waiter lifting a silver lid off a plate. 'Can I introduce Simon Hemingway?' she beamed. 'He's in the music business – don't ask me doing what, I lost track after Abba.'

Simon was wearing summery drawstring trousers and a T-shirt that clung to his torso. This in itself was pretty amazing: all the other men in Suzy's garden were wearing striped shirts and jeans one size too small, so that their paunches bulged over their waistbands. But more amazing still, it was a fabulous torso, solid but slender, so that you felt if you slid your hand under his T-shirt, you could feel all the individual ribs and the gristle between them.

'I told you about Julie,' Suzy reminded him. 'Her husband's left her. None of us can understand why, even though he's gone off with Emma Neil, because Julie's at least as pretty, wouldn't you say?'

'Rather older, though,' I pointed out, smiling through gritted teeth.

'And Julie has lots of glamorous friends,' Suzy went on, ignoring me, 'and she's *much* trendier than any of us.'

Simon caught my eye. His smile was lovely – amused and complicit.

'Simon's just moved to Langley,' Suzy informed me, 'and Dennis and I are wondering if he, too, isn't nursing a little bit of a broken heart. Is that right, Simon?'

'Er . . .' Simon looked nonplussed.

'Some Dark Lady?' Suzy winked roguishly.

'Wasn't the dark lady really a man?' I objected.

'Honestly, Julie! Poor man! Never mind her, Simon! Why don't you two go and get some steak?'

Simon caught my eye again; I nodded with relief, and we made our escape down the garden together. Any more of Suzy and I'd have to go and find somewhere to hide and not come out for several decades.

'Is she always like that?' Simon asked in amazement, as soon as we were out of earshot.

''Fraid so. She'll never get a job as an international mediator.'

Over at the barbecue, there was steak, chicken and sausages, plus a loin of pork. Dennis and the other men had moved on from beer to red wine.

'Don't tell anyone,' Simon whispered in my hair, rather sexily, 'but I'm vegetarian.'

We got some food – Simon rather less than me, but then it was mostly meat on offer and, in any case, he probably couldn't afford to eat much if he was going to retain that trampoline torso – and wandered off to sit on a bench at the bottom of the garden. It was one of the first really warm evenings of the summer, with leaves rustling softly above us and moths dancing in the light from the garden flares. I sat down, sank back and let the garden waft over me. There was a heady scent of honeysuckle tumbling from the side wall.

'So, tell me about your glamorous friends,' Simon said slyly.

'I don't know what she's talking about. The most glamorous thing I do is look at *Vogue* in the hairdresser's, and even then, I come out realising I've only really read the recipes. How about you: what are you doing in Langley?'

He speared a piece of radicchio. 'Running away.'

I thought grimly of what Ed McGregor had said about its anonymity.

'Suzy's right, in fact: there *is* a dark lady. Or was:

I've just come out of a long relationship. One way and another, I couldn't stand to stay in Manchester any longer. I inherited a house from an uncle, so I came down here. Notionally, I'm investigating the sounds of suburbia.'

'What are they?'

'You're not *that* trendy,' Simon said drily. 'It's a group of bands clustered around the M25. The next big thing. We think, anyway.' He looked up the garden, to where Suzy, surrounded by the other women, had her latest jewellery brochure out. 'You like it here?'

'It's become a habit. Some people smoke cigarettes, I live in Langley.'

He looked puzzled.

'It's relaxing, undemanding and quite pleasant in its way, and you only notice once every decade or so that your vital organs are atrophying.' I smiled. 'I can't quite understand how I ended up here. Still,' – I stretched my legs in front of me; he was very easy to be with – 'I have a rich fantasy life to compensate. I pretend to be Scarlett O'Hara as I go round the supermarket, or Joan of Arc as I do the ironing.'

He smiled. 'Oh, me too; I'm always pretending to be someone else. Oscar Wilde said – what was it? – "One's real life is often the life one does not lead." Something like that.'

I couldn't see why Simon would need an alternative to his real life. He was handsome – lean and lithe and athletic-looking. He had what sounded like a great job. And he had heaps of charm, and a dry, mischievous sense of humour. It was difficult to see how he could be more attractive.

'Actually – ' he stretched his legs too, alongside mine – 'I suspect we fantasists are happier than other people. We have a rosier view. Those boring old realists know how dreary life is; it makes them morose. It's why romantic love will never go out of fashion.'

I glanced at him sharply, suspecting he was trying to tell me something. But he raised his eyebrows wryly, and somehow I couldn't ask. Not yet, anyway.

We spent the rest of the evening together. Possibly there wasn't much competition at the Sharps' barbecue – I was the only single woman and the only one not sinking into the lawn under the weights of several kilos of garish jewellery – but it was still flattering. We talked about Langley, and Manchester, and his job, and the theatre. It was refreshing, after Ed McGregor, that he wasn't just interested in sticking his tongue down my throat and then buggering off back to work.

He didn't make me feel that sudden, overwhelming need to be seduced, but I'd had quite enough of that kind of over-excitement. Simon, I decided, was someone I could, potentially, have a proper relationship with. This time, if there was going to be another time, I was definitely going to do it properly. Swap phone numbers, have dinner, do the theatre maybe. Find out what the guy was like before I offered him my orifices.

I'd had enough instant sex. No more Pot Noodle fucking for me.

When it was time to go, because I'd promised Ginny I'd be back at eleven, he said: 'It's been great meeting you. I really hope we can get together again.'

I hoped so too.

While I was shrugging on my coat in the hall, Dennis lurched towards me with a bottle in one hand and a glass in the other, flushed from the meat and the flames and the Californian red.

'Whaddya make of him then?' he slurred, slipping his arm round my shoulder.

I tried to slide away, but he was holding my shoulder in a vice-like grip. I was convinced his hand was inching towards my breast.

'Very nice,' I said politely.

'Bloody good tennis player,' Dennis said, stumbling slightly and missing my nipple. 'But I think he might be a bit of a new man.'

'Really?' I inched towards the door. 'That's nice.' It would certainly make a change.

'Sort of bloke who'd not only give you a good seeing to, but clean your toilet and wash your smalls.'

'Lovely,' I said coldly. He still hadn't let go and he was breathing fumes all over me. I was terrified he was going to try to kiss me.

'Can't understand it myself,' Dennis said sorrowfully. 'All that getting in touch with your empathetic side.' Finally, to my immense relief, he released me. 'Still, you need a new boyfriend, and this one *looks* good, even if he is a bit of a poofter. S'what you need: pay Richard back. Bit of his own medicine. Come running soon enough then.'

Kate

Mum could smell the Lynx and cigarettes the minute she walked in from her barbecue. I explained that two boys we happened to know dropped in and she said how odd it was that they hadn't happened to do it while she was there.

Rachel and I took Darren and Joe upstairs. I told Ginny that Mum always let me go upstairs with boys, although this is the first time any have come round.

I don't mind Ginny. Before the boys arrived she told me and Rachel all about her boyfriend Gary. (She can speak. Mum just frightens her. God knows why.) Gary says he needs more space, but Ginny thinks he's gone back to his old girlfriend, who's called Sheryl. Ginny says she's a bitch.

The other good thing about Ginny is that she didn't come up when we were snogging and smoking. (I opened the bedroom window to let the smoke out, but you could easily smell it downstairs.)

She didn't tell Mum about us going upstairs either, so I only got a lecture about the smoking and I pretended that was just Joe. She didn't realise about the draw. The only trouble is that I'm worried now that Mum will go out and dig the garden – it is one of her ways of trying to get rid of all her bad feelings about Dad – and discover the fag ends that Rachel and I buried there.

Mum didn't give me a lecture about lying, although I could tell she wanted to. She tries quite hard to be understanding, even though she is permanently worried about me because she basically doesn't trust Dad to be a proper parent any more and she thinks he lets me drink wine and stay up late, which he does.

I think she must miss Dad, but she probably doesn't even know herself if she misses the old, strict Dad who insisted on early bedtimes, or the new one who opens a bottle of Valpolicella every night and forgets to wash up. I suppose he drank more wine and had longer hair and stuff when they met, and the new Dad reminds her of what he was like at university. Mum says when she first knew him, he wanted to lead the revolution, but not until he'd had a lie-in.

I don't know what happened after that to make him so straight. I can't believe it was Mum, because she always took our side when he was being strict.

Anyway, since he met Emma he has become pretty cool for someone who is still a history teacher. He doesn't see why I shouldn't get my ears pierced. And he told me last week that he and Emma are thinking of moving to Los Angeles for a while and if they do Ben and I could go with them and go to school there. It will be like *Heartbreak High* or *Beverley Hills 90210*.

Darren doesn't watch *Heartbreak High*, or *Neighbours* or *Home and Away* for that matter, so it's quite difficult to find things to talk about with him. He is dead serious and reads a lot of books, I suppose because of having a Saturday job in the library.

Still, he looks a bit like Leonardo DiCaprio, except with glasses and one or two spots. And he wears Airwalk trainers and kisses better than Matthew Armstrong, who has a slack jaw and dribbles into your mouth, or Jonathan Stark, who doesn't put his tongue far enough in but keeps darting it in and out like a lizard.

I am, however, a bit worried that he might think I am flat-chested. Rachel, who has big boobs, so it's all right for her, says I could stick socks in my bra. But what if he stuck his hand up my jumper and pulled out an M&S cotton and wool mix size four to seven?

I am also worried he will somehow find out I am the only girl in the class who hasn't started her periods. Rachel says that's brilliant because I can have sex and not get pregnant. But I could start ovulating at any minute and find myself with a baby without even having the warning.

Darren says the road protest is really important and we have a duty to get involved. People are going to live in a tree. I told him I thought Mum ought to recycle her wine bottles because she chucks away millions. He said that's terrible because they go in landfill sites. I got bored then and we pulled some more.

His parents split up too, when he was much younger. I hope he isn't interested in me because he thinks we're both sad.

Julie

I'm always ready at least half an hour before we're due to leave for Richard's. This afternoon I changed into a clean white T-shirt, put on some lipstick and doused myself liberally with the Poison that Richard bought me once in the duty-free on the way home from Majorca. He thought it smelled sexy, though on me the effect is always slightly antenatal. Perhaps I had my first whiff of it when I was pregnant with Arthur; anyway, it always makes me feel as if I'm going to have to stop the car any minute and vomit into the kerb.

Still, if he thinks it's sexy, that's good enough for me. God knows, I have to use what I've got.

I pottered around the kitchen, picking up the car keys, jangling them and putting them down again. Then when it was time to go, I lost them down the back of the breadbin.

Halfway to Richard's, Ben remembered that he'd forgotten his toothbrush.

'I'll stink at school tomorrow,' he wailed. 'No one will speak to me.'

Kate said: 'Do they anyway?'

'No, but they *specially* won't.'

'What d'you mean, people don't speak to you?' I demanded.

'Oh, nothing.'

'Ben, what do you mean?'

'Nothing.'

I sighed exasperatedly. 'The last thing I said to you before we left the house was "Have you got your toothbrush?"'

'I know, I know, I forgot. We'll have to go back.'

'No, we'll be late!' Kate shouted. 'We hardly see anything of Dad and then you two try to cut it down! Do you plan this?'

'You'll have to borrow Dad's,' I told Ben, then worried for the rest of the journey about orally communicable sexually transmitted diseases.

The flat that Richard and Emma are renting occupies the entire top floor of a 1930s office block on the edge of the City, in an area that, until recently, was down-at-heel and scruffy, full of shady import–export businesses, shops selling shoddy second-hand furniture and minicab firms with Formica counters and flashing red lights. Now it's seething with fashion victims, fantastically trendy bars – some of which pretend still to be minicab firms as a sort of joke – and loft apartments.

Richard and Emma's block still looks as though it ought to house a range of doubtful commercial enterprises. It's all orangey brickwork and metal windows on the outside; inside, you expect wire stacking trays overflowing with greying invoices and dustballs eddying along the skirting boards.

But there are no battered photocopying machines and fraying clerical staff, only rich young people without children. The hall is painted in brilliant white gloss and the floor's made of vivid blue-glass bricks. Every time I come here, I get depressed by the gulf between the cool-box atmosphere of this hall and the mayhem of the one at home, with the mystery black stain on the carpet by the front door, the rollerblades kicked off by the mat and Kate's trainers waiting to trip someone up at the foot of the stairs. If you left a pair of trainers in this hall, they would immediately assume an aesthetic significance, like a pile of old bricks at the Tate – an ironic statement, nothing to do with Kate being a slob.

As the glass lift whooshed us up through a steel tube to the fifth floor, I offered up a silent prayer that Emma wouldn't be at home. A part of me always secretly half-expects that Richard will open a bottle of wine, invite me on to his balcony to admire his view of the tops of the trees in Clerkenwell Green and tell me that he can't begin to understand what he ever saw in her.

He opened one of his industrial double doors and hooked it back while the children threw themselves at him. Emma was sitting on the long white sofa behind him, reading *Cosmopolitan*. She was dressed (just) in a filmy top which exposed her black bra, and tight pedal pushers that showed off her legs and the splendid curves of her bottom. I reluctantly admired her sleek, powerful physique. There was something magnificent about her. She must give some men the same sort of thrill they get from gazing at a classic car – though, obviously without the spare tyre.

Richard looked good too, in pale chinos and a dark blue silk shirt. When he lived with me he wore corduroys and sports jackets, as if he were taking the teacher role as far as it could go, to see if he could live up to it. He used to look as if he was going to seed; now he looked as if he had more seed than he knew what to do with, a surfeit of it, testosterone seeping out of his pores.

Still, what did they *talk* about?

I inched over the threshold, tipping Arthur into Richard's arms and explaining that Ginny would probably be there when he dropped him off in the morning.

'You got a job, then?' Emma asked, sashaying over to us. I could read the top cover line on her *Cosmo*. Ten Ways to Drive a Man Mad.

I explained briefly about the *Langley Advertiser*.

'D'you 'ave to pay for that, then, or is it one of them freesheets?'

'No, as a matter of fact, you buy it.'

'D'you want me to put in a word for you at the *News of the World*?' Emma folded another piece of chewing gum between her fabulous teeth. 'Or *Hello*!? They're beggin' us to do the flat again.'

To be fair, the flat *is* amazing. Three of the walls are actually windows, and the fourth is dominated by a huge painting in shades of off-white. A spiral staircase leads up to a platform; there's a stainless steel kitchen to the right and a built-in seating area around a sternly minimalist fireplace to the left. It's a perfect white space; all it needs is a pickled sheep.

'No, thanks,' I said icily. 'I'm quite happy with the job I've got, for the time being.'

'You gotta think big, though: you don't wanna go backwards.'

'That would be difficult, since I haven't started yet.'

Emma wrinkled her charming nose. 'Is that Poison you're wearing? Jools, let me give you a tip, those heavy scents aren't fashionable any more. Richard says – don't ya, darlin'? – that your trouble is, you're too inclined to settle for second best.'

'Oh,' I replied furiously, 'and what does that say about *him*?'

She laughed, gurglingly. '*Work*, he meant. You used to be quite a good actress didn't you, till you gave up?'

I wanted to hit her. The only reason I didn't do it was that I didn't want a full-blown row with Richard, and certainly not in front of the children. One day, though.

'I hope this Ginny person is going to be all right,' Richard said, emerging from the kitchen area and handing Emma a glass of wine. There didn't appear to be one for me. 'Shouldn't I have met her?'

'How could you, when you're not there?'

'You could have called me.'

'I did. You didn't call back. You never do.'

'I thought you wanted to complain.'

'I don't know why you can't communicate with me occasionally.'

This was a lie. I did know. He hated confronting me and his littered past; hated having to come down out of Celebrityland, the weird theme park that his life had become.

Richard frowned. 'You don't know anything about hiring people. You don't have any interview technique.'

Emma flashed him a brilliant smile. She probably thought it was something to do with sex.

'Ginny seems OK,' I lied. 'And if it doesn't work out, we'll find someone else.'

'You have to be so careful. One hears all these stories . . . nannies beating up children, even murdering them . . . Anyway, shouldn't *you* be looking after them? What about when they – you know – ask questions?'

'I'm not leaving home. Ginny can answer the can-I-have-chocolate-buttons? questions. The Is-there-a-God? questions will just have to wait until after six-thirty.'

Did they, though? Did they wait? Why was he doing this to me?

'We need to keep a close eye on it. Make sure they're not suffering. I'm not altogether happy.'

He ushered me back to the entrance, unhooked the heavy door and prepared to let it fall. ('Don't let Arthur get his fingers anywhere near that door!' I wanted to say.)

'It's interesting, you know,' he remarked conversationally (I never knew where I was with him these days; sometimes he seemed to have lost touch with reality altogether. Perhaps all those sex tips from *Cosmo* really have driven him mad), 'someone was saying at school today that this kind of arrangement is a great way for women to have it all. You get lots of uninterrupted quality time with the children. And, on the other hand, you get time to yourself.'

I got time to myself, and the terrible irony was I didn't know what to do with it.

I tried thinking about Simon. Would he call me? His behaviour at the Sharps' suggested that he would; but then Ed McGregor's behaviour on my kitchen table had suggested that *he* would.

I didn't want to think about Ed McGregor. How many women had he done that to while he was delivering those leaflets?

Simon, though, was engaging and wry. And I rather liked the idea of going out with a bloke who knew something about limescale remover.

The bathroom floor looked like the Top Shop changing room on the first day of the sales. I picked up Arthur's pyjama bottoms and Ben's boxer shorts. And then it occurred to me that tidying up other people's clothes wasn't really what you have free time for.

I wandered into the bedroom, picked up a book from the pile beside the bed and opened it. On the first page the hero got divorced, on the second his son died. Feeling faintly queasy, I put it back on the stack.

I considered the options. Go to the gym, apply a facepack, paint toenails. But the main attraction of all these activities is that they're child-free. When I didn't need to escape from small people demanding pocket money, a lift, or biscuits, they seemed somehow much less appealing.

It struck me that I've forgotten how to be on my own. I've got so used to keeping other people on track, I don't know how to do it for myself. What do people who live on their own *do* to stop themselves from picking their scabs or eating off the floor?

In the end, I spent the rest of the evening cleaning out the kitchen cupboards. And called Mel, who was out, and Fran, who still didn't know about Ed and probably wouldn't now, because too much time had elapsed *without* telling her – how to explain that? – and because it had all become too humiliating (I bet she threw out her mug-trees decades ago).

Fran said single people have to get themselves organised.

'I'll have to do increasingly eccentric things to meet people,' I complained. 'I'll become one of those strange middle-aged women who go to public lectures – "What next for UK railways?" or "Brazil's stabilisation programme" – and spends her time parachuting, or on murder mystery weekends.'

And then I went to bed, telling myself that Richard and Emma would surely get bored with one another sooner or later (there are, after all, only a limited number of sexual positions) and he'd realise that while he and I might not set off fireworks every time we removed our clothes, his absence wasn't doing the children any good. And then he'd come back.

Robin Cook dumped his wife at the airport when they were about to go on holiday, and Earl Spencer dumped his when she was in the bath (no wonder women have body-image problems) so, by comparison, I am really quite lucky. It is hard to ruin unpacking the shopping.

Ben

I am always being passed around like a parcel, or a chain letter that everyone would like to dump but they're too worried.

On Saturday, Mum went to a stupid party to meet a man and it was Ginny's turn to have me. After Arthur had gone to bed she played snap with me and I showed her Tomb Raider on the computer, so at least she took an interest in me, even if it's only because she's got a lot to prove owing to not being qualified. But I would still rather have my parents, ignoring me.

Kate said Mum went to the party because she belonged to the me-generation.

'What's that?'

'Spoilt,' Kate explained. 'It's the way they were brought up. Their mums stayed at home and had their tea ready for them when they came home from school.'

'Is that bad?'

'It was for them. Then in the seventies they let it all hang out.'

I didn't understand what she was going on about.

'Self-expression,' she said, which didn't make any sense either. 'Self-discovery, that sort of thing. Hippies, basically.'

'Oh.'

'And then in the eighties they had greed is good. The upshot is they're no good at responsibilities.'

Emma isn't much older than us, but I think she could be part of the me-generation. Tonight she spent the evening sitting on the floor drinking wine. She doesn't cook. I said I supposed she must be a feminist and she said, 'Certainly not!' Mum claims she is a feminist, but she cooks and cleans and does the washing and the gardening and everything. I don't understand women.

Emma has become famous so fast, according to Kate, that she couldn't cope without Dad to give her advice such as not to panic when photographers follow her around. It seems unfair that because she hasn't got a dad of her own (he left when she was little) she has pinched ours. She has made him be unfaithful to Mum, and also to us.

She did play four games of knock-out whist with me this evening, but she won every one. Dad was busy cooking pork chops, which took ages and they were still pink in the middle. He never used to cook anything at home, and he's still not much good at it. I shall probably get tapeworm. Kate will like having tapeworm as it makes you waste away and she's always saying she's fat, although she's not really: that's just something girls say so other girls won't think they're pleased with themselves.

Over dinner, I reminded Dad about the road and the house prices.

'I'm glad you're taking such an interest in it,' he said. 'It's a bit tricky for me, though, living so far away.'

'You could stay after school.'

'I'm not sure how much longer I'll be at school.'

He meant because of Los Angeles. But that's only a plan.

'I don't want to have to move because our house isn't worth anything,' I complained. 'And I don't want to live beside a motorway and get asthma.'

'I'm all in favour of the protest. I think you should do what you can. But I'm afraid I don't really have any time . . .'

'That's because you're always going to parties,' I said, and began to cry. I felt really stupid then, and had to leave the table and hide in the bathroom.

Later on, Dad came and tucked me up on my tatami mat and said I mustn't mind about him going to parties, which simply shows he doesn't understand what I was trying to say. I wouldn't mind if he went to parties with his own wife.

Kate

I love Dad's flat. There's a stone basin in the bathroom and the floor is made of white cement, which you'd think would be cold, but there's underfloor heating. All the shelves are hidden behind walls, so you can't see the books, stereo, etc. I don't think the architect had kids.

Dad and Emma haven't got much furniture but they have got a big white Guatemalan pot. And a couple of cement cubes, which can be stools or tables.

Emma did an interview with the *News of the World* today and she was wearing these really tight, sexy trousers. I said how much I liked them and she took them off in the middle of the room to let me try them on. She was wearing a tiny lacy black thong and I felt a bit embarrassed in my M&S pants with the pink cotton flower on the front. Anyway, they fitted, so she gave them to me! She is going to be in an article. And Dad is going to be in it too, including pictures, and she has mentioned us so our names might be too.

Dad let me have a glass of wine at dinner. Why

not? I am nearly as old as Emma and she drinks like a fish.

Arthur had to go in Dad's bed again, because we were making too much noise talking about television programmes and it's the only shut-off room apart from the bathroom. Emma insisted as soon as he was asleep he went back on his tatami mat. She said he cramps her style in bed. I hoped they weren't going to have any more noisy sex.

Dad said maybe the next time we came over, I could bring Rachel. Ben hates to keep moving around (but that's because he's always leaving things behind. His brain, for example). But I prefer being here. The only bad thing about it is being thrown together so much with my brothers. I'm expected to remind Ben to bring his homework and his PE kit, which is unfair because I am at an age when girls need to start breaking away from their families.

Later on, Emma sat on the sofa with me for what she called a girly time, which meant that she complained that her mum keeps wanting to come around and organise her and Dad.

I wanted to tell her that I knew how she felt, because my mum makes Stalin look forgiving. Now she's taken down all the photographs of Dad from the sitting room – and when I rang up Rachel to tell her about it, she said: 'Is it really necessary to spend forty minutes on the phone to someone you've been with all day?' I told her only if your mother is a dictator.

I didn't say any of that to Emma, though, because it would have been disloyal. Emma would like to think that Mum's a boring old teacher's wife from the suburbs, but she can't be sure, because she knows she used to be a really good actress, and she has her hair cut at this trendy place in Soho and wears granddad vests and still looks cool in jeans.

I think Emma's quite confused and insecure about Mum, which is surprising, and crazy when you think about it, because magazines are always asking to photograph Emma in her underwear and I can't think of anyone who would even want to see Mum naked, let alone have a picture of her. Lucian Freud, maybe.

Emma's mum also tries to lecture her about drugs, because she thinks everyone in television's doing coke, even though Emma says her mum knows nothing about it because she's never even had a spliff. I don't know whether my mum has had a spliff or not. She was at university in the eighties, so I suppose it's possible. Dad went red and changed the subject. I think he is less likely to have smoked cannabis than Mum, unless he has taken it up recently.

Julie

I had a dream about Simon Hemingway. At least, I *think* it was him; rather suspiciously, it was all mixed up with the road protest. But that's been my only association with sex for some time.

The action, of which there was quite a lot, took place in Langley Wood. In the dream Simon was less new-mannish than pre-mannish: practically Australopithecus, swinging from branch to branch and romping along rope bridges with well defined calf muscles and strong thighs. I was up a tree as well, and then it all became rather anatomically graphic.

I never used to have dreams in which body parts played such a significant role. This must be the consequence of having had no sex at all for a year followed by one lunchtime of wild-animal passion, then no prospect of any more, possibly for the rest of my life.

I feel rather sorry for Simon, having become the unwitting focus of my frustration simply for having been sweet enough to engage me in conversation for a few hours at Suzy Sharp's party. This is going to be my life from now on: it will only take a stray man to cross my path to trigger obscenity and obsession. If I'm not careful, I'll turn into a female version of a dirty old man, pursuing beautiful boys with flat stomachs and begging them to have sex with me in filthy underpasses.

Oh God, here we go again . . .

So I woke up feeling flustered, and then Richard appeared on the doorstep with the children at seven-thirty, claiming that Arthur had had them up since six and he'd had enough, so he was going into school. I hustled them indoors (Kate muttering that sleep deprivation was torture and what would social services have to say if she reported us?) and then the cat brought in a rat, which she deposited in the middle of the kitchen floor. It lay with glittering eyes and bright incisors in a puddle of Arthur's spilt milk and cornflakes, its coat matted with sewer foam, drain mould and guts.

'Ooh, dirty,' screeched Arthur, lurching towards it gleefully.

'Do *not* touchthatfilthyrat!' I shrieked, gathering him up into my arms and falling backwards, toes curled up in loathing.

'Sprout!' I ordered (Ben chose the cat's name, something to do with the colour of its eyes): 'Take that vile thing out of here.'

Sprout stretched, yawned, licked her paw and high-stepped off to find a nice warm place to lie down.

Where was a man when you needed one? Where, specifically, was my man, the one who signed up for my drain clearance, rat removal and sink plunging? Gone, taking his Dyno-Rod elsewhere.

I deep-breathed Arthur's smells of shampoo, cereal and perfect baby organs. Then I deposited him on a chair, collected the dustpan and brush, averted my eyes, clenched my teeth, exhaled and bent down.

It was only one rat, after all. They hunt in packs of forty to fifty, so I was lucky not to have a whole sewerful on my terracotta tiles. In London they are rarely more than six feet away. In New York there are twenty-five million, approximately four per person.

This was happening on my first day at the *Langley Advertiser*, and I knew why: it was cosmic punishment for leaving my youngest child with the silent woman of Springvale Avenue.

Ginny arrived just as I was tipping the rat into a bin bag.

'Oh,' she said sadly, 'are you throwing the sweet little rat away?'

I looked up in disbelief. 'Are you suggesting we should keep it?'

'My dad always used to bury my hamsters. I don't like the idea of them going in the bin.'

'Ginny, this is a rat. It *lives* in the bin.'

'Not any more,' she pointed out, reasonably enough. 'We used to have nice little funerals.'

'Oh, *please*!' Arthur started jumping up and down. 'Can we?'

'No!'

I tied up the bin bag firmly and put it outside the back door. Then I gave Ginny a list of instructions and important telephone numbers and showed her the Tupperware boxes of food I'd cooked for her to give to Arthur, after which I had about thirty seconds to put on my make-up, get Ben to school and drive on to work.

On the way out of the house I accidentally caught sight of myself in a mirror. Ivana Trump started cosmetic surgery when she was twenty-eight.

I needn't have worried about being late. Pete wasn't in when I arrived, and neither was anyone else except Tony, who was sitting at the end of a long, battered table covered with old newspapers and notebooks, press releases and plastic coffee cups. Poking up through the debris like a range of mountains through cloud were two lines of VDUs.

Tony was doing the crossword in the *Daily Telegraph*.

'Hi,' he said bleakly, barely looking up, 'welcome to the cutting edge of the media revolution. Get yourself a cup of coffee.'

So I made us both coffee. There were ants crawling all over the draining board. While the kettle was boiling I had to keep peering into the cups to make sure they hadn't got mixed up with the coffee granules.

Tony was right about the office not being plush. The floor was covered in grubby red and cream lino tiles, and exposed pipes lined the walls. The windows would have overlooked the High Street, if you could have seen through the grime crusting the panes. There was a persistent smell of fish and chips, which, I learned later, reached a peak of acridness at lunchtime and tailed off very slowly through the afternoon.

I sat down and read, in turn, the *Guardian*, the *Independent*, *The Times*, the *Daily Express*, the *Mail* and the *Telegraph*. At this rate I would soon be the best-informed woman in Britain.

Pete wandered in after about an hour, frowned at me, grunted, and retreated to his office. Then Tony's phone rang.

'Bugger,' he muttered into it: 'Bugger!'

He consulted a diary in front of him.

'How d'you fancy interviewing Ed McGregor?'

'What, me?'

There was no one else in the room.

'Victoria's ill. She was supposed to be doing it.'

'No!' I was horrified.

'You've got to start somewhere. I'll run through a list of questions, if you like. All you have to do is go up to the squats and ask them.'

'No! I can't!'

'Course you can. It's not difficult.'

'No, you don't understand. I *know* him.'

'That doesn't matter.'

'I hate him!'

He looked surprised, but said: 'That's an advantage. Honestly, Jools, it's often a good thing. You can be spiky.'

I shook my head in panic.

Tony looked at me sceptically. 'I *need* you to do this,' he said, as if to a small, stupid child. 'This is what the job is – I give you interviews to do, and you go out and ask people questions.'

I thought about blurting out: 'I had sex with him!' but that would have also entailed explaining that it had only happened once, and for perfectly good reasons – at least on my side – and that we hadn't spoken since because he despised my ornaments. It was all too horrible.

Incredibly, therefore, three-quarters of an hour later, I found myself in Cherry Drive, outside one of the four compulsorily purchased Edwardian villas on the north side of the green.

What was I doing? I'd made up my mind to avoid Ed McGregor for the next six months, or however long it took him to leave Langley. And here I was, less than three weeks later . . . My stomach was pulsing violently. It seemed to be on the point of prolapse. My hands were shaking as if with some terrible palsy.

I would be glacial. That was the only thing to do. Deep-bloody-frozen.

It wasn't difficult to identify which of the houses the road protesters were occupying. They'd painted the outer walls with murals of cars, flowers, death's heads, and grey lumpy objects that might have been meant to be lungs. I was too agitated to be able to take much of it in; crossing a front garden covered in old floorboards, broken tiles and empty cement bags, I pushed open the front door. A banner over the lintel proclaimed: 'No surrender in defence of Mother Earth.'

The hall of the occupied house was littered with plaster and piping. I picked my way over it and put my head round the door of a room on the right. Inside, the girl with the upwardly-mobile breasts bent her Gwyneth Paltrow neck over a trestle table, issuing instructions into a telephone.

She got up when she saw me. 'Hi, I'm Nettle,' she said breezily, not really noticing me. It was definitely the same voice as the person in Polly's. 'I'm in charge of publicity. Come through, Victoria.'

'Actually, it's Julie,' I said. 'Victoria's ill. I'm Julie Ellison.'

She frowned. 'Have you written about the road before? I haven't seen your byline.' She looked me up and down. 'Weren't you at one of the meetings? The first one?'

'Um, yes.'

Her scowl deepened. 'You're five minutes late, and you've only got half an hour. He's doing *Vogue* later this morning. Come on, I'll show you through.'

She led me down the hall to the room behind hers, where Ed McGregor had established a makeshift office. My ex-one-afternoon-stand was sitting at a trestle table in front of a phone and a laptop. Piles of books littered the floor around his feet. Even in frigidaire mode, my stomach lurched. He still had the same wayward hair, earring, and that air of dangerous, contained energy.

'Ed, this is the reporter from the local paper.'

'Welcome to the independent . . .' He looked up from his laptop and his jaw dropped.

'Julie!' he uttered, looking panicked. 'I was expecting someone called Victoria.'

'She's sick.'

'I didn't realise you worked for the *Advertiser*.'

'I only just started.'

At least he had the decency to look embarrassed. 'Well, er, have a seat. Coffee?'

'Thank you,' I said glacially, and looked down my nose at him.

A child was kneeling on the floor – a boy of about

ten or eleven, his tongue poking out of the side of his mouth as he painted some kind of banner.

'Phil, could you fix that?' Ed asked him: 'Two coffees.'

The boy got up off the floor and shambled away. Nettle remained.

Ed looked at me intently for what seemed like ages. Why didn't he *say* something? Offer some explanation for his vile behaviour. Apologise, even.

Nettle folded her arms.

I was embarrassed. I knew I was going red, so I scrabbled in my bag for a notebook and tape recorder.

'So, shall we begin?' I asked frostily.

He swallowed. At least he was discomfited. That was something.

But so was I. Nervous of letting him see what an amateur I was. He gets interviewed by *Vogue*; I, as Richard pointed out, have no technique.

'That boy looks very young,' I remarked coldly, procrastinating.

'He's eleven, I think.'

'Shouldn't he be at school?'

'Ideally.'

'So?'

Ed McGregor shrugged. 'He's been excluded. About four times.'

'Don't his parents mind him being here?'

Nettle shifted irritably. I knew I should get on with it. But I didn't actually *want* to know all those things I was supposed to ask about Ed's childhood and history. It would just be more things about him to forget.

'His last dad beat up his mum. No one's sure where she is now.'

Fran had told me this job would be easy. She'd assured me that the worst thing I'd have to do would be to sit through the odd bad production of Gilbert and Sullivan; other than that it'd be all church fêtes and prize vegetables. She hadn't said *I'd* feel like the prize vegetable.

Nettle said pointedly: 'You really haven't got very long.'

I glanced down at Tony's list of questions, then said stupidly: 'Doesn't he have social workers?'

'Perhaps they've taken the view that he's better off here than in Piccadilly charging ten pounds for a hand job. OK, Nettle, I'll handle Julie.'

'You don't want me to stay?' She seemed surprised.

'No, it's fine.'

She scowled. 'Well, don't let her take too much of your time. You've got that TV script to do.'

The boy returned with the coffees. Still glowering – irritatingly, it didn't make her any less pretty – Nettle left.

The boy, who was thin and pale, with over-bright, excitable eyes and stringy brown hair, squatted down on the floor again and reapplied himself to his poster. I consulted my notebook, took a deep breath, and started on my list of questions.

I asked Ed McGregor about his childhood in Australia and Aberdeen, his discovery of green politics at university, his several degrees in saving the world, his complicated postgraduate work on soil structure, and the Langley motorway. I did all this in a brisk tone

80

of voice; he in turn kept his answers brief and to the point.

'You won't be able to stop the motorway, will you?' I challenged him after about fifteen minutes, when I was feeling a bit braver.

I had, obviously, raised this point with him before, although neither of us mentioned that right now.

'Who knows?'

He was more practised at this than I was, and not easy to rile. He had a stillness, a ruminative quality, a deep sort of cool. My arrival had shaken him, but he'd recovered now, and he was in control. Unlike me, he did this all the time. 'We can – we know this from experience – slow down the construction by months and inflate the costs to the contractors. Maybe they'll give up; maybe no one else will want to take it on.'

A mobile phone was ringing somewhere, muffled. I looked around before realising it was in my bag. I stuck my hand in, trying to switch it off surreptitiously.

The ringing stopped, then started again.

Smiling, Ed McGregor said: 'I should get that, if I were you.'

I flushed again and retrieved the phone from the bottom of my bag.

'Mrs Ellison?' said a voice on the other end, 'it's Linda, from the comprehensive. Ben doesn't seem to have his packed lunch today and we're going to the borough music festival. We did send home a note.'

It all came flooding back. I'd told Richard about the packed lunch last night. But perhaps because of dropping the children off so early, he considered himself absolved of the responsibility. And what with one thing and another – the erotic dream, the unexpected early reappearance of the kids, the crisis over the rat – I'd completely forgotten it.

'Any chance of getting something over here for him in the next half-hour?'

'I'm sorry about this,' I said to Ed, flustered. 'D'you mind if I make a quick call?'

Ed McGregor shrugged and went back to his laptop. I dialled home, but Ginny wasn't there, and I called her mobile, which was switched off. I even tried her mother's house, and got no response there either.

'My, er, son doesn't have a packed lunch,' I muttered. 'I need to go and sort one out.'

Ed nodded and, I think, tried not to smile. 'You must be more or less finished anyway?'

'There were one or two more things . . .' I bit my lip. 'I'm terribly sorry –' I bundled my bits and pieces into my bag and got to my feet – 'is there any way . . . could we arrange to finish this some other time?'

'Call Nettle,' Ed McGregor said. 'It's very hectic here at the moment, but she might be able to fit something in.'

I gathered my bag under my arm and made for the door.

'Julie . . .' he said suddenly.

'Yes?'

He glanced at Phil, still squatting on the floor, and seemed to change his mind.

'Nothing.'

Ben

I was in the park, making the most of it while we still live here. I'm worried that now Mum is working Dad will stop giving her money and I don't think she's capable of earning very much, so we might have to leave our house. I'd like to move, if it was to the country and I could go to a different school and get away from Adrian Farr and learn to drive a tractor. But Kate says Mum earns so little it's more likely we'd move to a bed and breakfast.

I am already disadvantaged by having divorced parents because on the radio it said that family conflict makes children shorter. Mum said it was probably a good thing where Kate is concerned because she is already Amazonian. But the programme also said that people don't want to employ these people from broken families so much when they grow up. They must be the wrong height for the office furniture or something. You wouldn't want an office full of people whose chins only just reach over their desks.

I was on my rollerblades, practising going backwards

round corners, and the next thing I knew, I was in a puddle and Grandma was in a rose bed. I seemed to have hit her. She was all sprawled in the dirt with her legs stuck underneath her.

I was glad it was Grandma and not some other old woman, because she works with people who are even worse-behaved than me, and who take time off school just to go shoplifting. She didn't shout at me or anything, just got up and rescued her cake, which had gone flying and hit the netting round the tennis court and bounced out of its tin into the dirt. Fortunately it was in a plastic bag. (Grandmas are very keen on wrapping things up.)

Then she said: 'Well, Ben, we seem to have survived that. How is school?'

I told her that it was OK, although this is not true. Adrian Farr said Emma only got the part in *EastEnders* because she is pretty. Everybody agreed, because Adrian would beat them up if they didn't. Anyway, they think he is cool. It's not fair that people think they can make remarks about Emma just because she is famous. I don't say Adrian's parents are useless at their jobs. (Though they are obviously useless at bringing up Adrian, because he is a bully.)

I don't know why Adrian picks on me when I am bigger than him. Perhaps it's because I am no good at football. Or perhaps it's clothes. Adrian wears Nike T-shirts and Ben Sherman shirts and has a gang called the Trendies. I don't have anything designer.

The other bad thing was that I got my maths homework back today. I'd copied Sam, and he'd got them all wrong! Miss Millett called me over at the end of school and asked had I ever been to see an educational psychologist? I said yes, because I didn't want to go to one and I thought if I'd already been, they wouldn't make me go again. I once saw a programme on television about psychologists who deprived rats of sleep to see what effect it would have on them. (A not very good one!) So I don't want them doing that to me.

Miss Millett said could I ask Mum to bring in the report some time? So now I've got to keep Mum away from school. Fortunately she's got a lot on her mind.

Grandma walked back home with me. I told her that when Emma whinges, which she does a lot, she reminds me of Kate. You'd think one person like Kate would be enough for Dad. Emma mainly whinges about her mum. We haven't met her, although I personally wouldn't mind having a spare grandma. Grandmas are good for sweets and pocket money and spoiling you, so the more the better.

'And how's *your* mum?' Grandma asked.

'She's all right,' I told Grandma, remembering that Mum is her daughter and people worry about their children. 'But she's taking a drug Mel gave her and, sometimes, she drinks wine when she's on her own. D'you think she could be turning into an alcoholic?'

Julie

So now Ed McGregor thinks I'm an incompetent reporter who can't remember to switch off her phone and a ditzy parent who can't even get it together to send her son to school with his packed lunch.

Of all the billions of people in the world, why did he have to be the first one I got to interview? The one person I would have wanted to impress. If only to be able to say to him, 'So fuck off, with your stupid snobbery about my bric-a-brac.'

Afterwards, back at the office, I could have kicked myself. I should have said something: 'Was it the decor?' Or: 'D'you often take off your clothes, wrap yourself round another person, then get up and forget all about her?'

I was insecure about sex, that was the trouble. For all I knew, other people were gymnastic like that all the time.

I used to think – in my twenties, say – that I was probably quite good at sex. But as time passed I grew less certain that I had whatever it took. Sex with

Richard started to feel more and more like scratching an itch, and I began to worry about what it took to hold his attention, not helped by his evident preference for doing it on his own.

I minded, of course, but thought that this was probably what happened, mid-term in marriage. Sex was emotionless, apart from occasional irritation about bad timing. I fought down the feelings of loss and insult, and I hoped that some day, when the children were older and less demanding, we'd get over it.

So it's quite possible that now I'd have thought good sex was any naked physical activity with another person that didn't involve me in reviewing my list of things to do tomorrow. The brutal truth was that I was in no position to judge what was good and what wasn't. Except that, as I remembered it, I'd been in every position.

In the afternoon, Tony took me through my notes and told me how to turn them into an article.

'What *is* it between you and Ed McGregor?' he asked, frowning at his screen.

'What? Nothing.'

'Oh, well, if you always write with this much attitude you'll be great. We'll finish sorting it out in the morning.'

Driving home, I spotted a couple of teenagers on the pavement outside the British Queen. The girl was tall and striking, despite her rumpled school uniform. The boy was at least an inch shorter than her, and spotty, and they were holding hands so that their arms touched right up to their armpits, but looking in opposite directions, pretending casualness. I smiled, remembering what that was like, being driven together by crashing hormones and having nothing to say.

And then I realised that the girl was Kate and the boy was Darren Bredy, who works in the library. This is what happens when marriages break up: once-normal mothers become nymphomaniacs and their precociously sexualised daughters start shagging spotty boys with Saturday jobs.

I tried to remember at what age I'd started snogging. It must have been *quite* early, because there seemed to be years of being embarrassed about my boyfriends and pretending to myself that the introducing to friends and parents part of the relationship was happening in a parallel reality, and only the sex was in the here and now. Not that we actually had proper sex, because you could still be a nice girl then and get out of it. But since then, feminism has outed female desire. Now we know that the clitoris is enormous, and half the girl children in the country are on the pill, and the rest are teen mothers.

Ginny was cooking a sausage casserole for Arthur when I got in. It involved putting sausages and tinned tomatoes in a dish and boiling. I managed, just, to stop myself from asking what was wrong with all my lovingly prepared deep-frozen organic casseroles.

She said Arthur had been fine. They'd been for a walk and to the swings. She was afraid she'd got a bit muddled about the times and picked up Ben fifteen minutes late from school, but she'd try and remember it was three-thirty in future.

'Three forty-five.'

'Yeah, that's what I meant.'

She also promised to try to remember to switch on her mobile.

Kate came in, shortly after Ginny had gone home, looking blotchy and kissed out.

'Did you have a good time at Dad's last night?' I enquired, since she'd been too grumpy to tell me anything about it earlier.

'Fine. You know those trainers I told you about? The ones that were eighty quid? They're £49.99 in the sale.'

She picked up one of the beans I was slicing and chomped on it. I carried on de-stringing.

'Mum! That's under fifty quid. And my Vans are in a terrible state. I really need a new pair. Can I? Oh, go on, please!'

My mother arrived before this had time to develop into a full-scale row; she was accompanied, curiously enough, by Ben. She marched down the hall and planted a sponge cake on the kitchen table. For some reason it was dented.

'How's the job?' she asked, as she unwrapped the sponge and put it away in a tin.

'Today was my first day. I still don't know.'

'That doesn't seem a very positive attitude.'

My mother is an elegant model of third-age energy, with iron-grey hair and understated clothes. She's always being invited to Stockholm and Helsinki to give lectures about how she gets inner-city criminals back to school and work. In her spare time, she does yoga, sometimes in a monastery in Tibet.

She filled the kettle. 'Does this mean you can finally get divorced?'

'Mum, I don't *want* a divorce!'

'Oh . . .' She sounded faintly surprised, though I've never suggested the separation was anything but temporary. 'But if you did?'

'I *don't!*'

She drizzled hot water into the teapot, rinsed it round, poured it into the sink and dropped two teabags into the bottom.

'Anyway,' I said irritably, 'four days a week at the *Langley Advertiser* doesn't exactly give me financial independence. And there's no reason to get divorced. Richard and I have a tacit understanding that he's just temporarily . . . off-course.'

She raised her eyebrows. 'Like a homing pigeon, gone astray?'

'Sort of.' Why did she have to do this, imply that I'm credulous and self-deceiving?

'Oh, well – ' she whisked around with cups and saucers – 'I'm sure working is also good for your personal growth.' She said this without irony. 'And once you've got some experience, you can always go on to something a bit less . . . local.'

I said defensively: 'I interviewed Ed McGregor today.'

'The environmentalist? But that's great! That's a good start, surely?'

'Not really.'

'No?'

'He's a snob. He thinks anyone who lives in Langley is mediocre.'

I told her about his offensive conversation with Nettle in Polly's Tea Shoppe.

'Darling, has he been nasty to *you*?'

'What? No, of course not. I'm talking about his . . . attitude. As if he's above everything.' I took the tea she offered me. 'For example, he had an eleven-year-old child in the squats today, who seemed to be some kind of runaway, and he wasn't attempting to get him back wherever he came from. He didn't even seem bothered that he wasn't at school.'

'Some children have too much help,' my mother said, surprisingly, since she is one of the helpers.

'He's a rent boy. Or was. So Ed McGregor claimed. Doesn't sound to me like he's got much help.'

'You'd be surprised.'

'Then why is he on the streets?'

'Money . . .'

'Ed McGregor thinks you can't know anything about what's going on in the world unless you live in Chelsea or somewhere. Wherever it is he lives.'

'But you *don't* know anything about runaway children.'

'All right, there's no need to get all *political*.'

My mother took my cup and refilled it. 'Why are you so bothered about this boy?'

'I'm not!' I snapped. 'I was just giving an example.'

'Of what?'

'Why I don't like Ed McGregor.'

She ran water into the washing-up bowl. 'Well,' she said brightly, 'I'm glad you've got a job. I always thought that things might have been a bit better if you hadn't given up work in the first place. And if Richard had done a bit more domestically, of course.'

'*You* never . . .'

'It's every bit as good, you know, for children to

see their parents reading a book or playing a musical instrument as it is to see them wiping down a draining board.'

What was she talking about? I don't play a musical instrument.

She wiped down the draining board. 'Interestingly, the National Organisation of Women recently came out in favour of polygamy as a solution to childcare.' She picked up a scourer and started on a dirty saucepan. 'The career woman goes out to work, while the career mum stays at home to look after the kids, so the children never have to go to nurseries or childminders. And the husbands always have a clean shirt in the morning and dinner at night.'

This is the trouble with my mother. She is fascinated by theory which has absolutely no practical application. Since my father died and left her at the age of thirty-five with me aged four and almost no income, she has reinvented herself. But for as long as my father was alive she never so much as let him make his own coffee.

'I don't really know which one of those I'd be, the career woman or the career mum,' I said irritably. I was pretty certain she had me down for ironing Emma's tiny skirts, while Emma pursued the career I was trained for.

'No, well, you've never been able to decide. That's always been your trouble. You're not *drinking*, are you?'

'No. Why?'

'No reason. Anyway, if you do decide you need a divorce lawyer, I know someone who's good.'

After she'd finished washing up, she made supper, washed up again, put Arthur to bed with a story, helped Ben with his homework and advised Kate on her GCSE art project. I watched from the sofa as Kate described the technicalities of shading a drawing of her right trainer. Kate hardly ever shows me her art any more, but perhaps she was so unnaturally cheerful because of her earlier snog.

I watched my daughter as she sat under the lamp, engrossed by the movement of her pencil as it flashed across the cartridge paper. Her face was raw but beautiful, freckled and fine. I hoped that when Darren Bredy looked into it he was grateful, that he appreciated the unfinished quality in her as much as her assurance, and that her crazy hormones left her some dignity. And I thought about myself, and that if the long journey through fumbling and fingering and zits and flies and stained sheets doesn't lead to happy ever afters, I'm not sure what all the effort is for.

Kate

A man called for Mum. I picked up the telephone and almost fell over. I can't believe she has met a man. She never goes anywhere.

Anyway, it is much too soon.

He asked for 'Julie' as if we were sharing a flat or something, not as if she is my mother. I hope she has not concealed from him that she has a practically grown-up child.

She went red when I told her that there was this man Simon on the phone, so he was obviously not a complete surprise. I hope she knows what she is doing. Whole magazines are published on a regular basis to explain the difficulties of dating, and she never reads any of them. She can't have thought about it for years. Will she know what to do when he tries to stick his hand up her jumper?

That is a horrible thought. Do people do that when they have had babies? Their nipples are revolting.

Why did I have to get parents who started to go backwards in their late thirties? Some people's parents read *Country Living* and wear M&S cardies, while mine are looking more and more like extras from *Trainspotting*.

'So who is he, then?' I casually asked her later, wandering into the kitchen. She was having a row with Ben because his teacher has asked her to come in to school. Something about an educational psychologist's report. I didn't know Ben had seen an educational psychologist.

'Oh, no one.'

'What, like in the *X-files*? A disembodied voice, pure plasma?'

'No one important. Someone I met at the Sharps'.'

I might have guessed, although I wouldn't have thought even Mum was desperate enough to take up with a friend of the Sharps. They give the middle classes a bad name: they are snobbish and pleased with themselves, like something out of John Betjeman, needing to be flattened by friendly bombs. Simon probably wears Pringle jumpers and socks with golf-ball motifs and prides himself on having an eye for the ladies.

I asked if she was going to go out with him and she said she might. I hope she knows about making mistakes on the rebound.

We don't need a stepfather, especially one who would make us see more of the Sharps.

I wonder what they will do on their date. There is a limited number of things they can do at their age. I sincerely hope she will not bring him back here.

Julie

Miss Millett, Ben's tutor group head, was about twenty-three, with bubble hair, a beaming smile that never quite made it to her eyes, and a concerned voice, as if everything could be made all right by speaking softly.

I went to see her at break in her classroom, where we perched on adjacent desks and she inclined her head and furrowed her brow, adopting a professional, inclusive expression.

'You say Ben's never seen an educational psychologist? That's very odd.'

I rather resented that. 'Why?'

'He told me he had.'

'I'm sorry, that was very bad of him.'

'And that they found he had a very high IQ.'

'Oh.' I tried to adopt a grave expression.

'How long have you and your husband been separated, Mrs Ellison?'

'What, sorry?'

'Only Ben's teachers do seem to feel that, very often, his mind is elsewhere.'

I wanted to say: 'Oh, that's normal,' but felt it would be unhelpful.

'Eight months,' I said instead. 'It happened around the time he started here. You think it might be having a bad effect on his work?'

'We don't always see his work. I teach him maths, and in my lessons he tends to put it down behind the radiator and pretend he's lost it.' She smiled again: a weird, indulgent, and it seemed to me, defeatist smile.

'So you think it would be helpful if he saw an educational psychologist?' I said briskly, determined to take charge of this.

She nodded kindly. She thought I was feckless, I could tell. My husband has left me and my son's not handing in his work but I didn't even know. I'm a single parent, and from here it's a short step to not wiping my work surfaces and sinking into the underclass.

'Incidentally,' she said as I was leaving, 'he didn't seem very sure yesterday whether someone was meant to be picking him up. He was hanging around the playground half an hour after school finished, not knowing whether to wait or catch the bus. I think that person you've got helping out – Ginny, is it? – may have a rather erratic sense of timekeeping.'

'You spent an hour alone with Ed McGregor and neither of you mentioned the sex?' Mel said incredulously on the phone later that morning. 'What *did* you talk about?'

'We were very professional. We discussed his CV. Anyway, we *weren't* alone. There was a child making a poster on the floor.'

'Weird! You are *weird!* What does Fran say?'

I confessed: 'I still haven't told her.'

'Why ever not?'

'You know what she's like.'

'Thin?'

'Well, that. But sophisticated.'

'Jools, she's your friend. You've known her about twenty years.'

'She been everywhere, done everything, taken drugs I haven't even heard of. She probably *knows* Ed.'

'Well, it's a good thing you told me, given that you're both coming for supper. But now you've got Simon, you don't still feel rejected by Ed?'

'I haven't *got* Simon. He's asked me out to dinner and it's ages off because he's got to go to the States, and by the time he comes back I don't suppose either of us will still want to do it. And I know exactly what Fran would think – that I'm getting my knickers in a twist about Ed because he's famous.'

'From the sound of it, he made sure your knickers got very twisted.'

Several hours later, Fran and I sat in the kitchen at Mel's house overlooking Langley Wood, drinking Sauvignon Blanc while Mel whisked about throwing vegetables into a wok. Mel is mop-headed, voluptuous, and well-balanced: she claims she's done every diet ever invented and she's finally reached the conclusion that diets solve the problem of looking fat on social occasions by turning you into such a bore that no one asks you out.

She is also funny and warm, a combination I'm never quite sure I manage.

'So, tell us about Simon,' she urged me.

'He's good-looking. Blond. Ironic eyes.' I told them about the sexy dream.

'He sounds gorgeous,' Fran said, topping up my glass. 'I like the sound of his thighs.'

'I may have made that bit up. All I really know about him is that he works for a record company and he said he wanted something to look forward to while he was away on business, and that Dennis Sharp thinks he's a new man.'

'What,' Fran wrinkled her nose, 'with a duster?'

I don't know why she was being so supercilious: she's not such a great picker. She's been seeing the same man for ten years; unfortunately, he's married to someone else. When he failed to leave Karen after the first six months, it seemed safe to assume he never would.

Not that I think Fran ever really wanted the sort of relationship that Mel has with Ian, or that I mistakenly thought I was getting with Richard – passionate, devoted, demanding, forgiving. What she's most wanted from a relationship is for it not to get in the way – and the great thing about David is that he's never required her to change anything about her life, beyond occasionally assuming a concerned expression when she hears the words 'offside trap'.

'I don't know if I *want* to go out with him,' I said feebly. 'I'm out of practice.' Mel raised her eyebrows at me sceptically.

'Oh, for heaven's sake,' Fran said, 'you're only going out to dinner. You don't have to sleep with him.'

So you *weren't* meant to have abandoned, crazy sex on the first date! I was cheap.

'Don't I?'

'No!'

'That's it, you see: I don't know. While I've been married everyone may have worked out a completely different way of doing it. President Clinton seems to have suggested blow-jobs to anyone he spotted running round the White House.'

'At least you've got children,' Fran said, nibbling a crisp; 'that makes it much easier to attract men.'

I stared at her incredulously.

'Men are always terrified I'm just sizing up their genes.'

'Aren't you, though?' Mel joined us at the table. 'I think size does matter, actually.'

'Not their *jeans*, Mel! They think I want their babies.'

'You could have a baby anyway, without a man,' Mel told her, although I don't think this was quite the point Fran was making. 'You've got enough money. You could do it with a turkey baster and brilliant genetic material from a catalogue.' Then she went red, in case Fran thought she was implying that David wasn't brilliant genetic material.

'I don't *want* a baby; that's the point: men just think I do. Sigourney Weaver said being a single parent is harder than fighting an alien.'

'Though Richard's so strange,' I said thoughtfully, 'that often it feels like it *is* fighting an alien.'

'I just wouldn't mind being married,' Fran explained. 'Even nuns marry Jesus.'

Mel said there was no point in marrying someone who wouldn't do his fair share of housework.

'None of us,' Fran said, by now rather slurrily,

'knows what men are *for* any more. That's the real trouble. I mean, I must have read *dozens* of books about co-dependency and commitment phobia, and I still haven't a clue.'

I said: 'Getting rid of rats?'

'Perhaps everyone needs two men,' offered Mel. 'A new one and an unreconstructed one. One for the dust and one for lust.'

'Thing is,' Fran continued drunkenly, 'we don't believe in men any more. We want to, because we like the orgasms, but we're too cynical.'

'We don't believe in anything properly,' I agreed. 'We half believe in lots of things – happy ever afters, feng shui . . .'

'I think I might become religious.'

'Fran,' Mel objected, 'there really is no *point* in marrying Jesus.'

'I thought more like a scientologist, so I could maybe meet Tom Cruise or John Travolta. Or that thing Madonna's in – Kabbalah. It's a sort-of sexy Judaism. Anyway, it's got Barbra Streisand, Donna Karan and Courtney Love. Or maybe Buddhism. When Sharon Stone met the Dalai Lama she got to wear an Armani white shantung silk dress.'

We discussed the clothing possibilities of various religions for a bit, and then Mel asked Fran, 'How's David?'

'OK,' said Fran doubtfully. 'I think. He's talking about leaving Karen.'

'Uh-huh,' Mel and I chorused dutifully; no change there then.

'No, really: he *told* her. About me.'

101

We shouted together: 'He did *what?*'

'He finally told her about wanting to live with me. D'you think it's because I'm too old to have children?'

'Don't be stupid: of course you're not,' Mel said briskly. 'And *obviously* that's not the reason. How brilliant!'

'Is it? What if it creates a vacancy?'

We stared at her blankly.

'Having a mistress at least gives him the illusion that he's interesting.'

There was no answer to this, so I asked: 'How did she react?'

David's always given the impression that Karen is slightly unstable, which probably just means she's good at getting her own way. I bet *she* didn't stand in her kitchen thinking about cubism. She probably cut up his Richard James suits and poured paint on his vintage Jag.

'Don't know. He only told her last night.' Fran speared a forkful of noodles. 'Anyway. I suppose it'll be all right. Yeah.' She sighed. 'Nothing to say really. Yet. So. Hum. Tell us about your job.'

'Well . . .' I frowned. 'It's OK. Quite a lot of sitting around the office.'

'Done any interviews?'

'Um, not really. Ed McGregor.'

'Great! That's really great! Oh, of course, he's in Langley to fight this road thing . . . I bet that's made the natives restless. Damp knickers all over . . . 'Course, I know Ed from way back. He was an adviser to Greenpeace for a while when I was running their ad campaign. He's pretty cool.'

'Oh?'

'You've seen those eyes: to look lascivious, he only has to look.'

'Lots of women?' Mel asked casually, chewing a stick of celery.

'Quite a few. Not a great committer. Same old story.'

I was beginning to feel uncomfortable. It was starting to seem stupid, not telling Fran. We did once tour Australia in a camper van. How much difference did £500,000 a year make?

Still, I rather liked the idea that Ed McGregor's come-on-and-consummate-with-me eyes were inextricably bound to a stunted emotional life. For some reason, it reminded me of what Heidi Fleiss said when someone asked her why attractive men in Hollywood used prostitutes – that it wasn't the sex they were paying for, but the fact that the women went away afterwards.

Ben

A really terrible thing has happened. Mum has got a boyfriend. This is awful timing, because she and Dad are on the point of getting back together.

Grown-ups are always telling children not to talk to strangers, but as soon as they meet one at a party they go out in their cars and even to their houses without thinking about what might happen.

What does she want to go out with a man for? We've already got a father.

Kate said I shouldn't worry because any man Mum met at the Sharps' couldn't possibly be a serious prospect. But I'm worried that Mum is desperate.

To make matters worse, there was an article about Dad and Emma in the *News of the World* today. Kate sneaked out to buy it and brought it home in a plastic bag, in case it was upsetting to Mum, then read it out to me. She was disappointed because there was nothing about her.

There were lots of pictures of Emma, though, in a bikini – Kate said she had a very flat tummy – and in an evening dress with Dad lying at her feet. You couldn't see his face properly. Kate said you could tell he was handsome, but I thought he still looked like someone's dad.

The article was all about why Emma Neil, who could go out with pop stars or footballers, was living with a thirty-nine-year-old history teacher. Kate said it made him sound like a dirty old man.

There was also a photograph of Mum, which wasn't very flattering. I think Dad took it when they were decorating Arthur's bedroom. It looked like she hadn't washed her hair.

We tried to distract Mum so she couldn't go out and buy a copy but then Suzy Sharp 'dropped round' to remind Mum that local residents were meant to take some soup to the protesters, and she had one under her arm.

'Obviously, I never buy this old rag normally,' she said, 'but I saw this picture of Emma on the front page.'

Mum looked at the article carefully, then said: 'They're just writing about them like that so they can have more fun when it ends.' But she was very quiet for the rest of the day.

What if she thinks she's got to get her own back at Dad with this boyfriend? She could end up married to him before she comes to her senses.

I am quite pleased now that I am going to see an educational psychologist, because Mum and Dad will both have to come with me. Mum says he lives in Surrey, which means they will have to be together in the car for ages and there will be plenty of opportunity for them to rediscover their love over the shared problem of having a useless son.

Also, the psychologist is bound to say I am messed up because my parents are separated, because that is the sort of thing that psychologists think, and this might inspire Mum and Dad to try again for the sake of their children.

Actually, I don't think I am messed up at all, but normal, and it is schools that are wrong. Children have to spend too much time at school, which is all right for some, but unfair on those like me, who are not suited to it. I am very much suited to other things, e.g. skateboarding, playing computer games, listening to Capital Radio 98.5 FM. When Dad says I am lazy and do not stick at things, he is not considering activities like these.

Julie

I had another dream about Simon last night. He called me 'hot bitch', which was terribly exciting for some reason – if not completely convincing – and I woke up feeling flustered.

I suppose it *was* Simon.

At the office, I called Nettle to see if I could get to see Ed to finish the interview, and she promised to ring me back, but didn't. When I called again, three hours later, she informed me that she couldn't see how Ed could possibly fit me in again for at least a fortnight.

How demanding is it, hanging around a derelict house waiting for the bailiffs to turn up?

Tony said we'd have to finish the piece with what we already had.

'It's fine, honestly,' he assured me; 'funny.'

Which was worrying, because I was trying to be serious.

I sat putting in all the crucial bits of information that Tony had informed me that I'd missed out, and getting images of Ed's hands on my body. I was trying very hard to concentrate on what he'd said about the road contravening the government's commitments to stabilise carbon dioxide at 1990 levels at the Rio summit, but I kept seeing thighs.

We'd been writing this article for days, and I still seemed to have overlooked an awful lot of vital facts. Was I really competent to do this job? It was only one packed lunch, but it was symptomatic of what happens when you get older: your brain gets crammed with so much useless stuff – the name of your son's primary school teacher, the name of your daughter's primary school teacher, the name of your own primary school teacher, the titles of all the Spice Girls' number ones – that it crowds out all the really important stuff. One day I shall wake up knowing the names of all Rod Stewart's girlfriends and unable to remember how to walk.

'I'm not sure I'm doing the right thing,' I worried out loud to Tony over lunch in the High Street. 'Is this job worth the sacrifices? I'm not a proper career woman, like my friend Fran, and it's not as if I'm even earning enough to pay for high-quality childcare . . .'

'I thought the kids liked Ginny?'

'They do. Arthur loves her. But she's always late and she still doesn't say much. I know almost nothing about her . . .'

'W. H. Auden said children deserve as much neurosis as they can take. It makes them want to redress the balance in later life.'

'And did he have kids?'

'Er, well, no, he was gay.' Tony sat back in his chair and put his hands behind his head. 'You don't have to stay very long at the *Langley Advertiser*. Think of it as a stepping stone.'

This is all very well for Tony: he'll easily get a job in a television newsroom or a national paper as soon as he wants one. He's in Langley because his mother isn't expected to live very long. Besides, he's only just out of Cambridge; he's in no rush. But I could easily get beached here for the rest of my life.

What openings are there for a woman who's getting on for forty, with skills like mine? 'Top astrophysicist required. Must be good at dusting skirting boards.' I toyed briefly with the idea of writing a skirting boards book, of trying to become the Martha Stewart of the M25, but a tile has been missing from the bathroom wall for three months and my freezer's growing ice goitres.

'The trouble is, I don't know who I am,' I complained. 'I used to think I was a full-time mother, but I'm not even much good at that. I always have to pretend to be Boadicea when I'm going round the supermarket. It's never been enough on its own.'

'Exactly. You're meant to be working. And there are lots of things you could go on to do from here.'

'Such as what? All the opportunities are closing down. Kate wants to be a lawyer or a television producer or a graphic artist or an astronaut, but I haven't got time for any of that any more. Work is for young people. I'll never know now whether I could have been a pop star. I've fulfilled my biological purpose and now it's all downhill in support hose.'

'You could always go back to acting.'

'I'm too *old*. That's what I'm *saying!* Advertising's all

directed at eighteen to thirty-five-year-olds; Fran told me. I'm even too old to be a consumer. I'm supposed to be satisfied with the serviceable old skirts and slippers I've already got and not think about buying anything new.'

'Are you sure this is about work and not about your marriage?' Tony asked, chomping on a BLT. 'Or possibly some other relationship?'

'It's about everything.'

But he had a point. I was so restless mainly because my commitment to being part of a couple – coerced by domesticity, hustled by family – had been knocked sideways by Richard's decision to abandon me for Emma. I used to think looking after someone else and being fussed over in return was a state of grace. Maybe that's what I'd chosen, more even than I'd chosen Richard.

'God, am I glad you're here,' Marlene, our office secretary, said to me when we arrived back from lunch. 'Some woman from the *Daily Mail* has been ringing you every five minutes for the past hour.'

She called again, five minutes later. Her name was Mandy, she explained with the warmth of someone who was determined to be my new best friend – and she wanted to give me the opportunity to put my side of the story about Emma and my husband.

'You'll be amazed how much it'll help,' she said. 'You'll feel you've taken control.'

'Sorry,' I said feebly, 'I don't think I can.'

'We can offer £25,000. At least let me come and see you to talk about it.'

It was an awful lot of money.

'You're a journalist,' she said warmly, not realising how inaccurate that was: 'you'll be great.'

'No. Thanks, but I can't.'

'Just think about it. I'll call you again in half an hour.'

'There's your nanny-money,' Tony said, when I told him. 'Plus a degree of independence from Richard.'

'I don't want to be independent from Richard. My dependence on him is one of the few things still connecting us.'

'It'd be cathartic.'

Certainly, the most depressing thing about those pictures of Richard and Emma in the *News of the World* had been the sense they gave me that I didn't quite matter in the way that they did. They are of general interest. But I live entirely privately; it's a kind of loneliness.

I said no.

'It *would* be a cheap way of getting famous,' Tony said, after I'd fobbed off my new friend Mandy.

I guess it's better to be poor than cheap.

Anyway, I couldn't see how Richard would ever come back if I slagged him off across a centre-spread of the *Daily Mail*.

Half an hour later, when I was still totting up all the things I could have bought/paid off with £25,000, my mother rang. She'd seen the *News of the World* too.

'I know a lot of young girls these days think it's empowering to use their bodies to get on, but it's a dead end,' she announced. 'Looks fade. And it's not very sisterly, is it?'

'I don't think the notion of sisterhood has ever entered Emma's head.'

'I may be old-fashioned, but a woman needs something more to rely on than blonde hair and pouty lips. As she'll realise to her cost when she hits forty.'

Thanks, Mum.

Pete emerged from his office on the way to his late afternoon/early evening drink and said: 'That interview with Ed McGregor is a bit shrewish.'

Tony looked up from his keyboard and nodded. 'Good, isn't it?'

'She says he's a Don Quixote,' Pete said, for the benefit of the newsroom, 'tilting at windmills. Our readers won't know what that means. Not sure I do either. She thinks he's deceiving us into believing the protest can stop the road.'

'Well, it can't,' I said defensively.

'And he's only interested in his own career and leads the bunch of credulous hairies mainly because it gives him a sense of power and he gets on the telly a lot.'

All the sub-editors were staring at me.

I said aggressively: 'Not in so many words.'

Pete patted the top of my head. 'Don't worry, love, we don't mind a bit of controversy.'

'Is that what you really believe?' Tony asked casually, not looking up from his screen, when Pete had gone to the pub. 'Or is there something else going on?'

I thought back to the conversation in Polly's and to failing to switch off my mobile phone. I thought about Ed McGregor in my kitchen.

'Obviously, it's what I believe,' I said irritably. 'That's why I wrote it.'

Kate

Everyone was talking about the *News of the World* article at school. Dad's affair with Emma is the most exciting thing to have happened at our school in years apart from having two boys come in to act the male parts in *The Prime of Miss Jean Brodie*.

Single-sex education is a form of child abuse. I wanted to go to the comprehensive, but Dad said why did I think the price of property was so high in Langley? I had no idea, but apparently it is because of the grammar schools.

They let Ben go to the comprehensive. Not that they had any choice: he didn't even bother to sit the grammar school exam. It seems unfair that he should get the better deal just for being thick.

Anyway, Miss Hawkins, our head teacher, called me up to her office this morning and said if I ever wanted to talk about the publicity or anything, her door was always open.

I was like, yuk! because she is a governor or something at the boys' school and always having little talks with their headmaster. I'm sure she thinks Dad should be sacked, but Emma was over the age of consent and had already left school and everything, and though there's been a load of stuff about changing the law to stop teachers and pupils having sex, they haven't done it yet. Besides, the parents would probably riot because Dad's such a brilliant teacher. Most years his entire A-level set get As, so they couldn't care less about his morals.

I am certainly not revealing our family secrets to Miss Hawkins. She wears a hairband, even though she is fifty.

The article was stupid. There were no pictures of us. It went on and on about what a great career Emma had ahead of her.

They made Dad out to be a really old guy, then said how supportive he was, which made him sound like a Wonderbra.

I thought the tabloids were supposed to pay people to be in their papers, but this sounded like Emma had paid them.

I felt sorry for Mum. There was a picture of her, but it made her look like the drudge from the suburbs, even though lots of my friends think she looks fantastic. (Personally, I think she is rather average. She is average height and her hair is an average colour. I suppose she might be above-averagely pretty, but she definitely has some lines around her eyes.)

She is coping pretty well with being a single parent; but the *News of the World* didn't say so. They implied that *anyone* would leave her if they could go off with Emma Neil, which I don't think is true. She has more interesting things to say than Emma, who only talks about television.

Watching Mum reading the article reminded me of when she and Dad told me they were splitting up and I had to keep trying to think of nice things to stop myself from crying. But once I'd thought about Darren Bredy, and the party I was supposed to be going to the following weekend and getting an A star for art three weeks in a row, I ran out of ideas, so then I tried thinking unselfishly about people other than myself. Unfortunately I made the mistake of doing it about Ben, who was immature for his age even then. When Dad said he was going to live in a loft, Ben thought he meant like where people keep their Christmas decorations.

Now Ben has become a truant, though he does it without actually leaving the building, by hiding his work and daydreaming instead of doing maths. That is typical of him. He is incapable of doing anything properly.

Oh my God, I think I have an incurable disease, which is making me haemorrhage. Either that or I have started my periods. There is all this gunk coming out of my body. It doesn't look like anything you'd want inside you, but I have rung Rachel, who said not to panic yet, as it is unlikely that I have a terminal illness. (That would make my parents sorry, anyway.)

I have tried to use a tampon, but it seems my body is a completely different shape from in the diagram. (Maybe I have been deformed by the tragic virus?)

Instead I have got a pad between my legs, which I think is giving me a rash.

It is at least a relief that I did not take Rachel's advice and have sex.

Ben

Kate says the horrible new boyfriend is called Simon. She doesn't know his surname. I'd like to ask Mum, but I don't think she would be very pleased, as she is trying to treat it casually. I'm worried that it might begin with a W or a Z or something, because I don't want to go further down the register at school.

Actually, I don't want to have to change my name at all. My parents chose Ben specifically because it goes well with Ellison. Ben Ellison. It goes.

Supposing Simon's surname is Benjamin? Ben Benjamin would be plain stupid. Anyway, it is not as if Dad is dead or anything.

If I were a dad, I'd be really offended if my son gave up my name. (Not that I would split up from my wife if I was a dad. I am not even sure I would have children in the first place, because people make so many mistakes with them.)

Still, we spend more time with Mum and we will probably go on more holidays with her, and I wouldn't want us all to go on holiday with different surnames, because it would reveal to everyone that we are a fractured family.

(Dad and Emma are always talking about taking us on holiday but it hasn't happened yet because they need so much time to have sex. If Mum does marry Simon, I suppose they might want holidays on their own so they could have sex all the time as well and Kate and I would never get to go away.)

What if Simon has children and we don't like them? They could be like Adrian Farr.

Even if they were nice, I wouldn't want them playing with my Hornby railway. Some of the mechanisms are very fragile, and even Ginny, when she puts it back in the box, doesn't take enough care with the locomotives.

If Simon *doesn't* have children it is probably because he is no good at sticking with things, such as relationships, and will only make Mum miserable. It would be better not to get involved with him in the first place than to end up unhappy.

Another worry is that other people's houses always smell. Our house doesn't smell – at least, if it does it smells of us so we can't notice it – and I don't want someone coming in here and making us smelly.

Anyway, it isn't going to happen, because I am going to stop it.

Julie

Last night, Arthur asked if his daddy could come and kiss him goodnight, even though Richard hasn't set foot inside our house for months. I was only able to persuade him to settle down eventually by playing an elaborate game which involved all his Teletubbies jumping from the floor on to his bed, one after the other, and taking it in turns to sing 'Twinkle Twinkle Little Star' until he fell asleep. It took sixty-three goes, and it's not an easy song to sing without consonants.

When he finally crashed out, I sat at the top of the stairs wondering how I could possibly explain Richard's absence in a way that made sense to Arthur's three-year-old world-view. Daddy wanted to be a politician when he was younger but he ended up as head of history at Langley Boys' Grammar School and now he blames me?

Frankly, there isn't much about it that makes sense even to a compromised thirtysomething world-view. It isn't how I imagined ending up. When I was at university, I was considered quite desirable. More than one man wrote me poetry. These days, the only chance I get to be a siren is with Arthur, playing police cars.

Now Arthur and I were sorting through all the shirts and trousers and jackets that Richard hadn't wanted cluttering up his white hanging spaces in Clerkenwell. I intended to remove them from the wardrobe, put them into bin bags and offer them to him. Perhaps it might focus his attention.

There were trousers there still creased with wearing; I fingered them uncertainly. I picked up a lone sock from the floor and wondered where the other one was, shook out a jacket still faintly dribbled with Arthur's egg stains. Even now, my scent still hung around these masculine fabrics, corduroys and denims; our times together had seeped into them like sweat. I could press a sleeve to my cheek and remember steam rising in the kitchen from a pan of pasta on the hob, misting up the daffodils on the table as Richard snapped the top off a beer from the fridge and we talked about Kate's school report. I could rub the towelling of his dressing gown between my fingers and recall him sprawled on the bed with the newspaper while I trotted backwards and forwards to the bathroom telling him about Arthur biting Ben, and Ben wondering whether this meant that Arthur would have to wear a muzzle. Talking like this, offering up moments for his approval, I thought I was creating small, irrevocable, irreplaceable intimacies.

'Mummy,' Arthur said, jumping into a pile of old shirts, 'how was I made?'

'By a sperm from Daddy and an egg from Mummy.'

'Yes, but how?'

I backed out of the bottom of the cupboard, sat on

the floor and started to tell him. After about three minutes of explanation, he burrowed under the shirts. Two minutes later, he got up with one of the shirts still wrapped round his head and walked away.

'You were made from love,' I called out after him belatedly.

'Woooo!' he called back. 'I'm a ghost.'

At the back of the wardrobe, under a jacket that had fallen off its hanger, I discovered something called a Power Roller. I removed it from its box in pieces. 'Recover a flat stomach in only four minutes a day!' urged the instructions. 'Follow our exercise routine for as little as thirty days and achieve a super flat stomach and streamlined waist for £29.95 plus postage and packing.'

Richard obviously didn't need this any more: according to the children, he'd joined some swanky gym where personal trainers pressed hot towels on you as you arrived. 'Actually,' my mother said, 'what he needs is a personality trainer.'

I never even knew he'd bought the Power Roller. The thought of him working on it in private seemed somehow terribly sad.

'It's all to do with the umbilicus,' Fran explained later on the telephone. 'The umbilical cord represents softness and dependency. Richard's wanting to encase it in muscle is his way of trying to repudiate that dependency.'

'Maybe . . .' I said doubtfully. Richard's wanting to encase his stomach in muscle seemed to me fairly straightforwardly about wanting to sleep with eighteen-year-olds.

121

'Fran, are you all right?'

She sniffed, choked and burst out: 'David's not leaving Karen.'

'Oh God. Oh, I'm sorry!'

'David told her about me and she had a nervous breakdown.'

I was impressed – a nervous breakdown is much better than thinking your kitchen has broken up into a geometry of prisms and tilted triangles – although Karen doesn't, of course, have any children. If I'd tried to have a nervous breakdown – crawled into bed and cried for a week, say – Ben would have taken it as an invitation to eat sweets until his teeth dropped out.

'So what now?'

'Well, the thing is, there's something I . . .'

There was a deafening crash from downstairs, then an eerie silence.

'Hang on a minute.' I went to investigate.

Ben was on his hands and knees in the sitting room, surrounded by broken china. When I appeared, he hurriedly started scooping up the mess of lavender flowers on the carpet and mumbling sheepish apologies.

'Oh, Ben! *How?* It was right in the middle of the table.'

'I don't know . . . it just happened. I wasn't doing anything; only swinging Arthur's Postman Pat.'

The shattered bowl was hand-thrown and painted in rich blues and soft apricots. It was a present from Fran, so probably cost a fortune.

'Everything all right?' she asked, when I came back to the phone.

'Yeah, Ben knocked something off the table. What's

wrong with him? Why is he always crashing into things?'

'He's a boy.'

'Other kids aren't that clumsy. Oh shit, now they're having a fight. I'll have to go.'

Downstairs, Arthur was in tears because he'd borrowed – stolen, Ben said – a Lego dragon which had been guarding Ben's castle. And then Ben had reclaimed it, so Arthur had hit him and Ben had hit back harder.

I pulled them apart, put them in separate rooms and surveyed the mess of Lego and lavender pot pourri. I was a hopeless mother. I *resented* tidying up after them. If I were any good as a parent, I'd welcome the opportunity to keep bending down and picking up their toys in a spirit of happy self-abnegation. But I'm not and I don't, and as a result, they're all a mess. Kate's like a human hormone: if you lit a match near her, she'd explode and give off noxious gases. Arthur can't remember his parents sleeping together, so wanders off incredulously when I try to explain his conception. And Ben keeps falling over. Plus he's started getting other people to do his homework and claiming to have seen nonexistent educational psychologists. They all need a father.

I rang Richard and pointed out to him that Ben never used to lie and now he seems to be doing it all the time.

'Kids always lie. It's one of the things they do.' There was music thumping in the background; it sounded suspiciously like drum and bass. Once upon a time, Richard would have been yelling at Ben to turn it down. 'You have to make him understand it's not acceptable.'

123

'*I* have to make him understand?'

'One has to. I meant one. Anyway, it's all turned out OK. He's going to see an educational psychologist.'

'I'm worried he thinks things don't *matter* any more.' And why should he, when family members could be downsized when they were surplus to requirements? 'He thinks we don't talk to each other, so he can pretend to do his homework at your place and not do it at all. He thinks we won't notice.'

'I thought we were having a conversation about Ben's educational psychologist.'

'It's imperative that we all go, all three of us, show Ben this is really important.'

'Fine. Depending when it is.'

'No. Whenever it is.'

'Fine.'

'And when I see you next, remind me that I've got a whole load of your clothes in bin bags.'

'Huh?'

'Things you left here. I thought you might need some of them for summer.'

'Oh. In bin bags?'

'Just until you decide whether you want me to hang them up again.'

'I can't see that I'm going to need them after all this time. If I were you, I should give them to Oxfam.'

Ben

The appointment has come through for the educational psychologist. It's next Friday and I am dreading it because Mum says there will be tests and when we have them at school I always come bottom.

Mum still hasn't forgiven me for lying about it. I didn't know it was such a big deal. I don't think it really makes sense anyway, because our education is going to be cut short. Kate says what with our parents splitting up and universities charging fees etc, we will have to give up all thoughts of further education. I don't mind because I wouldn't have got in anyway.

Tonight I accidentally set an extra place at the table for dinner. Mum went all tight-lipped and took it away without saying anything, but afterwards she locked herself in the bathroom and came out with a blotchy face.

I don't know if it was because she misses Dad or because she worries about my brain. When I think of my brain, I imagine a bin full of screwed-up bits of paper. If I need a thought, I stick my hand inside, rummage around for a bit and pull one out. But it isn't always the right one.

Julie

Someone was blitzing the doorbell, as if they thought I was too much of a slut to respond to a normal ring.

Richard's parents stood on the step. June, her arms folded, was already tapping her fingers irritably.

'We were in the area, visiting Ikea,' she announced, 'so we thought we'd drop in.'

Ikea is miles away.

'How are you?' Alf tapped me awkwardly on the shoulder as I stood back to let them in.

'OK. Fine. I'm sorry I haven't called for a bit.'

Why was I apologising? I was mad. They hadn't called me either.

They always do this to me, make me feel guilty. It's because they think I'm not good enough for their son.

Now *he* thought so, too, but they'd always known. Right from the start they'd made me understand that Richard could, and should, have married better – that I was too uppity, to prickly, too ironic or something, and I spent too much time slobbing around the kitchen

126

table drinking tea while my children frolicked on the floor with bare bottoms.

'We just called on the off chance. We weren't sure you'd be here,' June said. 'We gather you've got a job.'

She made it sound like herpes.

'Yes,' I said, leading them down the hall. 'But I don't work on Mondays.'

Why had they come, if they expected me to be out? To miss me? To make a point?

'I'm afraid Kate and Ben are at school,' I said, apologetically again, although it was two o'clock in the afternoon and that's exactly where they should have been. 'Even Arthur's out.'

June marched into the sitting room. 'Yes, Richard told us you're putting him out to someone during the day.'

'She comes here, actually,' I said, through gritted teeth. 'She's called Ginny.'

I'm not sure June and Alf mind missing the children: their visits certainly seem to coincide very neatly with times when they aren't at home. The children shout and demand things and quarrel; June and Alf – who only had one child – can't stand the anarchy or the decibels. Every visit confirms their suspicion that my children are appallingly brought up.

June perched on the edge of the sofa and patted the cushion next to her to indicate that Alf should sit too. She touched her bright blonde hair and pursed her mouth. Her eyes had a challenging look, as if she was expecting someone any minute to start taking advantage. June believes that a woman's fingers should never be idle; she has crocheted more toilet-roll holders than anyone else in history.

Richard's father, mildly hangdog, blinky and apologetic, like Stan Laurel, promptly obeyed.

'Richard still hasn't taken any more furniture,' June remarked.

'No.'

'He'll be back,' Alf said. 'It can't last.'

I didn't reply.

I went out to the kitchen to make tea and do a bit of deep breathing. Fran, who is always sending me stress-busting tips that she gets out of newspapers or ridiculous self-help books, faxed me a list last week that claimed making porridge is very restful. I threw it in the bin. Porridge, even made in the microwave, is extremely time-consuming. It cannot be done unless you get out of bed the exact minute the alarm goes. Now, though, I was desperate, and wondered if a pot of tea might have the same effect, if you did it with a proper awareness of karma.

When I returned to the sitting room, I was almost certain that June was running her dust finger over a lamp.

'Alf's on a diet,' she said, looking at the cake I'd brought in. 'And sponges don't agree with me.'

Since when? Whoever heard of someone being allergic to sponges? Dairy allergies, yes; wheat allergies, fine; but *sponge* allergies?

She was allergic to the fact that I'm managing and that if she drops in unannounced I can produce a home-made cake. She should be pleased for me: I am the Jane Asher of the outer London suburbs; I have invented a second life for myself in cake-making.

I'd cut two pieces already, so I ate one of them.

'How is the job?'

I wiggled my head around, signifying 'fine', because I had too much cake in my mouth to speak.

'Of course, having a career didn't work out before, did it? Still, that *was* evenings.'

'She doesn't have to carry on when Richard comes back,' Alf pointed out helpfully.

'It doesn't give him much incentive *to* come back though,' June said doubtfully, 'if he thinks she's pre-occupied and has no time for her family.'

'I have plenty of time for my family,' I retorted, spraying crumbs on to the carpet.

I should be used to it by now. When I was an actress, she went on and on at Richard like this, until she persuaded him she was right.

'You don't think the children need you now more than ever?'

'I haven't moved out!'

'It's no coincidence, you know, that Britain has the highest divorce rate in Europe. People work very long hours.'

'But *I* don't work long hours.' I work part-time, so that Pete thinks it's a sort of hobby.

'I don't understand you young women, wanting to have it all.'

Have it all. As if we're talking a farmhouse in Tuscany with a kidney-shaped pool and a private jet to get me there and a personal masseur with his table already set up in the orchard.

'It's only a job. Actually, it's only a *part-time* job.'

'There's that woman at Pepsi, she was earning ever so much – two million a year. *She* gave it all up to be with her children.'

'It helps to earn the two million in the first place,' I observed mildly. 'And running Pepsi Cola was probably a bit more demanding than being a junior reporter on the *Langley Advertiser*.'

'It's sad, that's all, that you young women don't see running a home as your first priority. That was always quite demanding enough for us.'

Why was she doing this? I didn't want to fight with them; they were my children's grandparents. But it was a struggle.

'I was starting to feel I'd go mad if I didn't do something,' I said, with massive reasonableness, 'which wouldn't have been terribly good for any of us.'

'It's a pity that you don't count being at home as doing something.'

This was *so* typical: her son had left me and we were discussing the pros and cons of working women. When I was twenty, I'd admired Richard's ability to frame all his personal problems in terms of social issues. I thought it was because he was doing a degree in history and sociology. Now I knew it was displacement activity.

'There's Ben,' she went on obstinately, 'he ought to keep you busy enough. We were just saying on the way over, you can understand all that more now.'

'All what?'

'You *know* . . .' She nodded at me meaningfully. 'It's not even as if the work you do is *important* – you're not a nurse or anything.'

I looked towards Alf helplessly. I was going to be unforgivably rude in a minute if he didn't step in. June blamed me for the fact that her son was living in a loft in Clerkenwell, but it *wasn't* my fault. Or not, at any rate, any more than it was hers. She was the one who'd poisoned him with the family ambition – in her case, for respectability, in Richard's . . . well, he didn't know *what* his was for.

Alf blinked back at me sheepishly. At some early point in his marriage, he'd decided that women lived on some more vivid and intense emotional plane than men, and that to intrude upon it could risk upsetting their fragile mental health. This approach was a) patronising, b) a terrible example to his son, who learned to shut himself down, and c) made June worse.

After they'd gone, I sat on the sofa feeling crushed and leprous and fat, because, suffering from inlaws-rage, I'd eaten too much cake.

I was right and June was wrong. Wrong, wrong, wrong. Except that she may have been right in her sense that I had never been quite the right woman for her son.

Perhaps I should never have married someone who proposed in a china department.

But I *had* married him, and we had children, and now we bloody well had to get on with it.

I roused myself. It wasn't healthy to sit around mulling over past mistakes, such as failing to work out that someone brought up by June and Alf Ellison was bound to be a bit weird.

Later this week we are going to see the educational psychologist, where we have high hopes of finding out that Ben is dyslexic. Einstein was dyslexic.

Ben

Mum insisted on driving to the educational psychologist. She said she wasn't prepared to be a passenger any more. I didn't really know what she meant, but I thought it was bound to cause trouble because Dad gets impatient and shouts if she doesn't change lanes or overtake at the right time.

I took some tapes, choosing happy ones that I could remember us all singing along to on the way to the airport the last time we went on holiday together, which, when you think about it, was ages ago.

I also prepared some topics of conversation, in case Mum brought up the subject of her new boyfriend. This might, of course, make Dad jealous, but you can't be sure. He might just feel relieved. He might even do something stupid, like marry Emma. She is daft enough to agree, even though by the time she is in her thirties Dad will be pretty much dead.

My topics to distract them included the missing tile in the bathroom (to make Dad worry that the house is not being properly maintained); Kate wanting to get her ears pierced (i.e. she is unstable); and Arthur's fascination with the cupboard under the sink (the point being does Arthur secretly want to drink bleach because his parents have split up?)

Actually, I think Arthur may just have an obsession with cleaning. He likes the dustpan and brush as well, and he can identify four different brands of vacuum cleaner.

Unfortunately, I didn't get a chance to introduce any of them because Mum immediately started telling Dad about Grandma and Grandpa coming round to see her, and after that about Fran's boyfriend David, who is married but promised Fran he'd leave his wife and then said he couldn't because she was having a nervous breakdown.

Dad said that every boyfriend Fran had ever had was a bastard. (I would get told off if I said bastard.) I suppose Dad was implying *he* wasn't a bastard, because he *has* left his wife, but I don't see how this follows.

Then he told Mum about a film premiere he'd been to with Liz Hurley and Denise Van Outen and before I had a chance to mention the missing tile, we were there.

The educational psychologist was called Mr Phelps, and he had a soft, pink face and blue eyes. He shook hands with me and he was quite friendly. I hoped he wouldn't be like Miss Millett, who has been very touchy-feely since Mum went to see her, which I think might be the inappropriate behaviour you are meant to report to Childline.

Mr Phelps works in a big shed at the bottom of his garden. His secretary works there too, but he has his own room, where he took me. He left Mum and Dad together, which would have been a good time for them to sort out their difficulties, except for the secretary.

Mr Phelps and I did some reading and I had to draw the other half of a picture, and put some words in order and pair them up, then walk up and down and look through a camera and arrange some numbers. Some of it was easy, some wasn't, but he didn't mind when I couldn't do things. I kept wondering what he was deciding about my brain.

Then I had to go outside and look at books and comics (I chose the books, in case this was part of the test, though I really wanted to read the comics) and Mum and Dad went in with Mr Phelps. They seemed to be quite friendly to one another. I thought it was a good sign that although Mum had brought a book to read, it stayed in her bag. Afterwards, when they came out, they were behaving a bit like they used to when they had secrets about how awful Grandma was.

On the way back, I tried Arthur and the bleach and Mum told some story about how Arthur won't let the other children at nursery get on the bikes till he's cleaned them. They didn't draw the obvious conclusion.

Then, unfortunately, I fell asleep. But I am pretty sure that I have begun the reconciliation. It does not seem possible that they could get on so well and not get back together, if only for our sakes. Parents don't *need* children, and now that there are abortions, the pill, etc, they don't even have to have them by accident, so they obviously chose to have us and it doesn't make sense that they would then also choose to spoil our lives.

Julie

We crawled out of Langley along the new road, which is already a long muddy scar on the green belt; slowed by the roadworks, passing places where, until recently, there had been houses, trees, hedges, even fields, and now there was only a wide streak of churned-up London clay flattening the landscape into an eyesore. Bright yellow bulldozers dotted the muddy earth, and miniature men in hard hats moved around slowly on its surface like children's animated figures on a building site set. Soon they'd be replaced by screaming chunks of metal and rattling HGVs; a steaming trail of Tarmac and limp, denuded verges.

Richard's body beside me in the passenger seat was disconcertingly familiar. If I closed my eyes, I could remember exactly where his arms would come to on my back, and where he'd put his hands on my shoulder blades.

I wondered if we'd ever again find our heads on the same pillow, breathing in out-breaths from deep inside each other's bodies, ever slip back into breakfasting together and thinking nothing of it.

I could see, now that we'd spent time apart, that Richard and I had never been quite like Mel and Ian: a circuit, humming for and because of each other, believing we could never want anything else, because nothing more was out there. I was, in fact, no longer quite sure that I hadn't somehow *made do* with Richard. His mother, of course, would have said this didn't matter. She thought that making do was the highest calling, a cardinal virtue.

And perhaps she was right. Look where passion got you: exploited and ignored by Ed McGregor.

And it needn't necessarily be a bad thing to be pragmatic: in fact, I was thinking it was possible that my relationship with Richard might turn out to be *better* for this hiatus. At least being with Emma for a few months had helped him shake off his aura of chalk dust and disappointment. He looked good again today, in a dark, slightly oversized jacket – more like a television executive or a music journalist than the tweedy-seedy teacher he'd become in recent years. Tall and blond and alpha-male.

'Your parents came to see me on Friday,' I told him as we limped through the contraflow.

'I know, they came to us afterwards. How was it for you?'

'The usual. Your mother's developed an allergy to sponge.'

'She didn't tell me.'

'Perhaps you didn't offer her any.'

'No. We did offer her tea, but then realised we didn't have any.'

I bet June didn't make snide remarks, though. Emma

could get away with not having PG Tips and making people sit on concrete stools because she was on television and once met Des Lynam.

'They don't think I should be working.'

'No.'

'Do they have the same sort of reservations about Emma?'

Sometimes I think I am just not very nice.

('Don't be ridiculous,' Tony said bracingly, when I told him this. 'Niceness is a quality one looks for in wild flowers and children's zoos.')

'Emma doesn't have children,' Richard said. 'It's not the same thing.'

This was a route to nowhere, so I changed the subject, and told him about the latest developments between David and Fran.

'He *promised* he was going to leave Karen, *definitely* this time – and he did finally tell her about Fran – and then she had a nervous breakdown, so now he's staying.'

'Poor Fran.'

'I'm not sure, actually, that she really wanted his dirty socks . . .'

Whole schools of psychiatric thought are based on the premise that even the lowliest rat is capable of learning from its mistakes. Why should Fran be the one exception? Almost certainly, she sticks with David because he can be relied on to be a bastard.

'It suits her to pretend to be desperate for David,' I said. 'Like reading all those self-help books, it makes people think she's ditzy.'

'But the truth is that no man comes up to her standards?'

'I guess.'

How different, when you came to think of it, from me.

Deep down, I'd always believed – well, who doesn't? – that I was capable of all-consuming, passionate, utterly demanding love. Not only capable, but *destined* for it. And when it didn't immediately appear, it's possible I'd seized on Richard. He would have to do. It was like pretending to be Scarlett O'Hara as I went round Sainsbury's. Only with rather more serious consequences.

Mr Phelps lived in stockbroker-belt Sussex, in rolling hills studded with houses: enclaves of comfort along wooded roads punctuated by villagey high streets full of second-hand designer dress shops. It made Langley, jostled by inner London, feel almost on the edge.

Mr Phelps, who looked too young to be qualified at anything except women's tennis, took my sweet, nervous Ben off for tests, leaving Richard and me together in the waiting room with his secretary.

Richard having neglected to bring anything to read, I was left with the choice of reading anyway and ignoring him, or making conversation.

'Is Emma planning to stay in the current job?' I enquired politely, meaning *EastEnders*. This is the trouble with your husband living with a famous person; you have to speak half in code.

'It depends. She's up for a part in a film. It would mean going to Los Angeles.'

Los Angeles, *California?* Would Richard go too? If so, when would he see the children? Almost never, presumably.

How mad with love *was* he, that he was prepared to put thousands of miles between himself and his children?

'That would be an upheaval,' I said understatedly.

'But quite exciting for the children – to have access to all that.'

'The children? *They'd* come . . . ? How long exactly are you thinking . . . ?'

'Oh, I don't know,' he said airily; 'we haven't talked about it properly yet.' We, we, we. 'There's a possibility that they could come for a term.'

I nodded dumbly. Possibility. He only said possibility. That was what I had to cling to.

Even though Einstein was dyslexic and Ben is dyslexic, Ben is not Einstein. Inside my bumbling son, there is no rocket scientist straining to get out.

Ben is not, in fact, only, or even mainly, dyslexic, but also dyspraxic (vague, clumsy and disorganised) and dysgraphic (so that he couldn't write his thoughts down even if he could organise them, which he can't). Richard blames me for having a son who, as he says, has abilities just above those of a small swede. I tried to convince him that Ben has other talents, but could only think of growing mould on pieces of fruit left in his bedroom.

Mr Phelps took Richard and me into his little room and began by telling us how charming and willing he had found Ben. And then from there it was all downhill.

'I imagine he's often clumsy?'

'He didn't break anything?' I asked in alarm.

'No, Mrs Ellison,' he smiled. 'I am surmising. Professionally. Does he have a particularly active imagination?'

'Oh yes,' I said eagerly. 'He gets into games – becomes a pirate or a soldier or a train driver – and he's absorbed for hours. You can speak to him and he won't hear you.'

'That's because he doesn't want to,' Richard said sourly. 'He certainly does have an imagination: he's scared of heights, of boats, of planes, of theme park rides.'

'And a poor sense of timekeeping?'

Mr Phelps's assessment of Ben became more and more impressive as he reeled off a list of Ben's traits (his character flaws, Richard called them on the way home): '. . . a confusion between left and right, poor short-term memory, difficulty with complex oral instructions, distractibility, occasional hyperactivity, talkativeness, a too loud, possibly rather irritating laugh, an insensitivity to complex social cues.'

'Yeah, completely unstreetwise,' Richard agreed sourly. 'He gave his skateboard away to some kids in the park.'

'He was mugged!'

'Other kids don't get mugged. He's got no sense. He doesn't understand about keeping out of trouble.'

'I think that's quite astonishing, in an hour,' I told Mr Phelps, mainly to shut Richard up.

He smiled. 'These are typical symptoms of the dyslexic-dyspraxic continuum. There are certain things you might be able to do to help. Does he have a lot of fizzy drinks?'

I shook my head.

'Coke and Pepsi are particularly bad. So, funnily enough, is fruit juice, especially orange. Other things that seem to make the symptoms worse – we don't know exactly why – are Ribena, chocolate, highly flavoured and coloured sweets and crisps and Weetabix.'

'I see. He doesn't have much of any of that. Some fruit juice, but not a lot.'

His dyslexic-dyspraxic continuum is evidently sited deep within.

Mr Phelps suggested some further therapy, which mainly seemed to involve making patterns out of blocks of wood. For this, Ben would go to a special teacher.

'What's wrong with her just making him learn his tables?' Richard growled.

'Nothing,' Mr Phelps said patiently. 'But I expect you've already tried.'

There wasn't much conversation in the car on the way back, even when Ben fell asleep.

'Of course, you're dyspraxic,' Richard said eventually, having thought about it and absolved himself of responsibility for the fact that Ben is barely sentient. 'You practically have a nervous breakdown getting ready to go on holiday. And even then you forget your hairbrush. *And* you have the over-active imagination. You're always fantasising about being other people.'

'I don't see why it has to be one of us. He could be a throw-back.'

'To what? Baboons?'

*   *   *

'Is Dad coming in?' Ben asked sleepily, when we drew up outside the house.

Richard was already getting out his car keys. 'Sorry, son,' – he ruffled Ben's hair – 'not this time.'

Kate

I am really pissed off with Mum. She has written a vile article in the crappy local paper saying that the road protest is doomed to failure and Ed McGregor is only leading it to make himself feel important. She is just jealous because she is not involved, because, actually, the protest is the most exciting thing to happen round here for ages.

I have started going to the squats every day after school. I often bump into Darren Bredy there and we end up mixing concrete together. There is loads to do so we don't have to talk much, but sometimes we snog outside afterwards.

Fortunately, Ed McGregor hasn't mentioned the article to me. Ed is very friendly with everyone, even though he is a famous television personality (which shows that not everyone who's on television talks about it all the time). But Nettle, who does the protest PR and is having a relationship with Ed – Darren says they've been together for ages and some people even think they're going to get married – met me in the kitchen when I was making a herbal tea and said: 'That piece your mother wrote was absolute rubbish. Does she know *anything* about environmentalism?'

I replied that I wasn't sure, and went red. (But she doesn't: she thinks pierced ears are immoral, and most of the protesters have pierced eyebrows and even tongues.)

Darren said I shouldn't worry: Nettle can't bear it if anybody criticises Ed or has anything to do with him. But I don't see how this is supposed to make me feel better, because Mum *hasn't* had anything to do with him. All she has done is be rude.

Ed is pretty cool though. I'm not surprised he's in love with Nettle, because she's tall, beautiful, never wears make-up and often shows her midriff, which I wish I could get away with but I have too much flesh.

Mum ought to be grateful for the road protest. There was no point in living in Langley beforehand, and Darren says we were in danger of becoming alienated (that is what happens to young people in suburbia, he says).

Sometimes I think Darren is a bit peculiar. But he is right that Langley was really boring before: full of houses that look like other houses and little parades of dry cleaners and florists and greengrocers' shops. Suburbs were invented to be sociable places to bring up children, but they have no centre and nowhere to go so kids are forced to hang around bus shelters and at the swings being negative.

But now we've got the protest we've got all sorts of different people living here, like Nettle, whose dad is a barrister and who Mould says (he's a boy at the protest) lives in a big house in the country with her own ponies and a swimming pool in the garden. Or Phil, who is only a young kid, but has been chucked out of four schools and put in foster care and looks at you through narrowed eyes and hates everyone except Ed McGregor.

Adults are always saying young people should have more purpose in their lives and be more aware of the world around us. But now we've got a purpose – saving Langley, which we don't even like – and they're still not happy. Mum thinks I'm spending too much time at the squats, and Miss Hawkins said in assembly that she didn't want to hear that girls had been protesting when they should have been doing their homework.

The road is a difficult issue for most teachers, because even though they approve of saving the tree and stopping the road, they think the protesters take drugs and don't give a stuff about getting a place at a good university and a job in a firm of solicitors or accountants, which is all you're really supposed to care about if you go to Langley Grammar School for Girls.

Personally, I would rather do without GCSEs than trees. There is no point in spending your entire childhood worrying about exam grades if, at the end of it all, England is covered in Tarmac. The more I think about it, the more I am not sure that school is relevant to anything. How does knowing about conditions in the coalmines in the early years of the twentieth century help against the rape of the countryside by total consumerism?

Mould has done a really sensible thing and given up A-levels to become an earthfirster; he says exams no longer seemed important to him in the context of melting icecaps and burning rainforests.

Julie

I really quite like this job. I prefer being a reporter to sweeping the kitchen floor just so someone can mess it up again. I'd rather go into the office and gossip with Tony than stay in the house in jogging pants poking a brush down the lavatory. Besides, my first ever article has become quite a talking point in Langley. Wherever I go, people say to me: 'That was a load of rubbish you wrote about Ed McGregor.'

Pete is pleased with the reaction, in his slightly incredulous fashion (normally the only thing people are interested in in the *Langley Advertiser* is the classifieds), and Tony is very pleased, mainly because he now has someone sensible to talk to in the office. And I'm beginning to wonder (as if it wasn't actually the story of my life) whether I'd set my sights too low. Maybe I should have tried to get a job in the sort of office where they didn't have mice in the kitchen.

'What are you doing?' Fran asked, calling one morning when I was sitting over my keyboard, trying to summon up the enthusiasm to write photo captions for the Langley Players' production of *An Inspector Calls*.

'Thinking about alternative careers. D'you need any qualifications to go into PR?'

'I shouldn't think so. When is your date with Simon?'

'Tomorrow.'

'What are you going to wear?'

'I don't know. I haven't thought about it.'

This was a lie. I had tried every possible permutation offered by my limited wardrobe three times mentally and at least once physically. I had nothing to wear. Simon, on the one occasion on which I'd previously met him, had looked more fashionable than Richard's loft. I didn't own any of those kind of clothes. Everything I have makes me look like my mum in her Greenham phase – i.e., trying to look scruffy but basically too clean.

'Did you know that women who wear make-up earn 25 per cent more than those who don't?' I asked Fran. (I am still getting quite a lot of time to read the papers.) 'D'you think if I wore twice as much make-up, I could earn 50 per cent more?'

'You could earn 50 per cent more doing almost anything other than working for the *Langley Advertiser*. Are you planning to buy something new?'

'No!'

'Why not?'

'It's extravagant.'

'How many dates have you been on in the last fifteen years?'

'Er . . . none. Unless you count going out with Richard.'

'No, I certainly don't. Why don't you come late-night shopping with me?'

'Because I have three children.'

'Aren't they at their father's?'

'That's Tuesday, not Thursday. And even that's become very erratic. And if he does have them I often keep Arthur because Richard can't cope with him in the middle of the week. He wakes Emma up too early.'

'Can't you get a babysitter?' Fran asked, as if they were like shopping trolleys, stacked up and only waiting for a pound in the handle. 'Kate, for instance?'

'She could babysit for anyone else – she does – but if I'm going to put her in charge of Ben I might as well just douse them both in petrol and throw matches.'

'What about whatshername – Ginny?'

'She goes clubbing.'

'Not at six o'clock in the evening. Come on, you must need to get something new.'

'I don't see why. Anyway, I'm thinking of cancelling.'

'You're not to cancel,' she practically shouted. 'Being taken out to dinner by an attractive man isn't a thing you cancel for no good reason.'

'Taken out? Don't women pay these days? You see! I don't know how to do this. I shall screw up.'

'You eat meals with people the whole time: there's nothing *to* screw up.'

But as the moment approached, I was feeling less and less confident about why I was going out with him.

'He's probably got that date-rape drug.'

'What?'

'Rohypnol. Serial rapists use it to spike women's

drinks. And then they rape them. Serially. You must have read about it. No one believes the victims because they don't remember for two weeks afterwards.'

'You need to get out more.'

Perhaps Ginny is saving up for something – maybe, I thought hopefully, a round-the-world trip – because she was happy to stay on for a few hours. So I met Fran at her pink and silver office in Soho, and we took a taxi to Harvey Nichols.

Twenty outfits later, Fran was hopefully holding up a diaphanous Japanese shift, cunningly cut to reveal most of the left breast.

'The assistant said it was directional,' she said doubtfully. 'But I think you have to take off your M&S bra.'

'This is hopeless.' I pulled the dress over my head, threw it on the chair and pulled on my jeans. 'I'm too old for these clothes. They're not *for* me. I remember half of them from the first time around.'

What's ironic about wearing acid-green skinny-rib tops at thirty-eight when you've worn them at fifteen? Especially when skinny-rib described me in those days as well as the tops, and now it didn't. Now I had children and a caesarean scar and my body had become something to carry my brain around in, like a big bag.

We went up a floor and tried again.

'You're too obsessed with being past it,' Fran rebuked me, though it's all right for her: she thinks being nearly forty means opting for simple but elegant, which is fine if you can afford several outfits from Armani and Jil

Sander every season, but not otherwise. 'Pauline Kael said beauty often becomes more alluring as it starts to crumble.'

'She knew *nothing*.' I sorted irritably through the racks. 'The trouble is, I don't know what I want to look like any more. That's because I don't have a role. I am a middle-aged woman, a non-person.'

'It's called middle youth nowadays. And another way of looking at it is that you're old enough, and secure enough in yourself, to be comfortable with your own identity.'

But I didn't have an identity. The formal clothes looked too eighties, and the fashion-victim clothes looked as if they were designed for heroin-chic supermodels. They seemed to require a more starved, hollow-eyed and vacantly druggy look than I could manage.

'Prada?' Fran suggested.

Prada! As if I could afford Prada . . . This is what I mean about Fran being out of touch. But I tried a few bits on anyway – and there's a mystery: how come Prada makes Kate Moss look cool and me look like Olive from *On the Buses*?

Or perhaps I *have* got my own identity. It is somewhere between Oxfam and Army Surplus, and it isn't catered for in any of the shops along Knightsbridge.

Not that there weren't alternatives on offer. I could have gone out with Simon looking like a windswept poetic peasant in ruffly blouses and layered skirts, or a Tory MP in a day-glo suit, or a suburban housewife at the eat-as-much-as-you-like salad bar at the Langley Harvester.

'I think I must have outgrown fashion,' I announced,

when Fran and I were perched thirstily on stools at the Harrods juice bar, with not a carrier bag in sight. 'I'm too complicated. I've got too much past.'

'What are you going on about?'

'What I want are clothes that tell people that I'm wise, sexy, interesting, stylish, smart, complex and wild at heart.'

'Hmmn. Maybe you're asking too much.'

And then I found a jumper. (Jersey, June would have corrected me, because she thinks that's the upper-class word, and for all I know, she may be right. But if knitwear has classes, where do sweaters come? Above jumpers? Below jerseys?) Anyway, whatever this was, it was cashmere, sexy (slash neck, sleeveless – and my shoulders are possibly my best feature, which is not normally very useful) and £175. But given that you can easily pay £125 for a scarf, £175 for a jumper is really quite reasonable. And I don't shop in Knightsbridge often.

Then, to prove that I hadn't spent more than I could afford on the jumper, I bought a pair of black stretchy trousers for £200.

On the way out of Harvey Nichols for the second time, Fran dragged me over to the long-lasting lipsticks.

'Doesn't come off when you snog,' she said, dabbing at her lips with the assistant's lip-brush.

'I'm not . . .'

'This colour would really suit you.' And with no regard for hygiene, she stopped dabbing her own lips and stabbed the brush at mine.

I peered at her uneven daubs in the mirror. Then I

bought a long-lasting lipstick as well. It cost as much as four normal lipsticks, but women who wear make-up get paid more so it was actually an investment.

'Besides,' said Fran, 'it's always a good idea to be prepared.'

Ben

There's no obvious sign yet of Mum and Dad getting back together. Now that I've been officially diagnosed weird, I can't think what else to do.

It's called dyspraxia. I told Adrian Farr and he said did it make you crap at football as well? And I said yes, it did, actually, and then he pushed me over. After that he told all his friends that I had a disease and if they accidentally bumped into me they had to come to him for an antidote.

I've got to have special lessons for it. Mum says they won't be difficult – just like the things I did with Mr Phelps – but I don't think she knows anything about it.

I'm wondering whether it's worth suggesting to Dad that him getting back with Mum would help me more than even having the expensive extra lessons.

I can't really understand why he wants to stay with Emma, anyway, as she never stops whingeing about her mum.

Actually, her mum does sound a bit of a pain. She

rings up every day and asks Emma if she's had breakfast and what she's eaten because Emma was once a bit anorexic. And she wants them to have more furniture in the flat, and keeps bringing round books showing horrible comfy chairs and patterned curtains. She can't understand that the whole point is to keep everything white. Emma says she has no taste and can't think in an original way: she thinks all homes should look like the furniture floor of Marks and Spencer's, whereas Emma has got her own taste from *Wallpaper* magazine.

I wonder if Emma's mum has included guest beds in her suggestions? Kate and Arthur and I have to sleep on tatami mats (except Arthur won't put up with it and climbs in with Dad and Emma). They're a bit hard. Also, because there are no walls in the flat, the news comes on down the other end of the room and keeps you awake with a lot of stuff about earthquakes and politics. One very good thing about Dad coming home would be not having to sleep on the floor any more.

Now Mum is going out with this Simon bloke – Kate calls him her fancy man, as if it's all a *joke* – and I am really worried she might like him. *Someone* has got to keep the family together.

Kate told me about this boy called Phil at the squats, who's run away from home because his mum's boyfriend beat him up. He beat up Phil's mum as well. Someone should warn Mum that this could happen to her.

Julie

I was nervous all day. I sat at work trying not to think about having dinner with Simon and to concentrate instead on the Ducklings' Swimathon. If I felt like this later, it wouldn't matter *who* paid, I wouldn't be able to eat.

I was half-hoping Simon would offer to sleep with me (is that what normal people did, offer?) and half-hoping he wouldn't, because it had all been so mortifying the last time.

And if he didn't offer, would I have to? (Did I even want to? It was so long since I'd seen him, I couldn't remember.) And then how to negotiate all the niceties, all the would-you-like-to-come-in, would-you-like-to-take-my-bra-off bits?

I could see it wouldn't be as easy as it had been with Ed. His way of doing things is obviously quite particular to him. I'd decided now that Ed was one of those sex addicts you read about. They often live in Hollywood, but there's no particular reason why sex addiction should be confined to the West Coast of

155

the United States. People from Chelsea could have too much dopamine, or whatever it is that makes people capable of dragging just *anyone* off.

As behaviour went, it was a bit primitive. But then so was the sex, and Ed does live quite a lot of the time in a tree.

'What if I can't think of anything to talk to Simon about?' I asked Tony desperately. 'I don't have any interests. I have three children. My only interest is in whether Ben will ever learn his tables.'

Tony didn't even bother to look up from his crossword. 'Jools, you're being deliberately pathetic. It's not attractive. You're not normally short of words.'

He meant I prattled.

I left the office in good time to pack the boys' bags.

'D'you know what Dad's got organised for you this weekend?' I asked Ben, picking my way over a Lego village to get to his wardrobe.

'No.'

'Oh well, I expect it's something.'

'Yes.'

'Perhaps he'll take you to the Trocadero.'

'Mum . . .' Ben said pleadingly – but he didn't have time to finish because the doorbell was ringing. I heaved Arthur on to my hip and went downstairs to answer it.

Richard was standing on the step in jeans and a lilac linen shirt. More new clothes. No wonder he didn't want all those old Next jumpers.

Kate bounced down the stairs two at a time and stood to attention beside him, holding bags of clothing and homework, her violin and her minidisc.

Richard put out his hands for Arthur, whose legs clamped round my waist and whose arms tightened round my neck. Instinctively, I buried my face in his hair and squeezed his little sprite's body, smiling as it settled into the accustomed bumps and dips.

'Where's Ben?' Kate demanded.

'He's coming.'

Ben ambled down the stairs. Richard looked at his watch.

'Got your bag, Ben?'

'Oh. No.'

'Oh, come *on*,' Kate cried exasperatedly. 'Why does this always happen?'

'Here, I'll go and get it.' I handed Arthur to Richard and ran upstairs. Ben followed me disconsolately.

'Mum . . .' He shuffled into the bedroom behind me. 'Are you going out tonight?'

'Yes.'

'Why?'

'A friend asked me.' I put his bag down and looked at his screwed-up face. 'It's not a big deal, Ben. Really. It's . . . like having dinner with Mel or Fran.'

'I don't want you to get beaten up.'

I handed him the bag gravely. 'Honestly, I don't think that's likely. Come on, you take this.'

'It happens.'

'Not to me. I'm not that sort of person.'

I was glad my mother wasn't there, or she'd have pointed out that domestic violence can happen to anyone. She set up Letchworth's first women's refuge.

157

'Well,' Ben said, close to tears, 'just be careful, that's all.'

Simon arrived promptly, dressed in a black T-shirt, lime-green trousers and black Vans. Kate recently bought an identical pair. Perhaps he should have been going out with her.

I was glad now that Fran had dragged me to Harvey Nichols. The cashmere top made me feel sexy, and if I'd worn my old clothes people might have assumed that Simon was taking out his mother.

We drove into town in his black convertible Saab with the hood down. Simon wasn't *actually* young enough to be my son, obviously, but it occurred to me that I could well have been doing geometry before he could talk.

We went to a restaurant in Soho called Wave, where the furniture was designed without right-angles, and spiky-haired waiters served fashionable Pacific-rim food, yellowfin tuna and soy sauce.

He told me a little about his business trip: he'd been to Boston, New York, San Francisco and Seattle, briefed a lot of music journalists about what was happening in Britain, and heard at least three really great new bands.

'It was better than I'd expected.'

He had pecs of vulcanised steel.

Then he said: 'Dennis told me as I was leaving his barbecue that you were a great catch and I wasn't to be put off by the fact that your husband had left you.'

'How nice. He told me you were a new man.'

'I *did* tell him I'd never seen any lap dancing.'

'That'll be it, then.'

'Did Richard get on with Dennis?'

'Sometimes, in the part of him that got on with Langley.'

Simon chewed on his second chunk of walnut bread. He must spend all his spare time in the gym. 'But part of him didn't?'

And then I found myself telling Simon about June's constant anxiety that no one in her family should embarrass themselves, and how that had left Richard afraid of taking risks and of people he imagined to be superior, but ambitious all at the same time, and muddled.

'And now he's pushing forty, and thinks he's a failure, though no one else does.'

How was this happening? My first proper date for sixteen years, and I was talking about Richard.

Simon, though, was a good listener, and once I got started, it was quite hard to stop.

'When Richard first left,' I explained over my scallops in lemongrass, 'I thought it might have been because I'd failed to live up to some back-to-basics ideal of the suburban wife and mother. And then my friend Fran told me about this American craze for men to go back to the nineteen fifties.'

'What, like time travel?'

'Sort of. They have, these men, all these throw-back magazines, full of pictures of Harley Davidsons and Chevvies with tailfins, and structured cross-your-heart-bras and aprons.'

'How bizarre.'

'Oh, very. But apparently they allow men to feel like they felt before they were deconstructed by feminism and started feeling wimpish. The men who do feel wimpish, I mean,' I added hastily, in case Simon assumed that I was like Dennis Sharp and thought any man was a wimp if he could identify the useful end of a mop. 'I wondered sometimes if living in Langley was a version of that for Richard. It reminded him of his childhood – his mother in the kitchen, his father in the shed, as far away from her as possible. He wanted it, but I was no good at it.' I smiled brightly. 'But apparently that wasn't the problem, because now he's living in a loft in Clerkenwell . . .'

I'd now been talking about Richard for forty-five minutes non-stop. I drank some more wine, and said guiltily: 'Sorry, but you don't want to know all this.'

'I do.'

'It's your turn,' I insisted, embarrassed. He was supposed to be a boyfriend, not a therapist. 'You have to tell me about your relationship.'

'There's nothing to tell. My ex fell in love with a guy who manufactures plastic wheelie-bins. Which sounds boring – and is – but happens to be massively lucrative.'

He sounded rather bitter. I think he's even less well adjusted to it than I am to Richard.

'I'm sorry.'

He shrugged. 'You give up years of your life to someone, and then they go off with the most unsuitable person you can think of. The last person you'd think they'd ever be interested in.' He poured some more wine, then asked if I ever regretted giving up acting.

How did he know about that?

'Suzy Sharp told me,' he explained. 'Weren't you with the RSC?'

I nodded. 'I gave it up because I got offered a film and it would have meant six months in Ireland, and the kids were small.'

'You could have done something else, though, presumably?'

'Yes. I suppose. Though if I wasn't going to take opportunities like that . . . And Richard hated it. Of course, now he's gone off with an actress. He also hated the idea of me earning more than he did, and now he's living with someone who earns about five times more than him. Not that I *only* gave it up for Richard,' I added hastily, in case he thought I was completely wet; 'Ben seemed to be going backwards, and I was convinced the nanny we had wasn't singing to him or teaching him the alphabet or doing creative play. But I've been playing creatively with him for years and he's still going backwards. I realise now that it's innate.'

What was wrong with me? I had no proper conversation. First Richard, now Ben. What was wrong with recent developments in the Balkans or the Booker Prize shortlist or whether opera should get taxpayer subsidy?

Simon didn't seem to mind. Perhaps me talking about my failed relationship took his mind off his. Whatever, he was incredibly easy to talk to.

That's important, in a relationship, I think.

The only trouble with him being such a good listener was that by the end of the evening he knew practically everything about me and I knew next to nothing about him.

It wasn't that he was secretive, exactly – he told me

all about his business trip – but he encouraged me to go on and on about myself at such length that we sort of ran out of time to do him.

We were *still* talking about me on the way home. As we drove up Shaftesbury Avenue, he asked whether I was planning to stay at the *Langley Advertiser*.

'I don't know. I really like working. And the *Advertiser*'s not *that* demanding. I mean, I keep thinking that maybe I could do something else. Something that would actually cover the costs of the childcare.'

'Like what?'

'That's the trouble. I'm not really qualified for anything, so I was wondering about PR.'

He laughed, and then I remembered he was something to do with PR.

I stopped expecting him to spike my drink with the date-rape drug about five minutes into the meal. But if he wasn't going to take care of the next phase by doping me, then how?

Did I want to go on to the next phase anyway? Did he? He seemed very depressed about his former relationship; if he had sex with me, would he only be doing it to get back at her?

Did I even mind that? It wasn't as if I didn't have my own ulterior motives.

We pulled up outside my front gate. I took a deep breath and mentally rehearsed the words: 'Would you like to come in for coffee?'

But as I opened my mouth to speak, he leaned over, kissed me lightly on the lips and said: 'That was a lovely evening. I'd love to do it again. Some time very soon.'

And I gulped and replied: 'Oh yes, me too. It was great, thank you so much.'

And that was it. I got out of the car, unlocked the front door, gave him a little wave from the step, and went inside.

Would-you-like-to-come-in-for-coffee? I was still practising it the following morning. However many ways I tried it, I couldn't turn it into a difficult thing to say.

What was wrong with me?

I'd been nervous.

I'd spent the entire evening talking about my husband and children. This was not behaviour calculated to make me seem alluring, especially not to someone who was insecure owing to a recent dumping for a wheelie-bin man.

But perhaps it was simply that he wasn't a grabber. I had, after all, had a very uncivilised re-introduction to sexual activity.

Simon was merely taking all this at the proper, dignified pace. My sense that something about it hadn't gone quite right was simply the consequence of my recent experience with Ed McGregor. And he was uncouth, graceless and totally lacking in style.

Kate

I wonder how Mum got on with Simon. I hope she had a good time and got some sex.

Ben tried to persuade me to pretend I'd left my physics textbook at Mum's so we could go back and check she didn't have a black eye. I told him if she had Simon there and they were spending the day in bed, she wouldn't thank us.

I think Ben would almost prefer her to be beaten up.

He really wanted to go home because he was bored. There isn't much to do here at weekends, unless we go and see one of Emma's friends off the telly, and they never have kids.

It's not so bad for me, because I have so much homework and I can talk on the phone to Rachel. But Ben doesn't talk to his friends on the phone (I'm not sure how many friends he has, actually) and he ends up watching television.

Until this weekend, I've had to do my homework on my knees, but now Dad and Emma have bought a desk and put it in the gallery. It's made of glass, even the drawers, but I am not allowed to put anything in them because you can see through them. Emma has put six thick pieces of writing paper in one, and a bottle of Mont Blanc ink in the other.

It's a bit of a drag because the gallery is open to the rest of the flat, so the study area, as Emma calls it, is a bit noisy when you're trying to work. Also, people think they can talk to you because you're in the room. Emma was in a sulk with Dad about something last night, so she came to talk to me. There is nowhere else to go. I was in the middle of a human geography essay about tourism in North Wales, but I had to break off and answer questions about Mum, mainly about her acting career, which I know nothing about because she gave it up when I was six.

If we'd been at home, I would have gone out with Rachel and Darren and Joe last night. That's the trouble with having two houses: you're always in the wrong place at the wrong time. I love seeing Dad, but I need to fit in seeing people my own age. And it doesn't seem fair on Mum that I go out so often when I'm staying with her.

Still, there are a lot of absolutely vital things to do at the squats – mixing concrete and making lists of people who are going to help when the bailiffs come to storm the tree and the houses – and I have a duty to help the environment.

Darren says there's this fish called a barn-door skate (because it's as big as a barn door), only it's almost extinct, but no one noticed until about three weeks ago! If we can miss a species that big, how many species are we wiping out without realising? And half of them have got hidden cures for cancer, which is getting worse because of other environmental things, e.g. pollution and the ozone layer, etc.

I don't know how Ed McGregor stays so cheerful.

Julie

Mel appeared on the doorstep on Sunday carrying a Le Creuset tureen.

'Soup. For the protesters,' she hissed. 'It's just an excuse; I can go away again. Is he here?'

'Who?'

'Simon!'

'Oh. No. I screwed up.'

'How?'

I stood back to let her in. 'I spent the entire evening talking about Richard and Ben.'

'Oh.'

'Exactly. I think he was hanging back anyway, because he's on the rebound from some girl in Manchester. He didn't say a lot about her, only that now she's living with someone who manufactures bins or something.'

'There'll be another chance.'

'Maybe.' I sighed doubtfully. 'I only wanted a bit of raw, uncommitted, madly meaningless sex.'

'I thought you just had some.'

'That's why I want more.'

'It didn't make you very happy last time.'

'You weren't there.'

'The cold turkey bit afterwards, I mean.' Mel put her tureen on the kitchen table. 'You know what? We should have been cockroaches. They fall in love with every member of the opposite sex they meet and never get depressed.'

I made us coffee.

'I was too uptight,' I said. 'I was right when I thought I wouldn't know how to handle it. I was too married-mother-of-three.'

'I'm sure if you want raw mad uncommitted sex with Simon you can have it. Men never seem to turn that down.'

'But how do I let him know?'

'*Tell* him, if necessary. Anyway, not doing it on the first date probably makes you more desirable or something.' She blushed. 'Sorry, I don't mean . . .'

'I know *exactly* what you mean.'

'You should get out of the house. Come up to the green with me. I've got another pot of soup in the car.'

'I can't!'

'Why not?'

'I might see Ed!'

'You might see Ed any time you leave your house! He's living in Langley. You can't become a hermit.'

'I don't have to go up to the green.'

'He won't be there. It's Sunday. Someone – it might have been Suzy – told me he's *never* there at weekends.'

I looked at her suspiciously. 'Are you sure?'

'Yes, he has television programmes to make or something.'

'To go to his flat in Chelsea.'

'Well, he's not a kid; you wouldn't want to spend every night on the floor.'

'Mel, are you *sure*? Because . . . well, I wrote that article, as well.'

She looked at me blankly.

'About Ed,' I said impatiently. 'So it's no longer just that we had sex.'

'That thing people were talking about at school? Did you write that?'

There are serious drawbacks to Mel's being so wrapped up in Ian and baby Rose.

'Yes. And if you'd read it, you'd know why I don't want to see him again.'

'So you don't stand by this article, whatever it was you wrote?'

'Of course I do,' I replied irritably. 'I just don't want to see Ed McGregor.'

'He won't be there. I'll wait while you change.'

'Mel, there isn't a dress code for road protests.'

'Oh, I think there is. Nettle wears those tight tops that show her midriff. Of course, we can't get away with that – well, I can't anyway, I look like a Spacehopper – so otherwise, Suzy Sharp says our main value to the protesters is to be suburban housewives.'

'I'm certainly not dressing up as a suburban housewife.'

'All right. Are you sure you don't want to put on some mascara?'

'I'm not coming!'

'You're not against the road protest, are you?'

'No . . .'

'You don't want to see tens of thousands of pounds wiped off the value of your house?'

'No . . .'

'Exactly. And you haven't helped so far. Come on, Suzy said this was a really good way of showing solidarity before the bailiffs arrive. It boosts the morale of the protesters.'

'I don't want to help Ed McGregor.'

'You've got a warped perspective on this. Try to see something beyond Ed McGregor.'

She went on and on, until I let myself be bullied into trudging up to the green carrying Mel's second tureen of soup. We made our way across the green to the tree, which had once been beautiful, but was now festooned with junk. Tat of every kind spread through the branches like multicoloured mistletoe; an infestation of doors, pallets, canvas and plastic tarpaulins. In places it was yoked together to make platforms, on which people seemed to be living. Hanks of bright blue polypropylene rope dangled from the lower branches.

There were people up the tree, and more at the bottom, smoking roll-ups.

'Hi,' said a boy with a pierced upper lip and long, lank hair. 'Welcome to the free and independent state of Langlelia.' (The protesters had declared UDI, and written to the United Nations requesting recognition.)

'Thanks,' said Mel, blinking. 'We brought some soup.'

'Vegan?'

'Oooh,' – she frowned – 'er, not exactly.'

'Only, the vegans have set up a separate camp. In the third house. They were, like, disgusted by the high consumption of dairy products.'

Mel backed off from the protesters, turned to face me with a panicky expression and mouthed: 'It's minestrone!'

I drew her aside. 'Minestrone, as in, with bacon?'

'Pancetta. I wanted it to be authentic.'

'We could take it back and eat it ourselves.'

'They don't even wear leather shoes. How could I be such a klutz? Oh no, shit!'

'What?'

'Look, Ed McGregor's coming! Hide the soup!'

It was true. The environmentalist-world saver-sexual mishap was striding across the green in our direction. But it was not possible to hide two bright orange tureens full of non-vegetarian soup.

He was almost on top of us before he recognised me.

'Oh, hello,' he said awkwardly.

'We brought some soup,' Mel said brightly. 'But we made a mistake: it's not vegetarian.'

'Minestrone,' I added stupidly, thinking I ought to say something.

'Oh . . . great. Could you take it up to the houses?'

Someone called his name and he turned away, evidently relieved to escape.

'Bloody hell!' Mel exclaimed as soon as we were out of earshot. 'He was a bit offhand. For someone you've slept with.'

'I *told* you.'

What must he *think?* First I turn up to interview him, then I appear on the green with an offering of soup.

Mel was frowning. 'Was it *very* mean, what you wrote?'

'No. He just has a high opinion of himself.'

'Bastard.'

Up at the house, we picked our way across the cement bags and rubble in the front garden and pushed open the front door.

The only consolation was that, having seen us, Ed McGregor could at least be relied on to avoid the houses for the next half-hour. But I still felt sick.

Phil, the boy who was too young to be a protester, sat on the floor in the hall with his back to the wall, carefully distributing tobacco along a Rizla. We nearly fell over him.

'We've brought soup,' Mel announced. 'What should we do with it?'

Phil was smaller and weaker-looking than I remembered, with a solemn little face.

He looked us up and down, shrugged, and went back to his work.

'Can we take it somewhere?' Mel persisted.

'Mrs Ellison?' Another, older boy was standing on the stairs. Looking up, I recognised Darren from the library, Kate's friend. He was holding a hammer.

'Hi,' he said, coming down, 'I'm Darren Bredy. You're Kate's mum, aren't you?'

'Yes. We brought some soup.'

'It's not vegetarian,' Mel added.

'Oh, that's fine. Doesn't matter at all. D'you want to bring it up?' He turned and led the way.

Mel and I followed, stepping carefully on the rickety bare stairs and passing along through the upstairs hall. Ahead of us, in what must once have been the master bedroom, but which now contained half a dozen sleeping bags, a skinny boy in his late teens was standing just inside the doorway surveying what appeared to be a sculpture made of rusty petrol cans, a fire extinguisher and part of an old bedstead. It looked like an enlarged version of the junk modelling Arthur does when I remember to save the cereal packets.

Mel paused to stare.

'It's called "You Take Our Breath Away",' the boy said, puffing on a joint. 'It's about asthma.'

'Mrs Ellison?' Darren had come back to find us. 'D'you want me to get Becky to decant the soup so you can take your casserole dishes back?'

'Please,' Mel said eagerly. I could tell she had visions of her Le Creuset ending up in the asthma installation.

Darren took the pots away and returned them a few minutes later, emptied. He smiled shyly. He had a sweet, round face, plump and puppyish. 'Actually,' he said to me nervously, 'I've been hoping to meet you. I wanted to talk to you. Sort of about acting . . . Only, it's . . . I want to go to drama school, and I wondered if I could ask you some questions? Not now or anything. When it's convenient.'

'Sure,' I said, 'though I haven't acted for years. I'm not sure I can help.'

'I don't know anyone else who knows anything about it.'

'No, well, of course I'll talk to you.' I hesitated. 'Look, why don't you come round for supper one night next week?' I frowned, trying to remember what everyone was doing. 'Wednesday?'

'That'd be brilliant.' He flashed me another of his shy, bright smiles. 'Got to get back to my hammering now.'

'Why is it,' Mel grumbled, as we made our way back, avoiding the green, 'that in this radical insurrectionist alternative independent republic, a woman is in charge of the food?'

But I was busy wondering whether I should have invited Darren Bredy home without first asking Kate.

'Hippies!' she scoffed. 'They think if they all join hands and sing to the solstice then the crops will grow.'

'Darren seems all right, though.'

'Yeah, sweet,' Mel agreed. 'Is he the one who's got a thing with Kate?'

'I think so.'

'Hmmn. Well, he's much too nice for it to last.'

Ben

Mum hasn't said much about going out with the man. Kate asked her if she had a good time and she said: 'Yes thanks, very nice.' They went to a restaurant – which Kate says could mean anything.

I will have to put a stop to it.

I really need to get Kate's help, because she is better at almost everything than me, but right now she is only interested in going to the squats. She sees Darren Bredy there. Sometimes they snog. They call it pulling.

This afternoon I accidentally-on-purpose bumped into them in the High Street and asked if I could come with them. Kate said no but Darren said yes. He is too good for her.

I went anyway. The squats are actually a bit of a dump. There is no carpet on the floor and graffiti all over the walls. There are some very funny smells and everyone is dirty. I don't really know why Kate thinks it is so fantastic.

There's a boy living there who is only a year older than me. He's the one Kate told me about. His parents have split up too. He comes from Leeds and he has this strong accent so that sometimes you can hardly understand him. He doesn't have a dad any more. He used to have one, who wasn't his real dad, who was the one who beat up his mum. He beat up Phil too.

Phil says he doesn't want to see his mum because, when he last lived with her, she used to get money on a Monday (though she didn't seem to have a job) and spend it all on drink with her mates and then he wouldn't have enough to eat for the rest of the week. She used to stay in bed till the afternoon so Phil had to get himself up and make breakfast, if there was any food. Then he had to get himself off to school, except he gave up going because people used to bully him.

I told him about Adrian Farr bullying me, but what people did to him was worse. They used to burn his skin with cigarettes, and once someone set fire to his clothing and one of the teachers had to put it out. That was after he got moved to a children's home, which wasn't any better than living with his mum because the other kids used to steal his food.

He likes living at the squat because Ed McGregor keeps an eye out for him, he says, and it's the only place he's been where everyone under eighteen isn't on the gas. (I don't know what this is, but I didn't ask.) For a while he was living on the streets, sleeping in churchyards and shop doorways with some other kids, but he said there were horrible men out there and it used to make him sick, what they made him do. He wouldn't tell me what it was. He said I was too young, which is ridiculous as I am older than him.

Phil pretends to be hard. But actually he is quite shy and a sort of grey colour. He doesn't look very healthy. I don't believe he doesn't want to see his mum.

Kate

Half an hour ago, Ben came into my room and informed me that Mum has invited Darren to dinner on Wednesday.

How could she? It's so humiliating. He will think I put her up to it and I am serious about him.

Of course, I *am* serious about him, but not in a coming-home-and-meeting-my-mother way. That is what you do when you are about twenty and planning to move in together.

Why can't she mind her own business?

I went downstairs to the kitchen and asked her if it was true.

'Yes,' she said, completely calm. 'Darren wanted to come, so I invited him.'

'I don't believe you. Darren wouldn't have suggested it.'

'He wanted to talk to me.'

'Why? What about?'

'Acting, I think.'

'He didn't tell me.'

'Well, I'm sorry about that.'

'You asked him round here because you don't trust me! Why can't you leave me alone?'

'You're being silly,' Mum said, which is what she always says – it is a way of trying to put me down, as if my views don't count. 'The invitation doesn't have anything to do with you.'

Not much it doesn't. He is only my boyfriend.

She went on peeling potatoes. 'I'm sorry it's upset you so much. If I'd known, I wouldn't have done it.'

'It was up to *me* to invite him round! He's my friend. Where did you meet him anyway?'

'At the squats.'

'When you were doing your mean article?'

'No, when I was taking soup for the protesters.'

'You don't even like the protesters!'

She peeled potatoes harder.

'You can't bear not being in control of me!'

'I don't know what you're talking about.'

'You hate it that I make my own friends and you don't decide who they are and sometimes you don't even know them. Why else did you have to go and find Darren?'

She banged down the colander. 'Actually, he found me. I told you: he wants my advice.'

'You want to check him out, because you're nosy.'

And I slammed the door.

Inviting boyfriends home to meet your parents was the sort of thing they did in their day, and look where it's got them. They can't even keep their marriages going long enough to bring up their children.

They are useless. They have wrecked the planet,

driving round and round looking for parking spaces so by the time they've found one they could have walked. Darren says that a hundred years ago, when people had horses and carriages, the average speed of a journey through London was eight miles an hour, and today, with cars going from nought to sixty in six seconds, it's still eight miles an hour.

And they think they have made progress.

Mum would never have done such a stupid thing before she split up with Dad. She'd have known having Darren here would only cause trouble. Now she's welcomed him into the house as if she thinks it's about time I had a boyfriend. The next thing, she'll be sending us upstairs with a packet of condoms.

She has messed up her own life and now she wants to mess up mine.

Julie

'*Wave?*' Fran shrieked. 'But you can't get in there on a Friday night for months. I know: I've tried. *Who* is this Simon? How come I don't know him?'

'I told you at Mel's, he's called Simon Hemingway. He works for a record company. In marketing, or PR, or something.'

'He must be very well connected. You realise, Jools, that this Wave thing means he's quite important?'

'I don't know why you're so excited. I don't think I'll be seeing him again.'

'Let's go over this once more. You talked about Richard and Ben and he didn't talk very much at all ... Are you sure not having sex wasn't about him needing to go back to his cave and centre himself?'

'Huh?'

Sometimes it is hard to believe that Fran runs a multi-million pound business.

'Maybe *you* need to be more direct. Men don't always hear what women are saying, you see. You thought you were saying, "Please rip my underwear from my body with your teeth," and he thought you were saying, "Touch me and I'll claim you put Rohypnol in my chardonnay."'

I said faintly: 'Really?'

'You need to be more assertive. *Tell* him you want him.'

'That's what Mel said, more or less. Is that what you'd do?'

'Yeah, well, there's something I had to . . .'

'Mum!' Ben yelled up the stairs. 'Why's this saucepan gone black?'

I'd been wondering, vaguely, about the sweet, dark smell that had been wafting up the stairs for the past five minutes.

'I was stewing some apples for Arthur,' I told Fran. 'I must have left the gas on. I think they may've burnt dry. We're about to have a rerun of Three Mile Island.'

'OK,' Fran said wearily; she was used to my having to break off conversations to prevent the house burning down or the children electrocuting themselves. 'But don't give up. Bring him round to my place for dinner. Seriously. The week after next. There. That's your excuse to call him.'

But I didn't particularly want to show Simon off around town like a freak show – see the incredible frumpy woman and her unfeasibly handsome boy-friend! – and I certainly didn't want him to think that was what I was doing.

I wanted passion. A desperate, unable-to-keep-our-hands-off-each-other period – a phase, at least – before we started making social calls as a couple. I'd had years of respectability. I wasn't about to start all over again without an intervening bout of abandoned bad behaviour.

Perhaps Mel and Fran were right and I simply hadn't been upfront enough. How *do* postfeminists get sex?

But perhaps he wasn't very interested in sex.

Or women.

Or me.

The following afternoon on my way home from work, I somehow found myself driving past Simon's house in Oakhurst Grove. He'd told me which number it was. When there was no sign of his black Saab, I also somehow found myself slowing down outside.

The house was a pre-war semi, rather small, with a neatly clipped privet hanging over the front wall and a crazy-paved front garden with a diamond-shaped flower bed, tidily planted with annuals. No weeds. Nondescript curtains at the windows. And a 'For Sale' board outside.

He was moving. And he hadn't even told me. That was how little I knew about him. I am not normally a self-obsessed person. He hadn't told me because he hadn't told me *anything*; I am so egocentric and needy that I hadn't given him a chance.

It made sense, though, the moving. Number 54 Oakhurst Grove was a dull little house, too plain and cramped and uncool for Simon. He'd inherited it and he was just camping in it until he could realise the capital and move on, to somewhere more appropriate, more central, bustling, vivid, vital.

Living in Langley, for someone hip and worldly like

Simon, was like emotional pindown. If I'd thought about it at all, I'd have realised he was *bound* to move. He probably hadn't told me in order to spare my feelings. He recognised I was trapped here, and he pitied me.

It was an accident that I'd met him. Under normal circumstances – if he hadn't broken up with the girl who'd gone off with the bin man, if his uncle hadn't died, if his company hadn't been setting up in London – he was a person I never could have expected to come across. He was too damn cool. And soon he would have gone off somewhere more suitably stylish, somewhere his clothes didn't turn heads, but simply looked *normal*, and left me behind.

Ben

Before Darren arrived last night, I found Mum in the kitchen looking up recipes in the *River Café Cook Book*.

'I'm doing this for me, not for Darren,' she said.

Kate had already told Mum she wasn't to make a fuss of Darren, for example by cooking anything special.

'How will he know if it's special?' Mum asked. 'He hasn't been here before.'

Now she was frowning at a brightly coloured photograph of roast meat with bits of leaf stuck in it. 'This really needs a wood-burning stove,' she said, 'which, obviously, we don't have.'

Mad.

Kate also gave Mum instructions not to ask Darren questions about himself, his school, or his parents.

'Are there any things I *can* talk about?' she asked.

'He probably won't talk much. He doesn't.'

He arrived late. Kate kept going upstairs and putting on more blue eyeshadow, then taking it off, and afterwards coming down and saying: 'Right, that's it.

He's not coming, then.' But after she'd done this for the third time he turned up with a box of chocolates for Mum and some story about being delayed because he was feeding his neighbour's cat and he was worried it was lonely.

I was doing my maths homework when he arrived. Kate wanted to take him into the other room but Darren looked over my shoulder and realised I was getting it all wrong (it was fractions, which I don't understand) and he started to help me. He was quite good at explaining and when he did them I could see what he was going on about, although I still couldn't do them myself. But then it was time to eat, so Darren said he'd come over and help me with the fractions any time I wanted.

Over dinner he talked non-stop. He told us about his job in the library, and how librarians need to know a lot about computers, and about his GCSEs, which he is taking in a few weeks, and his dad, who is a dentist, and his mum, who is a school secretary, but they have split up.

But the most amazing thing was that when Mum served the meat (which I think was pork, though I don't know what the leaves were) he said: 'Did you get this recipe from the *River Café Cook Book*?'

'Yes. I did – though I've adapted it a bit,' Mum said, looking all pleased and flustered.

Darren reads cook books! For fun! He cooks from them as well! He reads all kinds of books, in fact, and the only thing he doesn't like about his Saturday job is that you're not supposed to read books if you're a librarian, only to file them. He agreed with Mum that it was ridiculous to produce a cook book in which so many of the recipes required a wood-burning oven, then he told her all about Tennyson, who is a poet he is doing for GCSE. Kate and I didn't know anything about him.

It was Kate who didn't speak. Darren hardly stopped. He asked Mum a lot of questions about drama schools and the best ways of getting in to them – he'd even brought a list of questions, written down, which impressed Mum, though Kate looked as though she might be sick – and he told us what's happening up at the squats, which Kate certainly never does, even though she spends so much time there. They are planning a phone tree, so that when the sheriff's men come to evict them, people in Langley can ring each other up and go over to the green and offer passive resistance. Darren is one of the main organisers.

He told Mum he disagreed with her article on Ed McGregor. 'He's passionate. He inspires people,' he said. 'He goes on television partly because it's a good way of getting his message across.'

'And he likes being a celebrity.'

'People watch his programmes.'

'He can't stop the road, though.'

'So do you think we should all lie down and just accept it? Let them tarmac us over?' Darren asked.

You'd have thought Kate would be pleased that Darren was explaining the environmental arguments, but she banged down her knife and fork and stared out of the window sulkily.

Darren has sent off for forms to join Friends of the Earth and Greenpeace and he's donating 10 per cent of his library earnings to the Stop the Road campaign. He tried to persuade Mum to do a covenant, I think he called it, obviously not realising how little she earns.

Mum liked Darren in spite of him being mad keen on the environment and on Ed McGregor, who she despises. By the end of the evening, she would have been happy for him to marry Kate. She probably would have married him herself if he'd been a bit older.

After dinner, Mum invited him to stay on for a bit, but he said he had to get back to revise for a physics test. He told me to ring him up if I wanted any more help with my maths.

Kate went out into the front garden to say goodbye (i.e. pull: I looked through Mum's bedroom window) but when she came back in she went straight to bed without speaking.

I knew Kate was furious with Mum, but I didn't realise how much until this evening, when she came in late from school with her nose pierced.

She now has a diamond stud in her right nostril. She paid for it with her babysitting money.

When Mum saw it her eyes went wide, like eyes in a cartoon.

'What on earth have you done to yourself?'

'Well, you didn't want me to get my *ears* pierced,' Kate said resentfully, although she looked hot and tearful.

'But you're so beautiful! Why mutilate yourself?'

'It's not mutilation. Indian women do it all the time. They think it's fabulous.'

'But you're not Indian!'

'Why are you always so racist?'

'I'm not racist! Why not your ears, if you had to put holes through a body part?'

'You said I couldn't have them done.'

'I know, but . . .' Mum sat down at the kitchen table with a tea towel in her hands. 'Miss Hawkins will never let you go to school like that.'

'She lets the Hindu girls, so she'll have to because she's not allowed to discriminate. Anyway, she'll never expel me because my marks are too good. She wants me in her stupid league tables.'

This is true. Kate is one of the cleverest girls in her year, and to get picked for the grammar school in the first place you have to be one of the cleverest girls not just in Langley but in about five boroughs.

Kate put the kettle on, slamming it down on the work surface so water spilled out of the spout. 'If you were a really loving mother, you'd say I looked nice. You'd try to make me feel good about myself and not like a freak.'

But Mum thinks nose-piercing causes Aids and several types of hepatitis. She only said: 'I hope you were careful about where you got it done.'

''Course I was. I did it at a place in Westfield. A jewellers.' She picked up an apple and took a bite out of it, as if she didn't care about anything. Then she switched the kettle on and added sarcastically: 'I know several people who've had piercings there, and *they're* all still alive.'

'I can't believe you did this without talking to me first.'

'Dad said it was all right.'

Mum stared at her. 'I don't believe you.'

'No?' Kate crashed the teapot on to Mum's polished granite work surface. 'Then ask him.'

Julie

I telephoned Richard.

'Yeah?' His voice was thick with sex, woozy with post-coital coatings.

It was seven o'clock in the evening.

I said primly: 'I need to see you.'

'Sure . . .' he said languorously; I imagined him emerging from a tangle of crisp, white, professionally-laundered sheets and young flesh; grunting as he heaved himself up on to his elbow. 'I was going to suggest lunch anyway,' he said surprisingly, since he never normally volunteers to meet me. 'You free tomorrow?'

Obviously I was free. We aren't big lunchers at the *Langley Advertiser*. Occasionally Tony and I get asked for a beer with Pete, but we lack the necessary willingness to carry on until we fall over.

Why did Richard want to meet me all of a sudden? Whatever the reason, it was unlikely to be good. All that night, I tossed and turned in bed, working myself into a stew. Was this about Los Angeles? Had Emma finally landed the film part, and they were off to

Hollywood for however long it takes to make a major motion picture? How long *was* that? Ages. Some of the madder directors take years. And the chances of Emma's having been cast by a mad director were high.

It had to be something serious. Normally Richard wants to see me about as much as he wants anaesthetic-free root canal dentistry.

Did he intend to break it to me that he wanted the children to go with them, even though Kate's halfway through her GCSE course and Ben's just been diagnosed dyspraxic and we've found a special teacher who claims she can help him?

Even if he found a British school in Los Angeles, they wouldn't be doing the same GCSE coursework.

But if I protested they shouldn't go, if I fought to have them stay in England, would I be doing it for low, selfish reasons? Would I be denying them a fabulous educational opportunity, for the loss of which they would blame me for the rest of their lives?

But could I bear to be without them for months? Could Ben, particularly, bear to be without me? Could Arthur?

Perhaps Richard wouldn't want Arthur to go. He often doesn't want him at the flat. Perhaps he thinks Arthur can just be left behind: perhaps, because *he's* a worm, he thinks we can all be chopped in half indefinitely and renew ourselves.

I was still going over this at work the following morning. And when I wasn't fretting about Los Angeles, I was gnawing away at my worries about Kate's nose-piercing.

'Why doesn't she realise how lovely she is – how

fresh-faced and luminous with health?' I complained to Tony.

'She's fourteen.'

'I want her to be perfect and unspoilt.'

'It's rebellion. It's what kids do.'

'I don't understand it, the politics of piercing. To her it seems to symbolise freedom, but how many free things have rings through their noses? I look at her and I see a pig.'

'Have you told her that?'

'I can't understand why she can't see what it *is* that makes her beautiful. Why she has to paint pink stripes in her hair and put metal through her nose . . .'

Tony shrugged. 'Different ideas.'

'*Why*, though? Why does she think I'm trying to thwart her? I didn't get down on my hands and knees enough.'

'What are you talking about?'

'My mother's ambitions for me were all about *doing* something in the world. Being someone. Not bogged down by children.'

'I thought you didn't believe in blaming mothers . . .'

'. . . So I spent too much time in the early years working. I didn't do enough Duplo. I didn't get down to Kate's level, and now she thinks I can never see things from her point of view.'

'It's nothing to do with Duplo. Stop beating yourself up. There are worse things she could be doing.'

'She probably is, and I just don't know about them. And the terrible irony is, I *didn't* ever achieve anything. I'm thirty-eight and working for the *Langley Advertiser*. And I'm not even taken seriously here.'

'I take you seriously.'

'And I'm *still* not a proper parent. And Richard *certainly* isn't: how does he think he's going to cope with them in Los Angeles?'

'I think we've been here before,' Tony said mildly. 'And you don't know that that's what he wants.'

But as I walked over to Pizza Express for twelve-thirty, everything around me – bus bells, my heels on the pavement, gears crunching at the traffic lights – seemed to jangle with threat.

Richard – it was obvious – wanted to take my children away.

Walking past the dry cleaner's, I remembered I still had the ticket for a pair of Richard's trousers. I had no idea if he'd ever collected them. It didn't seem likely. They were cast-offs, like me, with the difference that I couldn't even be flogged off to help fund aid projects in Africa.

Past the wholefood shop, the supermarket and the newsagent's, where there was a hoarding advertising this month's *FHM*. Emma Neil was on the cover: bent forward from the waist, looking up lustfully into the camera, dressed only in a lacy black basque. She pouted at me, eyes wide and nostrils flared, distinctly predatory. Slapper chic, I think it's called. When I mentioned this to Mel, she said: 'Well, she's got a cheek and you want to slap her.'

Richard was already in the restaurant, sitting in the corner table by the window, which happened to be the one at which we'd celebrated our fourth wedding anniversary. I wondered if he remembered; if he'd thought beforehand about the potentially distressing impact of this restaurant, this table, and decided it simply wouldn't be that distressing.

He still looked handsome: just dishevelled enough not to seem vain, his hair a fraction too long, touching his collar, his eyes blue and swimming.

'So,' he said, putting aside his menu and smiling as I slipped into my seat, 'what did you want to talk to me about?'

I did some deep-breathing, in the manner recommended by Fran's stress-busting tips. Then I smiled back politely and said: 'No, you first.'

I didn't want to start by getting into a state about Kate's mangled nostril, in case what he had to say was ten times worse. I intended to be perfectly poised and calm for whatever he might be about to hurl at me. At the outset, anyway. No point in wasting my anger on a bit of metal if my entire life was about to be upended.

He shrugged, and gave our order to the waitress without bothering to ask what I wanted to eat. We'd eaten enough pizzas here for him to know.

I couldn't stand it any longer. 'Is this about wanting to take the children to Los Angeles?'

'Huh?' He frowned and poured us both a glass of wine. Then his expression cleared. 'Oh, you mean the film project. That's not sorted yet . . . Emma hasn't definitely got the part, and then we'd have to . . . At the moment we're thinking maybe they could come out for the school holidays . . .'

I swallowed, and struggled not to let my relief show. So: they seemed to have dropped the whole-term-in-Hollywood idea. Give Emma a few weeks and she'd have successfully reduced the children's projected visits to manageable packages of a fortnight.

Richard chomped on a piece of garlic bread. 'No,' he said, 'the reason I wanted to see you is that I want a divorce.'

My hand slipped; my fingers momentarily gave way, and San Pellegrino sloshed from the glass in my hand down the sexy cashmere jumper, which had happened to find its way into my hands when I was deciding what to wear this morning.

Divorce? *Divorce*? I never thought it would come to this. Not quite. I'd always believed we'd find a way back before things got that bad.

And just like that, as if he was throwing out a suggestion that we might later try to catch a movie? I suppose this is what I should have expected from someone who proposed in a department store. If he couldn't even manage to manoeuvre me into a romantic spot and plead with me from a semi-recumbent posture when he was asking me to marry him (that was normal, wasn't it? A moving declaration of passion and unswerving devotion, rather than a decision that we needed a dinner service?) I suppose that when he was demanding a dissolution, I couldn't expect more than a passing mention through a mouthful of mozzarella.

'Why?' I uttered stupidly.

'Emma and I are thinking of getting married.'

He paused, staring at me, possibly because my jaw had dropped so far he could see my fillings.

'She thinks it would please her mother, and . . .'

I found it hard to credit that Mrs Neil really wanted

her beautiful, talented and rich daughter to marry a history teacher who was old enough to be her father.

'. . . So I thought we could do it – the divorce – ourselves.' Now Richard had got it out, he was relaxed. Almost enjoying it. 'Not bother with lawyers. It's very simple, apparently. You get forms from the County Court: they're pretty much self-explanatory. We thought perhaps you'd like to take charge of that. I don't mind doing it, of course, but then you could request the divorce. And I am fairly busy, one way and another.'

'You are?'

'Two jobs.' He smiled ruefully (the poor old thing, and having to perform sexually all the time too!): 'Teaching and trying to manage Emma's career.'

I walked out. I don't know why. I just didn't want to sit there any longer.

Unfortunately, I made the mistake of pausing at the doorway, working out where to go next – left towards home, or right to the office? – which gave Richard time to jump up from the table, follow me on to the pavement, and grab my elbow.

'Hey,' he said, 'there's no need to walk out. I realise it's a bit of a shock, but you must have seen it coming. You know what Emma means to me . . . And obviously we couldn't drift on like this for ever . . .'

'Let go of me!'

'Don't get hysterical.'

'I am not hysterical!' I shouted. 'I am absolutely *not* bloody hysterical. Did you say Kate could get her nose pierced?'

'Well . . .' he faltered, 'not exactly.'

'You did, didn't you? What's happened to your protectiveness of the children, your sense of responsibility towards them?'

'It's not such a big deal . . .'

I tried to shake him off. 'They *need* rules to chafe against,' I yelled. 'That's what you used to say – that if parents were too liberal they got confused and they rebelled even more. That's what you said!'

I finally pushed him off.

'I don't want them to grow up like me,' he answered, quietly but furiously: 'trapped by convention, too afraid to break out and be themselves.'

'Ha!' I shouted. 'That's the story that you're telling yourself about our marriage now, is it? That I trapped you and made you conform to some hellish suburban ideal? But I *wasn't* conventional when you married me. You were always much more boring than me! I think that's *why* you married me – because I offered you a fantasy of transformation. But it didn't happen: inside you were still the son of June and Alf Ellison from Acton.'

'Shut up!'

'No!' I shouted. 'It didn't work, did it? I couldn't change you, so now you're trying another fantasy, pinning your hopes for transformation on another person. Conveniently letting yourself off the hook yet again.'

'You're right: I should never have married you.'

'That's not what I'm saying,' I answered bitterly. 'You shouldn't marry Emma. You shouldn't marry *anyone* until you've decided what *you* want. Marrying Emma would just be another doomed attempt to stop yourself from falling into the black hole of existential angst, another distraction from the dreadful nothing-ness of being Richard Ellison.'

There was a buzzing in my ears that had shut out all other noise – the passing traffic, the shoppers hustling along the High Street, the aeroplanes locking into their approaches to Heathrow. Now I looked up and realised that everything really had fallen silent. I had been shouting so loudly and madly that people had actually stopped on the pavement to listen. Drivers had wound down their windows as they paused at the pedestrian crossing. A small knot of shoppers had gathered on the pavement opposite. And among them, pausing to watch, was a tall man with dark curly hair, looking amused. Ed McGregor.

I was a spectacle. Richard and I were having a domestic in full view of the residents of Langley. With the wet stain down my front and my hair blowing about in the brisk wind, I looked like an escapee from care for the criminally insane.

I didn't mind about the gormless passers-by, the shoppers with nothing better to do than stand and stare. But I was *furious* with Ed McGregor. How *dare* he stand on the pavement, cool as anything, and *laugh* at me? After the way he'd behaved?

I glared at him, long and hard across the street, as rudely as I could, then turned on my heel, marched back into the restaurant, and paid the bill.

Kate

It serves her right, anyway. She does things without asking me if *I* mind, like inviting Darren to dinner and sucking up to him and embarrassing me.

Then she had the cheek to ask why, if I had to stick pins through a part of myself, I hadn't had my ears done instead of my nose? When she'd specifically forbidden me!

She couldn't believe it when I told her Dad had given me permission, but it's true: we had a conversation about it over dinner at the flat. Emma agreed with me that it was cool and said she'd like to get a diamond in her belly-button, but her agent said it would give her too much of a certain image at this stage, so then Dad really *had* to say he thought it was cool as well. (Dad has to work quite hard to be as cool as Emma because until he met her he'd never even been clubbing.) So I asked if he'd disown me if I got my nose done and he said, 'Of course not!' in a really shaky voice – but the point is, he did say it.

Mum had lunch with him and I think they must have

had a row about it because when I asked what they discussed she glared at me.

Miss Hawkins doesn't like it either. She called me into her office and said: 'What is the meaning of that thing in your nose?'

I said it was a stud and it didn't have a meaning. It was purely aesthetic.

'In my view,' she said, 'jewellery makes a woman look like a chattel. Especially when it's in her nose.'

She sounds like Grandma. Same generation. Feminists.

'Perhaps the meaning of jewellery can change,' I said. (I was pleased with this afterwards.)

She looked at me sharply. 'Perhaps,' she said. 'But the meaning of the school rules doesn't change, and they say no jewellery other than a small pair of ear studs and a wristwatch with school uniform.'

'They don't mention noses,' I pointed out, because I'd checked.

'It's implied. What do your parents think?'

'Dad said it was OK.'

She looked really pissed off at that. I think she is reaching the end of her tether with Dad. He won't mind: he doesn't want to stay on at the stupid grammar school anyway. He's going to manage Emma.

'I shall be speaking to them.'

But she didn't threaten to throw me out. She knows I'd jump at the chance to go to the comprehensive, and she thinks Langley Girls has already given me such a superior education that I'd get brilliant results and push the comprehensive up the league tables, and that would be the worst possible thing that could ever happen.

Rachel is jealous because no way in a million years would her parents ever let her get her nose pierced. They'd ground her for a year. To make matters worse, things are not working out between her and Joe and she doesn't want Darren to be my boyfriend any more. She told everyone at school that he is sad and geeky and she doesn't really want him to come to her party because no one would like him.

I want to stay the night at the party, but I already know Mum's going to be difficult about it. I don't know why grown-ups think you are more likely to get pregnant and take drugs in the night.

Probably because fundamentally they are embarrassed about sex.

Ben doesn't like our parents being separated but it seems to me that it has some definite advantages. It is easier to identify points on which they disagree, so forcing them to be honest. And at least when Mum drives me mad, which she does quite often lately, I have somewhere else to go. Hopefully Emma will soon get her film role and we can go to school in Los Angeles and meet interesting new people.

I am hoping there will be more people like Mould in Los Angeles. He is seventeen and he has already dedicated his life to fighting for the environment. You never normally meet people like that in Langley.

Ben

I had my first dyspraxia lesson. It was with a Scottish woman called Izzie, at her house. She made a video of me, which I get to keep, and, at the end, she gave me a bag of crisps.

She is quite old and serious. First of all she made me copy a picture she'd drawn. She told Mum it was interesting that I only used the top right-hand corner of the paper, but I was being economical. If she'd wanted me to waste a whole sheet of paper copying a picture she'd already done, she should have said.

She had some magazine pictures, cut up, and I had to put them back together. She said it took me a long time, and I had to learn to think strategically. She kept saying, 'You see, Bin?' – which is what she calls me; Kate says it is apt – and I nodded because I could tell Mum was tense and I didn't want her to get any tenser.

Izzie showed me how to do it, then gave me another one, but by the time I'd sorted out the pieces into colours, I'd forgotten what I had to do next.

After the puzzles we did something called Mozi Blocks, which was making more patterns, only this time out of bricks. I thought this was a bit babyish – even Arthur is past bricks – but Mum said learning to organise the bricks will teach me to organise other things as well, such as getting ready in the morning. It didn't the first time round.

Izzie said she thought I might also benefit from physiotherapy. But what I would really benefit from is my parents getting back together.

Julie

'I'm having trouble getting my head round this,' I admitted to Fran on the telephone late the following evening. 'I mean, I can see that Richard and I might need at some point to clarify our relationship –'

'Or lack of it –'

'Or lack of it. But *divorce*? It's not my image.'

'Plenty of people do it.'

'It sounds so worldly and cynical. *Brassy*, somehow. D'you think I could somehow get through the rest of my life without mentioning it?'

'No.'

'You don't think I could vaguely pretend that Richard was dead? At least then people would regard me as tragic, rather than dumped.'

'Julie, it happens all the time. It doesn't make you a failure. Some people would consider getting rid of Richard a success.'

'I keep wondering if I misunderstood him . . .'

'What, and when he said "divorce" he really meant maybe you should take a holiday in the Bahamas?'

'Yeah, you're right. He seemed pretty sure.' I sighed. 'Time to draw the emotional stumps.'

'And let's face it, by now they are stumps. Anyway, you don't want to be married to him: he's ridiculous. He thinks he can be Emma Neil's agent even though he knows nothing about television, film or celebrities.'

'I suppose that must be love, not caring that he looks absurd. I don't think I ever made him feel like that. In fact, it's hard to remember now what I *did* do for him. I keep trying to remember how I came to be married to him . . .'

'Maybe you thought he was safe.'

That could have been it. Married to Richard, all the disruption out of the way, berthed in domesticity, I might have thought I'd be able to achieve more, *do* stuff. Get on with my life.

'Yes, but *what* life?' Fran asked acidly.

'Izzie, Ben's dyspraxia teacher, said the other day that he needs to develop his strategic thinking. And I smiled and nodded away, as if I agreed, and all the time I was thinking, Oh yeah, and where has strategy got me? My husband suggesting divorce between mouthfuls of pizza.'

'Have you thought about therapy?' Fran suggested. 'Or – I tell you what – a holiday where you swim with dolphins! They do special trips for depressed people.'

My mother thinks Richard and I split up because his idea of a good time was a trip to Allied Carpets then home for some Arctic Roll, and the answer is for me to get a job. Fran thinks it's something to do with umbilicus and I need to read more self-help books. Mel thinks the mistake was not to marry Ian, and I need to find a short, bald solicitor with glasses. Tony – who's gay, so what does he know about it? – thinks that when I thought I was having a relationship with Richard I was actually having it with carpets and curtains, and now I need to go clubbing.

Still irritated by Fran's imputation that I had no life, I said stiffly: 'Chekhov once said something along the lines that if many remedies are prescribed for an illness, you can be bloody sure there's no cure.'

I've been spending quite a lot of time distracting myself from the unpleasantness of becoming a divorced person by thinking of Simon, although it's tricky because there isn't much to go on. And he hasn't called to add anything. I know this for certain because I've checked my answering machine, and then rechecked it to make sure I haven't missed anything, then checked it again to make sure I hadn't forgotten how to work it. I've opened all the junk mail, just in case he believes in writing letters disguised as circulars from banks inviting me to run up large debts. And I've looked at my e-mail with a special little frisson of excitement, even though he doesn't know my e-mail address. (But he could have got it. There are ways of doing that, I think – and then what would he think if I didn't reply? He'd have sent his message off into the ether and he wouldn't be able to tell whether I was ignoring him or I just had no IT skills.)

It's been more than a week now. That's an awfully long time for someone who thinks I'm really attractive.

First Ed, now Simon. What is it with me that I'm incapable of holding anyone's attention for more than a few hours?

I bet even Kate would be able to handle this better than me. But then you're supposed to suffer these seasicknesses, these lurching waves of sexual possibility when you're Kate's age; at mine, you're supposed to be past it.

This afternoon I drove past his house again. He wasn't there. I expect he's spending as little time as possible in Langley. Too busy with his new London social life, with Friday-night tables at Wave and wasp-waisted girls who don't think pop music stopped with The Clash.

Ginny burst into tears this morning for the second time in twenty-four hours. It's the child who's supposed to cry when you leave for work, not the nanny.

It's more boyfriend trouble. She invited our window cleaner to the pub and he got off with one of her friends, so now they're not speaking. (Ginny and the friend, or Ginny and the window cleaner.)

'I don't care; I just won't let him in when he comes round!' she sniffed, clearing up Arthur's breakfast things noisily. 'That'll show him!'

'Er, not sure that'll be very good for the windows . . .'

'Why give him business when he's so vile?'

'Because, um, otherwise the house will get dirty.'

'Huh!' she said mulishly, kicking the dishwasher shut with her foot. 'I don't *care*.'

'I hope you're not exploiting that poor girl,' my

mother said severely, when I mentioned this incident later on the phone.

'Of course I'm not!' I answered irritably. 'If anything it's the other way round. D'you want me to stay at home, or what?'

'It's a conundrum, isn't it?' my mother said happily. 'I don't suppose Richard worries about it, though.'

Richard is so far from worrying about Ginny that he probably wouldn't recognise her if he met her in the street. He never has to explain to her that feeding Arthur sausages at every meal doesn't amount to giving him a balanced diet. And he certainly doesn't feel guilty about leaving Arthur in the care of a sobbing teenager, because as far as he's concerned, he leaves Arthur in *my* care, and the irresponsibility is all my problem. But *I* feel guilty, and Ginny knows it; both of us (all three of us, if you count Richard) think that I should be at home looking after the children.

'One in four separated and divorced fathers loses contact with his children within two years,' my mother remarked, à propos of not very much at all.

'I don't expect Richard will be one of them.' She was doing it again; I don't *want* to have to stick up for him.

'He will if he takes off to Los Angeles with Emma. Any news on the divorce front?'

'No,' I lied.

'You should do something about it yourself. The longer it goes on, the more unlikely you are to get back together. I know you want to think otherwise, and it's very loyal of you, darling, but at some point you have to face the fact that Richard's weak and simply not very centred.'

'You sound like Fran.'

'He should be clearer with you about what he wants,' my mother continued, 'and if he isn't, you'll have to force the issue. This lawyer I know is really excellent. At some point, darling, you *have* to get on with your own life.'

But as Fran so acutely pointed out, I scarcely have one. The nearest thing I've had lately to confirmation that I'm animate is, firstly, a brief sexual encounter with an environmentalist whose understanding of the verb 'to commit' doesn't extend beyond its use in connection with 'adultery', and secondly, supper with a music business executive, the meaning of which a professor of semiotics would be hard pressed to decode.

This is doubly cruel when you consider that I am probably now at my sexual peak.

'It's not fair!' I protested to Tony the next morning at work. 'Before I know where I am, I will be menopausal, and then dead. And I haven't had enough life yet. I haven't *earned* my death. I certainly haven't attained that zen-like menopausal state that Germaine Greer goes on about when you stop being bothered about sex. Anyway, it's all very well for her: she had a new lover every week when she was in her twenties. I haven't done nearly enough with my sexually active years.' Active was a bit of a misnomer where Richard and I were concerned.

Tony smiled gnomically and went back to his crossword. I glared at the top of his head and started compiling a list of ways to improve my life:

Stop shouting at the children for minor misdemeanours, such as leaving shoes on the stairs, but respond in a witty and provocative way, for example by hiding them.

Read the newspapers for the latest on Iraq or infighting in the cabinet rather than merely for articles about wives whose husbands have left them for younger women.

Stop resenting Arthur for waking me up in the middle of the night and then again at six o'clock in the morning, but be a welcoming earth mother wreathed in smiles at all hours of the day and night.

Stop being disappointed with Ben for not knowing his tables or being able to spell but simply accept him for the wonderful person he is.

Get a new job.

Stop fantasising about sex with Simon and his washboard stomach.

'Simon's not going to call,' I told Fran on Saturday morning. 'I've given up on that relationship. He's too young for me.'

'Did you ask him to dinner with me?'

'No, I . . .'

'Are you ashamed of me, or what? He might have heard of me, you know.'

'It's not you . . . I've decided that when he said he'd like to spend more time with me, it was just a way of escaping. After all, if I'd got frisky and, say, taken it into my head to sit on him, he wouldn't have stood a chance.'

'Don't be ridiculous.'

'Suzy Sharp probably put him up to asking me out in the first place. When she gets an idea into her head, she's like a Chieftain tank. I mean, what could be more improbable than employing Ginny? By comparison, even going out with me seems reasonable.'

'He's probably waiting for you to make the next move.'

'That's what Mel thinks. But there's nothing to move *on*. I know nothing about him.'

'The reason he let you do all the talking is that he was interested in you.'

'He was politely curious, that's all. To him I probably seemed quite exotic.'

'Sounds sexy.'

'Not exotic as in dancer; exotic as in remote tribe with disgusting social habits.'

'You don't have habits.'

'The point is that he's quite a bit younger than me. His frame of reference is different. It was incredibly arrogant of me ever to think he might be attracted to me. He could even be in his *twenties*. And when I was in my twenties I was *horrible* – insecure and ambitious, unrelaxed, grabby and childish . . .'

'Sounds like it's a good thing he waited until now to meet you . . . Look, Jools, there's something I have to . . .'

But the front doorbell was ringing. I promised Fran I'd call her straight back.

A boy stood on the doorstep, holding an enormous bunch of flowers.

'Julie Ellison?' he mumbled through a mouthful of chewing gum.

I stared down at the flowers, a tight mass of flower

heads wrapped in Cellophane and tied up with rough string: pale pink peonies, the colour of raspberry parfait; milky cream roses with pink-fringed petals, as if the outer edges had been dipped in strawberry juice and stained; and sticking up jauntily through the middle, spikes of loosestrife.

The boy heaved them into my arms, turned on his heel and sauntered down the path to his van.

I carried the heavy flowers indoors, laid them down carefully on the hall table and fumbled with a tiny envelope that was pinned to the Cellophane.

'Thanks for a lovely evening,' I read. 'Love, Simon.'

Ben

Last Wednesday, Grandma June came round with bags of what Mum calls cheap sweets – penny chews and milk bottles and gummy bananas. Mum's a sweets snob: she thinks anything beneath Cadbury's Dairy Milk on her own private Sweets Scale makes your teeth drop out. She hates Grandma June bringing round these huge bags of Woolworth's Pick'n'Mix. 'I don't know why she doesn't just bring a drill and make holes in your teeth. Save time,' she muttered grumpily when Grandma was out of earshot. We are only allowed a few sweets a day and Mum hates it when Grandma brings round her usual five kilos because she has to take them away and ration them. Either that or abandon her principles.

'You're still working, then?' Grandma remarked, pulling on the rubber gloves and looming over the pile of dirty plates. 'You're not worried that it makes the children feel insecure, having a whole lot of different people looking after them?'

'It's not a whole load,' Mum said. 'It's Ginny.'

'Poor Arthur must be wondering who his mummy is, what with this Ginny girl and Emma . . .'

'Emma's hardly my fault. Please don't do that, June. I'll finish it later.'

'It needs starting first!'

Mum glared at her. 'It's nice for the children that there are lots of people who love them and look after them.'

'Oh, I expect you think it's like in African tribes or something. But we don't actually live in Africa. Children need to feel that they're growing up in a normal family.'

'Well, they are. If you're talking normal, this is it. In ten years' time the traditional nuclear family will be in the minority.'

'You think, do you?'

'Look, please don't do that. I can put most of it in the dishwasher.'

'You'll only have to get it out again. And this takes no time at all, once you apply yourself. Now, you sit down and have a rest; you've been at work all day . . .' Grandma ran the water into the bowl noisily. 'You're very good at making *arguments* – you grew up with all those theories – but I *know* what children like. Dinner on the table, place tidied up afterwards, mother who's got time for them.'

'Then perhaps,' Mum said, 'you'd better address your comments to the person who smashed it up.'

I was sitting on the floor building a Lego castle and pretending not to listen. Secretly, I was hoping Mum would win, even though I agreed with Grandma that we'd be better off living as a proper family. I don't *mind* Mum working – I know that would be sexist – but it would be nice if she was at home.

Grandma went home quite soon after that. Mum banged saucepans about for a while afterwards and muttered under her breath about how she'd rather live in a commune than be like June.

I hope this is not her latest idea.

At bedtime, Arthur asked Mum if Dad was still his daddy now he doesn't live here any more. No one has explained to him properly why Dad moved out.

Mum told Arthur that he's got a mummy and daddy and they will always love him. But why should he accept that when everything else has fallen apart?

I tried discussing this with Kate, but she said we should be pleased, because otherwise we wouldn't have got the chance to go to school in Los Angeles or to the Seychelles for Christmas.

Kate's only concern at the moment is whether she will be allowed to stay over at Rachel's party. (In my view, she should have thought of this before she got her nose pierced.) She says everyone else is staying and if she has to come home it will be humiliating.

'Why do you need to stay out when it only takes ten minutes to get home?' Mum asked.

'I don't see why *I* have to suffer because you and Dad can't organise your lives! It's bad enough having separated parents who never have enough money for new trainers, without having to leave parties at a ridiculously embarrassing time. It's only because you're neurotic from being on your own too much.'

Mum said Kate could have a new pair of trainers as

soon as she stopped leaving the old ones where they trip people up in the middle of the hall. She said there are tea stains all over the skirting board where she's failed to dodge Kate's trainers.

Kate answered that she always leaves them in the same place, so if Mum falls over them it's her own fault.

Kate

Last night I finally got round to asking Mum properly if I could stay the night at Rachel's and she said no, which is so unfair I can't believe it. *Everyone* is staying and I will be the only person going home. Mum said she would wait outside and I could come out at midnight.

Midnight! Even if she doesn't knock, someone is bound to see her.

Darren's staying, which you'd think would make her feel better, since she thinks he is so bloody marvellous. But no, if we are together in the same house without adults for a whole night I will need an abortion.

Darren's parents don't worry about him, because they think he can't get pregnant, which if you think about it is the double standard because of course he can. This is the sort of sexist assumption the Child Support Agency was supposed to put a stop to, which just proves it has failed.

Mum is always going on about how I need to be responsible, but I think you're meant to get rights in return for responsibility. And at the moment it's parents who have all the rights.

For example, as Mould says, their generation think they have the right to travel at high speeds in cars, even though this means that children can't play out in the streets and are growing up physically and psychologically stunted as a result. (Look at Ben.)

Then they say we can't come home late at night because public transport isn't safe, even though this is because they are all zooming about in their cars, watching our morals.

So the upshot is that young people are indoors too much, which is something human beings are not genetically designed for. Soon we'll start adapting to this new environment: we'll get fat and start waddling and the Teletubbies will no longer be an amusing toddler entertainment with a lot of commercial spin-offs but a hideous sci-fi prediction of our future.

Julie

I arranged the flowers. Then I sat with a cup of coffee staring at them in bemusement for a good half-hour, marvelling at the summery lushness of the blooms.

I called Fran again, since she probably receives flowers all the time and knows why people send them, but she appeared to have gone out (rather rudely, I thought, considering we were in the middle of a conversation). So I tried Mel instead.

'That's fantastic!' she cried. 'Finally you find a man with a sense of romance: someone who knows how to do things properly.'

'You think?' I said doubtfully. 'I somehow have bad feelings about what these flowers are meant to signify.'

'*Signify*? Jools, what are you going on about? Honestly, you're always looking for trouble.'

'If Simon wanted to see me again, why not just pick up the telephone like a normal person?'

'Perhaps he's shy.'

'Why spend thirty quid on this amazing bunch of flowers?'

'Perhaps he thinks you're worth it. You said he was stylish.'

'Why wait so long? A whole fortnight. I've practically forgotten what he looks like. He's probably trying to draw a line under the relationship: "Thanks but no thanks"?'

'Why, when he could simply not contact you at all?'

'A misplaced sense of politeness?' Even to me, it sounded improbable.

'Anyway, why *not* wait a fortnight? There's no rush, is there? And he's probably nervous. You said yourself you went on and on about Richard and the children. He's playing it cool, and trying to take things at the right pace; he's worried that you're not ready to let another man into your life.'

'Maybe he was expecting me to call *him* . . .' I said hopefully. 'Maybe it's my turn, and he's trying to chivvy me along?'

'The general point is, you should take a more positive view. You got Ed McGregor wrong. You've probably got Simon wrong as well.'

'That's the positive view?'

'Are you really over the Ed thing?' Mel said suspiciously.

'Of course I am.'

'He can't commit,' she reminded me. 'Fran said. And he didn't like your Lladrò.'

'June's Lladrò.'

'Whatever. Look, you don't have to *fall in love* with Simon. He's just a way of boosting your self-esteem after Richard.'

221

'And Ed.'

'Whatever. Simon's a way for you to feel better about yourself: a distraction. A diversion. The ball's in your court. Pick it up and er, score.'

'What, ring him up?'

'I don't know ... ring him up, go and see him. Something. *Tell* him you'd like to have sex, if necessary. You weren't exactly a born-again virgin with Ed McGregor.'

'That was different. I was completely carried away. I didn't have to think about it.'

'So don't think about it this time. Just do it.'

I made myself another cup of coffee and stared at the phone. Then I went upstairs and stared at myself – sucking in, pulling back, pushing out. I looked fine. Terrific. It was a shame I couldn't breathe.

There was definitely a time when my breasts were perkier than they are now and my abdominal muscles made a whole lot more effort. And my hands are a dead giveaway: far too many knuckles and veins, a large freckle that looks alarmingly as though it might turn into a liver spot, and a bit of skin between my thumb and forefinger that resembles the dewlaps of a very large lizard. Richard always used to say, forget face lifts: you can tell a woman's age instantly, just by glancing at her hands. But perhaps Simon doesn't know this: he's young enough not to have given much thought to ageing. I did a couple of pelvic floor exercises, to prove I still had one.

I could always drop in to see him on my way back, as it were, from shopping. It was sort of on the way.

I just happened to be passing, and I thought I'd poke my head round the door and say thanks for the flowers. It was an afterthought, really – an unpremeditated, spur-of-the-moment thing, because that's the kind of kooky, spontaneous, fun girl I am.

It took me three-quarters of an hour to decide what to wear.

By the time I reached the corner of Oakhurst Grove, my throat was so dry I wasn't sure I'd be able to speak. I could feel the blood thudding round my body: a dulled thump, thump, like the washing machine when Kate uses it for her trainers.

Trying to park the car, I gently nudged it into the front of a Ford Probe belonging to one of Simon's neighbours.

I tried to breathe deeply, doing exercises I learnt when I was training to be an actress. But I must be out of practice; I sounded like a hippopotamus.

Simon answered the door wearing navy knee-length shorts and a white T-shirt with cut-off sleeves. He was wasted in the backrooms of the music business; he should have been a pop star in his own right, or on billboards, flogging jeans, or Y-fronts.

I smiled. 'Thank you so much. The flowers are fantastic.'

'I'm glad you liked them.' He smiled back. 'Come in for a coffee?'

I tipped my head to one side, to signal that I just might. 'Thanks.'

He opened the front door and stood back; I stepped inside, and, for a moment, we were uncomfortably close in the hall. I held my breath. Then his arms circled round me and he kicked the door shut with his foot and backed me up against it, murmuring as he kissed my face, my neck, and I moaned and scrabbled with the buttons on his shirt . . .

No, that was the other time, with Ed McGregor. Simon didn't do any of that. He set off down the hall to the back of the house, leaving me to close the front door.

I followed him into the kitchen.

'So you're moving?' I said.

'Yes.'

'You didn't say.'

I didn't mean it to come out like that.

He looked momentarily puzzled. 'Didn't I?'

'Where are you going?'

'Notting Hill. I've found a flat. It's very small – which is all I can afford, but a bit more central.'

Fran might end up meeting him after all. They'd probably bump into one another putting out their milk bottles.

The thought of milk bottles made me feel more determined. If Ed McGregor could stroll into someone's kitchen and seduce them, I could too. What did he have that was so special?

Simon's kitchen, now that I had the chance to look at it, was wholly unsuitable for him: too brown and ridged and rustic, too fussy, with twee corner shelves topped by scalloped pelmets – the sort of thing you'd have seen advertised in the back of a colour supplement about a decade ago.

Simon's natural habitat would, I imagined, be a cool urban space, a bit like Richard's, but less effortful – all stainless steel and 1950s-style fridges, with perhaps the odd amusing item: placemats with Kia-Ora graphics, or a blow-up tea caddy in coloured see-through plastic.

Several of the cupboards had been emptied of their contents, which were now strewn about the floor. Quite a lot of stuff seemed to have been decanted into two open bin bags by the back door.

'I'm trying to sort all this out,' he said over his shoulder, putting on the kettle.

'Your uncle left you the contents as well?'

He nodded. 'Pretty much. And it's awful, but there's almost nothing here I want. I keep imagining him looking down as I throw things into bags for Oxfam and *hating* me. I expect he regrets leaving me anything.'

'He's probably got more important things to think about now.'

'I hate it – all these possessions, once so important, and I chuck them out. It's the second time in a year: I cleared out my parents' house after my father died in February. I'm beginning to feel like, I don't know, a sort of one-man scorched earth policy.' He put a cafetiere on the table. 'How are the kids?'

'Fine. Did I talk about them all the time when we went out to dinner?'

'No.'

'I expect I did. And Richard.'

'No.'

'And my mother.'

'No. I had a great time. Honestly.'

'I talked and talked about me and I didn't let you get a word in edgeways.'

'That's not true.'

225

'It must be, because I realised afterwards I hardly found out anything about you.' I paused, meaningfully.

Simon poured the coffee, concentrating hard on not splashing.

Someone – an awfully long time ago – told me that my eyes over a coffee cup were incredibly sexy, so I tried it now. 'I'd kind of like to make it up to you.'

He blinked. 'Make what up?'

'Being a bore last time.'

He frowned. 'There's nothing to make up.' He got up and looked in the fridge for the milk, even though it was already on the table.

That wasn't the right answer. 'What sort of thing are you offering?' would have been better; or, 'Could I make a suggestion?'

'I've exchanged contracts on the house,' he said, locating the milk jug. 'It's taken bloody ages, because no one knows what difference the road is going to make.'

He was shy. Mel said so.

I let my sandal dangle off the end of my toes. Fortunately, for once they were painted. 'I'd *like* to get to know you.'

'It's a relief,' he hurried on, as if I hadn't spoken at all, 'because I've got to go to New York and San Francisco again next week and after that my solicitor's going away – to the Caribbean, for three weeks – and if it had dragged on much longer we couldn't have got started on the paperwork for months.'

Why was he telling me where his solicitor was going on holiday?

But I wasn't going to be put off. I'm too passive, that's what Fran thinks; I don't have the first idea about how to behave in the postfeminist, show-off-your-cleavage-and-run-a-multinational era. And Mel said I simply had to *tell* him. Come out with it. Did this apply even when he was making strenuous efforts to steer me towards the subject of house purchasing?

Still, I could be misreading him. I'd misread Ed McGregor: for about ten minutes, I'd thought he found me irresistible.

'It doesn't have to be complicated,' I blurted out, adding, as a sort of half-joke: 'you don't have to fall in love with me.'

He bit his lip. He looked up at the ceiling – for ages, as if he was working out whether it needed painting, and then how much it would cost, and who to get in to do it. Then he looked at the floor.

'Oh Jools, I like you so much . . .'

Oh God! I thought. He's going to say, 'But not in that way . . .'

I had made – it was now suddenly, but all at once glaringly obvious – a mistake. A terrible, awful, hideously embarrassing mistake.

'It's OK,' I said quickly. 'It was only a joke.'

But we both knew that it wasn't.

'Phew!' he said gamely.

There was a silence.

'Not a very good joke,' I said, half-laughing.

'Jools?'

'Yes?'

'I think you're funny and charming and *incredibly* interesting . . .'

'It's OK,' I muttered, swallowing coffee and almost choking. 'You don't have to go on.'

He took my hand. 'I think you're lovely,' he said earnestly. 'I'm sorry, I'm afraid I haven't been . . .' He stared out of the window.

'You're not over your other relationship,' I said quickly.

'It's not just that . . .'

'You don't have to explain.' I didn't need to be told that the other problem was that I was as attractive as a slug.

How was this happening – to me of all people? The most over-defended, ironic person I knew? How – when I can run a home and bring up three children and cook meals out of the *River Café Cook Book*, improvising in the absence of a wood-burning stove? When I can dispose of rats and hold down a job? Back in the days when I still acted, they used to give me the leads (I wasn't a character actress, dammit: I was *pretty*). And I have loyal friends who think I'm nice and generous and fun to be with. So how had I let Simon make me feel like a noxious virus? If someone had told me ten years ago that I'd get to the point of asking a much younger man for sex (*asking!*) and he'd turn me down, I'd have laughed.

'Julie, it's not . . .'

'I have to go.' I was already on my feet.

'No, let me –'

'Please, Simon . . .'

'Let's talk again . . .'

I'd rather be dead in a ditch.

It was only when I'd stumbled out of his front door into the still-bright morning that I realised I still had absolutely no idea why he sent the flowers.

Ben

Mum will go *mental*. We're at Dad's and it's Rachel's party, and Kate hasn't told him that she's forbidden to stay the night; in fact, she *lied*, and actually said it was OK.

Fortunately she did this when I wasn't around and, by the time I found out, she was already dressed up, including blue eyeshadow and pink lip-gloss, so it wasn't up to me to point out that Mum had said that on no account was she to stay the night. Kate can't have told Mum the date of the party, or if she did, Mum forgot it, probably because she was thinking about other things. That man.

This is what happens when mothers are only part-time.

In the past, Dad would have made Mum ring up Rachel's parents to find out why they were letting Rachel have an all-night party at the age of fifteen. And then Rachel's parents, who don't even know there is going to be a party, would have stopped it, or at least made everyone go home at midnight.

He never would have rung up himself, even before. He doesn't talk to other parents. And he can't get Emma to do it, because she is nearly young enough to have underage sex herself.

This is why people worry about divorce. It destroys the social fabric.

Emma even lent Kate a dress. She seemed dead keen on the idea of Kate staying out all night. Kate said the dress was very expensive (it came from the King's Road) even though there was hardly anything to it! Actually, I don't think Kate looks so good in pink silk dresses with lots of eyeshadow. She looks as if she is trying too hard.

But the pink streaks she put in her hair with dye were pretty cool. Emma said they were brilliant, so then Dad had to say they were brilliant too.

When Kate had gone I ate Dad's soggy shepherd's pie with too much gravy (it is a pity Emma doesn't cook, but she doesn't eat much either, which is probably why she doesn't mind Dad doing the cooking. She says television makes you look fatter so she has to be careful). I told Dad all about the effect of the road on house prices, and what Darren had said about everyone meeting at the tree and offering passive resistance, and I suggested to him that he ought to go on the list of people to be called at dawn when it starts.

He said: 'I'll think about it, Ben,' and patted me on the head.

So that's something.

Kate

Rachel was upset when I arrived because she'd had a row with her parents. They wanted her to come with them to her grandmother's and they couldn't understand why she wouldn't, or why, if I was coming round, I'd left it so late. She had to tell a whole lot of lies about Dad not being able to bring me out from Clerkenwell until after eight o'clock, when the real reason was that I didn't want them to see me dressed up for the party. I could have got ready here, at Rachel's, but then I wouldn't have been able to borrow Emma's dress. (Which is fantastic, though it's too dark for anyone to see it.)

Then Joe rang and said he wasn't sure he was going to come to the party, which was a disaster because he was the reason Rachel had organised a party in the first place.

She said: 'I'm not going to beg you, if that's what you want.' Then she thought about it and added: 'Anyway, you have to come, because it's mainly your friends and I don't know them.'

Joe said: 'OK, but I might have to bring someone.'

As soon as people started arriving I could tell Rachel regretted inviting them. Not that she *had* invited most of them.

Joe didn't turn up until the pubs shut, and then he brought a girl from the comprehensive with blonde hair and really cool skaters' clothes. She was also wearing an Animal watch, which is what Rachel wanted for her birthday, but her mum said they were too expensive for what they were.

Rachel drank five glasses of Dubonnet and lemonade and disappeared for ages. I don't know if she was being ill or sulking.

While she wasn't around, someone smashed her mum's best china jar from Tibet or somewhere and then a whole load of gatecrashers arrived and someone let them in.

Two blokes had a fight in the front garden and no one knew who they were. Then some time after midnight someone came round from the council about the noise and I turned the CD player down because I was worried about Rachel getting arrested, but one of the gatecrashers turned it up again.

Darren decided to go home at two o'clock. He said he couldn't see himself getting any sleep here and he has GCSEs in two months. He offered to walk me back, but Clerkenwell is miles away and I didn't see how I could go back to Mum's. I wanted to ring Dad and get him to pick me up, but I know part of the reason he didn't mind me staying was that he wanted to drink an entire bottle of wine with

Emma and probably have sex then fall into a stupor.

By then I was really tired, and I started worrying about my biology essay which I have got to do tomorrow, so I sneaked up to Rob's bedroom, which no one uses when he is at university. I thought I could borrow his bed, but there were two naked people in it and I'd never seen either of them before.

I was getting pretty desperate. I hadn't seen Rachel for hours and I had history course work to do in the morning as well, so I thought I'd sleep in her parents' room. It was supposed to be out of bounds – she'd put a 'No Entry' sign on the door – but I was only in there for half an hour before I was woken up by someone puking over my legs. It was a friend of Darren and Joe's. He was so drunk he thought he was in the bathroom.

I screamed and shouted: 'What the *fuck* do you think you're doing?' but he just groaned and wiped his face on the duvet cover. That was when I realised he'd been sick on Emma's dress.

I resisted the temptation to kick him and I left him there, moaning and looking pathetic, and went off to the bathroom to try to clean myself up. Unfortunately, when I rubbed water on to the dress it made another stain. It is Dry Clean Only.

Rachel was already in the bathroom, scrubbing at a red wine stain on the cream carpet. She said there was a cigarette burn on the Chinese rug in the sitting room as well. The whole house smells of draw.

We will have to kick everyone out early in the morning, because Rachel's parents are due back at lunchtime and it will take us hours to clear up.

Rachel says she *hates* Joe, and he ruined her party. I'm not that sure about Darren, either. He is very polite.

Julie

I woke up on Sunday morning, shifted in the bed, then remembered and pulled the duvet up over my head.

This was even more humiliating than being dumped by Ed McGregor. The indignity of throwing myself at a man who didn't want me, never *had* wanted me . . . ! At least with Ed I'd been able to console myself with the thought that for a minute or two, he'd found me attractive. The Simon episode was simply squalid. From not one single aspect could I rescue a shred of self-esteem.

How had I got it so wrong? I'm not normally naïve. Not like that, anyway. It would have been nice to be able to blame Mel and Fran for inciting me, but they'd only had my version of things to go on. If they'd encouraged me to be embarrassingly brazen, it could only have been because I somehow conveyed to them that that was what was wanted.

But *how*? I've never been one of those women who thinks everyone fancies her. Except, actually, that when I was younger quite a lot of people *did* fancy me. Men used to write me poetry and send me flowers and it was usually pretty clear what they were up to. They weren't, as a rule, trying to tell me that they were obsessed with someone else.

He must have been cleaning out his house, throwing things in the bin, disposing of the unwanted. All those things that he felt guilty about not caring about. He must have remembered that I was another thing he didn't care about. Send her some flowers, he must have thought: that'll tidy her up. I was a loose end.

It was still weird.

I shuddered at the thought of it, sitting politely among his dead uncle's G-Plan and *propositioning* him. This is what feminism has brought us to: disgrace and humiliation. How come Emma Neil can get in touch with her inner slut and make a fortune, but when I find mine I look imbecilic?

I got up eventually. I read the papers, ate a couple of croissants, had a shower, listened to the *Archers* Omnibus and thought about going to the garden centre for some bedding plants. Really, I'd have liked to *become* a bedding plant: I quite fancied being in a persistent vegetative state, all thought processes suspended.

When the phone rang, I almost left it, but then I thought it might be the children.

In fact, it was Fiona Wesley, Rachel's mother, who wears flouncy peasant skirts and dangly ethnic earrings, won't have a television in the house and has a way of always bustling about as if to imply that one is distracting her from important jobs, such as knitting a yurt or shredding bran fibre. I always think she despises me for being too materialistic and superficial, and can tell I sign Kate's homework diary without looking at it.

Now she said accusingly: 'I can't believe you didn't tell me!'

I looked up from the *Sunday Times* article I'd been half-reading about the Langley motorway extension. 'Huh?'

'If Rachel said *she* wanted to stay the night somewhere, I'd at least expect to *speak* to the parents. I wouldn't blithely assume that they were going to be there.'

'Stay the night?' I repeated idiotically.

'Yes. Your daughter and my daughter threw a party last night. Where did you *think* she was?'

'At her father's,' I answered, not caring, for once, whether our domestic arrangements looked chaotic and dysfunctional. Fiona, anyway, would probably only have approved if we'd conducted our separation according to the customs of the Yanonami. 'Rachel's party was last night?'

How had I forgotten? Had Kate told me?

Was it possible for senile dementia to be triggered by divorce, along with cancer and heart attacks?

'Rachel claims it was *their* party, hers *and* Kate's. And we weren't there. People were sick everywhere. There were *semen* stains on Rob's duvet, and God knows what on ours. Rachel says the stains were made by much older people, but what were older people doing here in the first place? I suspect there were drugs. There was certainly drink. Bottles and bottles outside the back door. Vodka and everything.'

'Oh, I am *so* sorry. Is Kate there now?'

'No, she just left.'

'She'll be going back to Richard's.' She wouldn't dare come here. 'Don't worry, I'll ring him. I had no idea . . .'

But I should have had. I was incompetent. I didn't know where my daughter was on a Saturday night. I couldn't imagine now – whatever had possessed me? – why I hadn't shown parental solidarity and called Fiona as soon as this party was mooted. I was a useless adult, unable to hold the line with other parents against the turbulent anarchy of adolescence.

It was because of Simon. I thought of the great gulf between my erotic fantasies of Simon's perfect muscle tone and the vexed and gummy reality of single parenthood, and I was ashamed.

'Kate did help clear up, at least,' Fiona acknowledged grudgingly. 'I don't think either of them had a great time. There were gatecrashers. My Balinese vase got smashed.'

I didn't really know what to say, other than sorry. I could tell what she thought – that my daughter, the product of a broken home, unfettered and unwatched, was leading her daughter astray.

I stalked up and down the kitchen, running my fingers through my hair, swearing at Richard. Why hadn't he called me to see what *I* thought about this party? Because he wanted to pretend I didn't exist.

I am constantly calling him, trying to trace missing sweatshirts of Ben's, confirming his shifting arrangements (cancelling the children here so that he can attend a film premiere, or there so they can make it to a fashion show); keeping him up to date with little developments in Arthur's routine (two books before bed and five nursery rhymes once he's tucked up) in an effort to diminish, a little bit, the disruption.

I can't remember him initiating a single one of these conversations. I am a part of his life striated with error and regret and anger. He thinks he can shove me out of sight; that if he never picks up the phone he can consign me to some emotional outer darkness.

I breathed deeply several times, then called him.

'Richard,' I snapped, 'where was Kate last night?'

He sounded half-asleep. Usually I assume he sounds like this because he's recently had energetic, multi-venue sex, but presumably this wasn't the case this morning with the children there. Perhaps he just yawns so much because I bore him.

He grunted something that could have been: 'Rachel's?'

'And what was she doing?'

'They had a party.'

'Fiona and Andy were away. They had gatecrashers. There was drink, and drugs. I'd expressly forbidden her to stay the night.'

'Oh,' he thought about this for a minute. 'Well, I expect she hated it. It's probably a good lesson.'

'In what? Parental neglect? She's *fourteen*. Anyway, what about Fiona and Andy?'

'Julie, this is a terrible habit, shouting at me. It's completely counter-productive. I am sorry if you think I've failed in my responsibilities in some way. But she's all right, isn't she? Still alive? The thing you have to remember about Kate is that she's very bright and quite sensible. We have to trust her.'

'I'd *forbidden* it!'

'She wasn't with you this weekend.'

'But I'm her mother!'

'And I'm her father. And I'm not prepared to be shouted at.' And he put down the phone.

I went out into the back garden, dug furiously for most of the afternoon and cried hot tears of rage and misery into the earth. There seemed to be an awful lot of fag ends in the flower beds. Fred next door must be chucking them over the wall.

On Monday, when Kate came home from school, she at least had the grace to avoid my eyes. She came in early, without going to visit the people Ben aptly calls the ego-warriors, but I think this may have had less to do with shame than exhaustion. She sank on to the sofa in the breakfast room, muttered something about having a headache, and groped for the remote control down the back of the cushions. It came out with a Lego dragon, which she threw on the floor, narrowly missing Ben. Then she started zapping through the channels.

'Mum, she's not looking to see what's on first.'

'I can see that, thank you, Ben. Kate . . .'

'I want to watch this.' It was the Jerry Springer show. Two women were pulling each other's hair.

Ben objected: 'When I watch that programme Mum says it's a set-up.'

'Shut up, why don't you?'

'And she says it's rubbish.'

'Mum, why is he always getting at me?'

Arthur spooned up a dollop of custard, turned the

spoon upside down so that it plopped on to his T-shirt, then pushed the bowl away so hard it fell on the floor. 'He's not getting at you,' I said, wiping the floor then rinsing the spoon.

'He's always trying to get me into trouble.'

'He hardly needs to do *that*.'

'Meaning?' Kate said aggressively.

'What happened on Saturday night?'

'Dad didn't mind.'

'I did.'

'But I wasn't *with* you.'

'And did you tell Dad I'd expressly forbidden it?'

'I don't know why you're going on about this. He's already given me one bollocking.'

'And did you have a good time?'

'It was all right.'

'Were there drugs?'

'Oh God, Mum, that's all parents ever think about! It's so *boring*.'

'No, but I don't want you to be in situations that are difficult to get out of. And you did exactly what I'd told you not to. How am I supposed to trust you?'

'Look, it's not my fault if you and Dad can't communicate ... and no, don't even *start* complaining to me about him. How do you think that makes *me* feel? Frankly, if you want the truth, if I want to take drugs or have sex, I don't have to stay out all night to do it. So don't patronise me. I've got a *headache*.'

And she stomped out of the room, slamming the door, so that the photograph of Richard that she'd insisted on putting up again after I'd taken it down wobbled on its shelf and fell over. On the television, one of the women had the other on the floor and was flailing her face with her fingernails.

Ben

A bunch of flowers arrived for Mum at the weekend. I'm hoping they are from Dad. Mum went pink when I asked and said it didn't matter who sent them. If they were from Simon the boyfriend, surely she'd say, in order to get us used to the idea of him?

They *could* have been from Dad. He needs to apologise, because he let Kate stay at the party.

If they were, they haven't worked yet.

Mum'll come round, though. After all, he was the one who left. She's angry at the moment about the party, although she says now that it's not the party she minds, so much as the lying. (Though if she'd let Kate stay the night in the first place, she wouldn't have *had* to lie. Grown-ups don't always see things.)

Anyway, Dad now thinks Mum considers him an inadequate parent. And Mum thinks . . . well, that he's an inadequate parent.

Despite the party fiasco, Kate quite likes Mum and Dad having different houses and different rules, because she thinks when one of them gets on her nerves she can move out and live with the other one. (People get on her nerves very easily, though, so she will be backwards and forwards all the time.) It's fine for her, but what she doesn't take into account is how bad it is for me and Arthur to have these different standards of behaviour, because we are still young enough to be confused.

I am trying to stay out of everyone's way on the computer, but I think I have made it crash. It keeps putting up messages saying 'protocol has been lost'. I looked up protocol in the dictionary and it said 'a body of diplomatic etiquette', which did not help me to re-start the computer.

I can't tell Mum, because she blames Dad for buying a cheap computer in Tottenham Court Road which has never worked properly, so if I tell her it's crashed again that will only be *another* thing to be irritated about. The people in the shop built it themselves, Mum says, out of paperclips and old car parts.

The other reason I can't tell her is that I was trying to get on to the internet because Adam says he does it pretending to be a lesbian and has sexy talk. I thought I'd try this, although I suppose I could have ended up talking to Adam. We would both be pretending to be lesbians when we are actually boys who go to Woodside Comprehensive. We wouldn't learn anything useful.

I was also worried that it might be a bit of a giveaway that I can't spell. But presumably there must be some illiterate lesbians? They must still want to take advantage of the digital highway to discuss breasts etc?

Mum is right that the computer's always crashing. It did it once when I switched it off without exiting Tomb

245

Raider and everything got wiped off the hard disk and Dad had to pay hundreds of pounds to get it fixed. I'm not sure Mum has hundreds of pounds. She said the other day that she couldn't even afford Kate's new trainers, even though Kate really needs them because of the fashion in her class.

She might just have been cross with Kate, I suppose, because trainers aren't *that* expensive. Still, it is a well-known fact that children are always poorer when their parents split up. Computer maintenance will probably be one of the first things to go round here: my education will fail to benefit from technological advances and I will fall behind children in Japan and Korea.

Maybe there is a computer programme that parents can secretly install that makes the system crash when children try to get on the lesbian line? In which case, we not only have a broken computer, no Dad to fix it, and poor educational prospects, but Mum will know I am interested in women.

Julie

I drifted downstairs on Tuesday morning, wearing my silk robe in an effort to look vaguely Greta Garbo, even if things here are really more Vera Duckworth.

I filled the kettle and switched it on, tipped porridge oats and milk into a bowl and stuck it in the microwave. Then I pulled the sheets from the washing machine, carried them outside and hung them on the line, trailing the hem of one duvet cover in the dirt. But it was mine, so that was OK. No possibility of anyone else's seeing that. Then I scurried back inside, shivering slightly.

The kitchen was dense with steam. You couldn't see from one end to the other; the vague shapes of kitchen appliances loomed at me through hot mist. It was a like a Turkish bath: all it needed was someone to pop out from behind the fridge with a stiff brush and start flailing.

I unplugged the kettle – which was still puffing away, but wheezily now, as if approaching meltdown – and peered inside. The element was crackling and beginning to go black.

'Bugger!' I rescued Kate's porridge from the insistently beeping microwave.

'Bugger,' repeated Arthur placidly, appearing in his pyjamas with his teddy, looking rumpled and smeared with sleep.

'It's foggy indoors,' he announced, and deposited himself like a small potentate in front of the television.

I carried Kate's porridge upstairs (she refuses to eat anything in the morning unless it's delivered to her room), and went into Ben's room and shook him a few times.

Richard, had he been here, would have had an opinion about whether the kettle could be fixed. It might not have been accurate, but who cares? A view about it would have been reassuring. He might even have got out his screwdriver and done it. But he wasn't here. And you can hardly call out a repairman for a thirty-pound kettle. On the other hand, throwing it away seemed a bit extreme, when it might be something really simple, like a fuse.

What did single people do when their kettles malfunctioned? I called Fran to find out.

'They get a new one,' she said from her office, where she'd been at her desk for at least half an hour. (She, though, doesn't have to run breakfasts all over her house; she has a croissant sent round from Patisserie Valerie.) 'Although there have been points in our relationship when I would have used it as an excuse to get David round. Can't you call Simon and pretend to be helpless?'

I *was* helpless; I didn't have to pretend.

I hadn't spoken to Fran since Saturday morning; she didn't know I'd solicited Simon and been rejected. I hadn't been able to face calling her.

'That's appalling!' she gasped, when I told her now. 'Why did he send the flowers, then?'

I sighed. 'I don't know; I've thought and thought about it, and I'm exhausted. I can't be bothered any more. Sex: it's too much effort. Anyway, one house can only take so much emotion, and Kate's got most of ours at the moment.'

'Men!' Fran scoffed. 'They don't know what they want. It's fine when you're grovelling for their affections, but they don't want the responsibility of a relationship.'

I said suddenly: 'Wouldn't you try to get David round now, if you had a broken kettle?'

'Mum,' Kate interrupted, coming into the kitchen, 'you didn't bring me up any tea.'

'The kettle blew up. Sorry . . . I'm on the phone.'

'If I get a migraine from dehydration it'll be your fault. Do you know Ben's still in bed?'

'Fran, I'm going to have to go.'

'Look, are you still coming to dinner, even without Simon? I've got someone for you to meet.'

Oh God, surely Fran isn't trying to pair me off with someone *else*? I'm not up to it. I'm the sexual equivalent of those pensioners who have to take another driving test. I need lessons before I'm let out again.

I drank a glass of orange juice, which splashed around acidically in my stomach, then yelled, 'Ben, are you coming?' up the stairs.

'Yeah,' came the muffled reply.

'Arthur, we're late.' I picked up his empty bowl and plate from the floor, where he'd taken himself off to eat, and stuck them in the dishwasher. 'We'll have to put you in the car in your pyjamas.'

'Can I stay here and watch *Wallace and Gromit*?'

'No, sorry, darling, you can't stay on your own.'

'Last week you said I couldn't go to Ben's school in pyjamas.'

'That was different. Today we're late because the kettle broke.'

'Why?'

'I don't know why. Things go wrong with kettles.'

'Why?'

'Because things go wrong. Everything goes wrong.'

'Like everyone dies?'

'Sort of.'

'I don't want to die. Make me not die!'

'Well, I'll do my best.' (I was in a hurry.)

Ben walked into the kitchen wearing boxer shorts and nothing else.

'Ben, you said you were ready!'

'No, I didn't . . .'

'You did!'

'Mum, I didn't. How could I be ready when I've got nothing to wear?'

I clenched my teeth in frustration. 'Trousers, T-shirts, jumpers . . . ?'

'I haven't got anything designer.'

'Ben, you're twelve.'

'At school they call me Marks and Spencer's boy.'

Ben got dressed, wailing as if his clothes were full of

250

tiny flesh-piercing pins. Still, at least the delay meant that I could get Arthur out of his pyjamas.

Ben sulked halfway to school, until he forgot, when he suddenly said: 'Mum, what's a particle accelerator?'

I tried to remember, but I wasn't sure I'd ever known. 'Um, a sort of tube I think. It shoots particles' – electrons, neurons? – 'sub-atomic particles towards each other at very high speeds.'

'What's a sub-atomic particle?'

'It's very small. Smaller than an atom.'

'How big is an atom?'

'Very tiny. Minuscule.'

'So what happens then?'

'They collide and make energy. I think.'

'How?'

'Isn't there something about this on *Encarta*? Can't you look it up?'

Ben said wisely: 'This is what you need a dad for.'

I spent the first hour at work thinking of all the things you need a dad for. Rats. Kettles. Putting out the rubbish. Or doing the ironing, if he prefers. I'm not sexist. As long as he did *something*. Simply being there would help: a last line of defence against the militant human rights activism that is modern childhood.

After that, I amused myself for a while by thinking about what I'd do if I won the lottery. My first buy – investment – would be a fifty-year-old Norland nanny, who'd exercise iron discipline in a charmingly grey-haired, apple-cheeked manner. My second was a housekeeper, to remember to remove the courgettes from the vegetable box before they deliquesced. There was a time when I'd have had a Lotus Elan and lots of Yohji Yamamoto, but it was a while ago now.

Tony said you're supposed to *do* the lottery to be allowed to plan your winnings. I told him he lacks imagination, and then I also told him the story of Simon, to show him that a lack of imagination would probably be a good thing. I was able to joke about it now, but it still hurt.

And then, because there really wasn't any journalism to do, I spent quite a long time considering whether I could possibly be qualified for anything else, and whether, for example, it might be worth sending off applications to PR agencies, or to whichever company it is – Hyundai, I think – that runs an internal dating agency. Except, as Tony reminded me, I'd just pledged to give up dating for ever.

By lunchtime there were still no exciting stories about chip-pan fires or large vegetables on the allotments. Tony and I had already finished all the crosswords we were capable of and more than exhausted all the possible interpretations of Simon's capricious behaviour. (Tony's favourite idea was that he was gay.) Partly to avoid being co-opted into drinking with Pete, I went to Sainsbury's and bought some cheese, fruit and olive oil that I only half-needed.

Standing outside the exit, wondering whether I could be bothered to walk up the High Street to Robert Dyas for a kettle, I felt a tug on my left shoulder; and, looking round, I was in time to see a lithe, leggy little figure twisting through the shoppers, running off down the street away from me.

The little bastard had got my purse.

I checked my bag. It was open. The purse was missing.

Without thinking, I set off up the High Street after him.

I was wearing DMs and, though he was nimble, there were enough people blocking the pavement to slow him down. He dodged across the road, through the traffic, and I followed, weaving in and out of the cars. I eventually caught up with him at the traffic lights.

I grabbed his elbow and pulled him roughly round to face me: Phil from the squats. Ed McGregor's charge, or familiar, or whatever he was. Our eyes met. His were dull and guiltless.

My purse was poking out of the pocket of his jeans.

'Can I have that back?'

He handed it over. 'You gonna grass me up?'

I hesitated. Still gripping his elbow, my fingers hard on his skinny arm, I said: 'What would happen if I did? If I took you to the police?'

'I dunno. They might caution me. They'd bring in the social workers, put me back in care.' He was defiant; he really seemed not to mind.

'And then?'

'I'd probably run away again.'

I made a decision. Gripping his wrist – it was thinner than Ben's – I marched him off in the direction of the squats.

Breathing hard with the effort of marching him along, I demanded: 'Do you make a habit of stealing things from people's handbags?'

253

'Not really.' He spoke listlessly, with a strong Yorkshire accent.

'Why aren't you at school?'

'It's boring. Don't teach you nothing useful.'

'How are you going to work when you're older if you don't go to school? Do you want to *have* to steal for a living, and end up in prison?'

'I won't get work anyway. There's no jobs.'

'Don't be silly, there are lots of jobs, if you're educated. Ed McGregor has a job.' Of a sort.

'He's different.'

'Look,' I said irritably, 'people in Langley are giving you lot money, food and help. That's because they think you're a good thing. What's going to happen if they find out you're stealing?'

We were at the squats. I marched Phil over the slabs of corrugated iron and cement bags in the front garden and through the front door.

Nettle wasn't at her usual post in the front room. I barged down the hall, opened Ed McGregor's door and pushed Phil through it in front of me.

Ed was standing by the fireplace: tall and dark, with dangerous eyes. Nettle was there too, about a foot away from him.

They were facing one another and she had one of his hands gripped in both of hers. I'd obviously interrupted them in the middle of some intense exchange.

I pushed Phil forward into the office. Ed looked up, recognised me, shook his hand free of Nettle's, and stepped smartly backwards.

'Oh, it's you again,' Nettle said unpleasantly. 'What do you want?'

'Your friend here stole my purse,' I said to Ed, ignoring Nettle and pushing Phil forwards.

Ed looked at me, then at Phil. He asked: 'Is this true?'

The boy hung his head. Ed winced.

I demanded: 'What are you going to do about it?'

'What do you want me to do?'

'You could start by insisting he goes to school like normal children. You're not exactly doing him any favours, letting him roam around the High Street all day with nothing better to do than nick things . . .'

'All right.' He held up a hand to silence me. 'Phil, could you go and help Mould in the attic? He's reinforcing the roof. I'll speak to you later.'

He nodded at me and I let go of Phil's wrist. There was a red weal where I'd been squeezing him.

'And you could return him to his parents, where he belongs,' I went on furiously – 'and if that's not possible, then to the appropriate authorities.'

'Julie, I'm really sorry,' he said, when Phil had clattered up the bare stairs.

Nettle stood in front of the fireplace, her head tipped slightly to one side, watching me coolly.

'Oh, I expect you are,' I said bitterly.

'But I *can't* return him to his mother, because he doesn't know where she is. And if he did, I doubt it would do any of us much good, because she drinks all day.'

'That's no reason for him not to go to school.'

'No perhaps not. Except that there's never been anything to give his life structure . . .'

'Don't preach at me,' I said irritably. 'I know all

that stuff. I read the *Guardian*. And I'm sure it's all very tragic, but there are proper ways of dealing with these things, without inflicting kids like Phil on people who are just going about their business and don't want their purses stolen.' I knew I was confirming all his prejudices about me, but I was too cross to mind. 'Anyway, I thought he was supposed to be in care?'

'Yes, he is. And one of his friends in the children's home died from sniffing lighter fuel. And it was also where he discovered if you gave a man a blow job you could get paid for it.'

I swallowed.

'I'm sorry,' Ed said, 'but the fact that he wants to be here seems to me the only hopeful thing about him.'

'You're not going to do *anything*?'

'Like I say, I can send him back to what is laughingly called his community. Or I can hope that by some process of osmosis he might pick up different values here.' He frowned. 'What are *you* going to do?'

'I don't know,' I said. I looked from him to Nettle. She gazed back superciliously. I felt hopeless.

I said coldly: 'I don't think all your supporters in Langley will be very impressed to know that your people are pinching purses outside Sainsbury's.' I turned on my heel. 'I'll think about it.'

Kate

I stuck Emma's dress in the washing machine to get rid of the sick stains and it came out half the size it was before and a different colour. All the shine has gone. I suppose it was a stupid thing to do, but Ginny said you could sometimes put things that said Dry Clean Only in machines, and I thought it might get rid of the water stain. It has, in the sense that now it's all water stain.

I could take it to the dry cleaners, but it would probably cost a lot of money and still not work – I don't see how they can enlarge it – and I could never afford to replace it, even if I could find another one, so I shall have to confess.

I hope this won't affect how Emma feels about me going with them to Los Angeles, as it seems to me that once the protesters have gone it's going to be my only hope.

There's certainly nothing to keep me in Langley. Darren is getting on my nerves: he keeps coming round to help Ben with his maths and then hanging around having ingratiating conversations with Mum.

Mum's annoying me because Phil stole her purse and you'd think the entire population of squatters had been involved in massacring shoppers in the High Street. She keeps saying things like: 'It's all very well for them to pool their property, as long as they don't assume everyone else wants to join in.'

Ben always annoys me, so no change there.

This evening Mum asked me what I thought would happen if she wrote up the story of Phil nicking her purse in her crappy local paper: would the squatters still be getting soup runs and Victoria sponges then?

She can't stand the protest, mainly because she doesn't like Ed McGregor, for some reason. She's jealous of my relationship with the protesters. She should accept that she isn't on their wavelength because she is a middle-aged woman who basically quite likes Tony Blair. She doesn't realise that traditional politics has nothing to say to my generation.

Mould – who is very thoughtful – says she has got to accept that I am old enough to have relationships that she has no jurisdiction over, or even involvement with. He is much more sophisticated than Darren and he also lives in a non-capitalistic and holistic manner in harmony with the planet.

Julie

I didn't want to go to Fran's dinner party. She'd only invited me because she wanted to meet Simon – she was probably only having the dinner in the first place because she wanted to find out how to get a table at Wave on a Friday night – and now I had to go alone. It would be all couples, reminding me that whatever it was that people did when they were having relationships, I hadn't got the hang of it.

As for being paired off with someone else, one more bad dating experience and I'd be ready to stick my head in the oven. I didn't dress up, so that whoever Fran had lined up (and knowing her, it would be another trendy person; I'd had enough of them) would not be under any misapprehension that I was interested. I had to change my T-shirt, because it was spattered with cooking oil, and then I thought I might as well put on the sexy cashmere top, but that was as big a concession as I was going to make. I would have put on another layer of mascara, but then Ginny arrived to babysit, and she was in tears.

'I think Gary's got another girlfriend,' she sniffed, as I let her in (she has keys, but she's lost them). 'I think it's that witch Debbie.'

'I thought she was called Sheryl?'

'No, this is the one before that.'

'He must have something, this Gary.'

'I hate her. How could she steal my boyfriend?'

I settled Ginny on the sofa with a cup of tea and the latest wedding pictures in *Hello!* and fervently hoped that Arthur wouldn't wake up. He is supposed to be growing up thinking of women as spirited and independent-minded individuals, not lachrymose gelatinous lumps. But by the time I'd calmed her down, it was too late for worrying any more about outfits or mascara – for anything, in fact, except getting in the car and hitting the accelerator.

Even so, it was nearly a quarter to nine when I pulled up outside Fran's five-storey stuccoed house near Portobello Road; I was more than half an hour late, and I was feeling hot, harassed and not at all like making conversation with some man who was so sad that he had to sit next to me.

Fran answered the door looking radiant in a simple but stunning full-length silver sheath. I instantly regretted my combat trousers.

'You didn't tell me it was posh,' I said crossly.

'Oh, come in.' She led the way into her yellow-striped sitting room, which runs the full length of the house, and which has been feng shui'd to be soothing and interior-designed to make the most of the light and the view over the garden from the big windows at the back. There was a bubble of noise in the room and I was aware of a flash of faces, but the first person I saw properly, sitting on one of Fran's lavender sofas, was Ed McGregor.

He looked up, seemed momentarily startled, and then, infuriatingly, he smiled. I was momentarily nonplussed: it was a proper, vigorous smile, as if he meant it; a smile to scorch the skin off you.

What was he up to now?

I flushed and sort of nodded in acknowledgement, although I was horrified. I wanted to spend an evening with Ed McGregor as much as I wanted to have my fingernails pulled out. And then I had a truly horrible thought – surely *he* wasn't the person Fran had lined up for me?

But he couldn't be, could he? She'd said she had someone she wanted me to *meet*, and she was aware that I already knew Ed McGregor. Even if not how well.

She introduced me to the other people in the room, who were called Paul, Sophie and Jamie. Sophie was an entertainment lawyer, mainly in the music business and, I suspected, had been originally invited to talk to Simon. Paul was her husband or boyfriend – I wasn't sure which, but they had a baby – and he ran an art gallery. Which left Jamie, who worked in Fran's agency and looked extremely young. He must be the one she had lined up for me, although he was probably only available because until now he'd been too young to get a girlfriend. Jamie was pale-skinned and fair-haired and somehow too tall for his body, with eyes undefined by very fair lashes, merging faintly into his freckly skin: the overall effect was of someone gangly and overgrown, like a bolted lettuce.

I followed Fran out to the kitchen, where she was collecting another bottle of wine and hissed: 'Why the hell did you invite him?'

'Jamie?'

'No! Ed McGregor!'

She looked puzzled. 'Why not?'

'We don't like each other.'

'Since when?'

'Since . . . I slept with him.'

'You *what*?' She crashed the bottle of wine down on to her stainless steel surface. '*When*?'

'The first time I met him. Well, the second. About eight weeks ago.'

'And you didn't tell *me*? All this fuss about Simon, who doesn't even *want* to have sex with you, and you somehow just fail to mention that you've actually *done* it with Ed McGregor . . . ?'

'It was a one-night stand. Er, afternoon.'

She wrestled with the cork, red-faced, saying aggressively: 'I thought he was going out with Annabel Wheatley.'

'Who?'

'Rhys Wheatley's daughter. You *know*, the left-wing lawyer.'

I didn't know. I said suspiciously: 'Does she call herself Nettle?'

'She might. She's one of those activists.'

'I know her,' I said wearily. 'There you are: he's a commitment-phobe – you said so yourself. They do that, don't they, men who can't commit? Sleep with other people to prove to themselves they still can? Is she coming tonight?'

'No, she couldn't. I suppose that's a relief, anyway . . . Honestly, Jools, I can't believe you didn't tell me! How long have we been friends?'

'I'm sorry.' I did feel guilty about it now. 'I hated it that I was so easy . . . and that I couldn't even *tell* it meant nothing . . . The thing is, Fran, I hate him. I'm ashamed of the whole episode. He patronises me. He patronises everyone in Langley. And then I wrote an article about him in the *Langley Advertiser* saying he was an egomaniac and a fake. And this week we had a row because some kid who's staying with his squatters nicked my purse.'

'That's terrible . . .'

'Yeah, well, he didn't think so. You should have told me he was coming.'

'You can't blame *me* for this particular fuck-up. This is what *happens* when you stop communicating with your friends. Anyway, I thought I did tell you . . . No, maybe I told him. I said you were bringing your new boyfriend. So that's something: he thinks you've got someone else.'

'That's why he smiled like that . . . ! He was pleased I hadn't managed to bring Simon. He was laughing at me!'

'Smiled like what?' Fran looked puzzled.

'You saw!'

'Jools, I didn't see anything. For someone who doesn't like him, you're curiously obsessed by him.' She picked up the bottle. 'Anyway, what do you think of Jamie?'

'He's OK.' I wanted to let her down gently. 'Very tall.'

She tossed the cork in the bin. 'Come on, let's go and eat. We've got to get through this evening somehow.'

I took my place at the table, carefully avoiding Ed's eyes.

By now, our session on and around the kitchen table had taken on a dream-like, parallel-universe quality. It was hard to believe it had really happened . . . except that his presence in Fran's house was still horribly inflammatory. The sight of him across the table made me feel hot inside, eaten up. It took me twenty minutes to pluck up courage to look at him, and, when I did, he was staring at me. He smiled again, and I immediately had to look away.

Bastard. Teasing, manipulative, game-playing bastard.

Over the first course, Paul asked Ed about some recent trip he'd taken to the Galapagos Islands for the BBC, about which, Ed was, admittedly, fairly interesting, although it is presumably a subject on which it is hard to be boring. This led to a more general conversation about holidays. I was the only person who hadn't been to St Lucia and the only one who had been to Center Parcs.

Then Jamie said to me, perhaps by way of cheering me up, 'Fran tells me you were at Greenham Common.'

'No, that's her *mother*,' Fran corrected him. 'You don't listen, Jamie.'

'Julie will have stayed behind with her home comforts,' Ed McGregor observed slyly.

'How fantastic, to have a Greenham woman for a mum,' Sophie said. 'My mum thought Margaret Thatcher was the best thing since ... well, Edward Heath.'

'I couldn't see it,' I admitted. 'I spent most of my childhood resenting the wages for housework banners in my bedroom and not being able to watch *Blue Peter* because the consciousness-raising groups were in the way.'

'So you didn't turn into a ball-breaking feminist harridan?' Jamie asked, it seemed to me in a quite unnecessarily flirtatious manner.

Ed McGregor made some kind of snorting, laughing noise. I steeled myself to glare at him.

'Quite the opposite,' Fran said helpfully; 'Jools has this terrible burden of guilt about not being feminist enough.'

This hardly seemed a very sexy way of describing me to my prospective new boyfriend: burdened with neurotic guilt. Besides, it's all very well for Fran: whenever she's trying to grapple with post-feminism, she's not doing it with leaking breasts or while pulling bits of fishfinger out of the sofa.

'And very exacting standards,' Ed McGregor said laconically.

I glanced at him dismissively – it was nothing to do with *him* what my mother had left me with – then did my best to ignore him for the rest of the meal. I also did my best to ignore Jamie, because I didn't want to give him the impression I was interested in him. Possibly I wasn't very good company.

At the end of the main course, I helped Fran clear

the plates. I had to lean over Ed McGregor's shoulder and, infuriatingly, he didn't shift aside to give me more space. Instead, he leaned towards me and whispered into my hair: 'I'm very grateful.'

I started.

'For not doing anything about Phil.'

I hesitated. I didn't want his gratitude. I didn't want him leaning anywhere near me. I hadn't done it for *him*. I still thought Phil should be punished.

But I bit my lip, nodded and carried on. In the kitchen, Fran was removing a lime cake from the fridge. I banged down the dirty plates on her stainless steel work surfaces.

'Everything all right?'

'Yes. No. Bloody Ed McGregor.'

'What's he done now?'

'Oh, I don't know.'

Her doorbell rang. She was still fiddling with her cake, so I went to answer it.

David stood on the front step. It had started to rain, and his Armani suit was clinging damply round his legs, the wide trousers sticking to his calves. Thick raindrops spattered on the pavement and made puddles in the tungsten sheen.

'David, come in! You're terribly late.' Though come to think of it, there hadn't been a place set for him.

He stepped inside. The whites of his eyes were shiny, his mouth was loose, and when he moved, a small cloud of whisky fumes moved with him.

'I assumed you weren't coming tonight,' I said; it was always touch and go with David, depending on Karen.

'I wasn't bloody invited,' he muttered thickly. He pushed past me rudely. 'Is *he* here?'

He lurched forward. I followed him anxiously down the hall and into the dining room. He was standing at the head of the table, feet apart, hair plastered to his head, looking menacingly around the table. In the candlelight, he looked like something out of a Victorian melodrama. A malign apparition.

He pointed menacingly at Ed McGregor. 'Is that him?'

'That's Ed McGregor,' I said, puzzled. Surely he knew that?

He swung round and pointed at Paul.

'David,' I tugged at his sleeve, 'let's find Fran. I think she's in the kitchen.'

Jamie stood up. 'If you're looking for me,' he began, 'you can't . . .'

He didn't get any further, because David swung his right arm and punched him in the face. Jamie reeled back, hand over his mouth. Blood seemed to be seeping slowly through his fingers.

David staggered sideways from the effort, crashing into me and knocking me off my feet. I hit my head on Fran's expensively painted red wall, muttered 'oomph!' and collapsed into a graceful heap on the floor.

David toppled on top of me; I pushed at him angrily, but he was a big man, and dead drunk. Then Ed McGregor was above us, pulling David off me, taking my hand, and helping me up on to a chair.

'Here, sit down,' he said to me, and dusted David down.

David slumped against Fran's sideboard, staring at

Jamie's blood drying on his knuckle with a puzzled expression. Puzzled and slightly frightened, like a child who's only just discovered how much impact he can have.

Fran appeared with the pudding and took in the devastation of her dinner party.

'What the *hell* is going on?' she demanded. 'How *dare* you come in here uninvited?'

'You're a little shit,' David told Jamie, who was hiding his face in a napkin, on which a red stain had appeared and was slowly enlarging.

'Don't you *dare* speak to him like that!' Fran snapped. 'Get out! I don't want you here.'

'I have to talk to you.'

'When you're sober. When I don't have people here.'

David stared at her resentfully. Whether it was this, or the groan that Jamie emitted from behind his bloody napkin, Fran suddenly slid her fingers between the cake and the plate, picked up the sponge, aimed, and threw it in David's face.

It caught him full-on. He shook his head in surprise, and the cake fell to the floor in three pieces, leaving fragments of sponge in his eyelashes and slivers of soft icing round his nose.

'Come on,' I offered, taking his elbow, 'I'll get you a cab.'

I hustled him out of the room.

'I'm sorry if I hurt you,' he said thickly in the hall. 'Fell over.'

'It's OK. Do you have a handkerchief?'

His face was flecked with crumbs; tiny lime gratings hung in his hair.

He found one and rubbed at his face. 'Karen needs me: that's what Fran's never been able to understand.'

'She seems to have understood it now. D'you want a cab?'

'No, I'll walk. It's only round the corner; might clear my head.'

'An umbrella?'

'Where would I have got an umbrella?' he asked irritably, and disappeared unsteadily into the night.

Back in the dining room, Jamie had lost a front tooth. Fran was sitting beside him, holding his hand and calling her exclusive dentist at his home on her mobile.

'He thinks he might be able to put the tooth back,' she announced, when she'd finished, 'but only if we go immediately.'

Fran, Jamie, and the dentist were all planning to drive to Harley Street, and meet for the attempted tooth-rescue in about half an hour.

'You have to hold it in there,' Fran instructed Jamie. 'Stay here as long as you like,' she added over her shoulder to the rest of us as she manoeuvred her lover out of the door. 'Have coffee. Jools knows where everything is. I'm sorry about the pudding.'

We all said it was fine about the pudding, and Paul and Sophie confessed that they'd eaten some of it anyway, when they were picking it up off the Persian carpet. 'We should go, actually,' they said awkwardly, 'rescue our babysitter.'

'I should rescue mine, too,' I said, although it was more likely to be my children who needed rescuing.

Ed smiled at me again. There was too much smiling altogether. It was completely untrustworthy. Not that I had time to give it much thought. I was too busy being furious with Fran.

Ben

The flowers weren't from Dad. They are really ugly and I hope they soon die.

I wonder if there is anything you can put in flowers to *make* them die?

How can Simon be keen on Mum without even meeting her children? We're part of it – you can't have her without also getting Arthur's runny noses and Kate's hormones. He might want *her*, but I bet he doesn't want us.

I've found out that we are going to be at Dad's on my birthday. Or rather, Dad is taking us away to Robbie Wade's house. Robbie Wade is the lead singer in Sump. We have never met him.

I don't mind being with Dad, because he is my parent, but sometimes it is pretty boring at the flat. I can't go rollerblading, because I don't know the area, and there are no other kids around, and I don't have my Lego or my railway. We still haven't been to the Trocadero, even though it is close. It's where I was really hoping to go for my birthday. There's an Imax cinema there, and the Pepsi Max Drop.

Still, going to Robbie Wade's might be better than having my birthday at the flat, I suppose, because I couldn't have a party there in case someone spilt Coke or pizza on the white sofas. Dad and Emma don't have a lot of furniture, but what they've got cost a fortune and it's all white.

Maybe it will be different in California with skate-boarding and softball and other things American kids do, but if nothing happens like in Clerkenwell and Dad and Emma still don't get up till lunchtime, I am not sure I want to go.

The other thing that is worrying me about my birthday is what is going to happen about my presents. Dad won't know where to buy things (I don't think he has bought me a birthday present in his life) but I am not sure Mum can afford a Nintendo 64, which is what I really want.

Darren came round tonight to help me with my maths. I bumped into him on the way home from school last Wednesday and we organised it but then I forgot! He was on the doorstep when I got home but it didn't make that much difference: we both had to wait to get in the house because Ginny was late. When Mum got in from work she explained to him about my dyspraxic short-term memory problems, but I don't think she was very pleased. She knew the fact he was there for the second time in a week would cause problems with Kate.

Kate was late – she'd been to the squats and she's still barely speaking to Mum – and when she saw Darren, she said: 'Oh, hi, it's you,' in a really offhand way, as if it was out of order for him to be living in Langley, let alone visiting the neighbours. So obviously they didn't have sex at the all-night party. Then she looked at the shopping Mum was unpacking and said: 'I suppose you used the car to get that?' and Mum said maybe Kate could get a week's shopping for a family of four on a bicycle?

Julie

On Sunday morning, Fran called to apologise and give me the good news that her dentist had managed to save Jamie's tooth. On Monday evening, she turned up at the house, looking sheepish, with a box of chocolates.

I was still sulking. 'I can't believe you didn't tell me.'

'I tried,' she said, feeding fragments of biscuit to Arthur as if he was a *pet*. He's not supposed to have biscuits once he's had his tea and bath and he's in his pyjamas, but he'd asked, and she'd gone straight to the biscuit tin and got one out as if it was her kitchen and they were her Hobnobs! – and of course the children think she's fabulous and can't see why they shouldn't be indulged like this all the time.

'When?'

'Lots of times. I kept trying to tell you, but something always got in the way. Besides, you're hardly in a position to complain about secretiveness.'

'Oh, so it's my fault, for being so self-absorbed?'

'No – like I say, I did try to tell you, but things kept happening: Ben was mugged for his skateboard, and then he was dyspraxic, and then there was Simon, and Kate hanging around with the protesters, and Richard and the divorce . . .'

I could see that it might perhaps have been Richard's fault: his relationship with Emma was a cancer, a rogue cell that infected all the other relationships it touched with its own diseased, self-regarding way of looking at things.

'. . . And finally, of course, Ed McGregor.'

I poured Fran a glass of wine and put it in front of her. Then I sat down across the table. 'What's happened to us?'

Until now, I thought I knew everything about Fran. I've *always* known about David – and not just that he existed, but precisely how Fran felt about him. At any point in the relationship I could have told you exactly how guilty she felt about having an affair with a married man, even one who claims his wife hates him and is mad anyway.

'Nothing's happened. Nothing serious. It's been a difficult few months. And you've got three children.'

That was it, then. No more sensible conversations for me.

I poured another glass of wine and instructed her to tell me everything.

It turned out that she and Jamie had fallen in love while they were working together on the Eaty Sweeties account; specifically, while they were in the process of launching the new pink Eaty Sweetie.

'I was crazy about him. I should never have hired him; it was unethical, I suppose, but I didn't admit to myself how attracted I was. Still, men do that all the time, don't they, hire people they fancy . . . ? Anyway, I didn't know what to do about it because he was the account director and I was the managing director, obviously, and I had no idea what he felt about me and I didn't want a lawsuit for sexual harassment, but then we both kept staying late and one of us would somehow always send the account manager home, and then eventually, about six weeks after he arrived, we got into a bit of a tangle when we were putting some transparencies on a light box . . .'

'Sounds romantic . . .'

'It was. He's great, honestly – I could tell you didn't take to him immediately . . .'

'That's not true!'

'You seemed a bit distant.'

'I was probably anxious. You know, about Ed.'

'Anyway, he's very sweet and incredibly enthusiastic in bed. I love that boyishness in him.'

I could see that; she'd taken charge very naturally over the broken tooth episode.

'So how long has it been going on?'

'A month. He's very young, though. Twenty-seven.'

I tried to remember exactly *how* unpleasant I'd been about people in their twenties.

She knocked back her wine. 'He's made it pretty plain he doesn't want to hear anything about biological clocks.'

He sounded exactly what she needed.

In retrospect, as I said when Mel dropped in the

following day, I could see that Fran had been getting slimmer and sleeker for weeks; 'more *refulgent*, somehow; more lit-from-within. But she's all gloss and polish even at the worst of times, when she's got flu or she's depressed, so I didn't notice.'

'I didn't notice, either, and you had a lot on your mind. You should stop blaming yourself.'

'She's my oldest friend. I knew about her plans to set up BCMI before two of her *partners* knew, for God's sake . . . What's gone wrong with me, that I've become so impossible to confide in? I'm so fantastically self-obsessed that I actually thought she'd invited Jamie for *me*.'

'Whereas you were really paired off with Ed McGregor.'

'Oh, very funny. He's going out with Nettle; Fran knows all about it. She's really called Annabel, and she's the daughter of some right-on lawyer.'

'So why is she such a snob?'

'I don't know. The point is, she was bred to be with someone like Ed. Someone who appears to be all green and . . . *democratic*, but goes round behaving as if he has droit du seigneur over any woman he happens to come across.'

'He hasn't slept with anyone else in Langley.'

'He hasn't slept with me,' I reminded her tartly. 'Anyway, how do you know?'

'He hasn't.' She waved her hand dismissively. 'No wonder he sprang away from her when you went in with Phil. If you got jealous and took it into your head to behave badly, you could cause him a lot of trouble.'

'I doubt he respects me *or* her enough to care.'

Mel lifted Rose on to her knee. 'What happened at the end of the evening?'

'I came back here. I expect Ed went back to his comfortable home in Chelsea, and Nettle.'

'Jools, are you really over him?'

'There's nothing to be over,' I retorted sharply. 'My only feeling is indignation that he's done nothing about Phil stealing my purse.'

'What can he do?'

I sighed through my teeth. 'How did we get on to talking about Ed McGregor anyway? We were supposed to be discussing why I've become such a terrible friend to Fran. Honestly, sometimes since Richard left, I feel *everything's* falling apart. Kate hates me . . .'

'No, she doesn't.'

'She spends an awful lot of time hiding from me in her room.'

'She's fourteen.'

'What must she think of me? No husband, an appallingly paid job . . .'

'Adolescents aren't genetically adapted to live alongside their parents. Until a couple of hundred years ago, you'd have had a 50 per cent chance of being dead by now.'

'She'd have preferred that.'

Mel raised her eyes to the ceiling.

'At least if we had lived a hundred years ago, she might have seen me doing something productive. Working alongside her in the fields . . . As it is, I don't feel I have much connection with her. She lives in a different world from me; I can't be always peering over her shoulder and telling her not to sleep with vile and stupid boys. I'm not *there*, in the places where the drugs and stupid boys are. And then there's Ben . . .'

'How was the dyspraxia woman?'

'OK. She said there were lots of different types of intelligence.' I frowned, remembering, ticking them off on my fingers: 'Linguistic, mathematical-logical, spatial, bodily-kinaesthetic, emotional . . . oh, naturalistic – that's about liking flowers, I think – and existential. The only trouble is, she didn't say which of them Ben had, and, thinking about it, I can't see that he has any of them.'

'What's existential?'

'The ability to think about the Big Things. Meaning of Life, all that stuff.'

'He's got that one, I bet. And emotional – he's got that as well. And he quite likes flowers, doesn't he?'

'But how will anyone ever know, if he hasn't got any of the others?'

'Can me and Darren have a drink?' Ben asked, coming into the kitchen and throwing open the fridge door so violently that orange juice sloshed out of the carton on to the floor.

Mel asked him about the lesson.

'She said people have all these different corridors in their brains,' Ben said, pouring orange juice into two glasses and over the work surface. 'For most people, when they get a maths question, their maths corridor lights up. But with people with dyslexia or dyspraxia, all their corridors light up, so they get in a muddle. But sometimes they get more imaginative answers, because they think about things in different ways.'

This was the most cogent thing I've ever heard Ben say.

'He's very charming. You should be proud of him,' Mel remarked, when he'd gone back upstairs to Darren and his maths.

And I am, I suppose. But he's about to embark on a period of his life when boys get worse exam results than girls, commit more crimes, get more depressed and suicidal – and all of this with a father, a role model, who can't make up his mind whether he's a suburban schoolteacher or a metropolitan minor celeb.

Ben

Kate's become a vegetarian. She's taken down all her Leonardo DiCaprio pictures and put up posters of whales and factories. I don't think factories like the ones in her pictures exist any more, except in television programmes about Victorian times. Nowadays factories belong to Japanese car companies and they are made of bright blue corrugated metal in the middle of fields.

I think she has got mad cow disease.

It would be really ironic if she had gone vegetarian too late.

She had fishfingers last night at Dad's even though Mum stopped them after there was a chemicals scare. They're the only thing Dad can cook properly apart from pork chops (and they are often red in the middle). She is not supposed to be eating fish, even though it is allowed by some vegetarians, and she made me promise not to tell Mould. I have never even met Mould.

She didn't slam the door and run out of the room, though, which she would have done if Mum had served some food she didn't approve of. (Dad has no doors to slam in his flat anyway.) Kate feels sorry for Dad, but I think he ought to buy a copy of Delia Smith.

When she'd gone to do her homework, I told Dad that Mum had a new boyfriend called Simon and he sends her flowers.

I am hoping this will make him jealous and realise he has made a terrible mistake and come back to us.

He didn't give much away. I expect it is difficult for him to absorb such shocking information.

Kate

Last night at the squat Mould grabbed hold of my hand as I was walking past the coal bunker and dragged me up against the wall and started pulling, without speaking or anything.

Rachel said he should have asked permission – men shouldn't simply grab – but she is jealous. Mould is older than the boys she has been out with and she doesn't understand how the more sophisticated type operates.

When I told Mum I was becoming a vegetarian, she raised her eyes to the ceiling and said that *that* would tax Dad's ingenuity. I should never have told her about the weekend when we sent out for a curry three nights in a row. Anyway, you can get vegetarian curries. I believe they are quite common in some areas of Indian cuisine.

I would like to become a vegan, like Mould, but that would tax *her* ingenuity, so I'm not going to. Actually, I don't really know what it is.

I am never going to get married. It turns you into

someone like Mum – bitter, and living in Langley. Mould says my parents split up because of the cult of the relationship. He says if we lived more communally (he says with a more relaxed attitude to sexual partners, though I am not sure about this) we wouldn't have so much trouble. It's only because society requires marriage for stability that we are made to feel it's such a brilliant thing.

As a result, little girls are brainwashed into thinking their lives will be transformed if they walk up the aisle in a white dress. Mould says it is called false consciousness. He says romance is a cultural construct designed to serve the needs of the status quo and that we would be better off acknowledging our desires frankly. I agree. I am going to reject bourgeois constraints, hopefully with Mould. We can have loads of fantastic sex and talk about green politics and go off together to plough up fields of genetically modified crops.

Julie

Ben chomped absently on a spoonful of Golden Grahams. 'Can I get my hair dyed?'

I was buttering toast for Arthur. Kate was sorting fussily through the un-ironed washing, trying to find something to wear to the squats when she goes there after school – she's taken to changing out of her uniform – and grumbling about being the only girl in her class who doesn't have a Map T-shirt.

I was trying to catch an item on the *Today* programme about paedophiles targeting single mothers and wondering if perhaps *this* explained Simon?

'No.'

'Why not?'

'Your hair's a perfectly nice colour as it is.' His hair is blond. It is exactly the colour I wish my hair was; it is exactly the colour my hair used to be, before it became blond sprinkled with springy grey and I had to start dyeing it.

'Can I get pink streaks?'

'No.'

'Mum, you can't just say no! You have to give a reason.'

'It would look horrible.'

'That's because you're stuck in the sixties.'

'Ben, how many times, I was barely born in the sixties,' I snapped, not quite truthfully. 'It's not my era.'

I turned up the radio, trying to hear John Humphrys, but Kate was elbowing me out of the way because I wasn't being quick enough with her second cup of tea, and Ben was muttering that because I have no fashion sense, he has to go to school looking like a freak.

'Ben,' I said wearily, 'it's very expensive to dye your hair.'

'I'll pay.'

'You don't have that sort of money. It'd cost – I don't know – fifty pounds.'

'If human beings had to pay for the services they receive free from nature,' Kate announced to no one in particular, 'such as pollination, water purification and, um, other things, it would cost \$2.9 billion annually.'

'I'll go without pocket money for the rest of the year. Or I could do it myself.'

'Anyway, it looks common.' I couldn't believe I was saying this. They do this deliberately, children, back you into a reactionary corner and turn you into a parodic parent.

I took Arthur upstairs to change him out of his pyjamas. Ten minutes later, when we came down, Ben was sitting open-mouthed on the floor in front of Children's BBC, being shouted at by hyperactive presenters (no wonder he has learning difficulties) and dizzied by cartoons.

'Please, Ben, could you get dressed? I've got a meeting after I've dropped you at school.' I was supposed to be writing a feature about the Langley Barber's Shop Quartet. They'd all taken time off work specially.

Ben ambled off disconsolately, muttering something about maybe hair mascara. Five minutes later, when I went up to check on his progress, he was stark naked and gyrating to 'I Will Survive' on his ghetto blaster.

So we were late.

'Have you thought about what you want to do for your birthday?' I asked once we were in the car. I was being conciliatory, because I regretted shouting at him for not having done his teeth. (He is dyspraxic, practically disabled; I am supposed to *help* him, not yell.) 'I wondered if you'd like some friends over and we could go out for dinner?'

'He can't,' said Kate, who was cadging a lift. 'We'll be away.'

'Away? Where?'

'At a party. At Robbie Wade's house in Sussex.'

'On Ben's birthday?'

Kate shrugged. 'That's when the party is.'

Richard was taking Ben out of reach on his birthday. How could he? My child. My Ben. He wouldn't be here on his birthday. He'd be away for the first time since the midwife laid him on my body, warm and sucky and soft, a little kicking peach. Tears prickled at the back of my eyes. I swallowed hard. We wouldn't be together on his birthday.

I was lucky not to drive into a bollard.

'Is this an actual arrangement, or a fantasy one, like Los Angeles in the summer and Mauritius at

Christmas?' I asked nastily, to cover the fact that I had nearly caused a major pile-up in the High Street by crying.

'I don't know what you mean,' Kate said coldly. 'We only didn't go to Mauritius last Christmas because of Emma's work. And I seem to remember that you kicked up a fuss. We still might go this year. And there's no reason to suppose that we won't go to Los Angeles. You're just being vile because you resent Dad.'

'No, I think he should keep me informed, especially if he intends to take Ben away on his birthday.'

''S'all right,' mumbled Ben. 'Really, I don't mind.'

'And how do you think dragging us into your fights makes us feel?' Kate demanded aggressively. 'If you want to have a go at Dad, then do it – have it out between you – but I don't want to get involved. You've done enough damage already!'

And with this – we were stuck in a traffic jam – she got out of the car, slammed the door, and stalked off into the crowd of commuters heading towards the station. I looked after her – admiring, in spite of myself, her long legs, her swinging hair, and her coltish body.

I did the Barber's Shop Quartet and arrived at work at eleven o'clock. It was break-time at Langley Grammar School for Boys, so I called Richard.

'Is it true you're going away for Ben's birthday?'

'We've been invited to Robbie Wade's for the weekend.'

'So I won't see him.'

'It is my weekend.'

'But it's his *birthday*. I assumed I'd have a few hours with him on Sunday. You might at least have told me.'

'I was going to.'

'When? You never speak to me! How can you tell me, if you never communicate?'

'Julie, I'm in the staff room. You can shout all you want, but it's not going to help. Anyway, I thought Kate had told you.'

'Why should she have to be the go-between?' I shouted louder. 'And it's right in the middle of her exams. She has physics on the Monday. It's her worst subject.'

'I know that.' He meant he knew it was her worst subject, not that he'd interested himself in her exam timetable.

'And I planned to take some of Ben's friends out for dinner. He doesn't *have* many . . . you know how difficult he finds it with other boys; I thought it would be a good excuse to invite some of the class.'

'I asked him if he minded going away and he said no. And it's quite a good birthday treat, meeting Robbie Wade.'

'Is it? And have you thought about presents?'

'No, not yet. What about you?'

'I want to get him a Nintendo 64.'

'Oh,' said Richard, 'that's a bit expensive.'

'He's right that it's quite exciting for Ben to meet Robbie Wade,' Tony pointed out after I'd slammed down the phone and complained bitterly for twenty minutes. 'And it's not as if it's Kate's GCSE year. It's

289

only her end-of-year exams, right? And she doesn't *need* to work; she always comes in the top three.'

'She's done much less work this term. She's always at the squats. People will think she's failing because her parents have split up.'

'No one will think anything.'

'The point is, he didn't *tell* me. He thinks if he ignores me I'll just disappear. He only ever calls when he wants to change an arrangement to suit him better. He never discusses how the children are doing at school, or Ben's difficulties . . . I don't think he even *knows* how few friends he has.'

'At least he sees them. It's better than a lot of men in his position.'

'And his relationship with Ben is entirely perfunctory. Ben sits in front of the television and gets fed, then has to fit in with whatever's going on with the adults. If you can call them that. Richard never takes him swimming, or to the cinema, or museums, or football, or anything. They certainly don't *talk*. He had the cheek to say Ben had told him he didn't mind going away for his birthday. Well, *obviously* he didn't mind – he's terrified of losing the thin thread of relationship he has with him. We all are. That's how he gets away with this sex-addled idiocy.'

'If he never had much in common with Ben, it's unreasonable to expect them to have developed some intense affinity simply because you two have split up.'

'It matters more now. Ben needs attention, and what he gets from his father is down-time. Richard doesn't even know how to talk to *me* any more. When he comes to collect the children he stands halfway down the garden path and avoids my eyes. Ben was rude to me the other day – he gets distressed by the handover – and did Richard tell him not to speak to his mother like that? No. Absolutely not. He got pissed off with me for making an issue of it and holding up their getaway.'

'He's terrified of confrontation.'

'Like his father . . .'

'He's morally gelatinous,' Tony said (though he barely knows him). 'He's aware that if he gets into a proper conversation with you, he'll have to confront the fact that he's tried hiding behind being a revolution-ary and a suburban throw-back, and it didn't work, so now he's hiding behind a cheap fantasy of fame and sex.'

This is comfort of a kind, I suppose.

Kate

I've got a love-bite! It's not huge – about the size of a two-pence piece – so if Mum sees it she might just think I have gone a bit blotchy with my period or something. I can't believe she knows about love-bites. Still, in case she does, I've borrowed one of her scarves. I look like Charlotte Ovenden's mum, who wears cravat things inside her shirts. Mum says Charlotte's mum is a bit Sloaney, or wishes she was. It certainly can't be that she has a lot of love-bites; she's built like a Jeep.

I don't know why love-bites are embarrassing, because they don't make you pregnant or give you diseases and I got mine in the course of a normal heterosexual relationship, but they are.

I'm hoping Mum will think scarves are suddenly hip. She wouldn't know either way: when she thinks hip, she thinks replacement.

I wonder if she knew when she was my age that she'd end up knowing people like Mrs Ovenden? I can't believe she *planned* to end up in Langley, being friends with the Sharps and worrying about mortgages and pensions.

She started out as an actress, so she could have ended up in California or New York. She must have had a self-destructive streak.

I called Dad this evening, partly to tell him about my A-star in chemistry, and partly to see if I could go over there. I thought if he saw the love-bite he might be more understanding because he probably has them himself these days. But he was out getting the shopping! When he lived here, I don't think he knew where the supermarket was. Perhaps that's why he left, because Mum wouldn't let him be a new man.

I hope he doesn't encourage Emma to have a baby so he can start changing the nappies he didn't change with us. He would be better putting his energy, and of course money, into the children he already has.

Come to think of it, a baby is unlikely. He's even borrowing Ginny when we go to Robbie Wade's because he doesn't want to be worried about putting Arthur to bed when he's meant to be partying with Emma. What he doesn't realise is that Ginny will be so starstruck by being at a pop star's house (which is pathetic, because famous people are just like everyone else, even down to wanting to be around famous people) that she will be even more incompetent than usual.

Julie

Kate has a love-bite. She thinks I don't know, but why else would she have stolen a scarf from my dressing-table drawer? Especially one so hideous that even I wouldn't wear it.

I am pretending I don't mind her taking my things without asking, or perhaps that I haven't noticed, and she's pretending there's nothing abnormal about my silence, so that neither of us has to confront the livid weal on her neck or the fact that she's a trollop.

It's like in our parents' generation, when they knew we were sleeping with our boyfriends but thought if they gave us separate bedrooms they didn't have to acknowledge it and, perhaps even, in some way, that it wasn't really happening. I never thought I'd get like this.

She's not speaking to me this afternoon anyway, partly because Darren's here, partly because I took the car to Sainsbury's again. In a way, I'm quite relieved, because it means fewer opportunities for horrible Freudian slip love-bite situations.

She's not speaking to Darren either (he keeps coming round to help Ben with his maths; I hope Ben recognises this is not wholly altruistic) so I don't think *he* can have given her the love-bite. (This would be the sensible thing, of course – to stop speaking to the person who'd given you the contusion – but this kind of logic is beyond Kate.) So I suppose we have to blame one of the protesters, and my guess would be Mould. She's mentioned him several times, in a sort of oracular way, and he'd appeal to her. For a start, he has rendered a perfectly pleasant, if not handsome, face ridiculous by sticking metal through his left eyebrow and lower lip. And he's a zealot: if he'd been born in Iran, he'd have been a revolutionary guard, zipping round on his scooter spray-painting the arms of anyone who wears a T-shirt.

I was sitting at the kitchen table feeling weary, watching Arthur unpack years of Christmas presents from Richard from the saucepan cupboard, and thinking that I have one child who has difficulty stringing his thoughts together sufficiently to speak, and another who doesn't want to anyway, when the doorbell rang. Kate hurled herself down the stairs and at the front door in case it was one of her friends, needing protection from her family.

But it was Mel again, on her way back from the childminder's with Rose.

'Has Kate got a love-bite?' she asked, coming into the kitchen and depositing Rose among the pans with Arthur, where they started a competition for who could make the most noise with a lid.

'I don't know why you're looking so disapproving,'

I answered defensively. '*I* can't control her. I wish I'd been born a hundred and fifty years ago.'

'Not that stuff about working in the fields again?'

'Pre-bloody-Freud. I wish my children could have just been rude, or a bit simple, or gone off the rails, and it wouldn't all have been because I fucked them up.'

'Some American woman now claims that your mum and dad don't fuck you up nearly as much as your friends.'

'Great. So now we've got to worry that they only make suitable friends. That's not much of a consolation, frankly, given that Kate's new best friend is someone who's dropped out of school, lives in a tree and despises her parents even more than she does.'

'I had loads of love-bites at her age,' Mel admitted. 'It's because I was fat.'

I frowned, trying to work this out. Something to do with the physiology of her subcutaneous deposits? So much flesh she couldn't keep it out of the way of people's mouths?

'I was unhappy,' she explained, settling herself at the kitchen table. 'Love-bites were a way of announcing that I was attractive and did have a social life, even if it was with Andy Walsh the Human Zit. So I think you should look on the bright side. It's when they go you need to worry.'

'I feel so powerless, as if I've already either succeeded or failed . . . After they had the drugs talk at school, she told me she already knew all that stuff.'

'They get lessons about it in infants now.'

'I wanted to warn her to make sure there was always

someone there to help her if things went wrong. But that's like condoning it.'

'You don't seriously think she's doing drugs?'

'Oh, I don't know. Mould looks completely out of it most of the time. And I barely recognise her lately, with the fluorescent streaks in her hair and fake nerdy glasses and this awful nose thing. I mean, she's so beautiful, why does she want to mess herself about?'

Mel shrugged.

'And then, if my job's more or less finished by the time they're fourteen, I need all the time with Ben I can get. I don't need him to be away at crucial times, like on his birthday.'

'The last time I was here,' Mel said patiently, 'we agreed that Ben's making progress. He *has* had a rough year.'

The doorbell was ringing again. Kate thundered down the stairs and threw herself at the front door.

'It's Grandma June,' she announced, coming into the kitchen and adding in a loud stage whisper: 'must be some kind of day-release scheme.'

I got up and welcomed Richard's mother noisily, in case she heard this; introduced her to Mel, and offered her a cup of tea.

'Please!' she gasped, fanning her hand in front of her face. 'What a day! First of all I went to Tesco's and they didn't have any strawberries, then I had to go to the wool shop, and they didn't have the wool that I'd ordered, despite saying they would, so I had a row with the woman in there, then I had to pick up some paint that Alf's ordered, because we're doing up the bathroom, then I had to visit Mrs Duncan in hospital . . .'

She looked around for somewhere to sit, though there was only the bench at the kitchen table. In the end, she perched reluctantly on the edge of it – but facing away from the table, as if to imply that it was inadequate, possible to sit on only with some discomfort. Mel had to lift her legs and swing them round, so that the two of them weren't facing in opposite directions.

June announced: 'I've brought Ben's present.'

'Oh, that's incredibly good . . . You didn't have to.'

'Well, he's not going to be here on his birthday, is he?'

'No.'

June caught sight of the milk bottle on the table, got hold of it, stood up and started opening cupboard doors. I handed her a jug silently. She decanted some milk, then replaced the offending bottle in the fridge.

'It'll be funny for you, not having him here.'

'Yes.'

'Still, you'll be able to get some tidying done.'

Mel said: 'Julie's coming to us for lunch on Sunday.'

'Yes, well, the main thing is to keep busy.'

I handed June her tea, thinking that this would be her epitaph: busy, busy, busy. Didn't matter what you were doing; in fact, the less you were doing the better: achieving something might stop you from being really busy. I had a vision of June as a person around whom the world swirled like dust motes while she effortfully swiped at them, arms windmilling pointlessly. Hustled, harassed, occupied – that was what she most wanted to be. She was like Richard in that respect: no sitting in a room and thinking for them. Too risky.

They were weird, these Ellisons. It wasn't that they had no inner life, more that they were scared of finding out they had too much. If June ever stopped crocheting, running errands, and fretting about shopkeepers' inability to meet her standards for the supply of goods or her neighbours' failure to follow her own high principles in the matter of not hanging out washing on a Sunday, she might have to admit that other people have a point of view. And (Tony was right) if Richard ever stopped striving towards some unrealistic idea of himself, he might have to *feel* something.

'Anyway, I've got to get to the post office before it closes, so is he around?'

I called Ben, who arrived with Darren and his geography project.

'Hi, Grandma, would you like to look at my drawings of Langley Wood?'

'I'd love to, darling – really love to – but I'm in a bit of a rush because I got held up earlier, so I'll just run out to the car and get your present.'

She came back in a minute later with a long, fin-shaped package wrapped in red and gold paper.

'Can I open it now, while Darren's here?' Ben enquired hopefully.

'It's up to your mother.'

I said I thought June should decide.

'Why not? After all' – her mouth set in a little line – 'neither of us is going to see him opening things on his actual birthday.'

Ben ripped off the paper and flushed brilliantly. 'It's a skateboard.'

'Wicked.' Darren inspected the underside. 'Hey, Ben, it's a really cool one.'

'I heard you lost your other one,' June said, looking approvingly at Darren. 'You'd better not lose this.'

'He won't,' Darren said. 'He can come skateboarding with me.'

Ben's eyes widened. 'Really?'

'Sure. Any time.'

Ben flung his arms round June and hugged her. She squeezed him back and, when she let go, her eyes were misty and she had to swallow and adopt an expression of false brightness.

Ben didn't notice; he was already dragging Darren towards the front door.

June picked up her jacket and handbag.

'The skateboard's fantastic,' I said.

'Yes, well, thanks for the tea, but I can't sit around here all day.' She kissed me with brisk efficiency and waved briefly at Mel. 'Got to get on.'

Kate

It's Ben's birthday. I got him a *Horrible Histories* book and a *Hot Hits* CD compilation. I didn't know when to give it to him, because in the past we've always given presents on Mum and Dad's bed before breakfast, but Dad and Emma needed to sleep after not getting to bed until five o'clock in the morning because of the party.

In the end I gave it to him in Robbie Wade's kitchen when we were making toast. We were the only people up and I was worried that if I waited for the others, his birthday might not get started until late afternoon.

In fact, Dad and Emma got up around lunchtime. Emma gave Ben a signed photograph of the cast of *EastEnders*, including herself, and Dad got him a book about football. Ben isn't sure whether he really likes football, and Dad certainly doesn't, although I think he wishes he did.

Still, Mum was brilliant and gave him a Nintendo 64, which was what he most wanted. She called early in the morning and left a birthday message on the answering machine, but Robbie didn't get up to listen to his messages until two o'clock.

I bet Mum is really missing Ben.

When Robbie did hear the message, he was cross with Dad for not telling everyone beforehand that it was Ben's birthday. He did it in a jokey way, but I think he was really annoyed because he hadn't got Ben a card or a present or anything. He made Ben ring Mum back straight away, but she'd already gone out to lunch.

Robbie fixed up the Nintendo 64 on his television and played it with Ben. In the end the birthday was quite successful, because we had a Diddy Kong Racing tournament and everyone was useless at it except Ben, who'd played the game before, so he won. Robbie secretly got his cook to make a birthday cake in a hurry and she managed to find candles from somewhere, so before we got in the car to come home, we sang 'Happy Birthday'.

I don't really think I'd like to have my birthday at someone else's house, although Ben doesn't seem to have minded, perhaps because he is dyspraxic. It's a bit like being autistic: he's not properly in touch with the world.

Robbie has got a pretty amazing house, with eleven bedrooms and a room just for snooker. Outside, there's a swimming pool, which he heated up to eighty-eight degrees for the party so people could swim even though it wasn't a hot night; and there are two tennis courts and a croquet lawn. But it was decorated by an interior designer and it's full of chintz sofas and velvety curtains, so it looks a bit like the Sharps' house, except bigger.

There were lots of other people staying. We got to meet them round the pool yesterday afternoon. (We couldn't swim today – which would have improved Ben's birthday – because it didn't stop raining.) There was Mac, Tone and Snoddy, from Robbie's band Sump, plus Tone's girlfriend Michaela; the model Jo Spitzeri, who doesn't seem that beautiful in real life – she looks like a stork because her legs are too long; her boyfriend Hew; and Jeff Speed, who plays Emma's brother in *EastEnders* and is always flirting with Emma. She says there's nothing in it, because they're brother and sister.

I am not sure where we fit in. No one else has kids. They have interesting pasts instead, which they are all recovering from. Everyone except us lot has spent time drying out or recovering from drugs or exhaustion. I expect Emma will do this soon.

Dad said it was all right for us kids to be there because although Robbie used to have a drugs problem he has successfully kicked it. He doesn't have an addiction any more and goes to therapy four times a week instead. His party was partly to celebrate having been off cocaine and vodka for a year.

I'm not convinced that cocaine can be as bad for you as they say at school. It seems to leave you fitter than having kids. Dad played Mac, the drummer from Sump, at tennis yesterday, and Mac just hit the ball from one side of the court to the other and kept Dad running about until he was exhausted (which didn't take long). Dad claimed afterwards that he lost because Ginny brought Arthur to watch (Ginny fancies Mac, who is the ugliest member of Sump) and Arthur kept speaking to Dad and distracting him. But I think Dad was lucky only to lose in straight sets and not have a heart attack.

Before the party started all the people who were staying plus a few special guests (including Gordon Rohmer, who's in the government, and his wife) had a posh dinner. Ben and I were invited. I sat next to Tone and talked to him about traffic problems, but I'm not sure whether he understood. He agreed that the congestion in London was appalling and then said it was putting him off getting a new Ferrari. On the other side, I had Jo Spitzeri, who's getting married on a beach in the Caribbean next month with exclusive pictures in *OK!* I asked her if she thought romance was a cultural construct but she looked a bit blank.

I wanted to wear jeans and a T-shirt, but Emma said I looked scruffy and should wear another one of her dresses. (I don't know why: she sulked for two weeks after I ruined the other one and Dad had to buy her two new outfits from Browns in South Molton Street before she'd speak nicely to me again. I suppose in reality she paid for the new clothes, because she's the one who's got the money, but she *pretended* Dad had bought them. She likes being made a fuss of in that way. I don't think this is very feminist. I can't imagine Mould buying me a dress.)

The dress Emma insisted on lending me was lemon, which is not my colour. It was also strappy, which meant I couldn't wear a bra. It was obvious I am flat-chested. I looked about ten. I wondered if she'd done it deliberately.

The other drawback was that you could see the love

bite, which has faded a lot, but still looks like a love bite. I tried a scarf with it, but it looked stupid, so I used spot concealer, extra-thick foundation and three layers of powder, but you could still see a blotchy red patch. I could tell from the start that it was going to be a horrible party.

No one spoke to me. I had to talk to Ben. We wandered around watching the guests arrive and spotting people off the television (except Ben didn't know anyone's name and he wasn't terribly good at faces either). We had a swim and then Ben drank three glasses of champagne when no one was looking and started skidding about in his socks on the dance floor with wet hair until Dad found him and sent him to bed.

I kept hoping someone would ask me to dance, but they didn't, not even Dad, so in the end I took up Ginny's offer of twenty quid to go and sit in Arthur's room while she had a look at the party. She was supposed to come back after two hours so I could go to bed, but I waited three hours, and then I fell asleep on her bed in Arthur's room. When I woke up, Arthur was kneeling on my pillow and the television was still on, showing *Breakfast with Frost*.

I thought Ginny must have gone to our room to avoid waking me up, but Ben said no one had slept in my bed all night.

I hope Mum has been OK today. She really loves Ben. She really loves all of us, but Ben is vulnerable.

Julie

It is my son's birthday and I'm not with him. What's worse, he's having a brilliant time with a load of people who are too busy or too famous to answer their phone. And I am loading the washing machine and making cups of coffee for something to do.

It's been raining all day – hard and remorseless, out of a solid grey sky. You'd never know it was June. There are puddles on the patio, piles of damp rose petals on the path and heaps of wet washing in the kitchen. The delphiniums have fallen over and the peonies look defeated.

My poor Ben. Sweet-natured, trusting, hapless Ben, trailing along so cluelessly. How is it possible to be so lovely – so warm and open and endearing – and yet to find it so hard to make friends? I feel anxious, almost desperate on his behalf, as if I have to make up for all the relationships, all the casual affection he doesn't have.

I went to Mel's for lunch, which was fine except that I missed Ben's call, and when I rang back he'd already left to drive to London.

'Ben's fine,' Robbie Wade said reassuringly, when I finally got through to the house. 'He's just left. But he loved the Nintendo: we played it all afternoon. He missed you a lot, I think, but he had a good day.'

I instantly made up my mind to buy all of Sump's records, singles *and* albums. But the fact that Robbie Wade was kind didn't alter the awfulness of knowing that my son and I spent his birthday failing to make contact with one another.

Besides, how could Robbie Wade know what Ben was feeling? He hides his unhappiness, tries his best to appear cheerful, because he doubts he'll ever really *be* cheerful. If he was feeling wretched, no one would know, least of all his father, who doesn't really look.

When we were tidying up the lunch, Mel suddenly asked: 'Would you go back to Richard, if he wanted?'

'It's a hypothetical question: *he* wants a divorce and I've sent off for the papers.'

'But you must think about it?'

I put down the tureen I was about to take into the kitchen. 'If you mean, do I wish he'd never left, then yes. I'd rather not have slept with Ed McGregor. Or tried to sleep with Simon Hemingway.'

'But what about now, if he wanted to come back?'

I shrugged. 'It's irrelevant. He doesn't.'

'He might wake up one day and regret throwing over everything you built up.' Mel gazed fondly at Ian's retreating back.

'I doubt it.' And then I rather surprised myself: 'And in a way I've got used to being on my own.'

Driving home, I thought about this again, and felt

it was true. I don't spend nearly as much time as I used to feeling resentful about the things that Richard isn't doing. I don't get so bogged down by petty frustrations: the pet smells in the carpets and the overflowing linen baskets and towels dropped on the floor ... When I tidy up now, I feel I'm doing it for myself.

I think, in a way, I must have conducted our entire relationship in the teeth of dissatisfaction.

But in the unlikely event that Richard were to have a sort of mental seizure and suddenly insist his life wasn't worth living without me?

I don't know.

Ben did finally get through to me when he got back to the flat, and he was obviously thrilled with his present. But the only way he can cope with having two homes is by trying to pretend the other one doesn't exist, shutting out one when he's at the other. Talking to me from Richard's is too bewildering. So he grunted monosyllabically for a couple of minutes and was evidently relieved when it was all over.

Later, I drove to the video shop. The rain had finally stopped, but the air was still dank, and the streets gleamed like grey patent in the headlamps.

I spent half an hour looking for comfort-viewing and eventually emerged with *The Bridges of Madison County*, even though I've seen it three times.

A slight, defiant figure was leaning outside the shop, one leg up against the wall, smoking with studied carelessness. He looked like a tart in film noir.

It was skinny, feral Phil from the squats.

I paused in the doorway. He was lounging: pretending to be relaxed, not on the lookout for anything. But he didn't fool me. I could see that he was alert with calculation, his little urban-weasel eyes flicking from side to side.

I went over to him.

'What are you doing here?'

He flicked ash at my feet insolently. 'Waitin'.'

'For someone else to rob?'

'Nah.'

'For what then?'

He blew smoke in my face. 'What's it to you?'

'It's eleven o'clock. It's too late to be out.'

'S'none of your business, though, is it?' he asked, taking another drag. And then he got up off the wall and strolled away into the night.

I went back to the car and slammed my bag down on the passenger seat. I knew what he was waiting for.

I drove home, and dialled Fran's number even before I'd properly shrugged off my coat.

The answering machine cut in before she had time to pick up the phone.

'I hope you weren't in bed,' I apologised, when her outgoing message had finished and the thing had bleeped and we could hear each other.

'No, I'm in a complete *state*. I've been trying to get hold of you. David left about three-quarters of an hour ago. He's been here all afternoon and evening. Tears, shouting . . . I'm shattered . . . *I* don't know what he wants. He seems to think he's entitled to pick me up and drop me and he doesn't have to make any commitment, but I have to –' she paused for breath, then gasped: 'Oh my God! It's Ben's birthday, isn't it? I'm so sorry. And here I am talking about bloody David . . . I can't believe I didn't call you earlier. Are you OK?'

'Fine. I spent most of the day at Mel's. Look, have you got Ed McGregor's number in Chelsea?'

'Jools, are you sure?'

'Yes, why not?'

'You're not going to do anything reckless?'

'Such as what? This is about Phil, not me.'

'Oh God, he hasn't robbed you again?'

'No, he's been soliciting outside the video shop.'

'In *Langley*?' Fran said incredulously. '*Are* there homosexuals in Langley?'

'It's not funny. He shouldn't be doing it here. Or any-where. But certainly not here: we don't want rent boys loitering in the High Street. It's not bloody Soho.'

She gave me Ed's number. 'Poor Ed,' she said drily. 'I hope he's feeling strong.'

I called him immediately, before I could have second thoughts.

'Julie!' he said in surprise, but not with any pleasure, not in his smiley mode; he sounded uncertain and rather distant. I expect Nettle was there.

I piled straight in: 'Why are you letting Phil solicit in Langley High Street?'

'Are you sure?'

'What *else* is he doing, I should like to know, hanging around at eleven o'clock at night outside the video shop? He's looking for punters.'

'I didn't think . . .'

'No, I bet you didn't. Because you're not supervising

him adequately. He's a *child*, and an immature child, at that; he can't just be left to his own devices.'

He'd recovered his composure a little. 'What do you think I should do?'

'Take him back where he belongs. I don't know *how* you can think you're a stabilising influence on him.'

'I've tried –'

But I was fired up now. 'I don't know how you can think he wouldn't be better off in care. What good is it doing him being with that shiftless bunch of squatters? None at all. It's complete anarchy at the squats. Since you arrived in Langley, *everything's* started breaking down. And it's your fault, because you encourage all the local kids to come there ... You *enjoy* having them all flock round you, thinking you're cool. They're all spending far too much time at the squats, being exposed to drugs and revolutionary ideas and ... face piercings ...'

And suddenly, unaccountably, embarrassingly, I burst into tears.

'Julie ...'

'Don't "Julie" me,' I yelled at him. 'Just do something about that bloody child.'

And I slammed down the phone.

I lay awake half the night, tossing, turning, trying to find a cool place on the pillow, a bit of it that wasn't creased, a length of the bed that wasn't lumpy, where the covers fell comfortably around me, all the right weight.

What was happening to me? Why was I letting Ed McGregor get to me?

I was over the ridiculous incident in the kitchen. I knew he'd used me. I didn't know why – maybe to settle some private score with Nettle – but it didn't matter.

The only way to deal with it was to be dignified.

Unfortunately, that would have been much easier if only Ed would leave Langley. I'd never been particularly exercised about the road, but my only interest in it now was in how quickly the contractors could get in the girders and spread the Tarmac. I wanted that road finished and humming with traffic. I wanted the protesters elsewhere, preferably at the other end of the country. I wanted my natural, clever, serious, *focused* daughter back. I wanted my son safe from the seductions of dirty houses and their louche, shiftless inhabitants. I wanted all those hairy people to go home and leave us in Langley, safe, circumscribed, suburban, where no harm could come to us.

Richard arrived this morning before school with a bag of dirty washing and Arthur, who threw himself into my arms, his head seeking out the usual places on my neck, his small hands settling on my back, face settling against familiar flesh.

I breathed in his adorable baby smell, kissed and tousled the weekend from his hair.

'Did you have a good time?' I asked Richard over the top of his head.

'Yep. Great.'

I hesitated, wanting to hold him there, to ask about Ben's birthday, Kate's revision, Arthur's sleeping. But he was all bustle, too busy to linger. He muttered something about having dropped Ginny off at her house last night and hurried off down the path.

So I carried Arthur into the sitting room and read to him – two stories, three, four – struggling not to look at my watch in case he thought I didn't want to be with him. Long before the children had broken the news to me about Robbie Wade's party, I'd agreed with Tony and Pete that I'd work this Monday, because Victoria and Steve, the other two reporters, were going to be away. Victoria was going into hospital for a mystery operation that everyone was trying desperately not to be curious about. I hoped Ginny hadn't forgotten.

She finally rang the doorbell twenty-five minutes late. She still hasn't found her keys. She looked terrible, as if she hadn't slept the whole weekend: bleached out, as if she'd left the photographically-developed Ginny somewhere else and sent us the negative.

She forgot to apologise. I told myself this didn't matter and it was unfair of me even to notice given that she'd been working all weekend. And uncharitable that it even crossed my mind she'd been paid double-time, because she was only half an hour late, and frankly, even with the others away, it was unlikely that anything was happening in the office.

She ambled into the kitchen and put the kettle on.

'Did Richard tell you about the weekend?' she yawned. 'Amazing!'

'Not really, no. Did Ben have a good birthday?'

'Yeah. It's a *brilliant* house. Swimming pool and tennis courts and a lake at the bottom of the garden. And they're great, the band. Have you ever met them?'

'No.'

'They're brilliant fun. Mac, he's the drummer . . .'

'What did Richard get him?'

She looked at me blankly.

'Ben,' I said gently.

'Oh, a book, I think. No, he had a great birthday, honestly. We had this Nintendo tournament yesterday afternoon and Ben won. Mac came second.'

'Did Kate get any revision done?'

'She was going to do some last night. She's brainy, though – now *me*, they thought I wasn't going to get any GCSEs at all. Well, I *did* have to retake them . . . I'd have thought they'd be stuck up, blokes in a band, but they weren't at all. I've gone right off Gary. That cow Debbie can have him. He doesn't know how to treat a girl . . .'

I nodded hastily; I'd got the message. Ginny had slept with Mac. I didn't want the details. I hoped she realised that sleeping with people is one of the things that boys in bands do. It's part of the point of being in a band. It might mean something, but then again, it might not.

By the time I got into work, I was so depressed about having abandoned my baby to a groupie that I just stared at my screen and wished I'd done something about getting a new job that paid for proper childcare. I didn't care what it was.

'Why is your head on your keyboard?' Tony enquired, draping himself over my terminal.

I explained about the awfulness of having been away from Ben on his birthday and having Ginny for a nanny. 'And then last night I did an absolutely terrible thing: I rang up Ed McGregor and *shouted* at him about his people having face piercings.'

314

'That *is* eccentric.'

'I found Phil soliciting outside the video shop.'

Tony frowned. 'And what's that got to do with face piercing?'

'OK. I was upset. Probably about Richard.'

'Are you sure there isn't something going on between you and Ed McGregor?'

'What d'you mean, going on? What could there be? Of course not.'

Tony shrugged. 'It's not like you to feel you have to stick up single-handedly for the values of middle England – an end to drugs and rent boys off our streets.'

'You can laugh, but I don't believe Ed McGregor is helping that child. And I suppose I was upset about missing Ben . . . The trouble is, I think this is going to be my life from now: lonely weekends without my children, interspersed with bouts of trying to keep the family together in the teeth of the massed assault of popular culture – nannies sleeping with pop stars and parties at the country mansions of recovering addicts. And to fight this I am going to become – although I don't want to – more and more traditional and Outraged of Tunbridge Wells and I am going to *hate* myself. I mean, why do *I* always have to be Captain Sensible? I don't want to turn into some mad old person fulminating about the breakdown of everything we used to value.'

'You're not mad, you're not old, and, from what you say, Ginny's been in love with some unsuitable bloke or other ever since you hired her. An unsuitable pop star could be a step up from an unsuitable plumber.'

'Rather less attainable.'

'She may not actually mind that. As for Richard, I bet there were loads of things he never bothered himself with before.'

He was right. Dental appointments. Children's teas with friends. Freezer bags.

'So why should you expect things to have changed? Why don't you go home and see Arthur? There's nothing happening and you're not even supposed to be here anyway.'

It was a good idea. A really good idea, as it turned out, because when I got home, Radio One was on at full volume in the kitchen doing something irreparably damaging to Arthur's eardrums. I walked in just in time to catch the opening bars of Sump's new single, 'Stuff It', and to see Ginny hurl down a tablespoon and run from the room in tears.

'Ginny, perhaps you should go home, catch up on some sleep,' I called after her, once I'd assured Arthur that her behaviour wasn't his fault.

She emerged from the bathroom a few minutes later, looking spectral and wiping her nose.

'Sorry, Julie. Honestly, I'm all right. It was the shock. He hasn't called . . .'

'He's probably busy with the band.' I hesitated. 'I'm not sure they're an awfully good bet, pop stars . . .'

'No! You haven't met him. He's lovely.' She blew her nose and finally registered that I'd offered her the afternoon off. 'Maybe you're right. He's got my home number. It could be that my mobile isn't working.'

So she left, and I fixed Arthur some lunch and tried

not to feel irritable about the fact that he hadn't already had it, even though it was one-thirty.

He didn't eat much. Perhaps he was too tired from his late nights. We settled down on the floor with a Thomas the Tank Engine puzzle instead, except that he thought it was more amusing to throw the pieces into the corners of the room.

I was trying to return them to the middle of the floor when the doorbell rang.

The flower delivery boy stood on the front step. The same boy, from the same shop, with very nearly the same flowers. And yet again, he dumped a crackly Cellophane-tied bunch in my arms.

In the background, in the breakfast room, Arthur fell over on to a little plastic knob on one of the puzzle pieces. It dug into his knee and he started wailing uncontrollably.

I quickly closed the front door and tossed the flowers on to the hall table while I dealt with Arthur.

Once he was settled on the sofa, sucking his thumb and padded around with cushions, I picked the flowers up again.

They weren't quite as sumptuous as the last lot. Pretty, though: scabious and cornflowers. I searched for a card, but there wasn't one. I opened the front door, to see if it had dropped off outside. The delivery van was already disappearing round the corner.

They had to be from Simon.

For one thing, no one else had sent me flowers for the past fifteen years. And they were from the same shop – a posh, non-Interflora place, where you probably had to pay as much for delivery as for the flowers themselves. Simon was the only person I knew who was stylish enough to go there rather than Fifi's Floral Displays in the High Street.

Anyway, it would have been too much of a coincidence – two bunches of flowers in a month, from different people but from the same obscure flower shop, miles away from where I live . . .

So now he'd sent me *two* bunches of flowers. But *why*?

Was he a stalker, specialising in horticultural harassment?

It didn't make sense.

On the sofa, Arthur had finally collapsed with exhaustion. He was breathing peacefully, except for the occasional sleep-sob, a susurration of escaping tiredness and over-excitement.

I picked up the phone, put it down, telling myself it wasn't worth it; then picked it up again.

Simon wasn't at home, but his answering machine recommended trying him on his mobile. It also gave the number.

'Julie! How nice to hear from you,' he said cheerfully. 'I was thinking about you this morning.'

Suddenly I wasn't so sure.

'You were?'

'A friend of mine was asking whether I knew anyone with kids to work on some PR campaign she's got going.'

'Is that why you sent me the flowers?'

'Sorry?'

'The flowers. The second bunch. They just arrived. They're very beautiful, but . . .' I trailed off.

He wasn't saying anything.

He didn't know what I was talking about.

I suddenly didn't think he could have sent me the flowers, after all.

I swallowed hard.

'You didn't send them.'

'Er . . . no.'

Was I always this mad? I used to think I was quite a sensible person, feet on the ground, rational, calm, that sort of thing. But here I was, telephoning a man whom I had only recently propositioned – *unsuccessfully* propositioned – in order to thank him for a bunch of flowers which, it was now horribly apparent, he had not sent.

I cause havoc everywhere I turn.

'I sent some flowers a couple of weeks ago,' he said, puzzled. 'Well, as you know. I was worried that I'd been, the whole thing had been . . . unfair to you. Misleading.'

'No, it was my fault,' I said in a strangulated voice. 'I jumped to conclusions.'

'I was worried after you came round that Saturday morning. It seemed a bit of a muddle. To be honest, I didn't know whether to call you about this PR thing or if you'd yell at me.' There was a pause, while I tried to work out a way of extricating myself that didn't involve slitting my wrists. 'But, er, I didn't send you any flowers.'

I wished I could have rewound the tape – back to the bit before I picked up the phone – and *not do it*.

First I ask this man to sleep with me and he refuses, then I ring to thank him for flowers he hasn't sent.

When I told him about pretending to be Joan of Arc in the supermarket, the poor man can never have imagined that the subject of my next mad fantasy would be him.

The doorbell was ringing. 'I've got to go,' I muttered, 'someone at the door.'

'It's OK,' he said, infuriatingly, 'I'll wait.'

It was the delivery boy again. 'Sorry, this must've fallen off.' He handed me a small envelope.

I tore it open – this was a nightmare – and read, in round florist's handwriting: 'With all my love, Richard.'

Richard?

'The flowers were from my ex-husband,' I returned to the phone and informed Simon, weakly. 'Mistake. He obviously uses the same florist. The card fell off.'

'Oh . . . good. Or I assume it's good? Anyway, I just wondered about this job. Were you serious? D'you want me to set up a meeting?'

I suppose I said yes. I don't really know what I said, because I was thinking about Richard – *all my love?* What the fuck was he going on about? He'd sent them to the wrong woman.

All I know is that in the middle of not thanking Simon for flowers, I somehow invited him to dinner.

I caught Richard in the staff room after lessons had finished.

'Oh, hello,' he said unencouragingly.

'What, exactly,' I demanded haughtily, 'is the meaning of these flowers?'

'What flowers?'

'The ones you sent this afternoon.'

'What would I be sending flowers to you for? We're getting a divorce.'

'I know that! And don't lie to me! I even checked with the shop because I couldn't believe it myself! You bought them on your credit card on Friday.'

'Julie,' he said, quite kindly, 'I know you had a really tough weekend. I'm sorry for taking Ben away on his birthday, but you've got to get used to it. I am not saying this to patronise you or put you down, or – well, suggest that you're going bonkers – but I think you should make an appointment with Dr Armstrong. See if she can recommend someone. You should get yourself some counselling.'

Ben

Mum realised the flowers weren't from Dad. She found out almost immediately. I knew she'd catch on sooner or later, but I hoped she might remember first how good he was at mowing the lawn and getting the wine, and flirt with him on the phone, because I heard this psychologist on the radio say marriages could spiral upwards very quickly, especially if they'd spiralled down quickly, and often all it took was one generous move from one side or the other.

But maybe our family is so dysfunctional we don't even meet normal standards of disturbed behaviour.

Mum sat me down and talked to me very seriously about borrowing Dad's credit card and impersonating him, although at the end she said brightly: 'Still, it was quite a feat of organisation!'

I am so useless that she is even relieved when I steal, as long as I do it strategically.

I don't know whether the flowers had put her in the bad mood, but later, she caused a terrible scene. It might have been that she's still sore about my birthday.

(My birthday was OK. I'd have preferred to go to the Trocadero, like Adrian Farr did on his birthday – which I wasn't invited to – and I sort of missed Mum, and it would have been nice if Dad had got up earlier. But it was fine.)

Anyway, what happened was that after school I didn't come straight home. I wanted Mum and Dad to have plenty of time to get back together, not realising she'd already worked out the flowers were from me. So I went to the squats to see Darren instead. He was tunnelling, but he promised to come out and help me as soon as the really tricky bit was finished, so I sat in Ed McGregor's office to wait and tried to start on my maths.

Ed was out making a documentary at the BBC, except that he finished early. I'd only been sitting at his desk for about ten minutes when he came back.

I tried to leave so he could have his desk, but when he saw what I was doing, he offered to help. Actually, he was even better at explaining than Darren. I thought we were going to get the sums finished in time for me to help with the tunnelling, but then the door of Ed's office opened and Mum was standing there. Her hair needs cutting and it had got all messed up in the wind and she looked slightly mad.

'I *thought* I might find you here,' she said in an accusing voice. 'What's going on?'

'Division,' Ed said.

'*Division*?'

I explained about Darren and the tunnelling.

'*Ed* is helping you with your maths?'

Why was she repeating everything?

Ed looked upset. 'I *can* do maths,' he said.

Mum opened her mouth as if to give Ed a piece of her mind (there is no explaining grown-ups: she *pays* other people to help me) but then Kate walked into the room. She looked startled and quickly slipped her hand behind her back, but not quickly enough to hide the roll-up.

'*This* is exactly my point!' she exploded at Ed. (What point? I had no idea what she was going on about.) 'Kate! Is that a joint?'

'Course not,' Kate replied in a really scathing voice. 'We're *working*.'

Then Mum snatched up my maths books and grabbed Kate by the elbow and dragged us both outside the house. 'That's it!' she shouted, when we were in the front garden. 'You are neither of you to go back there until further notice. It is absolutely forbidden.'

Kate shook her off and hissed at her that she was being embarrassing and how *dare* she show her up like this in front of her friends? But Mum was too mad to care.

Kate

I have never felt so ashamed. I used to think Mum was quite sensitive but lately she's lost it. Mould will think I am a schoolgirl who gets dragged home by her mother for having been caught smoking.

The only reason I agreed to come back here with her was to get her out of the front garden. She was perfectly capable of staying at the squats shouting and drawing attention to herself all afternoon.

'You told me you didn't smoke and I believed you!' she kept muttering like a mad bag lady all the way home. 'How am I ever supposed to believe anything you say again?'

There was no point in reasoning with her. I bet she smoked at my age, because everyone does. Most people give up in their twenties. It's not as if it's going to kill me.

The other thing she kept going on about was how irresponsible Ed McGregor was, which is a bit much considering he'd spent the afternoon helping Ben with his homework.

*　　*　　*

When we got back to the house, she was still in a temper and went through my drawers looking for more cigarettes until she found twenty Benson and Hedges in my underwear drawer.

'I suppose,' she demanded, waving them in front of me furiously, 'you think I wouldn't have found these sooner or later when I put your underwear away?'

I told her that she doesn't *need* to put my knickers away. Next thing, she will be covering up the piano legs.

This was probably a mistake, as she is now behaving completely unreasonably and saying I can't even go to Rachel's because I lie about that as well and actually I see Mould and get love-bites. I don't know how she found out; I kept it covered up the whole time.

She has violated my personal space, and I am going to ask Dad if I can live with him.

Julie

The room was bristling with small-hour silence when I woke up at 3.00 a.m., the darkness pulsing menacingly round the bed, thumping thick and black, like a birth canal.

I often used to wake up in the middle of the night when Richard first left, choking and gulping, feeling the tears slithering wetly past my mouth. Now, for an instant, I imagined the bristly softness of the hairs on his legs tickling my toes and felt a pang of hope. And then my foot moved over the bed into cool emptiness.

Ben sent the flowers. He picked up the card with Simon's message on it from last time, slipped Richard's credit card out of his wallet and made the call. It was actually quite impressive from someone whose PE kit's always in the wrong place, who's lost his fountain pen, and who last week picked up Kate's clothes instead of his swimming trunks and towel, so that when his class reached the pool, all he had to swim in was a Lycra mini skirt and a spaghetti-strap top.

But boys of his age shouldn't be driven to wage

campaigns on behalf of their parents' marriage. He's still hoping for the best, in spite of the evidence. If nothing else, it's an awful waste of effort for someone who has to use up so much energy simply not falling over.

I have to speak to him, and soon. Sit him down, tell him it's over. Richard doesn't want me back. He wants to marry Emma.

I would have done it this afternoon – I was meaning to when I went to find him at the squats – but I got sidetracked by Kate. How can a person change so much? She used to come home from school with tales of the colour of throat cancer and the texture of tar as it drips into the alveoli, and now she keeps packets of Benson and Hedges in her underwear drawer. And it's no use warning her about death, because she thinks that living after thirty-five is quite as bad as dying, and possibly worse: at least when you're dead you don't have to dust the mantelpiece. There's no point, either, in telling her that her skin will look fifty when the rest of her is only forty, because she's so beautiful, and her skin is so furiously healthy, that she thinks the worst that can happen to it is a blackhead.

Everything's gone wrong. And you don't have to look far to see why. My relationship with Kate started going downhill when she began to visit the squats and develop the idea that all you have to do to save the world is sit up a tree. We could all sit up trees if that was all it took. Kate should try making sure we don't run out of teabags.

'David claims the only reason I started seeing Jamie

was to get back at him,' Fran announced gloomily after work the following evening. 'And then I started *wondering* . . . I mean, Jamie's been a fantastically convenient excuse not to return David's calls and go out more . . .'

'I thought you were mad about Jamie?'

'And then I think, maybe I *want* to believe David because, actually, I'm *frightened* of how good it is with Jamie . . . ?'

'Look at me,' I warned her, 'I was so frightened of sexual euphoria, I married Richard. Now what's happened? I'm getting divorced, and Ben's so distressed by it he's sending me flowers and pretending they're from Richard, and Kate believes she's in the grip of an uncontrollable addiction to nicotine.'

The phone was ringing.

'It's Tony,' Kate called down the hall venomously.

'You see,' I said to Fran, 'she even resents me getting phone calls.'

Tony said: 'I hope you've got a good alarm clock, because you're needed at the tree in the morning. The bailiffs are arriving at dawn.'

I peered out of the window. It was raining again.

'Isn't this something you'd like to do?'

'It's your story. You're the one who's got the relationship with Ed McGregor.'

Kate bounded down the stairs and waved her arms at me, putting her fist to her ear and grimacing.

But Tony was still talking: 'Colour piece . . . police brutality . . . suburban solidarity . . . heroic struggle . . . little old ladies brewing up on camping Gaz stoves . . . Battle of the Somme.'

'Give me the phone!' Kate hissed. 'They've issued the *aruga*. I need to call ten people!'

'Knee-deep in mud . . . bailiffs with machetes . . . unfortunate grannies in the paths . . .'

'Tony, it's a tree-felling, not the Texas chain-saw massacre.'

'Very symbolic tree,' Tony said darkly. 'Anything could happen. You need to arrive soon after half-past four. Steve'll be there, but think splash and a piece across two and three. You'll need to come in straight away and write it up because it's press day, but that's great: we'll be first with the story.'

No other local papers cover Langley. We're always first with the story.

It was only after I put down the phone that I remembered I was a single parent.

'Sorry, I need that again,' I told Kate, who was already dialling some sympathiser's number.

'You've had your turn.' She consulted a list.

'I need to speak to Ginny.'

'You're not even on our side.' She tapped her fingers on the wall, willing someone to answer.

'Kate, the whole point of this is to get it reported.'

'No, actually, that's where you're *wrong*. The whole point is to save the tree.'

'The real point,' I said patiently, 'is to demonstrate the strength of local resistance to the road. The tree is just the focus. If I don't write about it, no one will know it's happened.'

She threw the receiver at me. Somewhere down the line, an unanswered phone was still ringing. 'You're so *old*!' she shouted. 'Old and cynical! You don't give

330

a stuff about the tree. You hate Ed McGregor, and you hate me believing in something, because your generation doesn't believe in anything at all.'

She stomped off upstairs, while I clenched and unclenched my fingers to ease the pain where the receiver had struck them.

'Oh, hallo,' Ginny's mother said vaguely, 'she's out, I'm afraid.'

'Can I get her on her mobile?'

'Er, well, you could, except it's here on the hall table . . .'

'Do you know when she'll be back?'

'She doesn't usually get in till after I've gone to bed.'

'Ah. Well, if you see her, can you ask her to ring me?'

'I can't promise – I mean, I can promise to tell her, obviously, but not that she'll call you back. She seems very upset about something. I only have to speak to her and she bursts into tears.'

'Everything all right?' Fran asked, emerging from the sitting room with Arthur on her hip, chocolate smeared around his mouth and plastered on his palms. She saw me staring at him and added unnecessarily: 'I gave him a chocolate.'

Underneath the chocolate – which was Belgian, from Godiva, and which Fran had really bought for me as yet another apology for the Jamie business – Arthur was looking faintly green. 'Hope you didn't mind me opening them.'

'Kate Adie doesn't have these problems,' I grumbled. 'She never has to say, "No, I can't catch the next flight to Sarajevo because I haven't got a babysitter."'

'That's because she hasn't got a baby.'

When I explained that I couldn't find Ginny and that anyone else I could possibly ask would either be looking after their own children or guarding the tree, she did, however, offer to stay.

Kate came back downstairs, scowling. 'I suppose she can have my bed,' she offered ungraciously.

'Where are you going to sleep?'

'The tree.'

I put my hand on the button, cutting off the call. 'Absolutely not. You have school tomorrow. Anyway, it's raining. You'll catch pneumonia.'

'So?'

'Kate, you are not spending a wet night up a tree!'

'I wouldn't do this for the NHS, you know. I don't *want* to catch pneumonia, but I'm prepared to do it because I really *care* about this tree.'

In the end, we compromised. Fran would share with me, Kate would spend most of the night in her bed, and I promised to get her up with me at four-thirty.

But when I went in to wake her before dawn, she groaned, turned over, grunted and burrowed deeper under her duvet.

I thought she wasn't going to make it. I made a cup of tea and drank it and was lacing up my walking boots when she stumbled down the stairs wearing her new denim jacket and Converse All-Star trainers.

'You can't go like that,' I whispered; 'it's raining. You'll ruin your shoes.'

'No, I won't,' she said loudly. Upstairs, I heard one of the boys muttering in his sleep; I bundled her out of the house exasperatedly. 'Only you would think about what people are wearing at such a time,' she grumbled, and then continued to harangue me all the way up The Limes about my lack of commitment to eco politics generally and the tree in particular.

There were already at least a hundred people on the green: bank managers and school teachers, estate agents and housewives, plus about thirty full-timers up the tree, most of them in the corrugated iron structure in the lower branches, a few on the lookout platform above, half a dozen more clamped directly to the tree. Someone above our heads was singing plangent folk songs off-key.

'This is really important,' a neurotically thin and druggy girl called Cat explained to me. 'You think it's about Langley, but actually it's the beginning of the eco-wars.'

'Oh yes, and what are they?'

'Well, in twenty years' time, right, everything's going to be concreted over. That's their plan, if we don't stop them.'

They appeared to be already on their way. If you listened carefully, you could hear the sound of revving motorbikes through the wet air. The few security guards who'd been on the green all night shifted nervously, waiting for the reinforcements. Dead-eyed from lack of sleep, they watched impassively as four coaches crawled up Cherry Drive and disgorged hundreds of men in bright helmets, a fluorescent yellow puddle in the mud.

I saw Kate in the phalanx of protesters that was

forming around the base of the tree. She'd linked arms with Mould.

'What are you going to tell your grandchildren?' she was shouting through a loud-hailer. 'What are you going to say when they ask what you did to stop the destruction of their planet?'

For a minute, I thought she was talking to me.

By eleven, the rain had stopped and there was even a streak of white cloud above the Taj Mahal Balti House. But most of the sky was still black, with the rainclouds humped low, squat, toad-like above us.

The guards and the police had already got most of the thousand locals away from the bottom of the tree and off the green. Then a cherry-picker arrived for the serious stuff, lumbering across the grass, heavy and threatening, lifting and swivelling its long neck like a mechanical Tyrannosaurus Rex.

'They've got *that*,' Suzy Sharp said acidly, 'and we've got sticks, rope and cooking utensils.'

I wasn't really concentrating, because I'd spotted Ben in the crowd about twenty feet away. I pushed my way through people watching the security guards being pelted with paint-filled rubber gloves.

'Ben! What are you doing here? Why aren't you at school?'

'Oh, hi, Mum. Have you seen Dad?'

'What would he be doing here?'

'He still owns our house, doesn't he?'

'Yes, but he doesn't know about the protest. *We* were only told last night.'

Ben bit his lip.

334

'Ben,' I said seriously, 'I have to talk to you about all this.'

'Christ, look at that,' someone said beside me.

A scrawny dryad was scrambling through the branches of the tree, stark naked.

'It's Mould,' Ben said, following his ascent, impressed.

'He's covered in Vaseline,' explained someone called Scouse Mick, who was standing nearby. 'They need to get hold of him and drag him down, but they're too homophobic. It'll take them hours.'

'Ben, you're supposed to be at school.'

'Oh, there you are!' cried Suzy Sharp, pushing through the crowd. 'I hope you're going to write about the fact that there's no ambulance. They're spending – what, millions – policing this, and they can't even be arsed to bring an ambulance.'

I stared at her.

Someone next to us said: 'They thought only protesters would be hurt.'

'Ben, you really shouldn't be here,' I said despairingly, and went to find the man from the Highways Agency.

'We did provide an ambulance,' he said, 'only the protesters sabotaged it.'

'When?' I held my pen over my notebook ostentatiously.

'It was one of the security firm's Range Rovers. It was clearly marked as an emergency vehicle.'

'Have you got proof that they sabotaged it?'

'No.'

'Where did this incident happen?'

'Don't know. Sorry.'

'No idea at all?'

'No. Wish I did.'

It took about eight hours from the arrival of the sheriff's officers to the rolling away of the crane from the muddy scar on the middle of the green. Mould was the last person to be brought down, still naked, greasy and white. He was reciting poetry.

It was only after the tree had been cut to pieces that I saw Ed McGregor.

He was standing on the opposite side of the green, across the ugly wound where the tree had stood, legs slightly apart, hands on hips, ankle-deep in mud and surrounded by debris – branches, twisted twigs, hanks of rope and salvaged ironmongery.

I took a deep breath and made my way over. The ancient tree lay in pieces all around, sorry chunks of timber on the churned-up grass.

Ed was talking to a couple of squatters; he broke off as I came up with my notebook and the squatters drifted away.

'How d'you think it went?' I asked briskly.

He looked at me very directly, in a manner I found slightly muddling. 'We lost the tree,' he said slowly, still staring, 'but the local support was wonderful. The contractors know . . .'

And then without warning, he broke off, bent over and kissed me.

Not again.

Who did he think he was?

This time, I wasn't hanging around long enough for Nettle to see, or whatever the point of this was. I slapped his face.

I did it really hard. I was incredibly angry. And then I turned on my heel and stalked off across the grass.

I had no illusions: I was covered in mud, red-eyed and bleary from having got up at dawn, and I was wearing a cagoule.

The bastard didn't even give me a quote first.

Kate

I cried when the tree came down. Scotch Billy played 'Amazing Grace' on the bagpipes and after that the rain started again, which seemed kind of symbolic. There was this real atmosphere of community and love and connectedness with nature.

I hate, hate the stupid guards. They only get four pounds an hour, so why don't they go on the dole instead of raping the earth? Mould is on the dole and he has a brilliant time. He says we have passion, so we will win in the end.

He was the bravest person of the whole day. He spent hours dodging the guards in the branches. They couldn't bring themselves to hug him and bring him down because they're disgusted by the human body unless it is wearing a Wonderbra.

Mould was arrested when they brought him down but Ed said the police will have to let him go. All he did was grease up and slow them down.

Perhaps Ed was upset about not having managed to save the tree, but after he'd reassured me about Mould being freed by tonight, he did a really weird thing. He said: 'Has he told you he takes his washing home to his mum every Monday?'

And then he walked off, so I didn't get a chance to ask him if he was joking. But it *must* have been a joke. Mould is anti-sexist and has repudiated bourgeois conventions.

Some of the locals were being very self-important: Suzy Sharp, for instance, was bossing everyone around as usual. She kept asking me to give out cups of tea, when I actually had much more important work to do, throwing rice at the guards and jeering at them for only getting four quid an hour and explaining to them how they were earth rapists.

Darren was also being bloody irritating. He led a group of residents who kept trying to breach the police cordon, but it was obvious they couldn't do it. They just looked amateurish. I saw him talking to Mum halfway through the morning, probably explaining his so-called tactics. And she is so gullible she probably wrote them down for her paper, as if he knows anything about direct action.

She's still not home. I expect she's writing another one of her vicious anti-protest articles. Ben – he bunked off school to see the tree come down – keeps coming in my room to ask why I think Dad didn't turn up. As if he'd care: he lives in Clerkenwell. Ben gets very muddled about things.

I've got a sore throat and I think I'm developing a temperature. But today was a brilliant day, and I feel part of the wonderful, organic cycle of nature.

I am thinking of changing my name to Bindweed.

Ben

Last night I called Dad. I had to wait ages, because Kate was on the phone to the tree supporters, and Mum and Fran were having a bottle of wine in the kitchen with the door open. It was quite late when I got through and I think Dad was surprised I wasn't in bed. (Actually, I was. I got up to make the phone call from Mum's bedroom.)

The conversation went like this:

Me: 'The bailiffs are coming to cut the tree down tomorrow.'

Dad: 'What tree's that?'

Me: 'You know, the one on the green. The one that's in the way of the road.'

Dad: 'Kate'll be upset.'

Me: 'Can you come to the protest?'

Dad: 'Me? Why?'

Me: 'Well . . . it will affect the house price.'

Dad: 'I have to teach tomorrow.'

Me: 'But people are taking the day off. All sorts of people. *Please* can you come?'

Dad: 'Oh, Ben, I'm sorry. Of course I'd come if I could . . . I expect Mum'll be there.'

Me: 'But Mum's no good on her own! She needs you.'

Dad (not really knowing what to say. Perhaps he realised this was true): 'Oh.'

Me: 'Will you *try* to come? Please? For me?'

Dad: 'I'll think about it.'

This morning I told Fran I didn't need a lift to school and I simply turned off in the other direction. I walked up to the green feeling really excited.

I know I was supposed to feel miserable about the tree, but I thought it would be worth losing one chestnut tree if it got my parents back together. Actually, it would be worth losing all the chestnut trees in Britain if my parents got back together.

I couldn't help feeling pleased, because Dad had promised to think about coming, and I felt sure that once on the green with all the community spirit, he'd realise that this was where he belonged and not in a white flat in a place where there are no kids.

There were hundreds of people milling round in the roads beside the green, and for ages I couldn't see anyone I knew, let alone my parents. Also, I kept getting distracted by what was happening in the tree. Mould climbed up without a safety harness, wearing only Vaseline.

'Brilliant, innit?' said Phil, that boy who lives at the squat and doesn't go to school. 'I love it when they tip paint over the guards.'

'Yeah,' I said. 'I might be a protester when I grow

341

up. You don't need any qualifications. I'm looking for my dad.'

Phil said he doesn't want to see his dad ever again. 'If I did, I'd probably kill him. He wasn't even my dad anyway.'

This is stupid: either he was or he wasn't. You can't have more than one dad.

'I like your mum,' he said surprisingly, because I don't think she likes him.

'Yeah, she's all right. She'd be better if she got back together with my dad.'

'They never do what you want. My mum's depressed.'

'Yeah, mine too.'

'No, your mum's not depressed.' He shook his head. I don't know how he thinks he knows so much about it. 'My mum could be dead by now, she's so depressed. No one'd tell me.'

'I bet they would.'

'They don't know where I am. And I don't know where she is. And she doesn't care because she's either on uppers or downers or she's drunk.'

I said I thought that must be terrible, not to know where your mother was. He shrugged.

Then I saw exactly where *my* mother was: right beside me! She didn't notice Phil, which was just as well because she thinks he's a bad influence.

But she hadn't found Dad.

Eventually, I realised that this was because he wasn't there. I suppose in the end he just had too much teaching to do.

Either that or I am simply not good enough at explaining myself. I'm not good at making an argument like Kate, who Mum says should be Secretary General of the United Nations. I have difficulty getting my thoughts out in consecutive order. Or maybe he didn't realise how important it was to me.

Sometimes I think I will never be good at anything. It's all very well saying I am going to be a protester, but if I tried to occupy a tree, I would fall out.

Julie

Ed McGregor is a sexual pervert who gets his kicks from kissing women with middle-aged spread. Or he's a sadist who can't bear it that I'm not grateful that he slept with me, that I'm not like all those other suburban matrons, simpering over him in public and hanging on his every word and delivering soup and cakes at least once a week in the hope of getting a quick sexual thrill from seeing him doing something in the back garden of the squats with his shirt off.

Whatever the explanation, the sooner the road comes through Langley the better. I don't want him here, striding about, outdoors and oxygenated, wearing jeans and a leather belt (which, Oh God, he once pulled off in a sexy, stripping manner), narrowing his eyes at me, and making me think of him catching my wrist and ordering me to have dirty sex with him, here, now, in the mud.

Back in the real world, the one in which people actually speak to each other rather than simply have animal sex,

I got into work late on Thursday morning and suddenly remembered that this was the day Simon was supposed to be coming to dinner.

'Oh, Christ, what am I going to do?' I muttered. 'What with the tree and everything, I haven't even *thought* about food, and I haven't invited anyone else.'

'Why did you invite Simon?' Tony asked.

'Tourette's Syndrome? I don't know. I was embarrassed about thinking the flowers were from him. Have you ever rung someone to thank them for flowers that they've not sent?'

'No.'

'Exactly. You can't understand what that makes you do. And I was embarrassed because of having thrown myself at him. I sort of wanted to normalise relations. But now if I don't invite anyone else he'll think I'm trying to do it again. And if I *do* invite someone else, they'll think they're coming to meet my new boyfriend.'

'You could cancel.'

'No, I can't. He might have fixed me up with a job interview.'

I explained about the friend in PR. Tony said it was worth enduring a lot for a possible alternative to employment at the *Langley Advertiser*.

'But I'm out of practice. And I'll have to pour the drinks and cook all at the same time. Plus he's a vegetarian.'

'You're used to that.'

It's true that most nights find me trying to do something with tofu to disguise the fact that it is grey and has the texture and taste of pond weed.

But while glaucous algae stew is all very well for the child formerly known as Kate, I don't particularly want to serve it to the most sophisticated man in Langley.

'And what with this tree coming down, I haven't got time to clean the house from top to bottom and use all my pans cooking something fantastically complicated that I've never tried before and get tearful because it doesn't work and there's nowhere to put anything down in the kitchen so that I have to open the wine early and start drinking in order to avoid having a nervous breakdown, and get slightly incoherent before my guests arrive . . . which is what I like to do when I have people round for dinner.'

Tony offered: 'Shall I come?'

I gazed at him gratefully. 'Would you?'

'Sure. Tell you what, I'll even bring the pudding. And I promise not to complain about lack of meat. Did you know, incidentally, that Tolstoy thought that eating carrots and turnips reduced lust?'

So there I was in the supermarket, buying carrots. Arthur, who had insisted on coming with me, had also insisted on getting out of the trolley and walking up and down the aisles with his fingers through the wire mesh, so that every time I stopped I threatened to dislocate his thumb.

I paused by the bottles of balsamic vinegar, trying to work out which one of the twelve varieties on offer I should buy for my salad dressing. How much did Modena matter? Aged or not aged, and if aged, how aged was aged enough? The bottles, thin and elegant, chunky and robust, swam before me in a meaningless kaleidoscope of consumer choice.

Actually, I wasn't really thinking about balsamic vinegar at all. I was thinking about evolution. Specifically, I was thinking that I have spent millions of years swirling around the universe being anonymous matter, waiting for my moment, that split second when a certain set of atoms would coalesce to make me. And now here I was. In Sainsbury's, on a wet Thursday afternoon, thinking about balsamic vinegar.

Evolution is clearly a giant cosmic joke.

And then I realised that Arthur wasn't there. He wasn't hanging on to the trolley any more. He wasn't by my side, on his sturdy, rather stubby little white legs; he wasn't looking up at me with blue eyes, wrinkled with perplexity and a certain weariness.

I called his name. I ran up the aisle in one direction, and down it in the other. I looked round the bottom corners and then again round the top ones. Sainsbury's was suddenly bewildering, its aisles filled with people, milling, distracted and indifferent.

My mouth was dry and the blood was pounding in my veins. For a moment or two – only it felt much, much longer – a string of ugly images danced through my head. The worst things in the world; a meteor shower of horrors.

And then round the corner came a tall man with gipsyish black hair and a disruptive smile, carrying a toddler in his arms.

'Where was he?' I gasped.

'He bumped into me; I almost trod on him.' Ed McGregor handed him back gravely. I pressed my face into his hair and neck. 'I realised it was Arthur.' He put his hand on my shoulder. 'You all right?'

I nodded. Even in my dizzy state of relief and thankfulness, my flesh flamed under his fingers; I was conscious of his deranging sex appeal.

'You knew it was Arthur?' I said stupidly. I wouldn't have thought he'd known Arthur's name. I wouldn't even have put money on his knowing that Arthur existed.

'Of course. I'm sorry about yesterday. You have to . . .'

'Don't.' I held up my hand to silence him. 'Thank you for finding Arthur, but I don't want to discuss it.' He looked as though he was going to start again, so I rushed on, quietly but furiously: 'The happiest day of my life will be the day you leave Langley. If I never saw you again, I could not be more delighted.'

'Julie . . .'

'For Christ's sake!'

'Sorry. Of course. Sorry. Well,' he glanced at my trolley, 'your family must really like turnips.'

Ben

This morning a brown envelope arrived in the post with Mum's name on the front and 'Langley County Court' printed in the corner. I happened to be in the hall when it came through the letterbox, and for some reason – I don't really know why – I picked it up. I thought Mum might be in trouble with the law. It is not unknown, when women of her age are upset, for them to begin a career in shoplifting.

In stories people are always steaming envelopes open with kettles, but the books don't tell you it takes three hours. Actually, I'm not sure it can be done at all, but it certainly can't be done in the morning when you're meant to be getting ready for school.

Mum kept bustling in and out of the kitchen when I was waving the envelope over the kettle (those stories must have all been written before the invention of electric kettles, which switch themselves off as soon as there's any steam) so I had to keep shoving the letter up inside my jumper and pretending I was trying to make a cup of tea. I don't even drink tea normally, let alone make it, but all she said was: 'Are you trying to break that kettle as well?'

I put too many bags in the pot but unfortunately I still had to drink the tea because Mum was hanging around looking suspicious. I also splashed water on my hand, which is still hurting a bit, and in the end I tore the envelope.

Mum is getting divorced!

How can she? *Why?* It's so final. Doesn't she realise how hard I have been trying to get them back together and that I have nearly succeeded now on several occasions? It's surely only a matter of time.

I wonder if Dad knows?

Just as bad, she seems to be doing it herself. This is mad. She doesn't know anything about the law. She doesn't even know when you can drive in bus lanes. She fails to make proper use of them after seven o'clock: Dad is always going on at her about it.

She will get ripped off and we will all end up living in the poverty trap.

They don't need to get divorced, anyway. Emma's only living with Dad because she doesn't get on with her mum and she hasn't got a dad of her own. She can't possibly be planning to marry him because he's so *old*. She needs to marry someone like her brother in *EastEnders*.

I hope Mum hasn't imagined that the next logical thing after getting flowers from that Simon bloke is to marry him. He hasn't even met us, so how can he know if he's going to like it here?

But perhaps it will be like with Dad and Emma, and we won't count so much any more?

I wish Mum'd go out with Ed McGregor, who knows exactly how many children she has and is really good at maths homework, even helping someone who is quite thick without getting impatient. Unfortunately Mum doesn't like him. She wrote something really mean about him in the local paper and now they don't speak.

Julie

Perhaps I was a bit rude to Ed McGregor in the supermarket, considering he'd found Arthur, but I've run out of patience. If I can just get through this dinner with Simon, in future I will be keeping myself to myself.

I decided to make roast tomato salad (Delia, very easy, can be done beforehand), courgette, pumpkin, and spinach coconut curry (*Sugar Club Cookbook*, sounds revolting but is actually delicious, have done it before), and I bought some strawberries and cream in case Tony screwed up with his pudding, because I'm neurotic.

At least, I thought complacently, drizzling olive oil over the tomatoes, Kate and Ben were at Richard's. It was a relief that they were going to be spared meeting Simon, because they'd be bound to imagine that there was more to it than there is, and that I'm having sex with someone who wears the same trainers as them.

Arthur was still around (Emma was doing a shoot for *Just 17* magazine in the morning and needed a good night's sleep), but I was well organised, and by seven o'clock we were curled up together on the sofa. I was reading *Thomas the Tank Engine* stories in a voice of narcotic calm, getting slower and slower and more and more stupefyingly dull. And, sure enough, by seven thirty, Arthur's eyelids were drooping and his long lashes were fluttering over his cheeks.

And then Tony arrived, half an hour early, saying he needed to set up his equipment in the kitchen. He crashed around with bowls and ingredients, plugging in his hand whisk and switching it on, presumably to check the current in our house was the same as in his, and generally whirling around theatrically.

I pursued him into the kitchen. 'You're making a soufflé?'

'Why not?'

'It's a bit labour-intensive.' His job was supposed to be placing himself between me and Simon, to ensure that I had no further opportunities to embarrass myself.

'You won't notice I'm here.'

'That's what I'm afraid of. I want you to entertain Simon.'

'It's a fifteen-minute soufflé, takes no time at all. It's my speciality.'

Tony's test procedures had excited Arthur, who was now once again fully awake and jumping up and down on the sofa, shouting, 'Want to see everyone!'

The oven-timer bleeped and I got out the tomatoes, looking round with the roasting tin for a surface that wasn't already occupied by eggs, chocolate, oranges and bottles of Grand Marnier.

In the end I balanced it over the sink.

'They smell nice,' Tony remarked, presumably because he couldn't in all honesty say they looked nice. They were cherry tomatoes, much smaller than the ones I'd used the last time. I'd forgotten that they shrank when cooked. You practically had to squint to see them: once I put basil leaves on top they'd be hidden entirely.

Simon arrived promptly, with an expensive bottle of wine, and kissed me easily on both cheeks. I led him through into the kitchen and introduced him to Tony and Arthur, who was by now sitting on the work surface, his pudgy little legs hanging over the edge, and sorting through Tony's eggs.

Tony and Simon shook hands; Tony, I thought, smiled at him rather lasciviously. Simon meanwhile displayed a reassuringly non-paedophiliac interest in Arthur (i.e. not very much interest at all), asking him about his *Thomas the Tank Engine* books, but with the air of one who wouldn't know a Henry the Green Engine if it ran him over.

He showed rather more interest in the preparations for Tony's soufflé (about which I felt Tony was being unnecessarily flamboyant; it was only one course). It turns out that Simon is very interested in cooking.

'While I remember,' he said to me, from his vantage point at Tony's elbow, 'd'you still want to talk to my friend Maisie about this job?'

Maisie? Only three-year-olds are called Maisie. I couldn't see how anyone so cool as to have a name that's only come into fashion in the last four years could possibly want to employ me. 'She's flying to New York on Monday so she wondered if there was any way you could make it tomorrow?'

'I suppose so . . .' I said doubtfully, while Tony nodded at me vigorously from behind Simon's back.

'You'll like her,' Simon promised – though I don't know how he thinks he knows *what* I like. He has an entirely distorted picture of me. 'I've told her all about you.'

So Maisie knows I am a suburban mother of three who has to hurry past mirrors in case of being surprised by a wrinkle, who asks men to sleep with her regardless of whether they've shown any interest and has no experience of PR. I bet she can't wait.

At this point, Arthur dropped one of Tony's eggs on the floor – which it had been obvious to me from the start that he would – got upset, and asked to go to bed. I took him upstairs, leaving Tony and Simon to bond, and settled him under his duvet with his arm curled tidily around Winnie the Pooh.

I was coming down again about ten minutes later, having sung several nursery rhymes, when I heard laughter from the kitchen.

I froze.

Tony and Simon were talking animatedly about something – techno-funk, I found out later, not that it mattered – and suddenly, in that instant, it all became horribly clear. I knew now why Simon had declined to sleep with me.

Simon may, perhaps, have been bisexual. He may even – I don't know – have *wanted* to be bisexual. But in quite a big part of him, he was gay. And, when you thought about it, this was glaringly obvious: the worked-on body, the chic clothes, Wave, the knitting-pattern looks.

I felt ridiculous. I went hot, then cold. I considered opening the front door, slipping out into the night, and leaving them to it. But my child was asleep in bed upstairs and, anyway, it was *my* house.

I was also furious. Why hadn't he been clearer? He'd deliberately deceived me. Asking me out, sending me flowers, cruelly exploiting my anxiety to believe that somewhere out there were other Eds.

A funny smell seemed to be coming from the curry. At least it gave me something to do when I returned to the kitchen. I smiled at them dazzlingly, relieved that at least they weren't actually pawing each other, and prodded the curry, uncovering an oozy brown mess on the bottom of the dish – which was when I remembered that this curry was really easy, so long as – and unfortunately, this was crucial – you stirred it constantly.

I tasted it to see whether the charred flavour was confined to the black bit at the bottom or had seeped through the whole thing, and burnt my tongue. 'Shit!'

'Anything I can do?' Simon offered.

'No!' I said brightly, switching off the gas, and thinking that I wouldn't be able to tell whether it was burnt or not now, because all my tastebuds were scalded. 'Let's eat.'

We had the very small tomatoes, during which Tony and Simon moved on from techno-funk to the films of Krzysztof Kieslowski. The last movie I saw was *Antz*, on video. I seemed to remember having seen one of Kieslowski's 'three colours' films once, and Tony and Simon made a rather laborious effort to include me by taking ages to work out whether it was *Red*,

White or *Blue*. But after that I had a limited amount to contribute.

I was pretty sure the curry tasted burnt all the way through. But I doubt whether Tony or Simon even noticed, because they were too taken with each other and their conversation about theatre. They'd both seen the new production of *A Doll's House* at the National. They had so many views about it they probably could have gone on discussing it all week. I sat spooning acrid liquid into my still-stinging mouth and thinking that before I had children, I used to cut reviews of films and plays and art exhibitions out of the newspapers. Now I cut out articles with titles like 'a workout for wistaria'.

'D'you mind if we come and watch?' Simon asked Tony when it was time for Tony to make his soufflé.

So we trooped off to the kitchen to watch him whisking and buttering and pouring and popping into the oven, all of which he did with faultless aplomb while continuing his canter through childless person's subjects. By now, he and Simon were on to their favourite jazz clubs. I don't even have one jazz club, let alone a favourite.

I was beginning to hate both of them. Tony was supposed to be *my* friend. So why so shameless about his avid interest in Simon? I mean, how fantastic a thing *is* it, to have a penis? And Simon had asked me out. Why had he done that? Why hadn't he done what he was supposed to, and gone to Hampstead Heath?

Every now and then I summoned the effort to try to work the conversation round to a subject on which I had something to contribute, and they'd humour me for a few minutes before returning to events that require a babysitter.

At one point I found my thoughts wandering to whether my well-woman check was this Monday or the one after.

Tony's soufflé was delicious. Simon and I both asked for copies of the recipe.

After that I got the coffee on as quickly as I could; and as soon as we'd all had one cup I yawned ostentatiously. Tony took the hint and said he really ought to be going, and Simon said he ought to be going too. They offered to help with the washing-up, but I declined. They each kissed me on both cheeks and set off down the garden path, like a couple.

I shut the door on them with relief and went back to the kitchen, where I filled the dishwasher and put the curry dish in the sink.

I crashed about the kitchen, banging spoons down on surfaces, clattering plates together, and thinking that I am never again going to invite Tony to dinner with only one other person, because he is basically much, much more interesting than me.

Kate

Over dinner (fish and chips again, even though I am not supposed to be eating fish) I explained to Dad and Emma that I intended to come and live with them full-time.

'She can't!' Emma exploded, almost choking (afterwards she pretended a fish bone got stuck in her throat): 'Tell her she can't!'

'It's not practical, Kate . . .'

'Bindweed.'

'There's no room.'

(That's crap: the flat is four thousand square feet with nothing in it.)

'And we're not here a lot of the time.'

'You could give me lifts into school in the morning,' I persisted, 'like you do now, except every day. And I could hang around after school until you're ready and you could bring me back.'

'It's not that simple . . . I often don't come back here till late. Anyway, Mum does loads of things for you that I couldn't possibly . . .'

Like nagging me about lung cancer and complaining about how much I use the phone? I am sick of Mum's disappointment in me, as if I'm a prize dahlia that hasn't bloomed at the right time for her, and my growing up is all about her and not about me at all.

'You don't realise how much of your life is in Langley,' Dad said.

'Like what?'

'Rachel. The road protest.'

'The road protest will be finished soon. And Rachel can always stay with me here.'

'We couldn't do your washing,' Emma said, 'we send all our stuff out.'

'I'll do my own.'

Ben said: 'D'you remember that time when you used the washing machine and flooded the kitchen?'

'Shut up, why can't you?'

'We never make dinner except when you're here,' Dad objected. Actually, they don't often make dinner when we *are* here. They can't cook.

'You must eat something.'

'We eat out,' Emma said.

'I could come with you . . .' I saw their faces. 'All right, I could make my own.'

'You can't boil an egg,' Ben reminded everyone. 'You left one on once and the saucepan boiled dry. The egg nearly exploded.'

'Ben, you're not *helping*.'

Ben glared at me. 'You can't leave Mum.'

'No, you can't,' Dad agreed. 'And I'm not sure what we'll be doing anyway. We might have to go to LA.'

'That's all right, you're taking us to LA anyway.'

360

'Well, we might, for a time,' Dad said cautiously, 'but it's not definite. And it probably wouldn't be permanent. You've got your GCSEs to do, and we need to be flexible, because of Emma's work.'

'It isn't a flexible *thing*, having children!' I shouted. 'I didn't ask to be born: you made it happen. The least you can do is look after me when I need it.'

'That's exactly what I want to do. And I see you as often as I can . . .'

I banged down my fork – I was sick of chips anyway – and ran into the bathroom, where I slammed the door and locked it.

After a few minutes Dad banged on the outside and begged me to open up.

'No, I'm not going to.'

'I need a pee!' Ben wailed.

I thought perhaps they'd put him up to it, but Emma started screeching about her carpet, so I opened the door just enough to let Ben in, then I locked it again.

'Dad wants to talk to you,' he said, peeing.

'We're not wanted.'

'Do you think?' He did up his flies and sat down on the edge of the jacuzzi.

'Mum's so tense, she's always complaining about something. She's got no one to make her relax and tell her the things she worries about don't matter. And Dad can't think about anything except Emma, who's got no emotions.'

'She's got a career instead,' Ben said.

'You coming out, you two?' Dad called heartily from outside the door, as if it was a Saturday afternoon and he was trying to get us outside for a bit of fresh air.

'We're just a burden, aren't we?' Ben asked.

'Yeah.'

I wasn't really listening.

'D'you think our parents could get therapy for it, like I do for my dyspraxia?'

Ben is always a half-tone off-key, mentally.

'You can't stay in there all night,' Dad shouted through the door.

I could have done, easily, but I'm not sure I could have put up with Ben, so I came out to see what Dad had got to say for himself. Basically, the story was that although he loved us, more than anything in the world, in fact, and wanted to include us in everything he did, it was kind of tricky at the moment, because his life with Emma was a no-kids kind of life. Not live-in kids, anyway. What it seemed he wanted was occasional kids, kids-for-rent, kids-by-the-hour.

He said that there'd be compensations for us, in time: we'd appreciate having this home we could come to for weekends and holidays, and we'd enjoy having an alternative lifestyle (honestly, they were the words he used). And meanwhile, he only wanted to be a good father, a friend as well as a parent.

At this point I almost threw up.

As I said to Ben as we bedded down on our tatami mats, there is very little in either of our parents' homes to keep us.

Julie

It was a relief not to have to go into work the following morning. I was dreading Tony's concerned expression, his sympathetic murmurings and the tension around his mouth as he tried to stop himself from falling about laughing.

To get to Maisie Guilfoyle's office, you had to climb a flight of stairs from the Soho street, past black-and-white photographs of cranes and half-finished buildings. The narrow stairway was brightly painted and lit by unnaturally violent, heat-generating bulbs in the ceiling.

Once upstairs and inside the office, the floorboards were washed-pistachio, the walls were white, and the modernist furniture – moulded plastic and uncomfortable-looking felt-covered benches – was in cleverly clashing oranges and reds. If you were feeling the slightest bit hungover you'd have to be incredibly careful what you wore to work.

Maisie, sensibly, stuck to black – a stiff, Japanese-looking dress made out of something resembling underfelt, which gave her an odd, triangular shape. She had masses of black wavy hair, tumbling on her shoulders with Texan volume, like Jerry Hall or Diane Thatcher, and she wore serious make-up. It took time to register all this, however, because what you first noticed was the mid-Atlantic accent and the effusiveness.

'*Julie*!' She clasped my hands between her own, which were soft and manicured. 'How fantastic of you to come in at such short notice. I told Simon it was ridiculous to expect you to drop everything just because I've got to go to New York, but he said I *must* see you.' She gazed at me, more appraisingly than the slightly hysterical manner might have suggested. 'He thinks you're great. Come through, come through.'

She led me through an outer office, cluttered with about half a dozen desks, at which a series of young women with short skirts and long hair were talking volubly on the telephone about photo-opportunities and lunch. In Maisie's glass-walled room at the far end of this space, I sat down on one of the hard red seats with no back and her secretary brought coffee for me and herbal tea for her.

'Pregnant,' she announced, sniffing the tea and making a face – which was a relief because underneath her sculpturally shapeless black dress she was at the awkward stage when it might have seemed rude not to mention the bump (implying one thought she was fat) or she might, in fact, have been fat. 'Accident,' she added cheerfully. 'You've got kids, haven't you? Were you very sick?'

We talked about pregnancy for a bit, which if she

364

had set out to do it, was clever and kind of her, as it made me feel as relaxed as someone with washing-up hands and no shapeless Japanese dresses could in this environment. I told her she'd soon be tidying out her cupboards.

'So,' she said eventually, 'Simon says you're the only person he's met in this place he's living – where is it . . . ?'

'Langley.'

She picked up a pencil and stuck the end of it into her dense hair; quite a lot of it disappeared. 'Where exactly *is* that?'

'Sort of near the M25. It's on the tube.'

'Really? Anyway, he said you're the only person he's met who's . . . well, he says you're a single parent and you do a job and you're funny, and you're a great *coper* . . .'

It was at this point that I realised I had a pair of tights down the inside of my trouser leg. They were large and lumpy, like a goitre on my upper thigh. I pressed my legs together in an effort to flatten them, but then worried that this might squeeze them towards the floor. I thought I'd probably be safe as long as I remained sitting down. But what if they fell out when I stood up? If I left the office trailing black Lycra legs?

'I don't suppose you'd have met Shane?' Maisie was still talking away. If she had this much energy when she was pregnant she must be terrifying at other times. 'Before your time. Simon never told his parents . . . they knew that he and Shane shared the house, but I don't think they *ever* went upstairs. I think personally that they *must* have guessed, though Si says not. Don't

365

understand it, myself – I mean, how difficult is it, these days? But there you go, I've never known anyone so secretive . . . My theory is, he's never been able to face his sexuality. Not completely. Still, he might be better now. He was very upset when his parents died, but it must have been liberating, *really*, in the circumstances. And London and everything . . . Anyway, what do *you* think?'

I flushed. How much did she know about my efforts to seduce her apparently famously gay friend? But she was gazing at me frankly, with furious PR sincerity in her eyes. I didn't think she was winding me up.

I muttered something about not knowing Simon well enough to judge, but guessing that he might perhaps have been – well, *muddled* – about his sexuality. Not wanting to be gay, possibly. I also told her I'd introduced him to my gay friend Tony and they seemed to get on brilliantly.

'He needs another good man,' Maisie said. (This was the weirdest interview.) 'It's odd, isn't it, for someone to be as hung-up as that in our generation? I mean, he knows a phenomenal amount about music and the club scene, especially the provincial club scene. I rely on him incredibly: he knows what's hot before it's even *warm*. But I guess it must have been his parents – he must have thought he was protecting them. *Anyway*,' she pulled the pencil from her hair with difficulty, 'he tells me that you can talk to anyone and you'd fit in anywhere. And frankly, that's what we need because we've got enough twentysomething Trustafarians, and they're *terribly* good, but, you know, they're sometimes a bit *Tatler*. And now we've got this account for One Potato – d'you know them?'

'No.'

'Oh, they're lovely. High-quality childrenswear and toys, mostly by mail order, but they're planning to open a couple of shops – Bath, Guildford, places like that. And we don't have anyone here who knows anything about kids ... and then we've got another account coming up, which I'm sure we're going to get, for an organic food wholesaler, which would mainly involve talking to retailers – but they're very big, so it would also be about pushing organic food generally – quite a lot of media as well ... What do you think?'

I said I thought it sounded interesting, though it was all a bit of a blur.

'Oh, *good*! Look, we couldn't offer you a fortune to start with – I was thinking about £28,000 – but if you really get stuck in and make a success of it, we could review that in about six months ...'

I almost jumped up in the air, risking depositing a pair of tights on the distressed floorboards. It was nearly three times as much as I was getting at the *Langley Advertiser*.

I removed the tights in the privacy of the ladies' loos in Liberty's, then caught the tube back to Langley.

I walked very slowly to the office, hoping to give Tony enough time to be called out on a story or to lunch, but when I slouched in, he was still sitting at his place at the head of the reporters' table. I did a bit of deep breathing, but it was completely pointless: I still went bright red.

I avoided Tony's eyes.

'How was it?'

'All right,' I muttered, looking through my diary furiously.

'Thanks for dinner.'

'S'all right.'

'He's lovely.'

'Yes, I noticed.'

'Julie . . .'

At last I steeled myself to look at him. 'OK, what d'you want me to say? I am thick as two short planks. I am a deluded fantasist; I think men fancy me when they don't remotely; I am so conventional that the possibility of their being, in fact, homosexual, doesn't cross my mind.'

'Why are you always so hard on yourself?'

'Oh, Tony! how can you ask? When I'm such an idiot?'

'It was his fault. He knows it was.'

'No. He invited me out to dinner and I assumed it meant we were getting married.'

'Yeah, well, perhaps he shouldn't have invited you out in the first place; it was just that Suzy Sharp kept nagging at him to do it . . .'

I put my head in my hands. 'Oh no! Let's pile humiliation on humiliation! He only went out with me in the first place because of Suzy Sharp . . .'

'He really likes you. He thinks you're brilliant. That's why he recommended you to Maisie. And I wouldn't want to make excuses, but he *has* had a very rough few months . . . his parents dying, and splitting up with his boyfriend . . .'

'Shane.'

'Yes.'

'The point is, Tony, it would have been easy enough for him to say, "I split up with my boyfriend." There needn't have been any misunderstanding. I needn't have wasted all those hours wondering whether the reason he was interested in me was that he was a date rapist or a paedophile.'

'I know it's difficult for you to understand, but for him it wasn't that easy . . .'

'He didn't even have to say *that* much. He could have just said "he" at some point, dropped it into the conversation, glissaded over it – only a syllable, barely a breath . . . And the irony is, *he's* the one who's moving out of Langley because it's too conventional.'

'I thought you handled it really well.'

He was trying to make me feel better, but I was in no mood.

'When did you realise?' I asked sulkily.

'I'm afraid when he walked in. You?'

'When I was coming downstairs after putting Arthur to bed. So,' I couldn't keep the sarcasm out of my voice, 'did you have a good night?'

'Yes. Simon thinks you're great, honestly. He feels awful about what happened: the misunderstanding. He should never have sent the flowers. He's a clot.'

'So why did he?'

'Because he likes you. Because he wanted your good opinion. Because he makes flamboyant gestures. Because he felt he owed you an apology and because I think he really, a part of him . . . wanted to . . . want to.'

'But not quite enough.'

'When it came to it, no. I can't really explain it: I never found it difficult to be gay. But some people do. Even now.'

'He treated me very badly.'

'He knows that. All I can say is that if only you'd been a bloke . . .' He grinned. 'Well, we all feel the same.'

'Oh, great, thanks.'

Halfway through the afternoon, Ginny erupted into the office, her big, pale face red and pocked with moisture, her thick fair Brunnhilde hair in chaos.

I was writing about the threatened closure of a pre-school group, and my first reaction was irritation. I thought it must be another Mac from Sump thing.

'I don't know where Ben is!' she yelped, lowering Arthur to the floor. Arthur ran over and hugged me, murmured, 'You're the best of the world, Mummy,' then plumped on to his bottom and began unpacking the contents of my wastebin.

'What do you mean?'

'He wasn't at school!'

'Has he gone home with one of his friends? – Sam? Or who's that boy he's always going on about, Adrian someone?'

'No, you don't understand! He wasn't at school all day!'

'But I dropped him off.'

'I know, I didn't believe it at first, but I made the secretary check with Miss Millett and then I spoke to her, too. She thought he was ill . . .'

I picked up the phone.

'Yes,' the school secretary said, 'this *is* rather worrying; we had Ginny in about fifteen minutes ago. I'm afraid Ben definitely hasn't been here all day. It looks like he's been truanting again.'

What did she mean, again?

She said: 'Well, I believe it's not the first time . . .'

'All right, thank you,' I said rudely, and slammed down the phone. That was different. The tree was coming down. He thought he was on the point of reuniting his parents.

'He must be at the squats,' I told Ginny. 'Arthur, please put all that paper back. You're making a mess.'

The phone rang and rang at the squats and, when, eventually, it was picked up, it wasn't by Nettle or Ed or anyone cogent, but by someone who sounded stoned – possibly the boy with the installation.

'Is Ben Ellison there, please? This is his mum.'

'Dunno.'

'About thirteen, sweet face. Blond hair like straw, blue eyes, often has a runny nose. Ed McGregor sometimes helps him with his homework. Could you check, please, ask around?'

'Sure thing,' asthma-boy said, and rang off.

I slammed down the receiver. 'I'm going over there myself. Ginny, you go home with Arthur. Call me on the mobile if you hear anything.'

Tony caught my hand. 'Is there anything I can do?'

I shook my head, but didn't meet his eyes, because mine were too frantic.

At the squats, Nettle was in the front garden, throwing

371

bits of old tile into a pile. She was wearing a black vest top that exposed her tanned shoulders and slender arms. 'Oh, hello,' she said, 'what do you want?'

'Is Ben here?'

'Who?'

'Ben, my son. Thirteen, blond, scruffy.'

'No idea. We're a bit busy, as you can probably see.'

I concentrated on the muscles in my face, keeping them still, stopping them from breaking up. 'He's disappeared.'

Nettle looked at me appraisingly for a moment, and did not comment.

'Is Ed here?'

'Ed McGregor? No, he's very busy.'

'I know, but is he *here*?'

'No, he's out doing an interview with the *Independent*. But I doubt he'd have time to see you anyway. We're expecting the bailiffs again.'

Mould appeared around the corner of the house. He'd shaved his lank yellow hair on one side of his head, so he was half-bald, half-greasy. He was carrying a length of piping.

'Oh, hello,' he said cheerfully, 'you come to do another hatchet job?'

Nettle said: 'She's looking for her son.'

'Oh, right. You seen one of these?' He brandished the piping. 'You fix it in reinforced concrete, in an oil-drum, say, and then there's a metal bar across the end that you attach yourself to with a coupling device, like mountaineers use. The bailiffs have to get cutters down the sides of the pipe or drill straight through the concrete.'

372

I had no idea what he was talking about. 'Have you seen Ben?'

'Your kid? What's he look like?'

I hope Kate was under no misapprehension about how interested he was in her.

'Can I go inside and look?' I pleaded with Nettle.

She leaned on a pile of planks. 'I told you, we're really busy.'

'Oh, let her, why not?' Mould said, waving his pipe.

I was already halfway to the front door anyway. I pushed it open and began searching the rooms, stepping over sleeping bags and blankets, withered vegetables and paint-tins, dog-eared paperbacks and candle stubs. I went up the splintered staircase. The squatters had already removed one in three of the treads. I went all over the first and second floors; I climbed down into the cellars. I even clambered up through holes and crawled around in the attics. I emerged dusty and streaked with grime. I interrogated everyone I met. But there was no sign, and no word, of Ben.

He hadn't turned up at home, either. I called Sam Everitt's house, but Sam only knew that Ben hadn't arrived at school. I looked up the Farrs in the telephone directory and got hold of Adrian.

'It's Mrs Ellison here. Ben's not with you, is he?'

'No.'

'I don't suppose you'd have any idea where he might be?'

'No.'

Even though Adrian Farr only spoke in monosyllables, there was something shifty about him.

'I don't know why Ben's so keen on that boy. He seems quite unpleasant to me,' I remarked to Ginny, trying to be normal.

I called Richard. 'Ben's not with you, is he? You haven't heard from him?'

'No.'

'He's missing.'

The relief of speaking to him was too much; I burst into tears.

'Julie, stay calm! Pull yourself together.'

'I'm going to call the police.'

'Hang on a minute, have you tried his friends?'

'Yes, and the squats. He hasn't been at school. Oh, Richard, I think he's run away.'

Ten minutes later, two police officers were standing in our front room. They seemed to take up all the available space, so that suddenly there didn't seem to be enough chairs. I don't know why this was, because I have a sofa and two armchairs and there were only two of them.

They told me their names, but I'm afraid I wasn't concentrating properly.

'You say he's never run away before?'

'No, it's completely out of character . . . he's quite vulnerable, you see – more than usual, I mean, for a boy his age. Guileless. Not very streetwise. He gets mugged. And he *knows* that, you see, which is why he'd be careful. He wouldn't run away. He's clumsy – he's dyspraxic, actually; it means he's not very strategic . . .'

I knew I wasn't making much sense. But it was beginning to feel nightmarish, as if any minute everything might go black and shut down.

'I know you've spoken to his friends,' the woman officer said, 'but we'd like a list of their names and addresses so that we can double-check. What sort of things was he interested in?'

'Nintendo. His skateboard, but that's here. He didn't go out that much. He was thirteen. He went to school and came home.'

'Shopping?'

'He quite liked Covent Garden. He was beginning to get into all that surfer-skater wear.'

I tried to think of everything, anything that could remotely be useful. But there was both too much – how was I supposed to convey the scope of Ben's hapless trustfulness? – and too little.

'How would you describe Ben's emotional state? Did he seem depressed at all?'

'No. Well . . . perhaps he was a bit sad about our separation. He was always trying to get us back together.'

The woman officer nodded. 'We'll fax all the details straight over to the Missing Persons Helpline. They're nationwide. And we'll follow up all the leads you've given us, talk to his teachers and friends and try his favourite places. Often, when a child is unhappy . . .'

'He wasn't unhappy. Not fundamentally . . .'

'No, sorry; when a child runs away, he often returns to places that he identifies with the happiest times. So the places you went on holiday for example, perhaps before your marriage broke up . . .'

I nodded miserably, accepting her judgement.

'I see you've got someone here at the moment, but would you like an officer to stay with you – or is there anyone you can get to come over and be with you?'

'Yes. Yes, there is. That's fine.'

'And I don't know how you'd feel about it,' she hesitated, 'but if he doesn't turn up very quickly, this would seem to be quite a good case for an appeal. A press conference, maybe. Still –' she snapped her notebook shut – 'let's hope it won't come to that. The thing to remember is that the majority of missing children are found safe and well within seventy-two hours.'

After they'd gone, I sat and sobbed. They thought I'd driven Ben away by not being able to stay married. His life was so dreadful, he'd been forced to go off in search of some happier past.

The seventy-two hours statistic was meant to cheer me up, I knew, but I wasn't sure I could stand even seventy-two hours of this feeling. It was impossible not to imagine, in graphic detail and livid colour, all the things that might have happened to Ben. His body broken somewhere; his sweet nature corrupted. His fear, helplessness, pain, his longing for home.

Ginny put her arm round me. 'They said I wasn't to leave until you had someone else here.'

'Sorry, you're right.'

I must pull myself together.

I tried to get hold of Fran, but couldn't find her, so I called my mother, who was impressively calm – being steeped in Dunkirk spirit, she never minds a crisis – and who arrived, half an hour later, with a bottle of scotch, four pints of milk and six M&S ready-meals from her freezer.

'I blame Richard,' she announced, dumping her eco-friendly shopping bags on the kitchen table and unpacking them. After the fourth chicken cordon bleu, I was half-expecting a Mary Poppins-style standard lamp. How long did she think she was staying for? 'It's all because he wouldn't face up to his responsibilities; he should never have *gone off*.'

'But Mum, you're a feminist,' I said wearily; I had no energy for arguments about Richard. 'You believe in people fulfilling their destinies. You can't have one set of rules for women and another for men.'

'Your generation is extremely *muddled*, if I may say so. I am in favour of opportunities, not selfishness. Anyway, it's a feminist *point*: Richard was a coward in all sorts of ways. If he hadn't bullied you into giving up work, you'd probably be more interesting to him now.'

Oh, great, thanks, Mum.

She was only doing it to distract me, I suppose. But I had no fight to point out that he didn't bully me; I was his accomplice. Besides, I'd only done what she did, and put my family before feminist theory. What she couldn't bear to acknowledge was that you ever had to make a choice.

But I couldn't say any of this; it was too much of a betrayal to think about anything except Ben, let alone talk about it. Fortunately, we were saved from more of it by Kate's return.

I met her in the hall.

'Hi.' She threw her jacket over the banisters and kicked off her trainers at the bottom of the stairs. 'What's all this about you going up the squats looking for Ben?'

'Oh, Kate, have you any idea where he could be? He didn't go to school.'

'It's serious, then?'

'The police are combing the streets. Possibly Langley Ponds as well, by now.'

I burst into tears again and she threw her arms round me. Crab-wise, holding on to one another, we went into the sitting room and slumped down on to the sofa.

I made an effort to dry my eyes, but the tissue was already sodden. 'What sort of mood was he in at Dad's, can you remember?'

She pulled away from me. 'Oh, God, I hope this is not my fault!'

'What do you mean?'

'At Dad's on Thursday I told him there was nothing in either of our parents' homes to keep us.'

I stared at her. 'Is that what you think?'

'Of course not.' She squeezed my hands. 'I was just being histrionic, as usual. I'm sure he'll turn up.'

But I could see in her eyes that she wasn't convinced; that she felt the same dumb incredulity I did that this was happening to us; and the same unease: if this could happen, then worse things could happen too.

The doorbell was ringing. I sat frozen on the sofa, not wanting the news.

My mother put her head round the door. 'It's Richard.'

I stood up as he came into the room. He looked like

Ben – same rough blond hair, same air of bewilderment. It's funny, but until now I'd never really seen the resemblance. I always thought Ben looked like me.

'No news?'

I shook my head and he fell into my arms. It was the first time we'd touched for a year. I hugged him awkwardly, unsure whether I liked the familiarity, the way our bodies settled into one another.

'I feel it's my fault,' he muttered into my shoulder. 'I should have come to that tree thing. That's what he wanted.'

'He was always trying to get us back together.' I pulled apart from him and brushed my hair off my face with my hand, avoiding his eyes.

He shook his head. 'I feel so helpless.'

'You could join the search. Take Kate: she needs something to do. At least it's light until late. I'd have gone myself, but I wanted to be here, in case . . .'

Richard nodded. 'The police wondered if we wanted to do an appeal tomorrow.'

'I suppose.'

It was difficult to think that far ahead, inconceivable to me that I'd be able to get through a whole night of not knowing where Ben was.

Once they'd gone, I wandered around the house, picking things up and putting them down – a photograph of Ben, a stone he'd given me from a beach, though I couldn't remember which one (why not? why hadn't I taken more notice of everything?), a battleship book open upside down on his bedroom floor.

As a baby, I remembered, he'd been sleepy and good-natured; as a small boy, imaginative, fearful, muddled. And since Richard and I had split up, less confident, more anxious. It was out of character for him to run away. He knew he was accident-prone. He may not have great insight (though perhaps he did; perhaps behind all that confusion he was far more sensitive and acute than any of us realised) but the one thing he knew about himself for sure was that he was ill-equipped to deal with an awful lot of what gets thrown at him.

He wouldn't have gone willingly, not alone. My real terror – too frightening even to talk about – was that he'd been taken.

My mother was trying to persuade me (for about the tenth time) to eat something when the inspector arrived. He introduced himself as Paul Ballard and said that he was in charge of the case.

'No news yet, I'm afraid. We'll obviously keep looking all night. What do you think about a press conference tomorrow? Think you'd be up to it?'

'I suppose.'

'It'd be more effective if you could bear to be there, but if you decide you can't, we'll do it anyway. We've more or less decided to do it at Scotland Yard, rather than the local station. We anticipate quite a bit of interest, which is good, obviously. Now, I know it's going to be difficult, but you should try to get some sleep. Do you want me to call your GP?'

'No, I'll be all right,' I lied.

Richard dropped Kate off at midnight. He said he'd be back at dawn.

I went to bed then, mainly to persuade my mother and Kate to do the same. But once I was sure they were both asleep, I got up and sat downstairs. Lying under a snowy duvet, head on a pillow, I felt as though I was letting Ben down. God only knows where he was sleeping, or if he was sleeping at all. I knew this was illogical – my being tired wasn't going to help him – but there was nothing I could do about it.

I dozed a little, but I was up before dawn, making a cup of tea. My mother padded into the kitchen soon afterwards, looking dreadful; she couldn't have had much sleep either. We sat drinking the tea in silence, while the sun came up on the garden, picking out the glistening dew on the rose petals, throwing apple-tree shadows across the sheeny lawn.

Richard turned up just after eight. He'd been with the searchers since first light, and he looked shattered too, grubby from the woods and the dump at the back of the furniture factory.

I twisted my fingers. 'Have they dragged the ponds?'

'Not yet. Today, perhaps.'

The inspector came for us in a police car at ten. Richard showered and put on some of the clothes he'd left behind, and I changed into a clean skirt and silk shirt. But we still both looked raddled.

No one said much in the car on the way. The police still had no leads. They hadn't even found anyone who'd seen Ben yesterday.

At Scotland Yard, we were offered coffee and biscuits – which we didn't touch – and DI Ballard took us through the procedure. He'd speak first, Richard would follow and then it would be my turn to ask anyone who might be holding Ben to let him go. (I couldn't see a tearful plea from me having the slightest impact on a vicious paedophile ring, but I wasn't about to argue.) Then Nicky, the woman police officer from last night, would say a little about the search so far and they'd open the floor to questions.

At eleven-thirty, they took us through into the room where the press were waiting. It was packed. There were rows and rows of chairs crammed with people with notebooks and hand-held tape recorders. From around the walls, photographers poked long fat lenses at us, and, at the back, television cameras whirred on tripods. The atmosphere was stuffy and tense with expectation.

The inspector began by saying how worried the police were about Ben's disappearance: he'd never gone missing before, hadn't left a note, hadn't taken any money, clothes, or other possessions. He was a vulnerable boy, not especially streetwise, trusting and open.

Richard asked Ben to come home. And then I did my bit. My voice through the microphone sounded strange and disembodied. I was amazed at myself, really, managing to utter those words without cracking; but I got through it somehow, even with the cameras flashing in my face.

Nicky described the search so far, explaining that a number of the neighbours and some of Ben's teachers were helping, which I hadn't realised – and then they invited questions.

A girl reporter stood up, said she was from the *Sun*

and then asked: 'Is it true, Mr Ellison, that you're living with Emma Neil?'

Richard looked taken aback. He didn't answer for a moment, then he said: 'That's right.'

'So Ben is Emma's stepson. Did they get on well together?'

I was horrified. I could see the headlines already: 'Emma Neil's Stepson Missing'. Not Julie Ellison's son, or Richard Ellison's son, but Emma Neil's stepson. That was why there were so many people here.

'Was Ben unhappy about the marriage break-up?'

Inspector Ballard answered that one, repeating that Ben and Emma had got on very well. Then he tried to deflect them by saying that Ben was mildly dyspraxic, but they weren't put off. More questions followed, about Emma, me and Emma, Richard and Emma, Ben and Emma, Kate and Emma.

I sat behind the desk in a daze, letting the inspector do most of the talking and thinking that I really shouldn't mind, not if it helped get Ben back. And a part of me really didn't care what it took: they could claim that Ben was Charles and Camilla's love child if it helped. But another part of me felt as though he was being taken away for a second time.

'Did you tell them?' I asked Richard outside, after-wards. 'Did you say they could do that?'

He shook his head.

'I'm sorry it was such an ordeal,' DI Ballard apologised. 'I had no idea it would be quite that bad.'

'Was that necessary?'

He looked at me compassionately, and I had to turn away.

Now that the press conference was over, waves of exhaustion swept over me. I was drowning in tiredness. I didn't have the emotional resources to take much more of this. Soon I was going to stop being dignified, start screaming and not stop. I sat in the back of the car and wept all the way home, staring out of the window, at the buses, the taxis, the shoppers pushing into Boots and out of Our Price, as though if I only looked hard enough, I might see Ben.

Outside our house, Richard caught my arm.

'I'm going to go out looking again . . .'

'Are you sure? Aren't you shattered?'

'. . . But there's something I wanted to say first. I'm no longer sure . . . I don't think I did the right thing, a year ago, leaving. I allowed myself to get carried away. But it all dwindles into domesticity sooner or later.'

'It does?'

'It all settles down and becomes humdrum. One relationship ends up much like another.'

'I thought you believed in euphoria. Exhilaration. Abandonment. Lasting passion.'

He kissed me on the forehead. 'I'll see you later.'

My mother met me at the front door.

'I took the liberty of ringing June,' she hissed. 'She watches all that daytime television while she's doing her ironing, and I didn't like the idea that she should find out from the news. I hope that's all right?'

I put my bag down wearily. 'I should have done it myself.'

'The only trouble is, she's come round . . .'

Bizarrely, I could hear the food processor rumbling

in the kitchen. Didn't she know my mother had brought enough food to last us six weeks?

'I accept what you say – I mean, I take your point,' she was shouting at my mother over the noise of the motor, 'but holding down a steady job and maintaining a stable family was *quite* enough for Alf. In our day, we didn't think we had to make it into the gossip columns by the time we were forty or we weren't worth anything. It's true that a few people might have harboured ambitions to get somewhere, but they always had a perfectly good excuse . . .'

'What *is* she going on about?' I asked my mother in horror.

'Absolutely no idea. Oh God, now there's someone else at the door.'

I stared at the gloss-painted door blankly, longing to run away and hide, put my hands over my eyes, to scream and scream if it meant not hearing; I wanted to die rather than live with this feeling of dread any longer, rather than have the dread realised, rather than hear anyone say, 'I'm sorry . . .'

But I didn't do this. I opened the door.

Kate

When I was small, I used to have nightmares of people coming into the house to get me. Sometimes they had guns. I don't know what I imagined would happen when they took me – it never got that far – but now I *can* imagine, because I'm old enough to read the papers and see the news, and I can't bear it.

I'm trying not to think about it. If I think too much, I could go mad.

Maybe that's what's happened to Mum.

It must be worse for her, because she always babied him. She did more than you should for a boy of thirteen, because basically, she never believed he was capable of doing it for himself. And now she has to think of him out there, by himself, or worse, with someone else, needing her.

I wish now I hadn't objected so much when she fussed him, and that I'd been a bit more understanding about his learning difficulty. I even told him I didn't believe in dyspraxia. But now I'd believe in anything if only he'd come back.

I don't even dare think what a relief that would be. If I allow myself to imagine what it would be like if he came back, I'll only be storing up more misery. Except how could the misery be worse?

Maybe this is what's driven Mum mad – not daring to hope and not being able to cope any longer with the fear. For nearly the first twenty-four hours she was fantastic. I could see that she was frantic with worry, and she wasn't letting Arthur see it, and she was trying incredibly hard for Grandma and me. Grandma Eileen was being very calm as well, but she has to accompany it with a lot of feminist ranting.

But then Grandma June turned up, for some reason – no one can have invited her – and I didn't hear how it started, but I suddenly heard Mum shouting: 'I know exactly what you think – that I should never have taken the job at the paper. I should have been around more.' And then she turned on Grandma Eileen: 'And you think I should have been around *less*. You think I should have been running a major multinational by now. But you set me the wrong example.'

Perhaps they'd been arguing with her about what she planned to do next, because, a minute later, she was stomping off down the front path and handing her car keys to Ed McGregor. Then he got in the driver's seat of our car and she got in the passenger seat, and they drove off.

God knows what Dad will say. He's out looking for Ben. Not that I think Ben can be in Langley. At least, not alive; they surely would have found him by now.

Julie

The motorway exit signs piled up meaninglessly on top of one another – Luton, Northampton, Leicester. The car flashed past the service stations with their knife-and-fork and petrol-pump graphics – Granada, Travellers Rest – their brightly lit bridges straddling the motorway, and their indistinguishable offerings of wrapped sandwiches, damp steaming burgers and fizzy drinks.

The fields rolled away from the road towards secret copses and hamlets nestling in hollows, with houses like toys and church spires poking up through the trees. There was a soft pink summer evening light on the fields; every now and then, you could see a stream shining in the distance and a big house beyond it – Jacobean, Queen Anne, Victorian. I imagined the inhabitants' lives protected and peaceful, stilled like the evening landscape, full for ever of twittering birds and mane-tossing ponies, hedges, and grassy knolls with sheep.

Lorries tore past us on fat tyres and cars roared

relentlessly up the outside lane – a great procession of contending traffic, belting north, belching fumes.

Now and again I dozed off. There were lots of things to ask Ed, but this wasn't the moment.

I was exhausted. There was clearly nothing I could do about Ben as long as we were in the car, but even so I always woke up feeling startled and guilty. I shouldn't be asleep when my son was missing. I shouldn't be here at all. Until Ed had appeared on the doorstep this afternoon, it had seemed imperative to stay at home, nesting for Ben. Now I was on the M1, on a hunch. I was away from the police, from Richard, Kate, and the grandmas.

I was already a bad mother who'd driven her son away. And now here I was halfway up a motorway, for no better reason than that Ed McGregor had suggested it. I'd tried to unpack my motives, and I thought they were the right ones, but it was hard to be certain.

'Phil's gone too,' he'd said without preamble, when he appeared on the doorstep.

'Oh my God!'

'Ben was fascinated by the idea that Phil didn't know where his mother was. They could've gone to find her.'

'Where?'

'The last time anyone knew, she was in Leeds.'

'We must tell the police.'

'Yes. I thought I might look myself.'

But he didn't have a car. So I'd lent him mine, and then – because I felt sure, somehow, that he was right – I came too.

Eileen and June both thought I'd cracked up. I shouted at them before I left. I can't remember what now, but it was almost certainly something unforgivable.

Ed drove north fast, and expertly. There was something comforting about being with him. Perhaps it was just that I finally felt I was doing something.

Or perhaps it was another illusion.

On the other hand, he *knew* Phil, and he knew Ben, and I'd always been sure that Ben wouldn't have run away by himself. It would be just like him to try to reunite a child with his mother. And just like him to forget to think about what effect that might have on me.

Leeds was a blur of grey buildings set back from the road, testaments to the civic pride of Victorian plutocrats; of traffic lights, one-way systems, and groups of excited girls in short skirts and summer dresses.

And then we were through the city and out the other side. We drove past row upon row of semis, grids of grimy back-to-backs, then a down-at-heel seventies shopping centre with boarded-up shops and sad, scruffy pubs.

I hoped Ed was right. I was risking an awful lot, being here. And though I now believed that Ben was with Phil, it was perfectly possible that they were somewhere else entirely – at King's Cross, being introduced to solvent abuse, or in Piccadilly among the rent boys and the addicts looking for their dealers.

We didn't talk much. There was plenty to say, but not immediately. There would be time, one way or another. The silence wasn't uncomfortable.

We found the estate where Ed thought Phil's mother had last been heard of. It was still light, and the evening was warm, yet the open spaces between the blocks were empty and echoing. We parked in one of them, a deserted concrete well that should have linked, but somehow divided, the tower blocks. I shivered, despite the summery air; the place was exposed, windy and bleak.

We got out of the car, looking around for someone to ask for information about Phil's mother. The only visible living things on the walkways or the overgrown grass were a couple of mongrels, humping. There were plenty of signs of human habitation – gold cigarette paper sparkling among the dog turds, broken wooden crates on the grass – but no actual humans.

And then Ed saw a young man loping along in the distance.

'I'll go and ask him.' He strolled away.

I watched from a distance; the man stared insolently as if Ed were a piece of meat, and gobbed on the grass.

I heard movement behind me and looked round. There was toddler play equipment on the grass – a slide, a low-slung climbing frame. A woman had just emerged from the building with a child.

'I'm looking for someone called Donna,' I called across to her. 'She used to live here.'

She shrugged. 'I only moved in last month. You could ask in there.'

She nodded at the door behind her. A plastic sign in red letters on white was tacked to the brickwork above the door. It said 'Family Centre' – so I went in and found myself in a kind of reception area, with lino floors and bare walls. The noise of women's voices and the high-pitched complaints of small children filtered through a door to my right.

I pushed open the door and peered round into the room. Six or seven women were sitting on plastic chairs in a circle on a patch of carpet, an assortment of babies and toddlers playing at their feet.

The mothers looked pale, with sagging faces and tired eyes. I went in tentatively; they didn't take much notice. I sat down next to one of them, and explained, again, that I was looking for someone called Donna.

She shook her head, but asked her neighbour, who shook her head too.

'The only thing I know about her,' I said, 'is that her surname used to be Reece, but she's changed it a few times. She had a son, Phil, but he was taken into care years ago, and she drinks.'

'Could it be that woman in Frimley Walk?' asked a woman across the circle. 'She drinks.'

'She shouts'n'all,' someone said.

'She makes a bloody racket.'

'Where did you say she lives?'

'Joanne lives at twenty-two,' one of the women said, 'so she must be – what? twelve?'

'How do I get there?'

They gave me directions – past the third tower block, then left – and told me to come back if it wasn't right.

It was only when I got outside that I remembered I'd gone off without telling Ed where I was going. He was pacing up the walkway towards me, looking alarmed.

'You disappeared!'

'Sorry.'

'I thought you'd been abducted.' He pulled me to him and held me tight for a moment. My head pressed into his shoulder. He smelt of woodsmoke.

'Come on,' I said, pushing him away. 'I've got an address.'

Frimley Walk turned out to be a scruffy three-storey building. The ground-floor flats, of which number twelve was one, had overgrown, scrubby gardens littered with old bedsteads and broken chairs. The whole block exuded deep depression.

I found the right flat and tried ringing the bell, but it didn't work. I banged on the door.

'Who is it?' a woman's voice called out aggressively.

'Is Ben there?'

'Who?'

'Ben.' My voice faltered and I turned away. I'd been hoping so hard. I'd allowed myself to believe in this wild-goose chase, and now we were here, and nothing.

'Is Phil there?' Ed was calling through the letterbox. 'Is that Donna?'

'No. Fuck off.'

'Do you know Donna?'

'Fuck *off*! Try number eleven.'

'Come on,' Ed took my arm; 'it's not the right place.'

I stumbled down the path and across the brambly patch of yard. Ed banged on the door of the next flat.

'Who is it?'

'Ed McGregor.'

A bolt slid back, and the door opened.

Phil stood inside, pastier and scruffier than ever, and swaggering weakly.

'Mum!' Ben screeched, hurling himself down the hall and into my arms. He collapsed into me, his body falling against mine and giving way to great, shuddering sobs.

I held his head against my chest, running my fingers ecstatically through his hair, covering his scalp with kisses, weeping down the back of his neck. He sniffed, rubbed his nose with his sleeve, tried to stand up straight and smile, and then gave in again.

'I'm sorry,' he managed to get out eventually. 'I didn't realise it would take so long to get here. I didn't know it would be so far. And then we didn't have any money to get back and I was so frightened . . . I didn't know what to do. I thought you'd be cross.'

'It's all right,' I soothed him. 'You're safe. It's all that matters.'

He was gabbling now: 'I thought if I left, you and Dad would realise you shouldn't be apart. But I realise now that was stupid. You're not going to get back together. But I don't mind, honestly, because I understand that you have to live your own lives, and I don't mind either if you marry Ed and, actually, I'd be really pleased.'

I laughed, embarrassed. 'Don't be silly. I'm not going to marry Ed! He just came to help me find you.' I looked at Ed apologetically over the top of Ben's head, but he only raised his eyebrows and tipped his head to one side.

'Ben thought it would solve all my problems, if I could find my mum again,' Phil was explaining, 'and I told him it wouldn't but he kept going on about it. Now he realises I was right. We were just about to try and hitch back to London.'

'Is your mum here?'

'She's asleep.'

'Can we wake her?'

'Do we have to?'

'I don't think we can simply take you away,' Ed said. 'She'll think she's been hallucinating.'

'I'm not sure how much she noticed we were here anyway.'

Ed handed me his mobile phone. 'You should call Richard.'

Still clutching Ben's hand, I dialled the number at home. Kate picked up the phone.

'She's found him!' she whooped joyfully. 'Mum's found Ben! And he's fine! She's found him!'

Richard came on the line. 'Julie! Where the hell are you?'

'Leeds. Well, actually just outside Leeds . . . Can you call Inspector Ballard and let him know?'

'Who with?'

'Ben! And he's fine. Absolutely fine. He . . .'

'Yes, but who else?'

'Ed McGregor. It was all his idea; he realised Phil was missing . . .'

'What on earth possessed you to go with him? What about Arthur, and your mother? What about *my* mother? And you didn't even take your mobile.'

'I forgot. And Ed drove the car. I'd have killed myself,

the state I was in.' Did all this matter? 'I *told* your mother, and mine, and Kate. You weren't there.'

'Can I speak to Ben?'

'Of course.' I passed the phone across.

'Yep,' I heard Ben say. 'I'm sorry . . . No, I realise that. Yes, I will.' He passed the phone back to me: 'He wants you to come home at once.'

Phil led us down a hall with a lino floor and damp walls. The interior of the flat smelt stale and sweetly rotting, as if there might be rancid food somewhere or as if everything, including the inhabitants, was quietly composting.

In what, I suppose, must have been the living room, although the only items of furniture it contained were a sofa, a television and a terribly stained carpet, a woman was stretched out, asleep. She lay on the sofa, underneath a patterned duvet, wearing a greyish T-shirt that might once have been white. She had purple bruising around her eyes, jowly cheeks and cracked lips, and her hair was thin and tangled.

Ben, still clutching my hand, whispered: 'She's like this most of the time. Occasionally she wakes up and swears. One time she screamed.' He pulled me lower: 'Phil says she doesn't have anything to get up for – no job and no family living here.' He stared at her, fascinated, this woman in her coma of sadness.

Phil shook his mother awake. He had to do it quite hard.

'What is it? What you doing? Get off, you great bugger . . .' She opened her eyes and registered that there were strangers in the room. 'You come to take 'em away?' she asked wearily. 'About bloody time, too.'

'This is Julie. She's Ben's mother. And I'm Ed McGregor.'

'Oh yeah? Well, they keep saying they're hungry. I haven't got any food here.'

'No, that's all right,' I said. 'We can feed them.' I stared at her helplessly. Her breath stank of alcohol and something else, something sweet and sickly.

'What you waiting for, then?'

Ed said: 'Is there anything we can do? Anything you need?'

'You a dealer?'

Ed shook his head, then handed her a twenty-pound note.

She sat up effortfully; she was a big, bloated woman. 'Not much for two boys, is it?'

He handed her another one. And then Phil started to cry, so we left.

Ben

We caught the 125 Express to Leeds. Phil had the money for the tickets, though he refused to tell me how he got it because he thinks for some reason I need protecting, even though he is the one who always looks grey and has no parents.

The train journey was cool – we ate sweets and changed compartments five times, even going in first class for ten minutes, till we were thrown out – but I had no idea Leeds was so far.

I think I enjoyed it more than Phil. The nearer we got to Leeds, the more moody he became.

At a place called Doncaster, he said: 'I don't know why you think this is a good idea.'

'You'll feel better when you've seen your mum.'

'You haven't met her.'

'I always feel better when I've seen mine.'

'Why've you run away then?'

'I haven't run away. I've just taken the day off school to help you sort yourself out.'

He raised his eyes to the ceiling, as if I was stupid,

but the point is, he hadn't told me it was so far.

We had to get two buses out to the estate where Phil used to live before he went into care, and by then it was quite late. He said no way could we expect to get a bus back tonight because this was a no-go area and after dark the drivers were afraid of being attacked by addicts.

I thought he was trying to shock me – he's always acting tough, as if he knows about a load of bad things – but, as it turned out, a bus wouldn't have been much use anyway, because as he now revealed to me, he didn't have the money for tickets back to London anyway!

I tried not to panic. 'Why didn't you tell me?'

'You didn't ask.'

'But what are we going to do?'

He shrugged. 'We could always hitch. We might get someone who'll turn us in, but it's only me they'll put into care.'

I said hopefully: 'You might want to stay here with your mum.'

He shook his head. 'You're wet.'

The bus took us to the edge of the estate, which was like the deserted cities you see in movies about the aftermath of nuclear explosions, meteor strikes, etc. All the buildings looked as if they'd been left untouched for months, and there was absolutely no one about.

'Can I phone my mum from the flat?' I asked as we walked along a passageway between a building and a wall, where weeds were growing out of the paving stones. 'If I don't come back tonight, she'll worry.'

Phil was now in a really evil mood. I could tell that

I was starting to get on his nerves. 'Don't be a *moron*,' he said, 'she hasn't got a *telephone*!'

He made it sound really exotic, like a swimming pool with a jacuzzi or something. What kind of person doesn't have a telephone? I tried to think of a single person I knew who didn't have a phone, and couldn't.

'A call box, then? I could reverse the charges.'

'You think you'll find a call box that hasn't been vandalised? On this estate?'

'I don't suppose your mum'd have a mobile?'

'Oh shut up, Ben,' he snapped. 'Stop being such a middle-class prat. The only people with mobiles round here are the heroin dealers.'

I didn't fancy asking one of them if I could borrow their phone, so I didn't say anything else.

When we got to where Phil's mum used to live, she didn't answer the door, but Phil said that didn't necessarily mean she wasn't there. I thought she must be a very rude woman, if this was true. He led me round the back, where there was a tiny toilet window that was open, which he said we could climb through.

'Couldn't burglars get in here?'

'They know there's nothing to steal.'

I thought he was joking until I got inside. The first thing you noticed was the smell. Burglars would easily be overcome by the fumes before they had a chance to make their escape. It was like rotten vegetables and wee, and maybe sick – but sweet, as well. It made me retch, though Phil said it was surprising how quickly you could get used to it.

Inside the flat, there was almost no furniture.

The kitchen floor was thick with grease, although this was pretty amazing considering that there was no cooker or fridge or any sign of any food – just a sink and some kitchen cupboards made of plywood and painted yellow a long time ago.

There was a small television in the sitting room ('Probably nicked,' Phil said. 'Bet she hasn't had it more than a few days.') and a lumpy old red sofa with a brown duvet screwed up at one end. There was a bedroom as well, containing a stained mattress and nothing else.

Phil seemed to think this was proof his mother still lived here. She must be a very odd woman: she didn't have any of the things women normally have, i.e. shampoos, body creams, spare pairs of shoes, pasta jars, etc.

He said we might as well watch the television until she arrived. We watched an old film about the Second World War and then a late-night discussion programme about nudists, which can't have been very interesting because I fell asleep, and I guess Phil did too.

At about two o'clock, I woke up. For a minute or two I couldn't think where I was, or why I was all tangled up on the floor with Phil. Then I realised that there was someone else in the flat.

I heard her open the front door, then crash into the wall and swear. She thumped down the hall and into the sitting room, swearing all the time. She was very heavy – every step sounded like a monster was coming towards us.

She was enormous. There were no curtains at any of

the windows, and as soon as she came into the room, I got a very good view of her.

Everything about her was swollen and flabby. She was grotesque, like a cartoon woman. Weirdly, she didn't see us – or if she did, she didn't realise what she was seeing. Her eyes were glazed, and she seemed to look right through us. She toppled on to the sofa and grunted a bit. And then, in seconds, she was snoring.

I shook Phil.

'Is that her?' I whispered.

'Yeah. You see now?'

'Should we wake her up and tell her we're here?'

Phil shook his head violently. I don't think he wanted to wake her at all, ever. 'Leave it till morning.'

I didn't get much sleep. I lay awake feeling sorry for Phil: he'd come all this way to see his mother and she was in this state. Also, she was snoring, which was really annoying. I thought about going into the bedroom and sleeping on the mattress, but it looked full of things you could catch.

We dozed until about half-past eight, which was amazing, considering how light it was in the flat. I guess both of us had spent quite a lot of the night worrying – me about Mum and Dad not knowing where I was; Phil about I don't know what – but whatever it was, by morning he was even more depressed than he had been before.

'Whose bloody stupid idea was it to come here?' he asked, rubbing his eyes viciously. He didn't bother to whisper; he probably knew she wouldn't wake up. 'Look at her.'

I didn't really want to look at her. She was a wreck. She was puffy and pasty and she was lying on her back with her mouth open, snoring and dribbling. She looked as if she was aged about a hundred, not like a mum at all, more like something in a Victorian freak show.

'Should we wake her up?'

But Phil had stopped speaking to me. The television was on from last night and he'd found some cartoons and was pretending to watch them.

'I'm hungry,' I said eventually. 'I haven't had anything since breakfast yesterday except for two packets of crisps and a Kit-Kat.'

'You should've thought of that before.'

'Can't we wake your mum and tell her?'

Phil shook his head at me and turned back to the television. But after a while – perhaps he was hungry too – he switched it off and shook the woman on the sofa. She didn't stir, so he shook her more violently.

'Fuck *off!* What the fuck . . . ?' she spluttered.

'It's me. Phil.'

But she just swore. She swore and swore, using every swear word I'd ever heard and some I hadn't, concentrating especially on the really bad ones, which she seemed to like best. And the awful thing was, none of it made any sense.

She seemed to hate him. I'd never heard anyone sound so violent. It was really scary.

It was a relief when she seemed to get tired of it. Phil turned away and she fell back on the sofa and back into her thick, deep sleep.

'You should have told me your mum didn't have any

food,' I said crossly, after we'd sat in silence for about half an hour.

Phil picked a scab on his head. 'You wouldn't have believed me anyway.'

Eventually, he said: 'All right. I'll go and get something.'

I jumped up eagerly. 'I'll come.'

'No, you won't. You'll just get us caught.'

He was going to steal it! I didn't want to have to steal things – he was right that I'd be useless at it – but I thought I'd almost rather be caught shoplifting than have to stay any longer in this horrible smelly flat.

He said: 'Look, if you come – if you even try and come – I'm not going.'

So I didn't have any choice. While he was gone, I hid in the bedroom, keeping well clear of the infested mattress. I kept worrying about Mum, who I knew would be frantic by now.

Phil seemed to be gone for ages. It even crossed my mind that he'd run off. If my mother had been like his, I don't think I could have behaved responsibly either. But he returned eventually, with ten penny-chews, two Mars bars, a Crunchie and a pack of playing cards. I'd been hoping for bread, but I expect it's difficult to nick a loaf of bread. I wouldn't know, because I've never nicked anything.

So we ate the sweets and played knock-out whist, while the thing on the sofa snored on.

'What are we going to do?' I asked Phil eventually. I'd decided I could always go to the police station, but that would almost certainly mean Phil would have to go back into care.

His mum must have heard me, in spite of seeming to be unconscious, because she sat up and said: 'You can't fucking stay here. I don't know why you came anyway.'

I suddenly felt angry: 'Phil wanted to see you!' I said. 'You *are* his mum.' Though even now, I could hardly believe it.

'Well, he's had a good look now,' she said unpleasantly, 'so you can both just bugger off.'

'We're hungry,' Phil said resentfully. I could tell he didn't expect her to do anything about it. He just wanted to make a point.

'There's nothing here.'

I stared at her great bloated shape on the sofa. Her face was all screwed up. I realised then that she didn't even *like* Phil.

What's more, I couldn't see how we could possibly both get back.

Julie

As soon as we could get to a service station, Ben and Phil demolished plates of bacon, eggs, sausages, chips, beans and mushrooms, followed by chocolate pudding and ice cream. Now they were sleeping on the back seat of the car, on top of one another, tangled up and snuffling like a pair of puppies.

'Can't we do something?' I asked, as we sped southwards. 'Get her into rehab or something? Couldn't we pay?'

'I never expected to hear you offering to fund some drug addict's rehabilitation.'

He was teasing, but only just.

'You're completely wrong about me,' I said offendedly. 'You don't even *begin* to understand where I'm coming from.'

'You wanted to send Phil back where he belongs.'

'OK, I admit I got that wrong. But I was provoked.'

'There's something I have to tell you,' Ed said abruptly. He was gripping the steering wheel; he looked, suddenly, very serious. 'Something I've been trying to explain for – well, ages. Pretty much since I met you.'

'Oh?'

His mouth was set in a hard line. He said: 'The week before we met, I asked Nettle to marry me.'

'Oh.'

I didn't know what to say. Perhaps, deep down, I'd already guessed.

I was relieved, at least, that I was prepared, glad that Fran had told me about their affair. No: relationship. It was a proper, grown-up relationship, in which she was called Annabel and was suitable – a *relationship*, not like his jolting half-liaison with me.

Even so, I felt unutterably miserable. I knew it was crazy, and it made me a cliché, but somewhere – not even consciously – I'd gone on hoping that all of this had amounted to something else. More than a fling.

I said stiffly: 'Then you behaved appallingly.'

'I know.'

'Mum,' Ben interrupted sleepily, 'is there any juice?'

I fished a carton from the plastic carrier at my feet. Then Phil stirred as well, and I gave him a drink. After that they wanted the radio on; and, once we'd sorted out a station that suited everyone, I wasn't sure if they were asleep or not. So, rather than make small talk with Ed, or even worse, listen to his excuses and worry that Ben was hearing them too, I closed my eyes and pretended to doze. I managed to keep it up all the way back to Langley.

It was three o'clock in the morning, but the lights were still blazing at the windows of our house. Richard must have been watching for us, because he opened the front door the instant we drew up, hurried down the path and stood shifting from foot to foot by the car.

'Come in,' I urged Ed, as he switched off the engine. 'Have a drink or something.'

He shook his head. 'I need to get Phil to bed.'

'Take the car then. Bring it back tomorrow.' I reached for the door handle, then turned back to him gratefully. 'Thank you.'

'Don't thank me. It was the least I could do.' He hesitated, then nodded at the pavement. 'Richard's waiting for you.'

Indoors, they were all still up – Richard and Kate, Eileen and June – and they all wanted to touch Ben, to hug and kiss him and be sure he was real – which he clearly was, because, befuddled by sleep, he was rather irritable with all this petting and kept trying to shrug them off and swat them away.

I tucked him up in bed, kissed him until he started grumbling again, then went downstairs to find that June had once again taken up her post in the kitchen, where she was bustling about making hot drinks.

'Nice cup of cocoa, everyone?'

'No thanks,' my mother said, adding pointedly: 'I think it may be time for us to go.'

'I'll just make a nice cup of something first.' June lit the gas and poured milk into a saucepan. 'Well, Julie, fancy you knowing Ed McGregor! I think he's very dishy. And how clever of him to work out where Ben was! Come on, Eileen, you can't go home without a drink.'

My mother raised her eyebrows to the ceiling. 'No wonder Alf spends all his time dibbing, or whatever he does in that shed,' she whispered, propelling me out into the hall. 'Shall I try to get rid of her?'

'I think it's beyond even you.'

'Well, I'm off,' she announced loudly. 'I'm sure we've all got things to do in the morning.' And then she added in a low voice, for my benefit only: 'Sorry I tried to stop you.'

'No, it must have looked insane.'

'But you were right. You often are. I'm sorry: I think I sometimes have too many expectations.'

I said with amusement: 'It would be fine if only they didn't conflict.'

'Still, it makes life easier, doesn't it, if they're self-cancelling? One thing I do agree with June about, though: Ed McGregor's lovely. I approve.'

'There's nothing to approve *of*.'

'No?' She picked up her umbrella. 'Oh, well.'

Once we'd seen my mother off, Kate retired exhausted to bed, which was exactly what I wanted to do, but, unfortunately, there were still various Ellisons scattered around the house. In the sitting room, Richard was lounging on the sofa as if he belonged there, drinking his mother's cocoa and flicking through last week's *Langley Advertiser*.

I said to him: 'Is your mum planning to stay all night?'

'Don't know.' He looked up from the article he was reading. 'D'you want me to get rid of her?'

Had I missed something? Some crucial develop-ment? Richard was behaving as if it was Saturday afternoon with cricket on television and he'd never been away.

Perplexed, I left him to it, temporarily, and went into the kitchen: 'Please, June, leave this. I can do it in the morning.'

June shook the water off her hands and dried them on a tea towel.

'Actually,' she announced, 'there's something I wanted to say to you.'

'Can it wait until tomorrow? I'm shattered.'

'It won't take a minute. I've been thinking about what you said, before you went off with Ed.'

What did I say? Something incredibly rude, I expect, about June's enthusiasm for finding fault. 'I didn't mean it. I was overwrought.'

'No, you were right. I *am* too critical of other people. It's a defence mechanism, I think – because I'm not sure that the way I live is the right way.' I frowned, and shook my head – we didn't need to have all this out – but she carried on anyway. 'What I mean is, what I do, I do well. But is it *worth* doing, that's what I often wonder?'

'Of course.' I touched her arm, a little awkwardly. 'It's the most important thing.'

She put down the tea towel. 'I wonder, though, what I'd have been like if I'd had more choice?'

I stared at her in confusion.

'If I'd been – I don't know, *political,* like your mother, and got into feminism; although of course, she was always eccentric. Or if I'd been born a generation later. I might have been quite different.' Her eyes were glittering, but I think with regret: 'I do love Alf, and I

410

enjoyed having Richard – I wish I could've had more, really – but perhaps the things I worry about now – keeping things tidy, having flowers in the window boxes, ironing underpants – just wouldn't have seemed very important.'

I stared at her.

'Oh well,' she sighed. 'I'm keeping you up. And of course what with all the time I've spent here, your mum's right, I'm way behind at home. Better be getting along.'

I rejoined Richard in the sitting room.

'Well done,' he congratulated me, meaning for getting rid of his mother. 'So. Here we are.'

I sat down opposite him and he put aside the newspaper.

'Sorry if I was ungracious about you going to Leeds.'

'It's OK. It was understandable.'

'I thought something might even be going on between you and that bloke.'

'Ed McGregor.'

'He's very attractive.'

'Yes.'

'Mind you, I suppose that means he could have his pick of anyone, more or less . . .'

I said nothing.

'Have you thought at all about what I said before?'

'Yes.'

Richard sat forward, clasped his hands: 'The way I see it, having really given it some thought at last, is that I've had a sort of mid-life crisis – which was actually, probably, as much about being a teacher as it was about our marriage. You know: other people coming up on the inside, making deputy heads at thirty-two, and me at thirty-nine thinking I might never be promoted again. My career seemed to have come to an end, and I wasn't even sure I'd ever wanted it in the first place.'

'Yes, I know.'

'But the good thing is, I've realised now.'

'Uh?'

'What's good for me. Where I belong.' He beamed. 'I'm back, Jools.'

I said shakily: 'I thought you wanted a divorce. I've sent off for the papers.'

'Well, yes, I admit I *did* think I wanted a divorce. But that was before. I can see, now, I was wrong. Look, I'm sorry, OK? I'm back. You didn't want me to go – I know that. But now Ben's done us all a favour. He's made me realise that the family needs me.'

I frowned.

'Come on, Julie, how difficult are you going to make this? This is my home. Half my clothes are still here.'

They weren't, actually. I gave them to Oxfam last week.

I said: 'I thought you believed in . . . I don't know, passion.'

He laughed dismissively, through his nose. 'We'd *all* like to believe we're capable of passion. I'm sure it would be very nice to think that somewhere out there there's all-consuming love. But I'm afraid it's only ever sex. And that all gets boring after a time. I told you before, all relationships dwindle into domesticity.'

I said doubtfully: 'Mel and Ian don't think that.'

'OK,' he said, spreading his hands in a gesture of openness. 'I'll be completely straight with you. Emma's a lovely girl, but she's very young. She's borderline anorexic, for Christ's sake! – and then there are the neuroses about not being famous enough, and the *other* neuroses about being followed around by photographers . . .'

I was startled. When we were together, did he talk about me like that?

'I'm a great support to her now,' Richard continued, 'but she'll find her feet sooner or later. Not that I'm suggesting I'm only leaving her because one day she'd leave me,' he added hastily, seeing my face. 'To be honest, I've got – well . . . I loved all that childlike egotism at first, but after a time . . . It's made me realise how different you are.'

'Is that meant to be a compliment?'

'Come on, Jools, don't be difficult: what I'm saying is that Em may be famous, but I don't want to be with some shooting starlet any more. I want to be with you. Funnily enough, you're *much* more seductive than weekends with Robbie Wade.'

'I'm glad to hear it.'

'Honestly, you'd be amazed,' he went on: 'they're really lonely, a lot of those famous people. They're incapable of having real friendships. People don't relate to them normally . . .' He frowned; he'd lost his train of thought. 'The point is, getting back together makes sense. For a start, it would be cheaper, and it would obviously be better for you and the children.'

'How d'you know? That it would be better for me?'

'You don't want to be a single parent. You've seen the statistics. Single mothers have high levels of depression. Their kids suffer. It's much healthier to bring up children in a couple. You wouldn't want to inflict those disadvantages on our kids.' He frowned at me suspiciously. 'Why are you making this so difficult? How much d'you want me to grovel? Perhaps you should just tell me, so I can get it over with.'

'Richard,' I said deliberately, 'I'm not interested in your sensible reasons for getting back together. You gave me practical reasons for getting married in the first place, and, at the time, I thought it was clever – awfully smart and witty and cynical. But I don't think that any more.'

'Sorry?' For the first time, a trace of doubt crept into his voice. '*Are* you having a relationship with Ed McGregor?'

'No, I'm not. In fact, I'm so far from having a relationship with Ed McGregor that he's about to marry someone else. This doesn't involve him, or anyone except us. But I've changed. I think now that you should only marry because it's imperative, because you can't imagine life otherwise, because it's the only thing you want and the person is the only one you could ever want. Otherwise, what happens when you meet a ten out of ten?'

Richard frowned. 'That's a load of claptrap. Ten out of tens don't exist, or, if they do, only for a few months, until the sex wears off.'

'I'm sorry. I don't believe that.'

'You're not in a position to be all romantic and self-indulgent. You've already got children with me.

414

Think about *them*. This disruption's already been terribly bad for them. Kate's gone a bit wild, Arthur's not sure *where* he is, and as for Ben . . . well, he would never have run away before. He's spent the past year trying to get us back together, one way and another. And now,' Richard stretched his legs out in front of him smugly, 'I guess he's finally succeeded.'

'No,' I said slowly, 'he hasn't. You've been sitting here for an hour, but you haven't once asked me if I want you back. That's quite phenomenally arrogant, and it's made me even more certain; but even if you'd asked me right at the beginning, the answer would have been the same: I don't. It's over, Richard.'

'You *can't* be serious . . . after all the reasons I've given you! You're not thinking straight. It's all the emotion of finding Ben. You'll see the sense of what I'm saying in the morning.'

'I'm sorry. I wish it could be different. But the real reason our relationship imploded was that there was too little emotion there. And I'm afraid there still is.'

'You're mad.' Richard got to his feet, shaking his head. 'Completely mad. I make you a great offer and . . . Sometimes I have no idea what to make of you.' He got to his feet. 'My God, Jools, what do you think is going to happen to you? You're not exactly in the first flush. And, frankly, you're weird. But there, my mother never believed you'd overcome your upbringing. She always said you'd end up batty.'

At six-thirty – by which time I had been asleep exactly one hour – Arthur jumped on to my pillow.

'Ben's home!' he shouted. 'I saw him!'

'I know,' I muttered sleepily. 'Good, isn't it?' I kissed his nose and he burrowed under the duvet.

'I'm a policeman. Nee-naw, nee-naw, nee-naw. I'm going to find Ben.' He climbed over me, sticking his knee in my stomach.

'Ooof!'

'Can I have breakfast now?'

So I staggered out of bed and made my way carefully downstairs; then I sat in a stupor, clutching a cup of tea, while Arthur ate Frosties, watched television and played a game that he called Emergencies, which involved toy cars running painfully over my toes to the accompaniment of loud, wailing noises.

Ginny arrived almost-promptly, only fifteen minutes late and remarkably animated.

'Wicked about Ben! I saw it on the news. How did the police know he was there?'

'They didn't. It was Ed McGregor.'

'The one you hate?'

'Well, not any more. Obviously.'

The opposite of love is not hate, I remembered someone saying, but indifference.

Ginny shook her head, as if other people were a mystery. I took the risk of letting her get Arthur dressed and to nursery, and went back to bed, where I slept until around midday, when I heard Kate and Ben padding around.

So I got up yet again, showered, and went downstairs to fix them brunch. Mid-way through making us all scrambled eggs, I switched on the radio. Ed McGregor was on some lunchtime news programme, talking about Langley. I couldn't quite make it out.

I leaned across the work top to turn up the volume and smeared my dressing-gown sleeve in the butter.

It was hopeless. I wanted to laugh at the preposterousness of it – Ed McGregor and my butter-smeared, marmalade-splodged, tea-splashed kitchen. Ed McGregor, three children and Sprout.

We hadn't long finished the bacon and eggs and bagels when he turned up. Kate and Ben had gone upstairs to shower, but I was still in my dressing gown. I'd been sitting at the table, surrounded by debris of smeared plates, staring out of the window at the sunshine.

'Your car keys,' he said, holding them out to me.

'Thanks. Coffee?'

As soon as I said it, I remembered what happened the last time and went bright red. How tactless can you get?

'Is Richard here?'

'No.'

'OK.'

As I led him down to the kitchen, I kept getting graphic images of the previous occasion we'd done this, and feeling hot and prickly.

'Is Phil OK?' I asked brightly, in order to stop thinking about it.

'I suppose. It's hard for him, though: his mother didn't come to get him.'

'You did. That's the next best thing.'

I wondered briefly what Nettle would make of Ed's responsibilities to Phil.

Ed sat down and pushed an eggy plate out of the

way. I hurriedly cleared it off the table. 'So, where's Richard?'

'I don't know.'

'I thought Ben had finally achieved the reconciliation.'

I looked at him sharply. It never stopped surprising me, the things he knew. 'No.'

He thought about this for a moment. Then he said: 'You were right last night, when you said I'd behaved appallingly.'

'It's all right. You don't have to explain yourself. You've more than made up for it, finding Ben.' I smiled. 'We don't need to have another fight.'

'I want to explain. You have to let me . . . That evening at the church hall, I was knocked sideways . . .'

I filled the kettle. Why was he inflicting this on me?

'. . . It was like a compulsion. I had to see you again.'

I raised my eyebrows. 'So you weren't really leafletting?'

'Let's just say I organised the leafletting very carefully . . . And then I did see you, and it was exactly the same. I've never done that before, walked into someone's house and . . . well.'

'You're not usually into speed-seduction?' I was determined not to get upset by this. 'You surprise me. You were so expert.'

'I couldn't work out what was happening to me.'

'I should have thought it was obvious.' I piled the plates by the sink. 'Suddenly you were marrying Nettle, and you were terrified. So you seduced me to prove to yourself, or pretend to yourself – I'm not sure how it works – that you weren't really tied to her at all.'

I put a cup of coffee in front of him.

'Is that what you thought?'

'D'you have a better explanation?'

'I didn't at the time. I was appalled.'

I filled the sink with water: 'I expect you *were*: so susceptible to a housewife from Langley!'

He looked surprised. 'That's not what I mean. Where you lived wasn't relevant. Or what you did – which, at the time, you may remember, I didn't know.'

I took my cup of coffee over to the table and sat down opposite him. I looked at him severely, then I told him all about having overheard his conversation with Nettle in Polly's tea shop.

At least he had the grace to look abashed. 'How much of that was me?'

'I can't remember. But you weren't exactly protesting.'

'The truth is, I probably did want to believe that Langley was dreary and, by extension, that you were dreary. I was trying to talk myself out of my obsession with you.'

'I think you found it remarkably easy.'

'No.' He shook his head. 'But I was committed to Nettle. I'd made her a promise and immediately broken it, and I was horrified. I wanted to believe that what happened with you was an aberration and that I could get over it.' He sat with his elbows on the table and put his forehead in his hands, shading his eyes. 'But I couldn't.'

I lowered my mug and stared at him.

'I kept telling myself I'd stay out of your way and simply not see you again. But you kept . . . cropping up. You came to interview me, and all I could think about was having sex with you again. Ripping off all your clothes. Stopping all that stuff about my qualifications and the motorway extension, and kissing you. But Phil was there.'

'I'd have hit you, anyway.'

'I know.'

'You laughed at me because I'd forgotten Ben's lunch and I couldn't find Ginny.'

He shook his head. 'I thought you were adorable. But when your piece came out, and it was so hostile, I decided you were still in love with Richard. I hadn't been using you; you'd been using me – you'd had sex with me to get back at him. For all I knew, you would have done it with anyone.'

'Be serious.'

'And then every time I saw you I felt so horribly upset. You turned everything upside down. But even though it was so unsettling, I couldn't get enough of it. I stopped going home at weekends; I took detours past your house. I met you on the green with your soup, I saw you fighting with Richard . . .'

'You laughed at me again.'

'I was trying to stop it hurting before it started. I thought if you and Richard could still have tempestuous rows like that, you were probably still crazy about each other . . . And then you got so angry about Phil . . .'

'With good reason.'

'Nettle guessed,' he said. 'That first time you turned

420

up with Phil. Or perhaps even earlier. But she only realised how bad it was around the time of Fran's dinner party. We had a terrible row: that's why she didn't come that evening. I was pleased, because I knew you were going to be there. Even though Fran said you were bringing your boyfriend.'

'I didn't have a boyfriend.'

'And then when he didn't materialise I decided I'd been right all along and you weren't over Richard. But it reached the point that I didn't care. When the tree came down, I saw you there and you were so lovely . . .'

Mad. Completely mad.

I said with satisfaction: 'But I hit you.'

'You not only hit me, you told me you never wanted to see me again. So then I took myself off for a week; I had to get away from you, from Nettle, from Langley, everything. I went to stay with some friends in Wales. That's why, for the first twenty-four hours, I didn't know Ben and Phil were missing.'

I pushed my cup away. 'You could have said some of this last night.'

'I thought Richard had come back, and that it was what you'd been waiting and hoping for. So there was no point. Why should I make it more complicated for you? Anyway, I did say it. I said it to Nettle.'

'Last night?'

'I haven't had any sleep. I decided in Wales I couldn't go on with Nettle when I'm in love with you. Even if you loved Richard.'

I got up and went over to the sink. I squirted washing-up liquid into the water, put on my rubber gloves (automatically: if I'd thought about how I looked, I wouldn't have done this) and whooshed up the bubbles energetically, struggling to absorb it all.

And then Kate bounced into the kitchen, and started pestering us to let her cement herself into the attics when the bailiffs arrived to evict the squats – which (and this was why Ed had been on the radio) everyone now thought was probably going to happen tonight.

'You have no idea how lovely you are,' Ed whispered, cornering me at the end of the kitchen while I made Kate another cup of coffee.

'*You* have no idea, actually. You only ever see me when I'm caked in mud and wearing a cagoule, or in an old dressing gown without mascara.'

'I think I quite like you dirty.'

I looked up at him and felt a surge of helpless lust.

'Cut it out you two,' ordered Kate. 'We need to get down to the squats and make sure everyone's in their tunnels.'

June spent the night at our house, looking after Arthur. She arrived announcing that she'd spent the day writing off to the Open University about foundation courses.

Ben and Phil stayed with Mel at her house, on condition that she promised to bring them down to the squats for six o'clock in the morning so that they didn't miss any of the action.

Kate slept on the first floor of 4, Cherry Drive, next to a burly welder called Scots Billy, who promised faithfully that no harm would come to her, before, during or after she was padlocked to a pipe. Mould slept, if sleep is possible in such circumstances, in one of the tunnels that honeycombed the foundations of the houses. Oddly, since Ben's disappearance, Kate hadn't mentioned him once.

And Ed McGregor and I spent the night on a mattress on the floor of what had once been his office.

'You deserve better than this,' he said. 'Venice. A four-poster.'

But I couldn't have cared less.

At dawn, we barricaded the door with three filing cabinets and the mattress. Before very long, we heard the slap of mallets and the scraping of chisels, the low grumble of the mechanical diggers, the corrugated sheets crumping down into the back garden, the rattle of roof tiles raining down on top of them. We knew more or less what was happening: we were in radio contact with other groups of protesters holed up round the buildings, and Geordie Bill kept up a running commentary through a megaphone from one of the attic bedrooms next door.

At nine, we heard machinery moving over our heads.

Ed gazed at me and said: 'I can hardly believe you're here. Twenty-four hours ago I thought I'd had everything I was ever going to have of you – one lunchtime on a kitchen table and eight hours of near-silence on a motorway.'

'Not only am I here,' I told him happily, 'but it's going to take seven hundred police, three hundred security guards and fifty bailiffs to remove me.'

Ed wrapped his arms round me and kissed me for ages and ages. And then a mechanical arm ripped through the ceiling, showering us in plaster.

Kate

A hole just opened up in the floor and there, underneath, were Mum and Ed. They have no sense of priorities. Here we are in the middle of the biggest thing ever to hit Langley, and they're hanging on to one another like a pair of kids.

Ben said to me last night that he thought the running away had worked, after all.

'This way we get four parents,' he explained. 'And Ed's much better at homework than Dad.' (He meant Dad was good at other things, just not particularly at homework.) 'Adults sometimes need help, don't they?'

All the girls at school will be jealous. And Ed's brilliant with Arthur. He doesn't even seem to mind being bumped into by Ben.

Things could be worse.